REN ROSSO

What Gives You Away

A Novel

for my husband

Contents

Acknowledgement

Though it stings, criticism is a gift. Receive it with humility, without rebuttal, and it will change your life for the better.

I am indebted to my early editor, Susan Roney-O'Brien for her supportive, gentle feedback and guidance. A heartfelt thank-you to Ann Lewis for permission to use a portion of Dan Lewis's poem *That Damn Apple Again* from his book *Intimations of the Focal Plane*. Dan was a talented and much-loved poet in Worcester, Massachusetts. My later editor, Lisa Findley, was terrific to work with and I'm grateful for her insight and skill. Thanks very much to Casey Gerber for her beautiful artwork. And with appreciation for the hard lessons life provides and the sunset at the end of the day.

Chapter 1

Pia first noticed Jeremy when he visited the registrar's office for an appointment with Ralph one March day. He didn't particularly stand out like the charismatic student who wore a cowboy hat and skirts or the friendly young woman with flowing curly blonde hair who reminded Pia of a mermaid. He was chatting with a work-study student named Larissa at the main counter. Jeremy had long, blond hair that reached the base of his neck and he had it tucked behind his ears. He had very pale blue eyes, almost gray. When he smiled his wide mouth took up most of his face.

It was noisy and busy in the office so Pia couldn't overhear the conversation, but she noticed that Jeremy asked Larissa several questions and he gave her his undivided attention. He looked completely focused on what she had to say.

"Most people aren't like that," Pia thought.

Larissa was a pretty young woman and Pia knew that might have had something to do with it, but still. Just as he was leaving Jeremy glanced up at Pia; he probably sensed her eyes on him. She didn't look away as fast as she'd have liked and she blushed.

Once he left Pia commented encouragingly to Larissa, "He's a cute boy."

Ever since overhearing a classmate in college refer to a guy Pia had a romantic interest in as a 'cute boy,' it had become a category to her.

Larissa swiveled her office chair around to respond to Pia, whose desk was behind Larissa's workstation at the main counter.

Larissa replied, "He's a nice guy."

"Maybe you two could...."

"I'm dating Corey again," she reminded Pia. "I can tell you don't like him but he's alright."

"I just don't think he's good enough for you," Pia said with a smile.

"You sound like my dad. Jeremy and I worked on a magazine project last semester. I wrote a piece for it and he submitted some photographs. He's in aerospace engineering but he takes great photos. He has an exhibit up now in the campus center," Larissa said, tossing her long, shiny brown hair over her shoulder. Pia knew it would slip forward again soon. Some students came in the office and stood at Larissa's workstation so she turned her attention to them.

Pia Sandstrom worked in the registrar's office at a small university near Boston. The office was responsible for all things related to students' course registrations. You wouldn't think that required an office unto itself but apparently it did, because it was usually a busy place. A large main front counter ran down the length of the large room, dotted with several workstations for work-study students. Behind that there were five low cubicles where the staff had their own space but could see everything going on around them. Behind that main space there was an office on the right for Ralph, the associate registrar, and a kitchen area to the left, with file cabinets lining the walls in-between.

A few weeks after his first visit to the office Jeremy had a meeting with Ralph again about something. They met in Ralph's office for quite a while. Ralph liked to talk. After Jeremy left, Ralph sauntered out into the shared space and looked at his staff.

"That kid is a pain in my ass," he said to no one in particular.

Pia was glad that there weren't any work-study students there to hear him, especially Larissa. Ralph, an older man with a sulky face, perceived every student as a liar trying to work the system. When Pia first began at the registrar's office, she thought that since Ralph had raised four children, he knew when a college student was being disingenuous immediately. Those qualities of being so intuitive and simultaneously remaining completely non-reactive impressed Pia initially, although it made Ralph difficult to read. Over time Pia realized that Ralph wasn't so much non-reactive as disengaged. It was his job to notify students when their academic standing had changed or their graduation requirements were not being met. He rarely allowed a student to complete a thought. When the conversation became complicated, he shot responses out of his mouth that sometimes didn't even address the issue the student wanted to discuss. His goal was to be rid of the student as quickly as possible.

Pia thought, "That poor bastard's not going to get much help from Ralph." What she articulated was "poor bastard" under her breath.

"Ha!" came from Shelly, whose cubicle was adjacent to Pia's.

Shelly Rosenblum was a recent college graduate with a quirky sense of humor. It made Mary, another cubicle resident, a little uncomfortable, but Pia found it refreshing and was glad that Shelly had joined the staff. Shelly kept a photo of Ben Stiller and she sometimes moved it around the office so it would surprise people. You never knew where Ben would turn up. Once Mary found him in her cubicle blocking a family photo. It disturbed and confused her until Shelly explained herself.

"What?" Pia asked Shelly.

"I love it when you say 'poor bastard'. It's funny."

Pia wasn't aware that she had this habit. "How often do I say it?"

"Pretty often. Thanks for handling all those emails this morning."

"No problem."

When she was younger, Pia had graduated from art school. Now she was involved with the arts in her town, even helping to promote and set up exhibits. One day when the spring weather wasn't great for her lunchtime walk around the nearby city park Pia headed for the campus center to check out Jeremy's photography exhibit. She ascended the stairs to the top floor gallery. There was something on display about the history of the university, which she gave some attention to although it wasn't really of great interest. Pia always appreciated the trouble someone took to arrange an exhibit, and so respected it on that level at least.

She returned to the main floor and was about to leave when Jeremy, of all people, greeted her hello as they were about to pass by one another. She thought that was nice of him; it was unusual for a student to say hello to a staff member they only recognized by face and didn't interact with. Possibly Pia had assisted him in the past and just didn't remember.

She asked him about his photography. "Larissa told me you have an exhibit of photographs up now, but I didn't see it in the gallery upstairs...."

Jeremy smiled and told her, "It's hanging in the café, right over there."

Pia's eyes followed where he pointed. She blinked at the newly constructed addition and stated the obvious: "That's new."

"Let me know what you think!" Jeremy said, adjusting a black courier bag on his shoulder.

He continued towards the exit and Pia walked into the café wondering if he actually wanted her feedback or if that was a figure of speech for him. Although she was a friendly person, she often felt unsure of how to navigate interactions.

The café was a fun, trendy new space crowded with students. There were about a dozen images, which a small placard indicated were from a trip Jeremy took to Nepal. All of the photographs were beautiful; they had vibrant color and were excellently composed. Jeremy seemed to value all his subjects equally, selecting equal numbers of shots featuring animals, scenery and people. Pia didn't personally and felt a little badly about it. She leaned more toward the natural world, although she did enjoy the endearing shots of children in which Jeremy captured them reveling in the attention and novelty of the photographer. There were great close-ups of wild animals. She wondered about his lenses as she looked at those. She enjoyed viewing art. A relief for one's eyes, really, from the constant onslaught of commercialization.

As she walked back to her office in heavy, wind-swept rain Pia pondered her favorite word, *serendipity*. That chance meeting with Jeremy seemed serendipitous indeed.

Pia passed Ralph as she made her way to her desk, shaking water off her coat, which she held at arm's length.

"You're soaked," he noticed.

"It's raining," she replied.

"That's why the rest of us are inside," Ralph explained to her as if she were stupid. He loudly included the other employees in the conversation. "We should've had Pia pick up lunch."

"Happy to," Pia concluded the topic.

That was the end of direct interactions with Jeremy for a long time, but he seemed to be everywhere. When Pia worked out in the recreation center on the top level she would spot him through the huge windows as he crossed the campus. His smiling face was on the main webpage right after commencement, so at that point she knew he had received his bachelor's degree. Pia's department watched a brief video put out by the residential life office and he was in a clip helping unload a car. One of the photographs he took hung in the provost's office.

Pia was a middle-aged woman with a small build, and fine graying hair that came down to her shoulders. She had small eyes and short eyelashes and always envied people with large eyes and long eyelashes. She thought it was funny how some women went to great lengths to have the opposite hair than what they were born with. Usually it went from curly to straight, but sometimes the other way around. And then there were all the colors to choose from. Pia wasn't worried about her graying hair, but if she could switch out her eyes for some big almond ones she'd definitely do it.

She was married to Gordon, a retired hardware engineer eighteen years her senior. Although she had always wanted them, Pia didn't have any children. Neither Gordon nor her first husband wanted kids, or, in Gordon's case, more kids, since he had an adult son. Also, Pia wasn't sure she'd be a very good mother. This way she'd never have to find out. Growing up, her own mother was always yelling at her two offspring and gave Pia the impression, which she carried for many years, that having children effectively ruined her mother's life. Her mother said "shit" all day long. Sometimes it was more of a bird call than a word: "Shit-shit-*shit!*"

In addition to her work at the university, Pia had been the primary caregiver for her mother until she passed away, three years back. In a lot of ways, caring for her mother, who had dementia, was a good outlet for Pia's maternal instinct. Except that with dementia, you aren't helping the person grow and develop more; you just take care of them and try to help them enjoy now. They aren't going to learn anything you teach them.

When Pia's mother died her older sister, Nancy, didn't attend the funeral for her own reasons. Pia knew she should've respected that but she couldn't. Pia told her that she should have gone to the funeral and this angered Nancy. Pia thought she would get over the criticism but that was a miscalculation on her part. She and Nancy were estranged from that day on. Pia's hair fell out. Well, to be fair, not all of it. Pia lost about a quarter of her hair from the shock and stress of the estrangement.

She mourned the death of her relationship with her sister more than her mother passing, but the friendships Pia had with other people grew more valuable. She had always felt love for her friends and Gordon's family but her appreciation of them changed dramatically without familiar Nancy to fall back on. Once pushed out of her comfort zone, she flourished.

Her life with Gordon was fine, although she wished he were a better listener. He was good-natured, though. Once when the two of them were struggling to set a gigantic air conditioner in the bedroom window, it dropped two stories down to a brick walkway and smashed. Rather than getting angry as Pia expected, Gordon just laughed out loud. As the years went by she learned to appreciate other little things, like that he would eat whatever she fed him for dinner.

Pia was also committed to her community. She appreciated that most of what was accomplished in a small town was the work of some dedicated volunteers and she wanted to do her share, so in addition to her work for the arts in her town, she sat on various committees over the years. The one she currently served on involved research and writing, which she enjoyed.

She also volunteered at the local wildlife sanctuary. It was an entirely different experience from her work week. She was raised by urban people, so moving to this quiet town with hundreds of acres of fields and forest was quite a change for her. Most of the acreage was forested, but the sanctuary was also an active farm with some sheep and hayfields. Pia helped with the sheep, corralling them into the barn at night, setting up the electric fence in new locations as they ate their way across the fields, and shearing their wool. One spring a young mother rejected her lamb after a particularly difficult birth and Pia helped bottle-feed him for a few months. She also assisted with large family events and led nature walks occasionally.

Most importantly, Pia learned that you're never finished with learning; there is always more information, more species and habitats and life cycles. This place attracted many knowledgeable naturalists who inspired her. The best thing about nature was that it didn't require a degree to be an expert in a specific field; you just had to pay close attention. To learn about the natural world just required the right level of interest.

She felt similarly about the university; professors were doing research that excited them and introduced it to the students. she imagined that igniting that spark of interest was rewarding. The students themselves were generally enthusiastic about learning and it made life more interesting, less static.

As time allowed Pia also became increasingly involved with a social justice group in the city, helping with protests and marches for racial equality.

Pia and Gordon went to parties and they hosted parties occasionally. She spent as much time outdoors as she could. She exercised regularly and was healthy. Life was really rather good.

Then, inexplicably, and so very gradually, she became distracted from her life.

One day in June an administrative assistant in the aerospace engineering department sent an email to all staff and faculty about one of their master's students selling his photographs. It read, "Many of you know Jeremy Ronan and what a great kid he is. He is selling prints of his photographs from his travels. If you are interested, please contact him directly. He is asking $250 each, framed." It included several attached images to select from.

Pia had been amassing quite a collection of friends' art. Jeremy had some nice images, but that was considerably more than she could spend, particularly for a photograph. She emailed him and said she would like the image of women in a marketplace, but she couldn't go higher than $150. She understood if he couldn't let it go for that. She hoped Jeremy wouldn't be offended by the negotiating. Some artists she knew would be.

He responded immediately, writing, "Of course I can sell it to you for $150, Pia. Thank you so much!" and they worked out a time for him to bring the print to her office.

Jeremy was very chatty when he brought in Pia's purchase. He told her that he was going to join the Peace Corps for two years beginning next month, working in Sudan. He spoke enthusiastically about the image she chose and what he knew about the people in it. She was charmed by how eager he was to teach her what he had learned.

Back at her desk Pia rationalized the expense to herself. She thought, "I'm glad I can help support him. It's great that he wants to go help make a difference in the lives of poor people in Sudan." She also thought about his handsome face.

Jeremy wasn't trendy. He wore clothes that did not attract attention to him: t-shirts, jeans. Pia had found students attractive before and felt it was somewhat wrong, because she was as old as their parents. Just a few days earlier, a handsome, muscular young man came into the office for some letters he had ordered, and Shelly and Mary had helped him. After he left Pia emailed Shelly and Mary that it had gotten very hot in the office. A man named Dave had recently joined the staff and Pia didn't want to be openly sexist so she didn't speak aloud about the student. Mary never responded, but after about two minutes, Pia heard Shelly burst out laughing.

"Ha! Definitely, Pia!"

The year before, Pia had been distracted by a student from Libya. He was, by anyone's gauge, gorgeous. There wasn't any harm in her appreciating these students' good looks. It didn't mean anything and it always switched quickly to something more nurturing and maternal if she got to know them. Besides, Pia considered herself rather unattractive, so she didn't really think that anyone would be interested in her.

After the office closed, she carefully packed up the framed photograph she had purchased and collected the rest of her belongings. On the way to her car, Jeremy ran through Pia's thoughts one more time.

"What a cute boy. Goodbye, cute boy, enjoy Sudan. Think of me, ha," she mused to herself. "Oh, I forgot my grocery list. I'll have to make it up as I go tonight. I have to stop for gas, too."

Eight months went by. In early February, Pia was spending more and more time on a document for the committee she was on. The Chair of the committee, Thatcher Livingston, wasn't particularly interested in it. Pia didn't fault him on that since no one was exactly enthusiastic about it. Whenever this project was on the agenda, Thatcher was fond of saying "We, and by 'we' I mean Pia." He thought that was funny. Thatcher wasn't a bad guy but Pia had trouble with his sense of entitlement. Pia didn't think she was too good for any job, which was great, but she didn't think anyone else was too good for any job either. Unfortunately, other people felt very differently about that point.

There was something else Pia noticed after her first several meetings on the committee. Thatcher didn't pay attention to women who were not beautiful and was consistently dismissive of them. It wasn't until a rather unattractive woman joined a meeting that Pia picked up on this. Mostly it took Pia awhile because it didn't matter to her what a person looked like if they had something of value to add. However, Thatcher seemed to be barely enduring them. In other instances Thatcher had mentioned women in town he had tremendous regard for, and they were beautiful, feminine, and very well made-up. "Living, breathing Barbie dolls," Pia thought. But she couldn't commit to that position because those women were also capable and accomplished. They were the whole package.

This bias of Thatcher's increasingly annoyed Pia once she caught on to it. She was quite confident in her assessment of Thatcher's attitude; usually she was filled with self-doubt and second guessing herself, but not on this.

The committee gathered in the Town Hall, set on the top of a hill, in a claustrophobic office space. One evening after Thatcher had made an insensitive comment about a woman who was absent from the meeting, Pia spoke up.

"Thatcher, something about you always gets me channeling Ani DiFranco."

Pia was different from other people Thatcher had known. However, her looks precluded her from being of much interest. He frowned.

A middle-aged professional man on the committee asked, "Who's Annie DiFranco?"

Thatcher knew who she was. "*Ah-ni*," he said, correcting the pronunciation. "She's an obnoxious, abrasive lesbian singer."

He smiled wryly at the man.

Thatcher may have intended for that to sting Pia, but she was pleased that he played so well into her hand.

She noted, "She's actually bisexual, like me." While that information stunned them Pia sang a little, staring directly at Thatcher.

"I am beyond your peripheral vision/ so you might want to turn your head/ 'cause someday you might find yourself hungry/ and eating all of the words you just said."

There was a subtle sexual innuendo to the interaction which Pia didn't intend. Everyone was silent for a beat.

A more diplomatic woman, Pam, piped up then. "Ooookay, let's look at the map of the watershed protection properties!"

Then they moved on.

Afterwards, as people separated in the parking lot to reach their cars, Pia stopped to breathe in the cool night air. It had recently stopped raining and Pia loved the smell of the sweet, fresh air. There were many frogs vocalizing rhythmically. Pia always thought it sounded like the earth breathing.

She found Thatcher and Pam waiting for her a little way from the town hall door, Thatcher to confront her and Pam presumably because she didn't understand the exchange during the meeting very well and wanted some insight on it. She got along very well with everyone in town.

Thatcher was very direct. "So Pia, what was up with that? Do you have some sort of problem with me?"

He wasn't confrontational; it was more like they were having a chat. Thatcher was so self-confident that he didn't perceive anyone as a threat. If you didn't like him it was your loss.

"Sorry, Thatcher, but you're the easiest person to read I've ever met. You just can't suffer unattractive women, can you?"

Pia held paperwork in a folder related to the committee responsibilities. She pivoted her torso in a little circle while her feet remained planted in place.

"I'm afraid I don't know what you mean."

Thatcher was getting his car keys out of his pocket.

"I'm not following either, Pia. What unattractive women?" Pam asked.

Kind Pam, she just didn't view people that way at all. She was entirely nonjudgmental and only saw peoples' contributions. Pia felt that she tried to be like that, but she couldn't help noticing the flaws in others. Maybe it came from seeing the ones in herself so clearly.

She didn't answer Pam. She certainly wasn't going to use herself as an example, because it would sound like she just wanted Thatcher to accept her. She couldn't really say who else was unattractive, as that wouldn't be charitable.

So she continued to Thatcher, "I think you probably do. I suppose you can't help it but it's really irritating to me. I'll refrain from calling you out on it if you refrain from insulting people, okay?"

"I don't think I insulted Arlene if that's what you're talking about. The woman is a total cow, that's just a fact."

Pam cried, "Thatcher! Geez, that's not very nice!"

"Come on, she's, like, three hundred pounds!" Thatcher was athletic and apparently disdained sedentary people.

He was amusing himself if no one else. Pia was glad Pam stayed and witnessed that interaction, since she now seemed to understand why Pia disliked Thatcher, but she had to get home.

"On that note, goodnight." Pia nodded to Pam, turned and went to her car.

She blared the radio when she was inside it. As she drove her car down the hill she saw in her rearview mirror that Thatcher and Pam were still talking. Pia might apologize to everyone at the next meeting. She was aware that she didn't have a filter but she also felt it was important to discuss the proverbial elephant in any given room. She couldn't understand why people avoided this.

On her drive home, Pia noticed the song on the radio was by The Police, from the '80's. "Don't Stand So Close to Me." It reminded her of her interest in Jeremy months ago. She turned it off.

Chapter 2

In late February someone named Linda from the university campus center emailed Pia. A man who had managed the art shows for that building had recently retired and suggested Pia as a possible addition to their new exhibits committee. Pia knew that it would involve more time than she could get away with during working hours and she would have to be prepared to do some volunteering. She enjoyed the university community as much as that of her town, so with her boss Sandra's approval, she wrote back that she would help out.

At the first exhibits committee meeting in March Linda handed out a matrix of what exhibits were planned for which spaces for the next three semesters. Several were a bit vague. It became apparent during the meeting that some of the committee members had been forced onto it and didn't really have the time or interest for this endeavor. It was essentially Linda and Pia splitting up most of the work.

After everyone took a few minutes to look over the paperwork, Linda began discussing her vision for how they'd begin.

"We have two spaces for artwork. There's the gallery on the top level and the new café on the ground floor. Obviously, the café has less space but it gets more foot traffic."

To Pia's surprise, Jeremy was one of the artists on her spreadsheet with a special theme he had in mind about an area in the city near the river.

"You plan to have each exhibit up for a semester?" Pia asked.

"That's the idea. We don't have the people power to switch them out any more often than that. The spring shows up now can linger into the summer if need be. I thought we could hang Jeremy Ronan's next fall in the gallery. We have a few options for the café. I've attached some descriptions from three artists."

A man from the marketing department named Steve asked Linda, "Do you have any preferences?"

"I don't, but you might. The one from New York might be too controversial for our administration's taste. Since you're our marketing representative, I think we should defer to you." Linda waited while he read about it.

"Hmm…yeah, you might want to skip that. They'd have a fit." It was photographs of body art.

Linda made an effort to delegate responsibilities amongst the group.

"We'll need someone to cover publicity. Anybody?" She waited. "How about you, Steve? I can write something if you can edit it and distribute it to the campus."

Pia thought this kind of thing was why the marketing department wanted him on the committee in the first place.

He accepted without hesitation. "Absolutely."

Pia's instincts told her Steve was entirely insincere.

"Great, thank you." Linda jotted some notes on her matrix. "Can someone contact the artists and work out logistics with them?"

No one spoke up. There was another man on the committee who worked in Linda's department. "Andy?"

He put his hands up in protest. "I honestly don't have any idea how to go about that."

Linda pursed her lips. Pia wondered if Linda had the same thought she herself did, that it wasn't exactly rocket science.

Then Pia heard herself offering her skills. "I've curated art exhibits on a few occasions. I can put the shows together. Hang them, make labels, and arrange openings…that sort of thing." Then her brain caught up and she thought, "What are you *doing*?"

Steve was surprised. "I thought you're an admin."

Pia looked at him without any emotion. "I am."

Andy asked her, "What's an 'opening'?"

Pia looked over at him. "Sorry. I should've said 'opening receptions.' It's basically a party for the artist and the exhibit."

Linda was clearly grateful that Pia had extended an offer to help in any way. "Pia, could you contact the artists? There's Jeremy Ronan for the gallery, and you can decide between the remaining two for the café. The current shows can remain through summer, I don't care. We can worry about next spring later."

Her face was pleading, and Pia thought she probably didn't have any time for this at all herself.

Pia nodded. "Okay. I can contact both of those other artists and maybe one won't mind postponing until spring. That way we can show both of their work."

"Super, thanks a lot." Linda made more notes.

They went over some basic details about the following fall and spring and then adjourned.

Pia and Linda walked out together. Linda asked Pia if she knew Jeremy, and Pia replied that she did. Then Linda made a face Pia didn't know how to interpret…a knowing look that she held for a minute. It made Pia uncomfortable, and so she quickly blurted out that she wished kind Jeremy was her own son. It was rather awkward.

Later in the week Linda forwarded emails from the two artists Pia could choose from for the café.

Linda wrote, "Thanks very much for volunteering to help me with this. I don't expect to have any assistance from Andy. We're rather like water and oil, I'm afraid. Jeremy should be on campus because he's finishing his master's degree. He was going to join the Peace Corp after he received his B.S. last spring, but the trip was indefinitely postponed because of political upheaval in the region. I really like both of the other artists. Let me know if you need anything clarified."

Pia checked Jeremy's schedule in the database and, while it was full, he didn't have enough credits to meet his aerospace degree requirements in time for that May. It was impossible to earn a master's degree in only one semester. Several weeks later, after many graduate students had submitted their applications for graduation, it occurred to Pia to review Jeremy's undergraduate courses. Then she found that he had taken many more courses as an undergraduate student than he needed and many of them were graduate level courses. Pia always felt a bit cautious in judging when to intervene and when not to. She was also having trouble determining if he really needed some help on this or if she just wanted to contact him because he was a cute boy. Eventually she sent Jeremy an email with a graduation application attached and asked him if he planned on graduating the following month.

"Hi Jeremy, someone told me you are planning on graduating this May. If that's the case, please fill out the attached form and send it back to me. I will print out an audit of your courses and forward both to your department head for his signature. Thanks very much."

Jeremy responded that afternoon. "Yes, thank you so much! I totally missed that I had to send this in. I will get it back to you very soon! Thank you."

As always, he was very appreciative and positive.

When her office and Jeremy's department head reviewed his courses, they discovered that he was missing just one course to meet his degree requirements. Jeremy was hoping to at least participate in the ceremony that was five weeks away. Pia knew that the proper protocol was for him to request special permission from a committee. She also knew that the committee normally took three to five months before they'd review a petition, because they had a great number of other matters to vote on in addition to those. Sandra, Pia's boss, was on the committee and Pia found no meetings for it on Sandra's calendar.

Pia was also working with several other students who needed help with special situations but were not getting any assistance from Ralph or Sandra. To Pia, Sandra and Ralph were a set, like salt and pepper shakers, because they shared the same mindset. They seemed to deliberately impede the students' efforts.

One of these students came to the office and explained to Pia about a very unusual and frustrating situation that was entirely not his doing. He was looking for a means by which to resolve it. Pia contemplated it and gave him some possible options, and he thanked her and left.

Immediately Dave spoke up. "I can't believe you listened to him for that long. I would've been like 'Dude, shut *up.*' You were too nice to him."

Pia wondered if Dave had even heard what the student was saying. How could you not help him with that scenario? He would need some intervention from the staff. Pia couldn't comprehend being "too nice" either. Months later, after Ralph dropped the ball on it and the dean of undergraduates fixed it, Pia and the student joked that he should have received three credits for independent study on navigating bureaucracy. But it wasn't really funny.

Another person, an international student, had lost his scholarships because he was not doing well academically.

One day when he was in the office pleading his case, he took the form Pia offered but was agitated by his predicament. Pia walked him out as they spoke to hear his case more. She could tell that, unlike other students she had assisted, his education wasn't a top priority for him and he was playing the administration. He said his daughter was sick, her mother was dead, and he was the only person to look after her. He didn't have a job. He complained that he couldn't get a loan because no one would co-sign for him.

Pia braced herself like she might before diving into cold water and then called his bluff. "I'll co-sign a loan for you."

The student abruptly stopped in his verbal tracks. He eventually collected himself and said he'd be in touch with her. As time went by he found another way, which was good for Pia but not for whoever gave him the money, as he failed most of his courses.

That fellow aside, Pia was helping students as best she could without being caught, so to speak, by Ralph and Sandra. Frustrated by having to work around her bosses, Pia finally decided it was also worthwhile in this case, especially since Jeremy would incur additional fees to take the final course he needed. She emailed Jeremy and suggested that he contact the new president of the university, since he could be persuasive regarding the matter.

"Hi, Jeremy. You would have to submit a petition to be allowed to participate in the ceremony without actually getting your degree. I can't say when it would be voted on, though. It's possible that the president could be persuasive regarding this. I think you should ask him for his help. Registering for the summer credits will cost you $4,100. There is a special scholarship fund to help graduate students finish up. You can contact Helen Johnson, the assistant director of graduate studies, about it." Pia hated being the bearer of bad news but Jeremy had to know this. She was afraid her emails were slapping him in the face though.

A few hours later, she received a reply: "Thank you so, so much Pia! You are the best! I will write to her now and copy you. I hope I'm eligible for the scholarship. I had no idea it would cost that much. Thank you. Warm regards."

Several days later Pia received an email from the president. The president forwarded a lengthy and, as always, extremely gracious email from Jeremy that began with "Pia Sandstrom from the registrar's office suggested I reach out to you regarding a unique situation." It hadn't occurred to Pia that Jeremy would not know that her advice had been covert and unauthorized. True, she had given the advice in an email so there was a paper trail of what she'd done, but if Jeremy hadn't highlighted it, no one might have known. This demonstrated to her once again that the students may technically be adults but lacked so much life experience. Of course, they don't know what they don't know. Or maybe Jeremy discussed it with his parents and they advised him to include that he was directed to the president by someone? She did feel that it was a wise choice on his part because otherwise he would have seemed quite presumptuous.

Nonetheless, Pia felt like she'd been hit by a bus. She had a small panic attack then and her hair began to fall out again over the next few weeks. The new president was a pleasant fellow who had graduated from the school, succeeded in his career, and had served on the board of trustees. He was just looking to Pia for some background on the policies and past practices regarding such a situation. He had copied the provost and would discuss the issue with some other key people. She replied to him immediately and he responded to her with appreciation for the information she provided. Still, Pia was certain she would be in serious trouble for the unauthorized advice she gave Jeremy.

And so she was. "Pia: Have you had any contact with a student named Jeremy Ronan regarding commencement?" was the email from Sandra the next day.

Pia decided she may as well fall on her sword. She forwarded her communications with the president including Jeremy's email to him. She did *not* use the opportunity to explain that Jeremy was in a bind that could have been avoided with better mentoring, or with more information, because in his written dialogues with Pia and the president, Jeremy himself didn't blame anyone for the situation. She included some of Jeremy's qualities that made him deserving of consideration.

Sandra was furious about the situation. It was decided that Pia would be given a warning rather than being dismissed. She was not getting any more chances, however. If she did anything as obviously against the policies again she would be fired. Pia thanked Sandra and Ralph for their generosity. She tried to make it a 'teachable moment' for Sandra when she was called into her office about the issue, explaining that the reason she advised Jeremy as she did was that he never blamed anyone for the situation and Pia thought that was astoundingly unusual.

"I really wanted to ask Jeremy's advisor where he's been all this time. He should have been guiding him and checking in with him—," Pia began.

"Yeah, you're totally right about that!" Sandra enthusiastically chimed in.

"— but Jeremy didn't try to hold him responsible, so I didn't either. Jeremy's taught me a lesson on being an adult; he just wants to know the best way out of the situation from where we are now. He isn't deflecting blame onto anyone."

"Hmm."

In the end the university permitted Jeremy to participate in the commencement ceremony. No harm was done, except to Pia by Pia. Jeremy had no knowledge of all this drama going on behind scenes. He was suffering enough stress about whether he'd be allowed to walk in the ceremony or let down his family. Jeremy had been redirected by the president to petition the committee, and the committee had him on their agenda for three weeks before voting on it. The meeting deciding on it coincided with Sandra having a time conflict, and so she was unable to cast her 'no' vote. Pia figured that was probably done deliberately for Jeremy, but the prolonged wait had to have caused him a lot of anxiety. It also left Ralph with only a week to get everything ready for Jeremy to attend the ceremony, so he wasn't too happy.

After careful consideration, Pia came to feel that she would not have done anything differently. The university failed Jeremy on several levels, but if he knew it he didn't say so. Almost everyone else on the planet would have deliberated that perspective, even if their arguments had no merit. Pia told herself that's why she took such a risk. She felt terribly that one email from her caused so much drama. Maybe she shouldn't have contacted him about it at all? Of course, being the type of person he was, as soon as Jeremy learned the petition was successful he came to the office. He leaned his tall, slender torso over the counter and looked at Pia directly.

"Thank you," he said earnestly.

Due to weakness in her knees and rising panic Pia was unable to get up from her desk. She glanced around quickly, hoping Ralph and Sandra were not there, because they would be unpleasant toward him. She flushed when she met Jeremy's eyes. She hated that but there was no stopping it.

Pia mumbled, "You're welcome" but couldn't be sure it was audible.

After a moment, as it became clear Pia was not going to engage further, he patted the counter lightly as his head bobbled slightly and then he left, his message delivered. Jeremy didn't know he had walked into enemy territory. Luckily the enemies were in a meeting, probably about him.

"Jeremy's a really special person," is how Pia rationalized her motives to herself. "It's *not* his big eyes and nice smile."

She had some sleepless nights over this. He was very generous with his gratitude, so sweet, but honestly 'with big eyes and a nice smile' could end every sentence in her head: "He's a really sweet kid with big eyes and a nice smile."

Rather like that guy she knew who put 'between the sheets' at the end of every fortune cookie note.

"You will have a long life with great success (between the sheets)."

So funny when you've had a few drinks. Then she gave that adaptation a try in her head.

"He's a really sweet kid between the sheets." That was followed immediately with "*God*, get a life, Pia."

She was feeling something for Jeremy. It was a pull like a gravitational force, totally ridiculous. In sixteen years of marriage to Gordon this had never happened. If she found someone attractive, she just expelled the idea from her head with no problem. For whatever reason that was just not working in this case. Pia really puzzled over it because it was so bizarre. Eventually she would fall asleep for a few hours before the next day began.

When Pia was married to her first husband, Neil, he came home from work one day and mentioned that a new woman had started working at the company and she was really cool. Like a new friend. Neil worked many miles from their apartment. Pia did not notice that he stopped mentioning her after a while. She did notice that he began showering more often. Pia was glad for that. Neil normally only showered once a week.

Anyway, she managed the bills and it didn't take long to notice that the phone bills began to include a lot of calls to a phone number in Salem. They didn't know anyone in Salem. Sometimes Neil would come home very late or not at all. She attributed this to his being an alcoholic. If he stopped in a bar for one drink all was lost. Pia preferred it when he didn't come home at all to his coming home in the middle of the night shitfaced and tripping over the coffee table, peeing in his pants. Neil had so many miserable stories and none of them were plausible, but she had to take his word for it if she couldn't prove he was lying. And when they were true it was all the sadder.

One morning she was in the bedroom changing and he came in. She asked where he had stayed. Neil said he came in late and slept on the sofa so he wouldn't wake her. She stopped what she was doing and held his gaze, which made him uncomfortable.

"I slept on the sofa last night," Pia stated sadly.

Confirming her suspicions did not feel good.

She discovered that in Massachusetts it was possible to obtain a divorce when nothing is contested without having to hire a lawyer. She just asked a lot of questions and did the paperwork herself. Somehow, still, it broke her heart to lose Neil. In hindsight she had been a fool to think the marriage would endure. It began to unravel in spring, and it wasn't until the following spring that she noticed one day she didn't feel quite as badly as she had a year before. That made her realize that she would pull through okay.

Thus, Pia learned to watch out when a name suddenly drops off the radar. She made a conscious effort to mention Jeremy to Gordon as frequently as anyone else she interacted with at work. They had his photograph of the women in a marketplace hanging in their dining room and Gordon was well aware of the warning Pia received at work for her helpful interference. Gordon's response to the situation with Jeremy's request to participate in commencement was somewhat juvenile to her mind.

"You should tell Jeremy that he nearly got you fired when he mentioned you in his appeal to the president. That wasn't too bright," he'd say over dinner from time to time.

"Oh, come on. Jeremy didn't do anything wrong, Gordon," Pia reinforced each time he brought it up. "He mentioned my name to Helen Johnson when he applied for the scholarship I told him about.

I should've foreseen that he would refer to me in the email to the president as well. I should've asked him not to."

Still, Gordon occasionally brought this up, and they would repeat the conversation until it vexed Pia.

Chapter 3

Jeremy earned his final three credits in August and then took a vacation with his family. He could receive his diploma in October, the next time the university confirmed degrees. When Pia thought he should be back in the area, she contacted him about having a photography exhibit in the fall in the campus center big gallery. She was anxious about contacting him but was charged with it by Linda. She realized that it was serendipity again that allowed him to walk in the spring ceremony; if Linda hadn't asked her to join the committee and mentioned that he thought he was graduating, none of that would have happened. Pia sent an email asking Jeremy if he would be willing to have a show up for a semester.

"Hello Jeremy, I hope you enjoyed your trip. I'm on the exhibits committee for the campus center. Linda Taylor thought you had an idea for a photographic exhibit on the nearby river and we wanted to see if you were interested in showing that this fall."

"Hi, Pia, our trip was amazing and exceeded all my expectations! Thank you for reaching out to me about this. I would be delighted to participate in some way in that exhibit."

Hmm, it seemed that Jeremy wasn't on the same page as Linda. When Pia pressed her for more details, Linda confessed that she hadn't talked with Jeremy about it, someone else had. Pia got the sense that they were hoping he would have his own show, since they didn't have much else lined up for that fall. Pia had arranged for a different exhibit in the café and that was simple to arrange, as the artist had asked them if he could exhibit there and he helped hang it. He was an attractive, soft-spoken, divorced man much closer to Pia's age. Luckily for him, she could only manage one infatuation at a time.

After some back and forth, Pia and Jeremy agreed on a number of images on his theme that would comprise his own exhibit. One day Jeremy phoned her, asking her to look at a sample of what he had in mind for his original concept in an email attachment. It was a photo taken right outside her office an hour before. Her heart beat faster.

"He was nearby just now!" her heart chirped with excitement.

"That doesn't concern you," her brain warned.

"How did you take that photograph? It shows you holding something with both hands," Pia asked him over the phone while she reviewed it.

"I use a tripod, and I have an attachment from the camera that I hold in my mouth and take the photo that way." Ah, his mouth.

After that day Jeremy was not able to take the photos as often as he had hoped because he was living at his parents' house two hours north and was spending a lot of time looking for work. Pia knew that without confirmation of his degree he wouldn't have much luck. She checked her database to make certain he had met all his graduation requirements and then quickly typed up a standard letter to scan to him. This would suffice for potential employers until he received his actual diploma in the fall. She sent it to him with that explanation.

"Perfect, thank you! If it isn't too much trouble, is it possible to mail the original? My mom wants to frame it, lol."

That made her laugh. "Ha, sure, it will be addressed to her."

"You are wonderful! Thank you! Warm regards."

Jesus, this would be easier if he didn't write that she was "wonderful." Did he really think she was wonderful? Did he always write to people this way? Knowing him was actually becoming painful; it made her ache. She sent the document off in the mail and very nearly added a note to his mother saying what a great job she had done raising him and explaining about his omission of blame with the graduation problem. But in the end she didn't include it.

Jeremy was also hoping to get some photographs taken from several rooftops on the campus. This would afford excellent and unusual views of the river. One morning he arrived on campus hoping to do this but hadn't gotten anywhere with the employee he thought could best assist him. Pia told him if he really wanted the photographs she might be able to help.

She made a call to the grounds department's administrative assistant Tess, who was always friendly. She said it would require permission from the head of compliance and the campus police chief. If they permitted it, someone from the grounds staff would have to accompany Jeremy. It turned out that there were two main concerns. One was that someone would fall to his or her death accidentally. The other was that someone would fall to his or her death deliberately.

As Tess put it, "Someone else has to go with you because, just as an example, you two might plan to hold hands and jump together. They would really like to avoid that."

Pia couldn't think of anyone who embraced life more than Jeremy, so she wasn't concerned about a suicide attempt on his part. Briefly she thought of she and Jeremy holding hands.

She sent an email to the head of compliance and the chief, both people she knew, respectfully requesting roof access. She copied Linda and Jeremy. Jeremy was given permission within an hour; someone from groundskeeping would arrange to take him up a few days later.

"John will meet with you Thursday morning. Good luck. Don't trip or jump," Pia wrote to Jeremy.

That was the sarcasm she had learned from her family. What she meant was "please be very careful," but that's not what she wrote. Jeremy didn't respond to it.

Pia rationalized his lack of a response this way: "Jeremy doesn't like me. I don't blame him; I don't like me either much."

She could be a little dramatic sometimes.

The trip to the roof was successful and Jeremy got some great photographs. He sent an appreciative email thanking John, Pia, and Tess afterwards.

Four days later, a student from their university fell to his death from a rooftop downtown.

Linda called Pia the next day. The head of compliance had just phoned her and vehemently rescinded his permission for Jeremy to go on any rooftops. Pia assured Linda he had already gotten some images.

"Pia, the student who died…he wasn't drunk or on drugs. He was a super kid. He," Linda exhaled and then continued, "he tripped as he was taking a photograph."

"Oh, no." Pia groaned. "Oh, no.…"

After she hung up with Linda, all Pia could think of was the email to Jeremy with her sarcastic comment about not tripping. She felt sick to her stomach. She had sent someone's son on a rooftop to take photographs and it could have ended up being his last day on earth. At the time she arranged for it Pia had visualized flat rooftops, but there were many more on campus that were slippery old slate slopes. She recalled watching a film with Johnny Depp running across quite a few of them in bare feet and pajamas. In real life he wouldn't have lasted a minute.

Pia attended the celebration of life on the campus a few weeks later on a lovely Sunday morning in September. She felt she should atone for making light of the university's concern over the safety issue involved in roof access. Before it formally began, there was video footage of the student's life running on a screen while people gradually filed into the auditorium. It was a moving and beautiful tribute. Many young people from the university and his high school spoke of their friendships with the young man and what made him special. His parents spoke. Pia could not imagine how they were going to continue forward without him. She could use some absolution, but she didn't find it that day.

Before she set off for home, she visited the memorial reflective pool on campus. It was for students who passed away far sooner than they should have. The campus was busy because it was homecoming weekend, but she had time to herself there. The reflective pool was in a serene area with elaborate landscaping because it was part of the formal garden to a very grand old house on the campus.

Initially, the campus consisted of a quadrangle of open green lawn and shade trees in the center, with a dozen buildings surrounding it on four sides. As it grew, a street encircled those buildings and on that street was another round of buildings, mostly dormitories and academic halls. Eventually the school expanded into the surrounding neighborhood quite a bit. The most recent additions were parking garages and sports facilities. So the oldest, most charming buildings were in the center, and the state-of-the-art structures were easiest to see from main avenues. Periodically the gardens would be the subject of debate because some administrators thought the land would serve the community better as a parking lot. Each time they had been spared, but Pia thought it was only a matter of time before the gardens lost the battle. A year earlier an enormous, venerable old sycamore tree was cut down without warning to make way for a new building.

Pia was seated on a granite bench thinking about how a reception was going on right then for the student's family and wondering if it was a flaw in her that she could not possibly go. She would not be able to say anything to them. Seemingly out of nowhere, two people came around the corner laughing about something one had just said. It was Jeremy with a male, Asian friend Pia didn't know. All three of them were a little startled for a moment, but then Jeremy said hello.

"Hi, Pia! I'm surprised you're here on a Sunday. You look very nice."

Pia was in a rayon, blue floral dress with a small cardigan over it in a paler blue that matched the little flowers. Her hair was done up and sprayed, which was rare for her. She was not surprised that Jeremy was on campus because it was homecoming weekend, and Jeremy had told her he would pick up his exhibit's promotional postcards that day. For once, Pia had hoped to avoid running into Jeremy.

"Thank you. There was, I was…at the memorial service. For the student who died? You probably got the email that went out from the president about it."

"Oh, yeah, that is so sad." Then he looked at her inquisitively; he tipped his head ever so slightly and knit his brow. "Did you know him?"

Pia smiled weakly and crossed her legs, arranging her dress over her knees.

"No, actually." She changed subjects abruptly. "I left the postcards for your exhibit at the main desk in the library, like you suggested."

"I picked them up when I got here. They look great! Thank you."

He motioned to his black canvas courier bag that was strapped over his shoulder. He was in good spirits. Almost as an explanation, Jeremy told her this garden was one of his favorite places on campus. Then Jeremy and his silent friend went on their way.

As she headed home from the gardens, Pia reflected that her feelings for Jeremy were a strange mix. She didn't know him well, but everything she saw of him suggested that he was a kind person. Pia understood that his public persona may or may not be completely authentic. Most people are inauthentic sometimes. But then he had invited her and Linda to view his photography website where he had a file for the upcoming exhibit. Jeremy included what he referred to as 'captions' to go with many of his images. There Pia found that Jeremy had a big, generous heart filled with affection for both strangers and friends. He took photos of many people as well as breathtaking ones of the natural world and described them all very poetically. To her mind, Jeremy allowed the world to see what was in his wonderful heart and that made her love him.

It also made her feel strongly that she wanted to protect him. Pia didn't want any experience to happen to Jeremy that would teach him to hide what his heart felt. It was difficult for her to comprehend that someone his age would allow himself to be so vulnerable. By the time Pia was ten years old she had personally had enough of mean girls making fun of any tender thought she expressed. She hid her feelings for many years and it was a long road back to sharing with kind people whom she trusted. She wondered if Jeremy was too naïve to know he could get hurt this way, or if he was confident enough in who he was that potential arrows would not inflict any damage at all.

Mixed in with all this were the romantic feelings she was developing for him. She still couldn't understand why she was unable to override them. On some level there must've been something she needed. Jeremy was so kind. He was, except for that Sunday in the garden, always solitary when she saw him. There was no indication that he had a girlfriend. That didn't mean that he didn't; Pia herself was rarely seen with Gordon, because Gordon didn't join her in many things. The blending of romantic and maternal feelings was particularly disturbing. She didn't feel creepy, but she did feel a little confused. Still, Pia thought of Jeremy a lot. There was no point to it, but there was nothing to be done for it either.

In late September Jeremy had a complete set of images for his exhibit.

Normally the artist would deliver the work ready to hang. Pia felt like Jeremy had been coerced to some extent and really didn't have time for this, so when he asked if she was able to take the photographs from him if he swung by one morning, she said yes.

Jeremy brought her the photographs, thanked her, and said he had to run, as he was late for work. Pia received them as if it were no trouble for her to frame them. Linda had the mats and frames for her to use, but Pia truthfully had no free time. She was responsible for an exhibit in her town and had some committee commitments and was under a lot of stress. She literally cried herself to sleep that night. Nonetheless, it was her own doing and she made the time after normal work hours. She made individual signs for each image's caption and printed Jeremy's short introductory statement. She framed and hung the photos, and bought a book for visitors to write their thoughts in. The show would hang from October through January.

On her way home late after hanging the exhibit, Pia was rewarded by coming upon a group of deer near her house. Where she lived was rural and the road home ran between two hayfields, with a pond beyond one field and a forest beyond the other. It was Pia's habit to roll down the window and, well, talk to the deer. She reasoned that this made them more comfortable because a predator would be silent. They would stop and turn their huge ears towards her and their noses twitched. The few deer in the field on the right side of the road waited for the one in the middle of the road to make a decision. She looked from Pia's car to her fawn in the left field a few times. The fawn waited for guidance. Then, determining it to be safe, the doe somehow communicated to the fawn to join her. It did, and together they vaulted over the old stone wall to the grass beyond.

That reminded her of a previous experience when her volunteer shift at the nature sanctuary had run way over time. A special needs adult didn't want to leave the event. Her caregiver's patience was worn but she didn't say anything. Pia sat and chatted with them, simultaneously picking up the craft supplies spread around them. Eventually Pia succeeded in coaxing the woman out. On her way home from the nature sanctuary, she saw a group of deer on the road.

That first time the hay fields for the nature sanctuary had just been cut and Pia inhaled the sweet scent deeply while she watched the deer. It was one of her favorite smells. There wasn't any hay this night in the fall, but there was the scent of cinnamon fern and the peaceful rhythm of the cicadas. In both instances, the moment with the deer was like a karmic reward for her overtime and it made her feel better.

In early October, Jeremy emailed Pia asking if she would be at work on a certain day. He was going to pick up his diploma and visit his exhibit. At lunchtime on that day, Pia headed down the hall to go out the main door for her walk. In the hallway she found Jeremy heading towards her.

"Hi! I'm on my way to see you," he smiled. His head bobbled ever so slightly when he talked.

So Pia turned and walked back toward her office with him, saying, "This is good timing. Have you seen your exhibit?""

"Not yet, but some friends told me it looks great! I'm going there next."

In the registrar's office, Jeremy waited at the counter and Pia went around towards the back area for his diploma. Shelly asked if she could help him but he stated that Pia was already. Shelly responded tersely that Pia was at lunch, so as Pia walked past Shelly's desk she assured her it was okay. Shelly knew that Pia had many favorite students and was willing to shorten her lunch for them, but Shelly frowned upon it on principle.

Pia returned with Jeremy's master's diploma and came around to his side of the counter. Jeremy thanked her for the exhibit, then held up the diploma and thanked her for that also. After a slight hesitation he hugged her. Immediately she felt her face blush, to her chagrin. Pia could only imagine what Shelly thought of it and she was glad that Ralph didn't come out of his office. Sometimes she'd get candy from someone she spent extra effort on but Pia couldn't recall when another student had hugged her. There was a work-study student *she* hugged, Etienne. He was a junior who had been working there his whole time at the university and they were buddies. Mary would sometimes suggest that they do less talking and find something else for Etienne to do.

Then Jeremy went one way and Pia went the other way for her walk. Pia took the hug for what it was, gratitude for her help, a kind gesture. She wasn't so crazed as to add any other meaning to it, but her spirits were high while she made her way along her route around the park. She felt that she had probably done the right thing by Jeremy.

The next time she would see him was at his exhibit opening reception in a week. She was looking forward to that. It was as if the rest of her life had a fine film over it and this obsession had more color, more clarity. She knew that in reality her life was full and busy and would normally be rewarding. She wasn't a spinster with only cats for companionship. This compulsive thinking of Jeremy was just dappled sunlight over everything. It was nothing real. But Pia was being drawn to the dappled sunlight in her life more than what it was shining on.

Chapter 4

The exhibit opened on a cold weeknight. Linda had arranged the food and Pia brought a flower arrangement. She knew the university wouldn't pay for it but it was a touch she added when she curated a show. Linda had sent out an email to the whole campus promoting the opening reception. Pia personally invited about twenty acquaintances. About six of them showed up, but that was to be expected. People are busy. Pia had been working out a lot more since the spring and had lost nearly twenty pounds. She told people who noticed her weight loss that the new rec center made it possible. No one asked further what the actual incentive was, thankfully.

Pia was wearing some new, smaller tan pants and a favorite dusky blue lace and silk shirt that fluttered with the little breeze caused by her walking. She had a new haircut she liked, although more actual hair would've been welcome. She felt about as attractive as she could. Jeremy arrived alone, wearing gray pants and a deep orange dress shirt. Although Pia was glad he didn't come with a date, truly, she would have been granted real relief if he had a girlfriend.

Linda and Jeremy chatted while they waited for people to arrive. Pia realized that she hadn't seen them interact before. They had music in common and they were talking about a venue in the city they both knew. Jeremy pulled up the place on his phone and showed it to Pia, but by the end of the evening she would forget the name of it. Then Jeremy told them that he had gone to the nearby art museum several times each week when he had attended the university. That surprised Pia. She told Linda and Jeremy about a new exhibit she had heard about that opened there, photographs of child soldiers in Africa.

"That would be really hard," Jeremy said. Pia assumed he meant to view.

"Yeah…but it's important," Pia mumbled and looked away.

She thought she mumbled. It was hard to know. She mentioned a Norman Rockwell painting on display there simultaneously with the child soldiers and hoped the juxtaposition of the two opposite worlds was intentional on the part of the curators at the museum. Linda wasn't so sure.

Pia said something about, "If you feel too saddened by the photography exhibit you could just go down the hall to look at the Norman Rockwell."

There she was trying to be witty again. Pia knew that, while the photography show was important and she was impressed that they were showing it, the very viewing of those subjects in the physical space of a grand old art museum would be difficult to reconcile. However, she didn't say anything about that.

Gradually people began arriving. Jeremy's exhibit had a good turnout as events go at the university, about thirty people over the course of two hours.

Pia's friend Diane, from the Computer Science department, dropped by, although she had a family to get home to and couldn't stay long. She marveled at most of the images and was impressed that Pia was involved in this committee now. Diane was generally social and knew some other people, and enjoyed the party atmosphere. Then Pia introduced her to the artist. Jeremy cheerfully answered some of Diane's questions. Afterwards Jeremy moved on to some other people waiting to speak with him.

"He's pretty neat." Diane smiled and nodded enthusiastically.

Pia concurred, "Oh, he's such a great person."

"And he's *so* cute, he really is."

Diane was always interested in handsome men and knew she was striking herself. She gave Pia that knowing gaze that Linda had given her months before.

"Uh-oh, cougar alert," Pia thought. Like she should talk. She responded to Diane's observation off-handedly while she looked at a photograph. "You think so? I hadn't noticed." Then she turned her head to Diane, grinned, and confessed with a sigh, "Getting to know Jeremy has been a gift…and a torment."

That wasn't too wise of her. Diane was a nice person but she was unable to keep secrets.

Diane said excitedly, "Is he interested in you?"

"Of course not, that's absurd!" Pia scoffed. She thought, "Diane's playing with me."

"Pia, it is not absurd. You're attractive, and you look much younger than you are."

She gave Pia a look that implied Pia should at least consider it. Good grief.

Then one of the faculty arrived, Jacob Katz. They both chatted with him. He was a great guy, in his mid-forties and married with children. He was also quite sexy; handsome and masculine, but with a charming boyishness.He didn't seem to know he was hot, which was part of the attraction. Diane flirted with him shamelessly. Pia had invited him earlier that day and thanked him for coming. She knew art wasn't really his thing and she wasn't surprised when he moved from them directly to the food table. Pia found Jacob attractive but had no trouble at all compartmentalizing that where it belonged. She resolved to make more of an effort to do that with Jeremy.

Later, a dear friend of Pia's arrived. She worked at a nearby hospital and they didn't see each other often, but Pia had sent her a postcard invitation. When Pia saw Ellen looking around after she stepped off the elevator, Pia went directly to her. They embraced and caught up for a while. Then they began to look at the exhibit together. When he had a free moment Jeremy came over to where they stood in front of one of the photographs.

"Hi, I'm the artist. What do you think of this one?"

Ellen told him, "It's terrific. You have an amazing angle. It makes the area look…enchanting. Better than it actually is!"

"These images were taken from a rooftop on this campus." Jeremy motioned to several photographs with a sweep of his hand. "I had hoped to get some that were timeless. That wasn't easy because of all the development in the past few decades. I wanted people to see the remaining nature and appreciate it."

"I'd say you succeeded. I'm Ellen," she said as she extended her hand.

Jeremy shook it. "Thanks very much for coming! I don't remember seeing you before. Do you teach here?"

"No, I used to work with Pia. She's one of my favorite people; she's a good soul," Ellen smiled. Pia sometimes suspected that Ellen added in her head, "Inept and can't remember something from ten minutes ago, but a good soul". Pia had filed in her memory the instances when she forgot to tell Ellen she had a patient waiting. Oddly, she remembered her errors indefinitely.

Jeremy absorbed what Ellen said and smiled at Pia.

A little embarrassed, she said, "Ellen, that's why I invited you. I wanted you to meet Jeremy because he's a good soul too," and the three of them chuckled at that.

Jeremy replied, "Thanks for saying that."

His head did that little bobble thing again and he looked at Pia a few seconds longer than she was comfortable with.

Pia just told him "It's true," and she flushed.

Someone else wanted Jeremy's attention. Pia and Ellen walked and talked some more. They promised to get together for dinner sometime soon, but Ellen had a family and lived a few towns away, so it was difficult to actually do so. To Pia's mind it was fine, it was enough that they meant to try.

At one point, Pia and a small, round Middle Eastern woman were reading the same caption. She was young so Pia thought she might be one of the eight or so young people who knew Jeremy.

"Are you a friend of his?" Pia asked her.

She turned to Pia and shyly answered, "Yes."

Her pretty face was framed by a blue scarf. Pia wanted to ask her if she was in love with him.

Pia overheard a nearby conversation Jeremy was having with his friends. They wanted Jeremy to spend time with them after the opening; he explained that he'd need a place to stay the night. A male friend offered his place so it was quickly settled. Later on Jeremy introduced that friend, Paco Hernandez, to Pia and Linda after everyone else left. Pia and Linda cleaned up and Jeremy and Paco stayed for a while chatting. Then Jeremy hugged each woman before he and Paco left.

Once Pia was in her car on her way home she picked up a scent around her she didn't recognize. It seemed to be coming from her. She was puzzled for a minute before she realized it must be Jeremy's cologne on her shirt. Pia thought it was a little unusual for him to wear cologne, but what did she know about twenty-three-year-old men really? Gordon had never donned cologne in his life.

When she was home Gordon picked up on the scent when he hugged her, which surprised her because his olfactory sense was negligible.

"Who've you been with? I smell cologne," he said.

Pia didn't care for his implication and matter-of-factly answered,

"It's Jeremy. He hugged Linda and I each about three times. He's very huggy." She flipped through the day's mail and changed the subject. "What did you do today?"

"He just hugged you, right?"

"Yes, silly."

Pia made it sound like he needn't worry. Later, when she was undressing upstairs, she held onto the shirt for a long while to inhale the scent before she reluctantly tossed it in the clothes hamper.

The following morning Pia attended an event at the local elementary school. She was invited because she chaired the local cultural council, which provided funding for the performance. The main speaker had mentioned at the beginning that it was made possible by the council's funding, as was the protocol. He pointed Pia out to everyone as the chair of the council, and had all the children say, "Good morning, Mrs. Sandstrom." That made Pia laugh.

She sat in the back so she could watch how the schoolchildren responded to the show. Pia enjoyed the event and as it was ending some parents thanked her for funding it. She felt good; it was a successful presentation. She left feeling a little melancholy though, because it reminded her of how much she'd wanted children. As was often the case for Pia, she had several emotions simultaneously. She didn't know if this was normal for others, but she was both happy and sad together as she drove to work.

She was at her office by noon. When she turned on her computer there was an email from Jeremy with the subject line "Good morning!" written at about seven that morning to her and Linda. "Thank you both so much again for the exhibit and reception. It went really great, a total success! Thank you for all of your hard work. Please choose an image from the show that I can give you."

He was just too sweet.

So that was that. Pia would communicate with Jeremy when the show came down. She made a concerted effort to focus on her real world and suppress any notions about that boy. Then about two weeks later, Jeremy stopped by her office late in the afternoon. She got up from her desk and went up to the counter to talk with him.

Jeremy said, "Hi! I was wondering if you would be interested in going to the art museum with me tonight? It's open until 9:00 and it's free on Thursdays."

This was one of those times Pia wished the wide counter wasn't separating them. All conversations there were public.

"Oh! Hmm, sure, I would like that. I work until five o'clock, though."

"Okay, great! I'll come back then." He smiled and his head bobbled slightly.

After lightly tapping the counter surface, Jeremy went on his way and Pia sat down. She didn't know what to think. She was excited but rather stunned and began chewing her nails. It occurred to her that it was lucky again that Ralph wasn't in the office that afternoon. She called Gordon and said she wouldn't be home until about eight so he should make himself dinner. Whenever she was going to miss dinner Gordon never really minded because then he could eat exactly what he wanted. Pia knew he would pick up a submarine sandwich.

"Do you have a date with that student?" Shelly asked with a laugh, after she heard Pia hang up the phone.

"It definitely sounded like a date to me," Dave added. Dave was an easygoing fellow with a good sense of humor.

Mary had just come in from a meeting and in a cheery voice she asked, "Ooh, who's got a date tonight?"

Shelly and her boyfriend had split up a month ago. Dave was also single. When she learned they were discussing Pia, her face fell and she went directly to her desk. Mary was a skittish, old-fashioned mother of two young girls.

Nell, a kind, older woman who worked there part-time, pointed out, "I met my husband here thirty years ago. Oh, but he wasn't a student," she remembered. Then she considered something else. "Oh, and you already have a husband, Pia. There's that little matter."

"It's not a date. He's my 'nephew,'" Pia said.

She referred to about a dozen students as her nieces or nephews, so they knew by now that he wasn't really her nephew but rather it was just how she felt about the students.

"I dunno. I think it's a date," Dave teased. "That must be against school policy, isn't it?"

Shelly added, "I'm sure it is. Pia's gonna get in trouble!"

As long as everyone was having fun, it was all good. Pia laughed with them.

After the office door was locked Pia hung around in the hallway and Jeremy came by a few minutes later. Pia had parked on the street and she didn't have to take them out of their way to leave her bento box and sneakers in her car. Her office was one of the buildings on the outer, secondary ring around the quad. They walked over to the museum together, about five blocks away. It was a cool and breezy evening. The leaves rustled periodically as they were swept up by the wind. Most of the trees had released their leaves by now and they were tumbling along the lawns and sidewalks. Jeremy had long legs and a quick stride, so Pia nearly had to jog to keep up with him.

He said his job was going fine when Pia asked him about it, but he didn't elaborate. He enjoyed living in the city and saw a lot of bands in small clubs. His brother was living with him and they got along well.

Pia didn't really know her way inside the museum because she had only been there twice before in eighteen years, although when she was in art school she visited there regularly Jeremy was familiar with the layout so they declined the maps offered by the visitor services staff. Several wings had been added to it since Pia had last visited. She didn't care much for most of the old sculptures and paintings, but she knew and appreciated their value in the history of art. Pia enjoyed new art much more, so she went to regional exhibits and places that featured current artists' work. She loved to see new concepts and artists finding their own language.

They came upon an exhibit of recent work first; the artists' work was creative, unique, and fun. It was probably best that they saw that gallery before the one featuring the child soldiers. As far as Pia knew, it was a visit to see whatever they could, not a specific exhibit. Jeremy enjoyed showing her some of his favorite paintings as they meandered through the halls and he greeted the docents, all of whom were familiar with him. Jeremy seemed to appreciate all of it.

"So you're interested in art. Do you make any yourself?" he asked.

"Not really anymore. If someone gives me a drawing assignment I'll do it."

"Did you used to draw a lot?"

"Oh, sorry, yes. I have a bachelor's degree in art. Now I make signs for non-profits I volunteer at. But I don't make art for myself. I feel like it's too…well, self-indulgent," Pia said.

She was being honest but she probably insulted every artist she ever said it to, possibly including Jeremy.

She changed the subject then. "It's great that you can use both sides of your brain; you're a scientist *and* an artist. I only use one side and even that's pretty sporadic. Linda told me you play the piano."

"Yeah, and the guitar sometimes," he said. "I really love music."

"Your parents must be so proud of you. I was hoping to meet them at your opening," Pia said.

This made Jeremy looked a little puzzled and almost displeased. "Too far for them to travel. I don't know…I hope they're proud of me."

Pia faltered a bit. "You graduated with high honors and received A's in extra courses. And you're a great person. Don't your parents think so?"

She felt like she was slipping in mud.

"I forgot you have access to my grades." Jeremy smiled briefly. "My dad is in finance, and he's very competitive, whereas I'm not at all. We have different values, so I think I might not be what he wants in a son. My brother Adam does a little better by him, but he tries harder than I do to please him. Like, I'm not cutting my hair to look like a banker for him. My mom is really great, though!" He perked up a little when he mentioned his mother.

"I could tell you didn't want to let her down during that commence-ment trouble," Pia offered.

"My father is kind of…oh, a little hard to live with. I think my mom would have a happier life with someone different."

"I'm sorry. Anyway, if you were my son I would try to take all the credit," she said assuredly.

Jeremy had been looking at the exhibit off and on while they talked, but when she said that he turned his head to her.

"How do you mean…credit for what?"

She couldn't read his face; she hardly knew him.

"For you being the fine person you are. Probably the credit is all yours but I'd be all like, '*Hey, I raisedthis guy!*'"

This got a laugh out of Jeremy and he shook his head at her. "That's a really nice thing to say. Thanks, Pia."

They found the exhibit of photographs of former child soldiers. It was uncomfortable, as they both expected. Descriptions beside each photograph explained not only the awful conditions that forced them into it, and told of what they endured, but also highlighted the precarious circumstances they were in after their service. Because they had been forced to kill their neighbors or watch their families brutalized, they were not welcome in their former communities when the war ended or when they ran away from the militants. So they had no families, no tribe. In modern cultures families often spread out and away from each other, but in these more traditional cultures the village community is vital. An individual alone has no place.

Some images showed the dilapidated huts they lived in, in abandoned villages. The vines, mosses and grasses were overtaking the thatched roofs. One young woman was so beautiful and had been through unspeakable things. She was only fifteen, living in a solitary hut in the jungle. One little boy believed wearing a garland of leaves on his head would protect him from bullets. Pia contemplated, as she always did with photographers and reporters sent to cover atrocities, the moral tension of the job.

"I know I couldn't do this work," she said. "I couldn't bear witness and not feel compelled to help these people. Just looking at these images here, in contrast to our surroundings…well, it seems like an abomination."

Jeremy had been quiet. He still didn't say anything beyond "I totally agree," but he gave the exhibit his undivided attention.

When they were at opposite ends of it, Pia was looking at an image of one of the huts, and the words to a song she hadn't heard in years seemed to be manifested in the photograph and welled up in her. The huts were made entirely of natural materials and were in the process of being reclaimed as earth again. And people lived inside them.

She sang it quietly, although others may have heard her.

"Well I've seen them buried in a sheltered place in this town/ They tell you that this rain can sting, and look down/ There is no blood around, see no sign of pain/ Hey, no pain, seeing no red at all, see no rain…."

Pia continued viewing the images and eventually made her way back to Jeremy. He had sat down on a bench and she remained standing next to him. She thought he looked emotionally drained. Pia felt obligated to absorb as much of their experience as she could here. But he was so young. Maybe he wasn't prepared for this reality.

"Are you okay?" Pia asked.

Jeremy just sort of tossed his head about, as if to shake out his thoughts. Pia felt badly.

"We're honoring them by learning about their lives. It's not much, but it's something. That you care about them is something. Even if they don't know you do."

"I don't know…." He sighed and got up.

Pia left it at that, since she felt she had contradicted what she had said thirty minutes earlier.

Jeremy walked her back to her car. Beneath the streetlamps, Pia noticed that the wind had cleared the sidewalk of many oak leaves, and their tannin had left impressions on the light concrete surface after a heavy rain bled them.

"Isn't this pretty?" she paused and asked Jeremy, pointing to the leaf designs under their feet.

They stopped to look all around the sidewalk.

Jeremy smiled. "It is! I always think only the maple leaves have something to offer in the fall, but this is cool, too."

Pia thought of how vibrantly crimson the poison ivy turned in the autumn, but since people hate that plant unequivocally she didn't say anything about it.

When she stopped and unlocked her car she asked Jeremy if he wanted a ride. He said he would catch a bus. She got into her seat, turned the engine over and lowered the driver's window. She looked up at him.

"I hope you didn't view that exhibit just because I wanted to see it," Pia said, referring to the photographs of the former child soldiers.

"No worries, it was excellent photojournalism. I'm glad I had you with me. Thank you. Goodnight!"

Pia wondered on her way home how much weight to put on that: 'I'm glad I had you with me.' She turned her phone back on and had three messages from Gordon. The neighbor's horse had just broken a leg in a freak accident in front of their driveway and had to be put down. What a night.

Sandra scheduled a meeting with Pia. When Pia arrived at Sandra's office, she found that Ralph was seated there. And to her great surprise, so was Jeremy. She had the sense that this was not going to be a pleasant experience. Sandra didn't give Pia much time to contemplate what was going on.

"Thank you both for coming. I'm going to get right to the point. The vice-president has asked me to meet with you because the university wants to know exactly what your relationship to one another is."

Pia and Jeremy just looked at her in surprise.

"Hello? Did you hear me? Jeremy, why don't you answer first. Then we'll see what Pia has to add."

It was more of a demand than a request. Pia's heart was in her throat; what on earth was Jeremy going to make of this strange inquisition?

Jeremy's head bobbled a little. "Sure. So, we're friends. I feel that we're friends."

He smiled at Pia. She nodded and returned a small, brief smile. Pia had the idea that Jeremy might have thought they were finished and could leave soon.

Sandra was clearly vexed by the simple response from Jeremy.

"Pia, what is your relationship to Jeremy?"

"Jeremy was a student here and I work here, and sometimes I would help him if he came to our office."

Pia was thinking in the most basic terms of the meaning of 'relationship' as well.

"Well, *duh*. That's inadequate. You haven't answered what your relationship is," Sandra said.

Pia elaborated after giving it some thought. "We both love the university and consider ourselves part of this community. So we have that in common. We're both involved in the arts. I curated an exhibit of his photography in the campus center. I think that's about it."

Jeremy nodded, as if she had covered everything.

"There's nothing more you want to add?" Sandra pressed.

Pia confirmed, "We are friends."

Inside, Pia felt sure that her infatuation with Jeremy was plain to see.

"Are you *more* than friends?" Sandra asked.

"There you go," Pia thought. "Plain to see"

Pia should've seen that coming but she hadn't. She thought this had more to do with the issue with the president in the spring. She was mortified and wished Jeremy was not there. But the fact that he was made Pia more inclined to push back.

"Sandra, you're embarrassing—" Pia began.

Sandra interrupted her. "I'm embarrassing you?"

Sandra seemed pleased, as if she had Pia boxed in. Jeremy's eyebrows were raised and he looked back and forth at Sandra and Pia. He shifted in his seat a few times.

"You're embarrassing yourself. Your implication is completely baseless and offensive." Pia hoped she was convincing. "This is totally inappropriate."

Pia stood up to leave.

"Wow, yeah! I'm not sure what to say to that," Jeremy added.

Sandra pressed on. "Are you *lovers*?"

Then Pia's alarm clock went off next to her face from the night table.

Pia's dream lingered for a few minutes. She reviewed it... eww, terrible. Pia believed that dreams aren't so much a message, but just a messy jumble of recent thoughts and preoccupations. She didn't put much weight on this dream, other than to be careful with Jeremy. On rare occasions like that, when the dream was awful, getting up was preferable to remaining asleep.

The cat jumped on the bed and began her ritual of annoying Pia until she would get up to feed her. In her old age the cat was going deaf and meowed very loudly all the time. On more than one occasion she had saved Pia from oversleeping. Time to go to work.

On the drive to work Pia realized that throughout the past months, while she was so distracted by Jeremy, she was being short-tempered with Gordon. During the weeks surrounding the issue with the president, she told Gordon that was what her trouble was. More of what he did annoyed her and her mind was elsewhere when she should have been paying attention to him. When it came to small decisions such as what to have for dinner, she was much less creative than usual because she really didn't care.

She did her best to behave normally. Gordon was eighteen years her senior with a bad back and sometimes his legs would go numb while he walked. So he would take country drives as something to do and she'd join him if she had free time. He didn't usually listen to Pia when she talked so oftentimes she didn't. Sometimes she'd worry when they were silent for a long time. Then Gordon would begin to whistle and she knew he was fine.

She couldn't understand how Gordon could not see what was going on, even as she did her best to conceal her feelings. She thought that if she was with a woman, that the woman would sense the shift. She told herself that Jeremy would not ever be interested in her, but she had been wondering if it was theoretically possible. Diane's remarks gathered strength in her mind.

At Thanksgiving, between dinner and dessert, the family, including Gordon's son, daughter-in-law and others, sat around talking and drinking wine while the children ran wild or watched a movie. Pia told their daughter-in-law and her sisters that she was "having a mid-life crisis." For many years she had looked much younger than she was, and so was always fine with her age. Now at forty-four, she had suddenly understood that she was truly, irreversibly middle-aged. And that she had been for several years, and that any young person would know that with one look at her.

They tried to understand it, but they knew her well and they didn't think she was the kind of woman who cared about what she looked like to other people. She didn't wear make-up, expensive jewelry or even nail polish. She didn't color her hair. They were too kind to mention the deplorable condition of her feet. Pia thought of her body as the ultimate Swiss army knife, an amazing set of tools to help you get through life. She was glad to be healthy and strong, especially since Gordon was not. Pia mowed the lawn, did the yard work, shoveled, and brought the trash down to the curb. She valued being useful. She could not fathom why women put so much effort into their looks while men generally did not.

Still, her description of her emotional situation seemed acceptable. Everyone told her it would be fine.

Chapter 5

At the next committee meeting with Thatcher the group tried to hash out some differences of opinion about a community project they were slowly working on. They wanted to create a snowboarding/skateboarding park in town. It had been in the works for years and recently the town had approved partially funding it on the condition that the state provided substantial grant money towards it. Unfortunately, the land designated for the park had recently had a change of use. The owners had been getting a tax break for keeping it open to the public for non-motorized recreational activities but recently they sold it to a private entity that restricted the use to hiking only.

Thatcher wasn't deterred. "I think if we talk to the right people we'll be able to convince them to allow the park as originally conceived."

A sensible Black woman named Carla reminded him about the new restrictions. Carla was a somewhat chubby physician. Pia had the same figure as her before she started working out a year ago.

"Thatcher, they've told us before that we won't be allowed to snowboard on that land. And certainly not build a skateboard park there. There's lots of town-owned property we can consider."

Thatcher shook his head as he said, "Look, we're talking about over four hundred acres that isn't currently being used for anything. It's a total waste of the land."

Pia cut in, "It isn't wasted by any means. It's preserved habitat for the animal and plant species that live there. It's also an important piece of the wildlife corridor that runs through this county."

Thatcher made no effort to conceal his disdain for that rational. "It's a waste if we can't use it for anything. The taxpayers should be able to have access to it for recreational purposes."

Arlene pointed out a few facts. "It isn't owned by the taxpayers; it's private land and it's open to hikers and birders now."

Pam and Pia nodded in agreement.

The normally neutral man, Alan, sided with Thatcher on this. "That isn't allowing very much. This proposed park's been a goal of the town for five years now. We have the designs for both the snowboarding area and the skateboard park ready to go and we have a contractor."

Pam asked, "Can't we look at other parcels in town? What about Ravens Hill?"

"Not the right slope. It's no good," said Thatcher in an irritated tone. "And what the hell is a wildlife corridor?"

Pia explained, although she had done so at the last meeting. As with Gordon, it was difficult to get Thatcher to listen to her. Fortunately, they were not similar in any other way.

"It's a long stretch of undisrupted wild land that animals can use to move about without crossing roads. The more of those we have, the fewer incidents there are of collisions with vehicles."

Thatcher responded, "I don't care if we lose skunks and squirrels to traffic, to be perfectly honest with you."

"We know that, Thatcher," said Arlene with a sigh. "If your car hit a moose you might reconsider your perspective while recuperating in your hospital bed."

Carla added quietly, "Might be your coffin. I lost a pregnant patient to a moose collision two years ago."

Thatcher looked smug but everyone else gave that a minute out of respect for the deceased.

Pia persisted with the animal support even though she suspected only Arlene and Pam really appreciated what she was saying.

"An adult male fisher has a range of four or five acres and each one needs his own space. It's similar for bobcats."

Thatcher had just about had it. "I'm not entertaining a conversation on animals right now. Focus on the project, please!"

Carla showed more diplomacy. "If you'd like I can invite them to our next meeting to discuss this again. We can approach it as an opportunity. Most people in town are looking forward to the park."

Thatcher was glad someone was being positive.

"Good, please do. I think that with the right public relations campaign we can shame them into supporting our plan. When they're the only hurdle to making the park a reality they'll look bad."

Pia's advice was, "If you aren't careful that might turn around and bite you on the ass."

Alan had heard enough. "Let's keep it civil, please."

"I apologize," Pia said, and around it went for another fifteen minutes without further input from her.

The snow came early that year. One cold night with a full moon Pia joined a night hike with a group of people from her town. With the snow on the ground the forest was quite beautiful in a totally different way than on summer nights. (Also, this time of year there wasn't the perpetual pitter-patter of caterpillar feces falling from the canopy, where hundreds of them were dining on leaves.) It was only a matter of waiting fifteen or so minutes for the eyes' rods and cones to shift, and then one could see fairly well, particularly with snow on the ground.

Two women decided the snow was too deep and went back. They had driven a third woman, Mattie, so Pia told her she'd give her a ride home. She and Mattie were acquaintances from years back but hadn't seen each other in a while. While they all carried on with the hike, Pia and Mattie's conversation turned to age and Pia again confessed to being in a mid-life crisis. Mattie described her slow-paced divorce a few years before as likely a mid-life crisis as well.

When they were in the car they caught up a little bit. Pia got the sense that Mattie felt a little judged by the community for divorcing her husband. It was a small town and she and her husband shared many friends. That might have been what prompted Pia to share the truth with her: Pia was not in a position to judge anyone. She revealed that she had an infatuation with a twenty-three-year-old boy. Since Mattie had twin sons that age, Pia wasn't sure how this would go over.

"Hey, that's fine. It is. You're interested in them and they're interested in you." She was so casual about it.

"I don't think he's interested in me."

"He probably is. They think it's cool that you have so much more experience. They do. Hey, thanks for the ride. Do you want to come in?"

Pia declined. She thanked Mattie and they said goodnight. While she waited to make sure Mattie got in the house she became aware of a sense of relief. It was so nice to have told someone. On her way home it occurred to her that Mattie might have been talking from experience. Regardless, Pia felt a little less like a pervert.

A few weeks after the trip to the museum, Jeremy came by again in the late afternoon. His workday began much earlier that Pia's, so he was free after three-thirty.

"Hi, Pia! How are you?" Jeremy was very upbeat, all smiles.

By now Shelly had learned to let him default automatically to Pia. Dave avoided the front counter whenever possible and Nell was on the phone.

Pia smiled. "Hi, Jeremy! I'm good. How are you?"

She approached the counter. Then from where she was, she saw that Ralph was nearby and regretted saying Jeremy's name.

"Great! Your song in the museum has been haunting me, though."

Pia wasn't sure if he was serious about that, as he was smiling when he said it.

"So, I have to get a document notarized and I was told I can do that here. Are you a notary by any chance?" he asked pleasantly.

He began to pull paperwork out of his courier bag.

"I'm not, but Dave—" Pia began but stopped mid-sentence when she saw Ralph.

Ralph had abruptly finished his conversation with Mary and was approaching the counter. The theme to the movie *Jaws* played in Pia's head.

"Jeremy Ronan," Ralph said.

Jeremy turned his attention to Ralph and nodded in a friendly way. Pia tensed.

"What brings you here?"

Ralph sounded like he was being helpful but Pia knew better. Jeremy began to explain but Ralph cut him off. "You should never have contacted the president about graduation in April," Ralph said with his stern face.

Poor Jeremy looked dumbfounded.

Pia warned Ralph, keeping her voice down as a hint he should as well, "Ralph, that's not appropriate."

Ralph was speaking loudly enough for the whole office, and three students who just came in, to hear him.

"You almost got Pia here fired, y'know," Ralph continued.

Jeremy looked to Pia and back at Ralph with a confused look.

Pia raised her voice loudly then. "That's privileged information! You were not at liberty to share it with the whole office!"

She felt her cheeks redden. Ralph lifted his eyebrows at her. She shouldn't have yelled and he didn't like it when Pia used fancy vocabulary like 'privileged' and 'liberty,' because he thought it made her sound like a snob. In any case, the damage was already done. Jeremy was processing this and the other people all paused to do the same.

"Just sayin'," Ralph finished, and asked the student waiting behind Jeremy what she wanted.

Jeremy hesitated as if unsure what to do. Then his expression went dark and he quickly gathered his paperwork and turned to leave. Jeremy didn't put the paperwork in his courier bag and he didn't look at Pia.

"Jeremy, wait!" Pia didn't mean for him to stay, but to wait for her, as she was moving around from behind the counter to him.

Many more students had come in to get forms processed but she left them to Shelly and the others while she went to clean up Ralph's mess. She moved pretty quickly but Jeremy's long legs propelled him way ahead of her. She picked up her pace and saw him ahead, weaving through a stream of students. She nearly caught up to him in a hallway that led directly to the street.

"Jeremy!" Pia called out to him.

He stopped when he heard his name and turned to her. Pia's expression was very apologetic when she reached him.

"I'm sorry about that. Ralph had no right to do that to you."

"What was he talking about? Did I almost get you fired? How?" He was perplexed and agitated.

"No, you did not. You had nothing to do with it." Then she clarified for him. "I almost got myself fired when I advised you to go to the president."

"Why? I don't get it."

"That was the wrong channel to go through. As a general rule, staff aren't really supposed to tell students to go to the president. It's frowned upon." Understatement of the year.

"Then why did you tell me to contact him?" Jeremy asked pointedly.

Why. That was a little more difficult to answer. Because she was infatuated with him wouldn't be an ideal response.

Pia sighed and then explained, "I thought it was your best chance. And it did help. You're the only graduate student who's ever walked in the ceremony without having met all of the requirements. In any case, it was a calculated risk on my part; I own it."

She might be stupid, but she was strong.

Pia figured what happened back in the office was confusing and possibly humiliating for Jeremy, so she gave him some time. She started to chew her nails but forced herself to stop. There was a ton of work on her desk waiting for her. Jeremy thought about what Pia was telling him.

Finally he said, "You risked your job to help me out?"

She made light of it and shrugged. "Well, I do that for students occasionally. A few times a week, actually. I just got caught this one time."

Pia hoped Jeremy wouldn't connect the dots and realize how her advice was discovered. Then she remembered the atmosphere in her office back in April, so she leaned against the wall and ended up giving Jeremy more information than he needed or probably wanted.

"Honestly, there were several students getting absolutely nowhere in my office with problems they had back then. If I can redirect them to a dean or someone in academic advising, those people will go to bat for students with extenuating circumstances. Ralph and our boss, Sandra, don't care about the students. I try to help. I just don't have any authority because I'm only an administrative assistant."

She gazed out beyond the glass doors for a minute. There was a young red-tailed hawk on a lamp post. Any other time Pia would go out to greet it. Still, its presence was a salve. She snapped back to the present and her tone softened.

"Anyway, it's all good. I didn't get fired, did I?" Pia was still mortified thinking about how Ralph spoke to Jeremy. "I'm sorry Ralph did that to you. I'm going to file a formal complaint."

"That's not necessary. Sorry he told your colleagues."

Jeremy began to shake it off a little but he was still somber. Pia thought it was nice that Jeremy considered she had 'colleagues.' They were all just staff, she and her co-workers.

"Hey, come on, it's fine," she coaxed Jeremy.

He wasn't listening to her; he was considering something.

Then he said earnestly, "Pia, what can I do for you?"

Oy vey, Pia thought of what he could do for her. There was a broom closet only a few feet away. But then she had a better idea, under the circumstances.

She pushed herself away from the wall, folded her arms, tipped her head to one side and asked, "Could you smile for me, please?"

Then Jeremy did smile. Further, he shook his head and laughed. They walked together to the doors on the other side of the building, which faced the inner road and, beyond that, the quadrangle in the center of the campus. Pia directed him to another notary's office nearby. Before he headed out Jeremy turned to her.

"Thank you again."

"You're welcome. You remind me of an old lady I met once when I worked for some surgeons."

"Sorry?" Jeremy asked.

Pia told him a little story. "She was a very sunny person and when she was leaving the office, she told me we were all *so* nice even though I, for one, was rather grumpy at that moment."

Jeremy told her, "I can't picture you grumpy."

Pia cocked an eyebrow at that and then continued. "For once my mouth waited for my brain before talking, and I told her that she brings out the best in people. She waved that off cheerfully but her sons nodded and smiled behind her back. You're like her. You bring out the best in people." Then, mostly to herself she added, "I wish I could remember what happened to her."

Jeremy gave Pia the tiny head bobble and a hug for that.

Pia went back to her office, where everyone looked up from their work but no one spoke. A student followed shortly behind, so Pia remained at the counter to process a registration form for her before she returned to her desk. Pia was nice to her but mechanically entered the numbers in the database. It wasn't until after the student left that she read her name in order to file the form correctly. Pia realized she was the sister of the student who fell from the roof.

Later, in the break room, Pia talked with Nell.

"What was that all about, if you don't mind my asking?" Nell said in a low voice as she wrapped up half a cake.

There were people in the office Pia would definitely mind, but not Nell; Nell was the best.

"That student, Jeremy, was short one course for his grad degree, even though he'd taken lots of extra courses here. I think he just had a brain cramp and dropped one he should've stayed in. Since I knew he wouldn't get anywhere with Sandra or Ralph, I told him to talk to the president." Pia acknowledged where she erred. "I had lunch last week with someone who told me she does that sometimes, but she remembers to always add 'but you didn't hear it from me.' I forgot that part."

Pia washed her coffee cup and set it aside on a towel to dry.

Nell's tone was supportive. "Yes, that's an important part to add. But I understand; we do have to find alternate routes for a lot of them. It's unfortunate that it has to be like that here. How did Ralph find out you suggested that to him?"

Pia sighed. "Jeremy told the president straight up about my advice, since I didn't tell him not to, and the president told the provost, who I assume raised hell about it."

Nell's eyebrows went up.

"Yeah, I didn't see that coming. Stupid me." Pia was disgusted with herself about that.

"No, you're not stupid. You just care about the students. You'd think that would be expected, or at least appreciated, here. Unfortunately… well." Nell ended with a knowing nod. She patted Pia's arm. "You're a good person, don't worry about that."

Pia was deeply grateful for Nell's support. "Thanks, Nell."

"It just occurred to me," Nell said thoughtfully, "you know how Joan left the university because she couldn't work with the provost anymore?"

"Yes." Pia had gone to the farewell party held off-site for Joan, a wonderful person who had worked there for over twenty years. Many great people showed their support for her at that bittersweet event.

"Well, I just wonder if it had anything to do with that. If he made a big stink about this and Joan was frustrated with him for it. If that was the last straw." Nell pondered this idea and so did Pia. The timeline made sense.

The weight of the possibility hit Pia then. "God, I hope not. I wouldn't want to have anything to do with *that*, on top of everything else. I wish Joan were still here."

"So do I, she was terrific. In any event, it was the provost's behavior that caused Joan to leave, not yours. I better get back to my paperwork."

Nell patted Pia's shoulder before returning to her desk. Pia had to let that idea go; she was getting confused by all the possible ramifications of what she had started.

Shortly after that, Jeremy emailed Linda and Pia to invite them to hear his friend Paco's band at that place he liked. Linda and Pia had lunched together awhile back and talked about the band Linda was in with her husband, Ethan, and three younger people. They'd talked about how they both liked to dance. Linda was a vibrant, interesting woman and Pia was glad she signed on for the exhibits committee just because she got to know her.

So Pia emailed Linda about Jeremy's invitation to see if she planned on going. Linda wasn't sure Ethan would go but she'd ask him about it. In the meantime, Pia had friends who were usually up for a good time and she asked them if they were interested. Sam had graduated from the university Pia worked at and he and Jane were both fun, laughing easily. She enjoyed spending time with them and was glad when they accepted.

Pia and her friends took one car in together since they lived on the same road. Jane admitted that they hadn't been out to hear a band in many years. Pia hadn't either. It was amazing how fast time went by. Pia wore a blue camisole under a sheer gray sweater and jeans. She knew nothing she wore would make her look cool in a bar filled with younger people so she didn't put a lot of energy into coming up with an outfit. She chose clothes she felt good in. Because they were older and not in the habit of going out late, they arrived well before the band started playing.

Linda and Ethan were there and they had a big table so Pia and her friends could join them. Pia made the introductions and it wasn't long before they could all find common ground. Sam was a real rock music fan and so he and Ethan got to talking. Linda asked Jane about herself and they chatted about Linda's background. Jane was funny and Linda liked her quickly. There was music playing in the background but it was not too loud, so they could carry on a conversation.

After a while Pia saw that the band was setting up. Eventually, Linda spotted Jeremy helping them with their equipment. When he looked around at the audience, Jeremy saw them in the back corner. He smiled and waved to Linda, as she was best situated to see him. After a few minutes he came over to them.

"Hey, Linda! Thanks for coming," Jeremy said cheerfully and they exchanged a hug.

He glanced around at the three people he didn't know with a smile and a round of "Hi"s, and then he saw Pia and said to her, "Oh, hey!"

She was out of hugging range in a corner but she smiled. "I'll pretend I'm young tonight," she thought.

Linda began the introductions. "Jeremy, this is my husband Ethan. You know Pia, and these are her friends Jane and…oh, I've already forgotten!" she said somewhat embarrassedly.

"I'm Sam, pleased to meet you," Sam shook Jeremy's hand heartily.

There was an extra seat so Jeremy asked, "Is your husband here, Pia?"

"No, you're welcome to join us if you'd like. Gordon…doesn't like music much. He's also somewhat disabled—"

"She means he's a lousy dancer!" Sam piped up.

"—so he stayed home," Pia explained. "But I did invite him."

Jeremy went to get a beer since everyone else was all set in that regard and talked to Paco briefly. Then he returned to their table.

"Jeremy, Sam is an alumnus from the university like you and he loved it there," Pia began.

Sam added, "A long time ago, in the '60's. It was much smaller then. Different."

"Hey, those were fascinating times," Jeremy said. "I'm aerospace engineering, what about you?" he asked Sam.

"Chemistry. It was fun," Sam mused, "It still is."

"Oh, Sam, you have to tell him about the bands that used to play there! Please tell Jeremy who you saw perform on the quad," Pia enthused.

Sam was happy to oblige. "Pia's talking about Janis Joplin."

"Wow, you're kidding!" Jeremy said.

Linda and Ethan enjoyed hearing about that show and the other bands as well. They were big names and they played right on campus. During a pause in the conversation Pia tried to think of some other things they might have in common.

"Jane does some photography. Jeremy's a photographer, too."

"Is this the fellow with the exhibit you were working on?" Jane made the connection.

"Yes, that's right. Jane's also a poet. She's gotten me interested in it. Reading it, that is," Pia told the group.

"That's neat. What do you write about?" Linda asked Jane.

"Oh, it varies a lot." Jane pondered that question. "Let's see…nature, current events, and homeless women."

She chuckled at the incongruity of her topics.

Sam thought of one of her poems suddenly. "Hey, you wrote one for Pia."

Everyone looked athim expectantly then.

"It's called 'Turtle Mother.'"

Pia covered her face as everyone began to laugh at that. She knew she was blushing as her face heated up.

"That's really the title, I swear. That's what everyone in our town calls Pia, you know."

"God, Sam was a ham," Pia thought to herself. Since it rhymed, she decided to share that.

"Sam the ham," she teased him, tipping her beer mug to her lips.

"Sam the ham I am!"

More laughing. Linda rolled her eyes. Her sense of humor was a little more sophisticated than everyone else's.

"I did; I did write a poem for Pia, to thank her. She let me help with the release of her hatchlings into the pond near where we live," said Jane, who was more serious now.

"What do you mean?" Linda asked.

"Pia, would you like to tell about that?" Jane asked.

Pia sighed. She didn't like the attention on her. "I'm going to need another Guinness after this. Okay, so on two occasions I've jogged in the morning by painted turtles actually laying eggs in their nests. Usually they're scouting, and when I go by they call it quits. But once they've begun laying, they have to stay put. The first time was about seven years ago and a friend of ours who's an excellent naturalist told me how to excavate the eggs and take them home to incubate them."

She stopped to see if she should continue.

Linda said, "Go on."

"The first time I did this everything went perfectly. This last time it was trickier. Do you really want to hear about this?"

Jeremy said, "Yeah!" as Linda said, "Definitely."

Pia continued, "So I marked the area with some twigs, because after the turtle has finished you can't tell where the nest is at all. Then you leave her to it. Later, when you return, you take a piece of tall, dry grass, and start poking the soil near the twigs you left. It won't penetrate the hard soil. Where it submerges is where the nest is. Then you dig down ever so carefully. Eventually you reach the eggs about four inches deep, and you brush away the sand and soil. You take them out, carefully, without turning them at all, and place them in a quart ice cream container—"

"Without the ice cream," Sam interjected.

"Right. You put moistened vermiculite in there instead. Then you leave them in a very hot room until September and keep checking it. One day you will find cute little baby turtles staring up at you! Unless you don't. I had two eggs that weren't viable this time, but three were fine."

"I love the little egg tooth they have," Jane said cheerfully. Pia nodded in agreement.

"What's an egg tooth?" Jeremy wanted to know.

Jane explained, "They have one tiny tooth they use to break out of the egg, and it falls off after a few days."

Sam added, "Then you leave a dollar under their pillow."

"Ha!" Pia found that funny and she and Sam toasted.

Linda frowned at Sam, then asked, "How'd you know they weren't, what was it, 'viable'?"

"I called our friend Annie distraught over them. She said that if I hold an egg up to a light and it's still clear, it was never going to turn into a turtle. I don't know if she was just trying to make me feel better. She's a real sweetheart. But I know I handled them correctly."

"Wow, that's so cool! Then you let them go?" Jeremy asked.

"No, then I kept them over the winter; I fed them and kept them warm and active. That way they grew a bit before I released them in early summer. It's a Head Start program for turtles."

"Huh. Interesting," Ethan said. "Why did you take the eggs?"

"Oh, great question, Ethan. Sometimes I've jogged by and seen the nests predated (that just means ransacked). More often, I will see hatchlings in the road flattened by cars. One morning I stopped jogging because I realized there were many of them around me in the road, trying to reach the pond. Mostly snapping turtles but some musk turtles, too. So I picked up as many as I could to save them from an oncoming school bus. That's a lot of excitement before you've had your coffee."

"Pia had a dinner party and before she fed us, we fed the hatchlings some shrimp." Jane was trying to reach the finish line to her point. "So I asked her if I could join her when she released them into the pond," Jane continued.

"They had a little ceremony. They walked down to the pond each holding a turtle. Annie went with you, didn't she?" Sam said.

"Yes. Then I wrote a poem about it, ha!" Jane laughed so often; she was good medicine. Then Sam had everyone toast to turtles.

The band began to rev up. Paco was the drummer. They played a few songs Pia and the others didn't know, and Jeremy disappeared into the crowd. It was definitely music for a younger generation but Pia enjoyed it. The singer took a break to address the crowd. He was good-looking and shaggy. He wore a tight t-shirt with a retro graphic image on it and current style jeans hung low, with superhero boxers visible above the jeans. Tattoos covered his arms.

"Hey everybody, thanks for coming to hear us! We are Alchemy! So, those of you who follow the band know that we try to have a theme for each show. Today is my birthday…" He was interrupted by cheers. "…and the theme for tonight is *romance*. Hopefully that works out for me!"

More cheers, particularly coming from young women. Then they started to play something with a steady beat.

"Oh, I love this song." Pia set down her beer and headed to the dance floor.

Pia enjoyed dancing and she was good at it, but if she weren't she would still do it. In a minute Linda and Jane joined her. Then they noticed that Jeremy was dancing with them. They danced to a few more songs. Sam joined them, but not Ethan. Then there was a short break. Pia quenched her thirst with beer. She didn't drink very often so she was getting inebriated quickly.

The singer stopped by their table with Paco and they picked up Jeremy, who had been sitting between Linda and Sam.

The singer said, "Thanks for coming. We're going to play stuff geared more to your era in the next set – stick around!"

He was serious. When the three young men were far enough away from the table the group feigned being indignant about his comment.

At least Pia thought they were feigning, but they might have been genuinely offended.

When Pia went to the crowded bar for another beer, Jeremy came over to her. He ordered another for himself. Pia could smell Jeremy; his own natural scent, not any cologne.

"Are you having fun?" he asked.

She wished she could say something clever.

"I'm glad you like to dance," she said. Not clever.

When the band resumed they played love songs. Jeremy came back to the table as one song ended and took the seat next to Pia. He drank some of his beer and listened to the next song, watching the band.

"Who's this by?" Pia asked him loudly.

Unfortunately, Pia could hardly hear what her friends were discussing over the band.

"Kaleo. It's great, isn't it?" Jeremy said.

Pia nodded her approval. "Yeah, it is. I've heard it on the radio. Is that a person or a band?"

"A band." Jeremy looked directly at Pia while he enjoyed the beat, but Pia looked away toward the band. Too much for her while listening to sultry, romantic lyrics.

Then Linda and Ethan were calling it a night. Pia thought it was the type of music prompting this rather than the hour. That wasn't their era after all.

As the next song began Jeremy wanted Pia to dance with him. Pia was surprised but she followed him to the dance floor. She felt it was not the best song for them to dance to, sexy and suggestive, but she was drunk and felt free. The song had an energetic, fast beat.

Pia had lost enough inhibition to go with the moment, without caring if she was being responsible. When the song ended, the band segued smoothly into another. She saw Jeremy glance at the band, and followed his gaze, but when she looked she didn't see any communication from the band to him.

The new song was slow and plaintive. Jeremy took Pia's hand in his and put his other behind her back, his expression asking for her permission. Pia nodded ever so faintly and slid her free hand tentatively around him. Jeremy held her a little tighter then as they danced. Pia felt a surge of want, like a toddler near a cookie. After a minute she tucked herself closely into him. Jeremy responded right away by enveloping her while they turned slowly. Pia was so grateful for this moment with him.

She let her face rest on his chest, and her lips were by the base of his neck. She shut her eyes and kissed Jeremy's neck lightly then. She lifted her chin and gave another kiss just under his jaw and left her lips there while she inhaled his scent. Jeremy made a soft sound like a purr and dipped his head down to hers.

"Thank you, Pia," he murmured in her ear.

"For what?" Pia said with her eyes still closed. She was becoming sleepy.

"For kissing my neck," Jeremy told her.

Pia's eyes blinked open. She was not aware she had done that.

"I kissed you…on the neck?"

Pia moved her head off of Jeremy to look at his face. She then realized she might have.

"You did."

Jeremy smiled at Pia and his head bobbled slightly. They contemplated each other, and their mouths were only a few inches apart.

"Knock it off, kids!" Jane hollered with a laugh.

She and Sam were watching from the table. Pia came to her senses then and felt her arms, then her hands, and finally her fingertips slip away from Jeremy's body. Pia turned to go back to the table and Jeremy followed her. She noticed that there was only one other couple dancing to that song.

"Pia, I think we were right in the middle of a transfusion of some sort."

Jeremy had his elbows on the table and was leaning close to her, so Sam and Jane might not have heard him. He was smiling, as he always seemed to be.

In her head Pia responded with, "Good grief."

She finished the rest of her beer immediately, set the glass down, and licked her upper lip. Jeremy seemed to enjoy that. Pia looked at him but didn't know what to say. She bit her lip while she thought and Jeremy waited.

"Excuse me, please."

She left to use the restroom. Jeremy looked a little disappointed then. When Pia saw herself in the mirror, she knew she had drunk too much, although what had transpired on the dance floor should have sufficiently informed her. When she returned to the table, Sam and Jane gathered their things and paid their tab. Pia slung her handbag over her shoulder and draped her jacket over her arm.

"Don't leave yet. Stay and hang out with me," Jeremy said to Pia. His eyes were optimistic.

"Pia has to come with us because we gave her a ride into town." Sam said it gently, being rather fatherly with him.

Jane was not particularly impressed by Jeremy or Pia at the moment and said nothing.

"I have to go home but thanks, it was fun. It's pretty late," Pia told him.

In the car, Jane turned towards the back a bit to converse with Pia. "So, was that a spontaneous situation or is there more going on?"

"He's my mid-life crisis," Pia confessed forlornly. "But it's just an infatuation on my part." She tried to change the subject. "Clearly I can't keep up with that kid. He has so much energy."

"Does Gordon know about this?" Sam asked in a lighthearted tone.

"I could have told Gordon eight times and he wouldn't have heard me. Y'know, the last time I saw Jeremy he asked me what he could do for me. I don't remember Gordon *ever* asking what he could do for me! I'm just there for his needs. I'm a habit more than anything else." She exhaled after her rant. Then she feebly added, "Sorry."

"I hope you're not angry with us, Pia. We just thought that you were about to make a bad choice. One you might regret," Jane said kindly.

"Oh, not at all, thank God you were there. I'm grateful to you, really." Pia was tired. They dropped her off at her house. As she got out of the car and into the frigid night air she said, "Thank you, guys. I'm really sorry about that."

Jane called from her open window, "Are you coming with me next Saturday to snowshoe at the sanctuary?"

Pia thought she heard Sam say something about "childish."

"Sure! If you could remind me later that would be good, since I'm half in the bag now." Pia teetered a bit.

"No shit," Sam and Jane said in tandem.

Then Jane laughed and rolled up her window as Sam put the car in reverse.

Chapter 6

Now Pia was more distracted than before by Jeremy, if that were possible. Even though he had graduated and wasn't on campus anymore, Pia looked for him everywhere she went. When she rode the subway, when she walked in her favorite park at lunchtime, when she hiked the trails of the hill near her home. She had hoped Jeremy would follow up after that night at the bar, but he didn't.

After many days spent thinking about the details of that evening, Pia realized that she might have been giving it more meaning than it actually had. In fact, it might not have any meaning. It also occurred to her that she had made a move, whereas Jeremy really hadn't. Perhaps she owed him an apology? Now Pia debated whether she wanted to contact him to apologize or just to be in touch with Cute Boy yet again. She really wasn't any good at this. Without determining her true motive, she wrote him an email.

"Jeremy, I think I may owe you an apology. If so, I'm sorry."

She sent it. It was a hectic day and Pia didn't have time to mull this one over, but she knew that was pretty lame.

She hoped for a reply. Pia had never known Jeremy to communicate anything negative. In instances where she thought Jeremy might not have liked something she wrote, he just didn't respond. The silence was deafening, as the saying goes.

Pia was exhausted when she left twenty minutes after the office closed. She didn't mind staying late because she didn't have to get home to cook; Gordon had gone out with an old friend who was in town visiting. She planned on picking up Indian food for dinner. Some interactions with Ralph had been frustrating and her nerves were frayed, and besides that there were volumes of paperwork to get through.

Pia had recently begun carrying a book of Billy Collins' poems in her lunch bento box, because he had some charming poetry that always made her feel better. She thought Billy Collins was a cute boy, too. The building that housed her office included a big public space with pub-style tables and chairs for the students and before Pia went out into the freezing, dark night, she remembered the little book. She stopped at a table to pull it out, thinking that a light-hearted poem would improve her mood.

There were many students buzzing around. The campus atmosphere changed after work hours. It became more electrically charged, like a storm, which made Pia's exhaustion more present to her.

"Hi, Pia!" Suddenly, Jeremy was looking over her shoulder to see what she was reading.

She jumped. "Geez!"

"Sorry," he smiled. "What are you reading?"

Jeremy was very focused, like he had been while talking to Larissa that first time Pia saw him.

"Oh, I just needed a Billy Collins poem kind of urgently." She was so weary she wasn't able to snap out of it even with Jeremy there, but she did make an effort. "I take him medicinally."

Jeremy replied, "He must be a great poet if he's a like a drug for you."

"I like him very much. A poet friend once referred to him as 'accessible,' which I took to mean the average Joe would understand him."

In this conversation, with Jeremy being strong and Pia feeling defeated, their roles seemed to have shifted. She was the one in need of some support.

"Was that Jane?"

"Oh, yes. I forgot you've met."

"Would you read me one you like?" Jeremy was encouraging her.

Pia flipped through the book and found one that she almost knew by heart so she would be able to read it the way she wanted to.

"This is called 'I Chop Some Parsley While Listening to Art Blakey's Version of Three Blind Mice'. Do you know who Art Blakey is?" Pia asked.

"No, do you?"

"Well, I didn't until I read this poem, so I Googled him. He's a jazz musician and the piece is really cool. He might be dead, I'm not sure."

Pia did her best to give Jeremy a sample of her interpretation of the music. It was enough to give him the general idea.

"Okay, so the title is so long that I decided it was also the first line of the poem: I chop some parsley while listening to Art Blakey's version of 'Three Blind Mice'/ … and I start wondering how they came to be blind./ If it was congenital, they could be brothers and sisters/ and I think of the poor mother/ brooding over her sightless young triplets./ Or was it a common accident, all three caught/ in a searing explosion, a firework perhaps?/ If not,/ if each came to his or her blindness separately,/ how did they ever manage to find one another?/ Would it not be difficult for a blind mouse/ to locate even one fellow mouse with vision/ let alone two other blind ones?/" Pia looked at Jeremy for this next part: "And how, in their tiny darkness/ could they possibly have run after a farmer's wife/ or anyone else's wife for that matter?/ Not to mention why./ Just so she could cut off their tails/ with a carving knife/ is the cynic's answer,/" Pia looked to the poem again "but the thought of them without eyes/ and now without tails to trail through the moist grass/ or slip around the corner of a baseboard/ has the cynic who always lounges within me/ up off his couch and at the window/ trying to hide the rising softness that he feels./ By now I am dicing an onion/ which might account for the wet stinging/ in my own eyes, though Freddie Hubbard's/ mournful trumpet on 'Blue Moon',/ which happens to be the next cut,/ cannot be said to be making matters any better."

Pia tipped her head a little to one side when she finished and let the poem have its moment.

After a pause Jeremy said, "That's neat. A little melancholy though."

"Is it? I think it's sweet. Well."

Pia packed the book back into her bento box. She made her way out into the bitter cold and Jeremy followed her. The wind was blowing in intermittent batches. They were each bundled up against the weather.

As soon as they were through the doors Jeremy finally explained his presence.

"Pia, I'm here because of your email."

His hair, animated by the wind, was obscuring parts of his face. Most of hers was anchored by her scarf, wrapped up to her ears.

Pia stopped abruptly and turned to him. "Oh, I completely forgot about that!"

Her glove came up and its fingers covered her mouth. She wore bulky Andean cotton gloves that didn't match.

"Yeah, that's why I came by."

As usual, Jeremy was making eye contact that held without wavering. It made Pia nervous.

"You don't owe me an apology," he told her.

"Oh."

She was really not doing well today. They continued to look at one another, Jeremy with his shoulders hunched by his neck and his bare hands in his pockets.

Eventually Pia said, "I'm afraid my intuition has left for the day. Anyone else would understand you, but I don't really know what you're trying to say."

Her tone made it clear that the difficulty was definitely on her end. Pia felt rather pathetic compared to her normal self and Jeremy looked a bit concerned. He hadn't met winter Pia.

"Hello!" One of the faculty hailed Pia on his way by. "Great work on the parking committee!"

"Thanks, Ken. Have a good night," she half-heartedly called to him.

People were moving briskly due to the cold conditions. Something else was going on with her but she didn't consciously know exactly what it was. Pia realized that she had attempted to read that poem to Gordon without success. Halfway through it he had said, "You said it was short. Is it almost over?"

When she looked back at Jeremy he was still looking at her.

Pia sighed and shook her head once, saying, "Sorry."

Jeremy's head gave the nearly imperceptible bobble as he said, "You look like you could use a hug."

He slipped his arms around her and held her close and even rocked her slightly. Pia held onto him; she surely needed this embrace. Because of her current emotional state, Jeremy's arms felt like angels' wings covering her. She was certain that if he asked her to walk away from her life and leave with him she would absolutely do so. This felt good.

With her face buried in the folds of his thick coat, she said, "You are so very wonderful."

Then Pia found her heart lifted and realized that, to her mind, this was the best possible place to be. She should enjoy it now before it was gone.

Jeremy released Pia and then his hands gently guided her face up towards his. Their breath was steaming together in the cold air. He looked as if he was contemplating a big decision. Jeremy bent his head down and kissed Pia on her mouth, delicately twice, then once a little more firmly.

"Oh, shit," Pia thought.

Jeremy paused to assess her response. She took one step back. She was impressed by his bravery but still quite surprised.

"Jeremy, I don't think…." Pia knew she should say something to thwart this, but she didn't want to.

"Pia, why do you always blush when you talk to me?"

She understood that Jeremy knew the answer and was trying to make a point. Nonetheless, she thought it was time to speak it.

"Because…I have…a crush on you."

Pia was very embarrassed but it was good to be rid of her secret.

Jeremy made an exaggerated grimace then. "Oh, now you're *really* red."

"Well, I'm deeply ashamed of myself!" Pia scowled as she said that and shifted her feet.

"There's nothing to be ashamed of. I'm flattered, actually."

Jeremy kissed her again. Finally Pia kissed him back, delicately at first, indebted to his courage. Pia's mood was such that she was very submissive that evening; she was drained. She would never have initiated this with Jeremy, and any other time she might have had the strength to object rationally. Tonight she just needed someone to treat her tenderly. Pia crossed a line. She was hungry and he was her food. She kissed him and kissed him and kissed him some more. There was nothing before this and nothing after it. Just this now, and all the reasons why this should not be happening were nowhere in sight.

Still, they couldn't kiss on the sidewalk under a streetlamp indefinitely. Jeremy asked her to come along with him. He took her hand and they walked across the street and around another building. As they went to cross the quadrangle in the center of the campus Pia dropped her hand from his as a precaution, since there were people around. They took a back route toward the secluded gardens of the elaborate old house on the school grounds. Pia was a realist despite her excitement, and so dearly hoped the gardens weren't his idea of a destination on this frigid evening. Jeremy led her through them, and beyond to the carriage house next to the grand house. In the back of the carriage house there was a staircase sorely in need of repair that led to rooms on the second floor. Pia knew that at one time the space was used for an office suite but it hadn't been occupied recently.

On the landing at the top of the stairs, Jeremy leaned far over the right railing and reached to the gutter. Pia grasped his coat because she didn't have much faith in the old railing. After a minute he found what he was looking for and produced a key on a string. He glanced at Pia. She tried to enjoy the mischief they were getting into, but her heart was racing. As she expected, the key opened the door and they went in. As soon as Jeremy secured the door behind them, he turned and kissed her again. Apparently he interpreted Pia's behavior at the bar as an accurate representation of her feelings about him. He was right, of course. Pia, for her part, intended to completely consume Jeremy. After a few minutes, Jeremy took out his phone and hit a few keys. Before Pia could question him, he explained the interruption.

"We shouldn't turn on the lights, but there's an app for making this candlelight."

In a minute he had that ready and used the phone as a flashlight to quickly scan around the room. Then he set the phone on a desk by the door, leaning against something, so it shone on the meager space between them, illuminating their forms.

"There!"

"Our eyes will adjust fine if we give them fifteen minutes with the dark," Pia told him.

Jeremy said playfully, "I don't think I can wait fifteen more minutes, Pia," and kissed her again.

He took off his coat, his shirt, his hiking boots, and then his jeans. Pia had dropped her bento box and handbag. Now she removed her scarf, gloves and coat, and slipped her feet out of her shoes. Practical, earthy ones without laces. Boy, life could change fast.

"Here, let me help you catch up."

Jeremy smiled and helped Pia with her sweater and hesitated briefly at the bra. He paused to kiss Pia's face and neck, put his arms around her, and soon it was on the floor with the rest of her clothes. Before she knew it, they were dressed only in their socks. It was much warmer here than outside, which surprised Pia. She was briefly modest. Jeremy took her hand in his and they moved to the sofa. Before they sat down on it Jeremy put the light on a side table and looked at her body.

"You wear clothes that hide your figure. You're beautiful."

Pia believed Jeremy was being sincere but was still glad for the poor lighting; probably he meant she didn't look as bad as he had expected. He hopped onto the sofa and encouraged her to join him. She didn't have a vocabulary for this experience. She used touch instead with him. They were both startled by a loud knock on the door and Pia was slightly panicked. She was also beginning to think this was not meant to be.

"Come on out. Don't make me call campus police on y'all."

Whoever it was sounded like he had run into this scenario before. He must've seen them going up the stairs.

Pia recognized the voice. It was Tobias from the grounds team, a handsome, middle-aged fellow with dreadlocks worn tied back. A week ago, when everyone worked through a snowy day, Tobias had helped Pia shovel her car out. Later she had brought him a cake in return for his generous assistance. Hopefully that gesture would serve her now. All their clothes were in a heap over by the door, so Pia called to him loudly from the sofa.

"Hey, Tobias. What's up?"

She glanced down at Jeremy, who was biting his lip with his eyebrows raised. That almost made her grin.

There was a pause, then, "Pia? Tha'chu?" from Tobias.

"Yes."

"Well, I'll be damned. I though'chu was married."

Pia just couldn't reply to that at the moment, which gave Tobias his answer.

He sighed and considered the situation. "Alright. Well…have fun. I gotcha back but just this once. I'm not, y'know…condoning. Don't forget to lock up."

Tobias to the rescue again!

Then he looked in the window momentarily and added, "And you *might* want to pull the shades."

Jeremy stifled a giggle but Pia was quite embarrassed. Just how many people were going to see her nude tonight, she wondered. Before she went over to close them she heard Tobias reporting on his radio.

"It's just an employee bedding a student."

A static response followed.

Then Tobias again, "Yep…right. Over."

Apparently when the truth is preposterous people assume you're not serious. Then he made his way down the stairs and around the corner to the driveway in front of the carriage house.

"Wow that was close. It helps that you know everyone." Jeremy marveled at their good fortune.

"I've worked here ten years. He's good people…." Pia said reflectively. She knew she was disappointing Tobias.

Jeremy and Pia were alone then. Still, Pia could not initiate anything because this was rather surreal to her. It became more real for her though as they each spent some time enjoying the new terrain of the other person's body. Jeremy was very tender with her. She didn't think about what they shared, she didn't analyze it or compare it to Gordon.

The old sofa was proving to be too soft, so they slipped to the floor, with Jeremy carrying most of her weight so she landed softly on the carpet and he was over her. She couldn't say what he thought of her for certain, but he made her feel overwhelmingly cared for.

At the very moment Pia realized he was hard against her thigh she let out an unintentional gasp. He wasn't being pushy, it was just... there. In a second Jeremy was looking in her eyes with one hand caressing her face lightly.

"Is everything okay?"

Pia nodded but her face indicated some worry.

"Why the furrowed brow? If you have any concern please tell me. I can stop...."

Pia sputtered, "I don't want to take advantage of you."

She realized that sounded inane since he was on top, but the notion was still disconcerting to her.

Jeremy laughed, "I can assure you, you aren't."

One of his fingers followed the contour of her jaw.

"Are we good?" he smiled.

"Mm-hm."

Pia placed her left hand behind his neck to draw him in for a kiss, and her right hand meandered down his back to its base. There was no sense of a performance from him; what they did was, well, organic.

Afterwards Pia became aware that Jeremy was actually still. Normally he was very kinetic, always moving at least a little even when he didn't mean to be, like children are. That stillness didn't last long, though. Jeremy lifted his head to look at her and he stroked her hair.

"Sorry, I meant for that to take longer. What you did with your hips,

I didn't expect it. That was new for me. It was incredible." Then he told her softly in her ear, "I lost control."

Then he kissed all around her neck. Pia knew that maneuver wouldn't be a novelty for long.

She was having a difficult time processing the fact that she had just had sex with someone who had seemed unreachable only a short while ago. They stayed on the floor for a while but then moved to the sofa. The phone app wasn't as romantic as real candlelight but it served them well.

"Would you tell me about your travels?" Pia asked Jeremy as she sat down next to him.

She wanted no more student/staff conversations.

"There's a lot to tell! Let's see. My first trip out of the country was to Angola with the school for a semester. That was totally fantastic! I met so many interesting people. They're different there; they're just more…real, I guess I would say. It's hard to describe. Maybe their lives are more genuine than ours? I'm generalizing, of course. The culture here is so oriented towards material wealth. People there have to work so much harder than we do to take care of basic needs but their lives satisfy them. It just seems ridiculous to work for money to buy so much junk that we don't need at all."

"I agree it's pointless…I have trouble respecting it," Pia said. "Did you have a favorite food on that trip?"

Pia thought she sounded like a classic American then; always talk of food or weather.

"I liked dried fish a lot. Mmmm." Then he nearly crawled in her lap and said "Yummm" on Pia's cheek and began to play eat it.

Jeremy was back to being lively already.

"Eee, that tickles! I'm like dried fish?" Pia pushed him back a little.

"I really like dried fish, Pia! You should feel honored," he laughed at her.

He was sitting with his legs wrapped around her waist and his arms around her.

"How about your favorite experience on that trip?" She tried to be serious.

"Hmm…hard to say." Jeremy thought about it. "Oh, I had a lot of fun swimming with penguins! That was so cool. A bunch of us went to the beach and after we were in the water a…flock? A school? I'm not sure about what to call it. Anyway, a group of free, wild penguins swam with us. They were really inquisitive and came right up to us. That was fabulous!" he recalled happily.

After a pause he followed with, "You're the first person I've told that to who didn't comment about penguins in the warm water on the coast of Africa."

"I know they don't all live in cold climates."

Pia didn't want to let on how little she knew about geography. She had never heard of Angola until she worked at the university.

"You must know a lot about animals."

"Yes. I can tell you that Atlantic bottlenose dolphins have eighty-eight teeth and a common periwinkle has over three thousand teeth. But that isn't information anyone really needs to know," Pia lamented.

Jeremy smiled, looking entranced by this information. She didn't let herself dwell on the possibility that maybe he was entranced by her.

After a silence he told her he was trying to think of what kind of animal she reminded him of. Apparently they were playing a game together.

"Hmm, this is tough. Maybe a honey bee, since you're always working for the rest of the hive."

He pondered his selection as though he weren't committed to it yet.

"Funny you should choose that. I kept honey bees for many years." Pia liked the comparison.

"Why does that not surprise me?"

"A bear finally found them and ate up the hive. Anyway, I'd like to be an animal that lives in the sea, please."

"You can't choose, Pia." Jeremy was having fun. "You could be a cat, like an ocelot…or a snow leopard. They're so cool."

"They are, and they're so beautiful. I hate winter though," she pointed out.

"You wouldn't if you were a snow leopard! Problem solved! What kind of animal am I?" Jeremy had so much energy.

"Well, that's really a trick question because you already are an animal." Pia was buying some time.

"I thought I was pretty gentle with you." Jeremy laughed and leaned over to kiss her face. "Okay, we are animals, that's true," he conceded.

Then Pia thought of the right animal to describe Jeremy. It may have been prompted by her remembering photos she'd seen of snow leopards. They could blend with their environment so well their prey couldn't see them in plain view.

"You're like a blue morpho butterfly. Yes, that's it." Jeremy's questioning face told Pia he needed this explained to him. "On the outside you appear to be an ordinary person. At rest your wings are folded together, brown to blend with their surroundings. The tops of your wings are visible only intermittently when you fly. Then a glimpse of the vibrant iridescent blue is spectacular. You're spectacular."

"That's so nice, thanks! Do you mind if I look it up on my phone? I want to see one."

While Jeremy did that Pia enjoyed the chance to watch him, although she felt weird when she glimpsed his body. It was so foreign to her and she thought it wasn't her place to do so. It was good that they had almost no light to see by. She rolled a curl of her hair in her fingers and thought of him swimming with penguins.

"It's 'blue morpho', m-o-r-p-h-o. I think that if an indigenous North American tribe made you an honorary member, they might call you 'Swims With Penguins,'" she suggested.

Jeremy nodded but noted, "There aren't any penguins in North America."

"Oh, right, of course," Pia remembered. "Damn," she thought.

He had a mischievous look that let her know he was trying to think of a retort and he tapped the back of his phone on his jaw lightly. Then his face lit up.

"Swims With Penguins loves Turtle Mother!"

He chuckled when he said that, kissed her quickly on her cheek, and then took a look at the butterfly on his phone. Pia was stunned. She considered that he could mean it several different ways. After a minute Jeremy looked up because she had gone over to get her clothes.

"Wait, don't get dressed yet. We're not finished, are we?" he entreated her.

"We're not? What did you have in mind?"

"More."

Jeremy came over to her and began enticing her back to their makeshift nest. But Pia had to pause.

"Jeremy... 'loves'?"

She didn't know how this would play out and so she was nervous.

"I don't sleep with people I don't love. I love you," he said matter-of-factly.

Jeremy's face was very close to hers and his hands were on her rear, holding her against him, making it terribly hard for Pia to focus.

He smiled and added, "I hope you don't mind."

This was possibly the strangest thing Pia had ever heard. She looked around the room while her mouth changed shape a few times.

"How can you love me?"

That didn't come out quite like she had meant it.

"Pia, you're always so kind to me and I like your values. Students talk to each other and you're the go-to person for your office because you're so helpful to all of us. You know Ning Zhou? You're, like, her shero!"

Pia thought that might explain why she was always so busy.

She said, "Ning is so sweet. She told me her name means 'tranquility.' What's a *shero*?"

"It's a new word I learned recently for women heroes," Jeremy explained, and then he continued. "Your friend said you're a good soul and I trust her on that. Also, I saw you out my lab window once, when you stopped your lunchtime walk to talk with a homeless man leaning on his cart full of cans. You talked for about ten minutes. I thought that was pretty cool. You are a good soul." His hands were exploring.

There was more to that interaction than what Jeremy saw but Pia didn't feel like elaborating on it. Three policemen on motorcycles had pulled over and she wanted to make sure the Black man with the cart wasn't of interest to them.

"I'm not so sure about that. Society's 'throwaways' are sort of my people. But Jeremy, I don't really think…I'm really not…I don't know."

She ran her fingers through her hair and tried to explain her thoughts without sounding like a cynic. He can't love her; they hardly know each other. Jeremy wasn't asking for anything reciprocal back from her.

"Don't overthink it. Love is love, Pia. Love is good."

He sounded quite confident in his philosophy.

"You're very wise, you know that?"

Jeremy grinned and then kissed her. She couldn't remember ever feeling this way with anyone else, though surely she must have. Her body ached for him and she kissed him like he was treasure. She still could hardly believe she was being physical with Jeremy. This time they took longer and he was more involved in Pia's sensations.

When their lovemaking finished he rolled off her so they were both looking at the ceiling, saying, "I know there are many facets to life and I appreciate them, I really do. But I don't know why people don't do this, like, all day long."

Pia wondered silently how often a twenty-three-year-old male could actually do this. No wonder the world was overpopulated.

"I hate this side of it, right after," Pia lamented.

"The French have a term for it: *la petite mort*," Jeremy informed her.

"Of course, they would. *La petite mort* indeed."

He turned onto his side to face her, with his head resting on one hand. With his free hand he pulled his hair away from his face and then firmly ran that warm hand along Pia's torso.

Pia heard Jeremy's stomach growl so she wagged a finger at him.

"That's why you can't do this all day long; you'd starve. But also, you have so much to offer the world. You have important things to do. That's another reason."

"Hmm. Do you really think so?"

There was no question in Pia's mind. "Oh, yes. I don't know much, but that I do know."

Jeremy's eyes lit up. "Like what?"

Pia frowned. "Like what what?"

"What do I have to offer the world?"

Jeremy was making it more of a request for Pia's thoughts. He was young and optimistic and she knew from the brief tour she took of his website that he hoped to be a positive change in the world. Maybe he just wanted some confirmation from someone else about it.

"I'll bet you know, but I can give you a list of what I've seen. You're extremely intelligent; you have an awareness…it's like a righteous consciousness. Compassion, energy, optimism, courage (I just recently discovered), and many talents. I've probably left some things out. Oh, you also have grace. Gotta get me some of that."

The last sentence Pia said more to herself than to him.

Jeremy seemed to not believe her about that. "You don't have any grace?"

"I'm afraid not. I didn't handle Ralph very well the last time you were in the office, that's for sure," Pia said contemplatively.

They lay together on the floor for a while. Finally Jeremy's growling stomach nagged them to move on. They got dressed. Jeremy asked for another poem so Pia retrieved her book and perused the pages.

"Let's see, the one about the Victoria's Secret catalog is pretty funny. Oh, this is a good one, too."

"He has one about the Victoria's Secret catalog?" Jeremy asked with his little head bobble.

"I'll let you take this book with you. Okay, this one is called 'Another Reason I Don't Keep a Gun in the House.'"

Jeremy made a surprised face and Pia smiled. She cleared her throat and held the book up high in mock seriousness.

"The neighbors' dog will not stop barking./ He is barking the same, high, rhythmic bark/ that he barks every time they leave the house./ They must switch him on on their way out./ The neighbors' dog will not stop barking./ I close all the windows in the house/ and put on a Beethoven symphony full blast/ but I can still hear him muffled under the music,/ barking, barking, barking,/ and now I can see him sitting in the orchestra,/ his head raised confidently as if Beethoven/ had included a part for barking dog./ When the record finally ends he is still barking,/ sitting there in the oboe section barking,/ his eyes fixed on the conductor who is/ entreating him with his baton/ while the other musicians listen in respectful/ silence to the famous barking dog solo,/ that endless coda that first established/ Beethoven as an innovative genius."

Jeremy smiled, pulled his hair back and said, "That's dope."

Pia hoped that meant 'good.' "I visualize a Weimaraner for some reason," she said, handing him the book. "Those large, short-haired gray dogs photographed by William Wegman on notecards and calendars where he has them all dressed up?"

"Ah, okay, I've seen those. I had a beagle in mind," Jeremy answered.

They were quiet then. Pia didn't know when or if this would happen again, and she was fighting thinking about that. To her surprise all of this took less than three hours. They collected their things. When they were sure they had everything they came in with, Jeremy zipped Pia into her down coat, locked the door and returned the key.

The moon was almost full and small, fast-moving clouds blocked it occasionally, taking round bites of the cold, brittle disc. All the trees and buildings back on earth looked black against night sky, except for some little yellow windows and lamps on the campus. They walked briskly to her car because of the temperature. They each kept their hands in their pockets, Pia's in her coat and Jeremy's in his jeans. In the quiet of the freezing night Pia heard him chuckling.

"What?"

Jeremy was recalling something she'd said earlier. "'Hey, Tobias. What's up?' That was *so* funny!"

When he laughed his whole torso was involved, lurching forward and back. Soon they were at Pia's car.

"Do you want to get something to eat with me?" he asked her.

Pia knew that her window of opportunity to reach home before Gordon was quickly closing so she declined. Before she opened the car door Jeremy gave her a little quick kiss. Pia was anxious because she didn't know what was in the future. She couldn't really conceptualize it at all now.

"I'll see you again soon?" Jeremy made it a question for her to answer.

Pia said, "I hope so. I would like that. Can I give you a ride?" This felt awkward.

"No, thanks, my car's a block from here." He waited until her car turned over and then went on his way.

On her drive home Pia reviewed the night. At first, she couldn't get past the fact itself: "I just had sex with Jeremy. I just had *sex* with Jeremy!"

Then in a panicky shame she admonished herself, "What were you thinking?"

Pia had absolutely no idea how to manage this situation. Jeremy was consistently one of the nicest people she knew, and she knew many fine people. But if he and she were such great people they shouldn't have done what they just did. Pia didn't know what the next step should or would be. She was ever so bad at chess and life, socially speaking, was basically chess.

She arrived home about twenty minutes before Gordon. That was just enough time to put the outside light on for him and clean up the kitchen after whatever daily activities caused him to leave debris strewn about. Gordon reminded her of a woodland rodent, leaving piles of midden on stone walls after eating. It was always clear what he had done and eaten during her absence. She had long ago given up trying to get him to clean up after himself. He couldn't help his habits and scolding or nagging only made them resentful of each other. Pia fed the cat and went upstairs to change into pajamas.

When Gordon came home she asked him about how his dinner went with his friend. They sat at the kitchen table under the warm light talking. Pia found it particularly harsh on her eyes this evening. She knew that they probably went someplace like a strip joint and not where he said they went, because his friend was that type. She thought that Gordon didn't share much with her and she respected that. He was welcome to keep secrets from her; she now had one of her own. But it made her a little sad.

When she went to bed Pia thought again about how things transformed that night. Then, seemingly randomly, she remembered someone she used to work with years ago. Wanda was a strong, solid, rational lesbian, and for the summer there was a pretty blonde college student interning. Before long those two were an item. Wanda talked about the relationship with Pia one day. Wanda said she knew that she was a novelty to the young intern, who would go on to live a straight, traditional life after the summer. In the meantime, Wanda was going to enjoy her while she could. Pia never forgot that; she thought Wanda was like an old sage for knowing full well how the relationship would evolve, and then devolve, and peacefully resigning herself to it.

Pia tried to apply that situation to herself and Jeremy, but it caused her heart to constrict and she didn't like it at all. Finally, she fell asleep.

Chapter 7

The next day it seemed to Pia that there was more than the usual whispering in the office, and it seemed to stop when she passed by people. Maybe it was her imagination.

Later that morning Pia received an email from Jeremy.

The heading was "Good morning!" like once before. The body of the email was simply "when?"

Pia's response was "When what? My cell number is 975-903-5768."

She took a break from her work and walked down the hall.

Jeremy sent a text that read: "Hi Pia! When can I see you again? Tonight perhaps?"

Pia breathed deeply. She was thrilled that Jeremy had contacted her so soon, but then she had to navigate her schedule in a way she wasn't accustomed to. How and when could she see him? Tonight would not be possible unless she lied to Gordon, which she hated partly because she wasn't a good liar so it could go badly, and partly because she felt guilty. She wasn't feeling guilty regarding what she would be lying about though. She texted him back asking if she could call him. He wrote that would be fine, so she did.

"Hi, how are you today?" Jeremy said cheerily.

"I'm fine. How about you?"

Pia felt bashful with her new lover. She'd considered the possibility that she was a one-time lay, but here he was calling her already.

"Good, but I would like to see you again. Is tonight a possibility?"

"Um, well, I don't see how. I have ingredients for dinner on my kitchen counter for tonight. I don't know how to explain not following through on that."

Pia was avoiding mentioning Gordon for as long as she could.

"I understand. What about this weekend? Do you want to do something together then?"

She was pleased that Jeremy might be expanding on what they could do together besides sex, although she could hardly wait for that again. Today was Tuesday.

"Saturday afternoon I'm leading some snowshoe hikes at the nature sanctuary in my town. We're having a winter open house, with a bonfire and family activities. I have to be there from noon until at least four. You're certainly welcome to come if you think you might like it."

Pia hoped that wasn't too different from what he had in mind.

"That would be cool, I'd like that." Then he added, "I don't have any snowshoes, though."

"No problem, we have lots of them at the sanctuary. You can use a pair of ours. It's part of the program to get people trying them out. It can get a little hectic, like herding cats, as they say. I hope it's not too cold Saturday."

"Okay, great! Is there any way we can see each other Friday after work? I kind of miss you," Jeremy told her.

Pia didn't know how to read him. She thought about it. At some point she would be lying to Gordon. Maybe she should just dive into the deep end of the pool now.

"I suppose I can. But not for too long. Maybe a few hours? Oh, I have to get back to my office for a meeting." She was becoming uncomfortable with this conversation.

"That's great! I'll text you Thursday afternoon then if that's okay?"

Pia was walking back to the office so she wouldn't be late for the staff meeting. "Okay, 'bye."

Back in the office everyone gathered for the staff meeting. Again, the chatter died down when she arrived. Sandra explained that this was a special meeting to go over protocols with everyone together so they would all have a uniform response to any given situation. Of course, in reality there were too many to cover but this was a start.

"Okay, we have some scenarios we'll describe and then ask you what the correct answer is," Sandra stated at the beginning.

Ralph gave the first situation. "So, a kid comes in after the add/drop period to add a physics course. What do you do?" Ralph said.

"He can't add it after the deadline. That's an easy one!" Shelly offered.

"What if the instructor told him he is in the course?" Pia asked, since this happened frequently.

"It's too bad, Pia. They have to check their schedules," Ralph responded.

"Okay, next question," Sandra carried on. "A grad student has a hold on her account. It's because she registered for a course and never went but didn't drop it during the window to do so. What can they do?"

"They could petition the graduate committee, couldn't they?" suggested Nell.

"They can, but we really want to discourage petitions, or else we'd have too many of them," Ralph explained.

"So that's $4,100 they lose?" Pia said.

"Exactly. Very good," Sandra said.

Surely she understood that Pia was pointing out an enormous burden on the student. Sandra was making her own point by ending the possibilities there.

"A grad student doesn't register for his research credits and then comes in ten weeks into a semester wanting to do so now. How do you respond?" asked Ralph.

"They're shit out of luck," Shelly said.

Everyone except Nell and Pia laughed.

"One student told me that he tried to do that in the database himself and couldn't so he gave up. I've been sending the grad students email reminders since then explaining the process," Pia said.

"He should've contacted us when that happened," Sandra maintained. "Please forward me the email template you send out. You should have sent it to me to review it first."

And so this continued for another fifty minutes. Before they wrapped it up, Ralph and Sandy reiterated that everything done in the database has a name and date stamped on it and people will be reprimanded for disobeying the policies. Pia knew that the meeting was a diplomatic way of warning her and Nell to stop being soft on the students.

On Friday night, Pia waited out on the sidewalk for Jeremy to pick her up. While there she said hello to various staff and faculty walking to their cars. Jeremy pulled up across the street a block away and crossed over to meet her.

"Hi!" He gave her just a quick hug since there were many people going by.

In fact, one staff member she was friends with stopped right then and said, "Hey, Pia! Nice job on the parking committee. You're really brave to take that on."

"Honestly, if that's the biggest worry someone has they're pretty lucky," Pia answered, shaking her head.

"I know, right? Shameful how that professor threw the rest of the committee under the bus. Take it easy!" And she was on her way.

Pia and Jeremy crossed together to where his car was parked. The interior was a bit messy with several coffee cups strewn about. Not terrible, though.

"Nice to see you again," he told her once her door was shut. "What's up with this parking committee? You seem to be a celebrity."

"There's a shortage of parking spaces. Everyone thinks they're entitled to their own spot right outside their building. It's ridiculous how much of an issue they make out of it. So, a committee was formed. I was selected by Vice President Blodgett because in a campus-wide email she took some grief for it and I emailed her privately in support. Not surprisingly she wanted me on her new committee. My boss was a little surprised when I told her Blodgett specifically requested me."

"The students are completely out of that loop. I wonder what else we don't hear about. Sometimes we lose sight that it's a workplace because it's where we learn and live. What was that about someone throwing the committee under the bus?" Jeremy asked while he turned onto a main road.

Pia noticed that he spoke as if he were still a student.

"Oh, Professor Michaelson wanted it to be known that he had nothing to do with the committee. His name was on it but he never attended the meetings. So he sent out an email to the whole campus, well, staff and faculty. I responded, telling everyone they can contact me with any questions or comments on the topic. A few people responded to me with 'bless you.' Ahh, that was funny!" Pia smiled remembering those emails.

"That woman just now said you're brave." Jeremy seemed impressed.

He nearly ran a red light but decided to stop, sending Pia forward in her seat.

This bone had been chewed on for so many months by the faculty and staff and Pia found it absurd, but she only said, "Bravery is not necessary for dealing with parking issues."

She gazed out the window at the passing businesses as they drove through an intersection. In a few minutes Jeremy pulled into a spot.

He reasoned, "If we don't have much time tonight, we should probably not go to a restaurant for a real dinner. Unless you want to, of course."

Pia agreed with him. "No, something quicker would be better."

They were in a neighborhood that had many eateries for several blocks. Jeremy had been fortunate to find a parking spot at all.

"Okay, how about some hot wraps? There's a place a block away that makes them with Mediterranean spices and sauces," Jeremy suggested.

"Perfect!"

Pia was glad that was easy. They walked up the street to the place he had in mind. When they were in the tiny restaurant, Jeremy ordered the food to go.

They waited in a booth near the cashier.

"What's your job like?" Pia had been wondering because he hadn't talked about it.

Jeremy seemed surprised by the question.

"My job? It's not bad. I work with a team on some projects developing new prototypes for lightweight equipment to use in space exploration. Unfortunately, I get pulled in a different direction each day depending on which project manager is actively participating in the process. It would be better if they had us work on one project at a time."

"Why don't they?"

"It's really driven by the clients and their deadlines. We may have taken on too much at once, but those decisions are made at a level I don't have any access to at all."

"What do you mean by no access? That you don't interact with the top brass?"

"We don't work in the same buildings and I have no communication with them. I work for the Wizard of Oz. Anyway, the testing is interesting. We have space-like scenarios to subject the prototypes to, like zero gravity and extreme cold. I work mostly on materials science."

"Do you like the people you work with?"

"They're okay. Two guys, Hamish and Milo, are really funny! But… I don't know. I feel like an outsider sometimes."

That was as negative as Jeremy ever got. He was a little squirmy in his seat.

Pia nodded in confirmation. "I get that. You're different from most people. You're uncommon, which is great when people appreciate it, but probably not when they don't."

"Actually, I just meant that everyone goes home to their families. I'm the only one without those responsibilities."

"Oh."

Pia felt rather stupid then, but she'd stand by what she said. The man behind the counter told them the food order was ready. They collected it and walked back to the car.

"Where are we going to eat these?" Pia asked as she got in the passenger seat.

She took the package from Jeremy and put it on her lap.

"My apartment if that's okay with you? Adam has gone home for the weekend and my two other roommates are going to a concert, so they left about a half hour ago." Jeremy looked at Pia and then back at the road.

"I'm surprised you didn't go to the concert with them. You like music so much."

"They're going to a Slipknot concert. Not my taste," Jeremy said. "Besides, I would much rather spend time with you," he added cheerfully.

That made her smile.

Jeremy lived on the second floor of a solid old apartment building in a neighborhood that was transitioning from run down to becoming more gentrified. It made Pia sad for the original neighbors because they would be priced out soon. The building had what she would call 'good bones,' with solid hardwood floors, granite stairs and thick doors. The living room and kitchen had clutter but it wasn't as messy as Pia imagined an apartment with four young men might be. Posters were on the walls instead of framed art, except for two photographs that Pia assumed were Jeremy's. The place was well worn and could use a paint job. It had some fine old light fixtures and the living room had a fireplace, although it didn't look functioning.

Jeremy took Pia's coat and offered her a choice of beer, wine or some funky sodas that were made locally and in bizarre flavors. Pia chose a beer and he had one with her. He lit a chunky, partly consumed candle in the center of the kitchen table. He reflexively brought one foot up on the seat of his chair and Pia tried to but failed. She crossed her legs.

She was uncomfortable being transferred suddenly into Jeremy's private life. It was noticeable in his car but stronger here. She felt she had crossed another line. He sensed it.

"Thanks for seeing me tonight," Jeremy told her while they ate.

She finished chewing, swallowed, and then articulated her thoughts, albeit poorly. "This is really weird, isn't it Jeremy? I mean, I'm glad to be here, but it's so weird."

"I suppose it is a little bit. Just think about you and I getting to know each other better. I would like you for a friend."

Pia tipped her head and smiled. They finished eating the sandwiches and Jeremy cleared the table. He opened a canister on the counter and took something out of it. He put five Hershey's Kisses down in front of Pia.

"Dessert. I made them myself!" he said with a grin.

He went to the refrigerator and took out a second beer for each of them.

"Let me show you the rest of the place."

While they each rolled chocolate around their mouths, Jeremy showed her where the bathroom was and then they passed a very neat bedroom and two with the doors only slightly open. Soon they were in his bedroom at the end of a hall. Like the car, not too neat, not too messy. A folk guitar in a corner, many books, a desk and chair, the bed left unmade with deep purple sheets. The closet door was ajar. There were four more framed photographs on his walls. He had many camera lenses and other related equipment in several woven baskets on one shelf of a deep, heavy oak bookcase. On the top of the bookcase were some paper origami figures, mathematical abstractions, not animals and such. Two were quite large, about a square foot, with many different colors.

"These are so amazing! Did you make them?" Pia said when she saw them.

"I did, a few years ago," Jeremy said. "They're fun to make, really challenging! There was an origami club at school for a while but it faded out. People were too busy." He held one out for Pia to look at closely.

She took it and turned it all around trying to grasp how it was made.

"I think this would be impossible for me."

She handed it delicately back to Jeremy so he could place it the way it belonged. She thought it remarkable that he found a difficult challenge fun. That was something he had in common with Gordon. They had patience for mental challenges. She didn't at all.

Jeremy put his beer and the last two chocolates on his desk, next to his computer and some speakers. He looked at Pia and moved closer to her. He put his hands on her hips and kissed her once.

"So, welcome."

His head bobbled and he smiled.

Pia was a little uneasy in the lit room, surrounded by his belongings. She found courage enough to kiss him back and the process became familiar to her. Then Jeremy paused to pull his sweater and t-shirt over his head together. He tossed his hair out of his face and proceeded to remove the rest of his clothes. Pia hadn't begun yet and was having a hard time with his being nude in front of her. Her instinct was to not look. When she glanced at him briefly she saw that he was very lean.

"You're going to need my assistance again, aren't you?" he said as he pulled off his socks.

Pia nodded shyly while holding her beer to her lips. Jeremy thoughtfully switched off the overhead light so there was just one bedside lamp currently lit.

"Okay, we start here, with these buttons, right? First this button… then this button…aaannd this one…."

As his knuckles grazed her breasts lightly, Pia's senses began to heat up.

He got an idea. "Hey, this might help," he said as he quickly un-wrapped a Hershey's Kiss. "Try to get this from me!"

He popped it in his mouth and held it between his front teeth as a lure. Pia tried to lick and suck the chocolate from Jeremy's mouth while he helped her lose some clothes. Chocolate kisses indeed.

He bounced onto the bed, which included a box spring and mattress but no frame and reached for Pia. She joined him and he pulled the covers up around their waists. Then he looked her in the eyes.

"We can take this much slower if you want. I have the whole night, but I thought you…don't."

"No, you're right." She looked down and then began to look all around Jeremy's body. "Huh."

"What, did you lose something?" Jeremy glanced around but turned back to her face to follow her eyes.

"I just realized, you don't have any tattoos, do you?" Pia noticed. "That's a little unusual these days. You don't follow trends much, though. That's good."

"Maybe you should check more closely. I might have some little, tiny ones that are hard to find," Jeremy grinned.

Pia made a face at him but then continued to search around his skin. "I have a birthmark," Pia said.

"Do you? Where?" Jeremy asked, so she turned to show it to him.

He ran a finger around the area on her lower back.

"The French have a term for this, too. It's a 'café au lait' spot, which is accurate. It looks just like my mother's coffee, medium brown. Actually, it might not really be a French term. It might be like French fries." Pia wished she knew when to stop talking.

Jeremy seemed okay with her babbling.

"My brother Adam has a small, purple birthmark. I hope you meet him sometime. You aren't permitted to see his birthmark though," he warned her.

"He can't see mine, either! I don't think your brother would like to know you're sleeping with someone who's forty-four."

Then Pia realized she had just divulged her age. That was probably the last thing she wanted him to know. No more beer, she decided.

"Forty-four?" Jeremy pushed aside the covers, moved to the edge of the bed and put one foot on the floor. "*Forty-four?* I had no idea you were that old."

He was looking away from Pia; it seemed he couldn't believe it.

"Okay, that's enough already. How old did you think I was?"

"I don't know, I guess I figured you were about ten years older than me. But not forty-four. You're, like, almost as old as my mother, Pia."

So this was a big deal.

"Oh, that's great. As old as your mother." Pia sighed and looked down at her hands. "Well, I am. Sorry."

She was starting to feel everything crumbling and was thinking she should get dressed and leave.

Then Jeremy swung himself over and sat on Pia's lap, startling her, and he took her hands in his, entwining their fingers together. Jeremy lifted them over her head on the bed behind her, laying Pia down under him in the process. His face was locking down at hers then, and through his mop of hair Jeremy was grinning. Pia was immensely relieved to see that.

Jeremy was being playful with her again. "You're almost as old as my mo-ther."

While he teased Pia he rocked on her hips steadily, speaking in rhythm to his movement.

"You're almost as old as my mo-ther."

"Ohh."

Pia was aroused by his movements. Still, she was conscious of something indecent about mentioning his mother during sex. Perhaps kinky was a better word for it. Jeremy kissed Pia deeply. When their lips parted she sighed.

He feigned a scowl. "It has come to my attention that in sexually-charged situations, like the one we're in now, your vocabulary becomes substantially compromised. Tsk."

He continued rocking on her and she made a sound.

"Mmmm."

"Sorry, I can't understand you!" Jeremy smiled. "Are you interested in doing something? Whatever could it be?"

Pia begged him to stop teasing her, "*Please*, Jeremy."

He got serious and she clung to his shoulders. Then they rested.

"Thank you," Pia simply stated as he pulled the covers up over them.

Jeremy replied softly, "You're very welcome. Thank *you*."

He encouraged Pia to rest in his arms. It was nice to have a whole bed together. Pia took in the scent of his chest. They just stayed that way quietly for a few minutes, stroking one another tenderly.

Pia was curious about something. "How much of that was acting? Are you bothered by my age or were you totally kidding?"

"I was surprised for sure because you don't look that, um, age."

Pia caught that hesitation and she gave him a little nudge. "You almost said 'that old.'"

Jeremy ignored her and continued, "But I really don't care about it. I was kidding but then you sounded *so* sad, I had to give it up. Anyway, let's talk about something else. What's your favorite color?"

"I don't have one favorite. I like yellow, gray, blue and green best."

"My favorite is orange," Jeremy said as he played with Pia's silver necklace.

She asked, "What's your favorite word?"

"I don't have a favorite word. Hmm… 'peace' is a good one. What about you?"

"'Serendipity' is my favorite word. I like its meaning and it's a fun word in and of itself. 'Peace' is an excellent choice, however."

"Se-ren-di-pi-ty…it is fun to say. Dare I ask if you have a least favorite word?"

"Well, 'rape.' But after that it would be 'exclusive.' I've been spending some time with people who are making me aware of my privilege and I dislike exclusiveness."

This made Jeremy reflect for a bit. "That's good that you don't like exclusiveness. Exclusivity? I'm not sure I understand what you mean about your privilege, though."

He was giving Pia his concentrated attention. Way back in a tiny corner of her mind was a flicker of concern when he said that about exclusiveness but she addressed the other issue.

"Well, I'm part of a group trying to even the balance for the Black community. I'm becoming much more aware of the fact that, as a white person, I'm treated differently than those friends. On many levels. I suppose I was always aware of this, but it's prominently on my mind now so I want to be part of the change."

"Can you give me an example?"

"Well, I can feel relatively sure that if I get pulled over for speeding I won't end up dragged to the ground and killed by the officer."

Jeremy replied, "If it's racism, it's totally wrong. I meant —"

Abruptly, they heard some sounds in the apartment.

"Remy, are you here?" someone called out.

Jeremy lifted himself up from Pia and hollered, "Hi, Adam! Don't come down to my door! I have company!" Then he lay back down on his stomach and said to Pia, "So you can meet my brother after all."

Adam called back, "I won't, I promise." He began making a lot of noise in the kitchen cabinets.

Pia asked Jeremy in a hushed tone, "Shouldn't we close the door?"

Jeremy answered her in a normal voice, "No worries. He promised."

That made Pia think about promises.

"Promises are tough to keep. I'm afraid to make them."

"Hmm, I suppose it depends on the promise. I know Adam won't be at this doorway because he said he wouldn't." Jeremy thought for a minute and then told Pia solemnly, "I can promise you I'll never lie to you."

He stroked her hair.

As a disclaimer he coyly added, "I didn't really make the Hershey Kisses; that was just a joke."

She had to laugh at that. But Pia was surprised by what he had said about promises and was focused on that.

"I don't know what I could promise. I don't know."

"You don't have to promise me anything."

"Remy, got a minute?" Adam hollered.

"Do you mind?" Jeremy asked. Pia shook her head. "I'll be right back. Another beer?"

"No, no."

Jeremy put his blue underwear on and went down the hall to talk to Adam. Pia could hear the conversation. She thought she must get dressed and head out soon.

"I got stuck late at work. Mom called me shortly after I headed up to visit; she wants me to bring back her Tupperware. I guess we have almost all of it now. I can't find the small bowl with the yellow lid. Do you know where it is?" Adam asked Jeremy while he continued the search.

"It should be behind the cereal bowls in that cabinet. Yeah, right there."

Jeremy was getting a little chilled, so he crossed his arms.

"Got it, thanks. Are you still coming up Sunday? She asked."

Adam was packing up the Tupperware in a bag.

"I will, definitely. We have some things in the freezer from her. Should we dump the food and return the containers?" Jeremy let Adam decide.

"Um…yeah. Crap." Adam looked like he wasn't up for the task.

"Give me a sec," Jeremy told him and then returned quickly to Pia.

"Sorry, Pia. Do you mind if I help Adam for about ten minutes?" Jeremy asked sweetly.

"Of course not. I'm going to use the bathroom if that's okay."

Jeremy grabbed his sweater and went back to the kitchen, where the young men poured hot water over some Tupperware containers until the blocks of mystery food landed with loud thuds in the sink. Then they transferred the food to a big pot. That way they could wash and dry the plastic to pack with the rest of its kin.

Pia dressed and then called Gordon on her cell phone to tell him she'd be home in about an hour. He was watching a favorite show and had an Italian club submarine sandwich for dinner. Gordon didn't doubt her, so that made everything easy.

Soon Jeremy was back in his doorway, leaning against the jamb.

"May I introduce you to Adam?"

Pia looked at him, considered it, and rose from the chair to follow him. Jeremy pulled on his pants and then they went down the hall to the kitchen.

"Adam, this is Pia. Pia, this is my brother."

"Hi, Adam. Very nice to meet you," Pia said and extended her hand.

"Nice to meet you too, Pia. Sorry for the interruption! I'll be on my way in a few minutes."

Adam shook her hand and they each made a visual assessment of the other. Jeremy walked Adam to the door carrying one of the bags. At this point Pia hung back out of sight but was deliberately eavesdropping.

"She has a wedding ring on, Remy."

"Yes. I noticed that as well," Jeremy admitted.

Jeremy's romances were a recurring topic between them. "Why can't you ever date college co-eds?"

Jeremy grinned at his older sibling. "Because they're always attracted to my handsomer brother!"

That made Adam smile but then he was serious. "Well, use some caution. I wouldn't want her husband to kick your ass."

"I will."

They hugged and Jeremy gave Adam his bag of Tupperware.

As Adam headed down the stairway he hollered back up, "And 'handsomer' isn't a word, bro!"

When Adam was gone Pia and Jeremy sat on the sofa in the living room.

"Are you going to eat that food you took out of the Tupperware?" Pia asked curiously.

Jeremy shook his head. "No. I love my mom, but she can't cook. We don't usually eat what she sends us away with." He made a charmingly apologetic face. "Pia, is 'handsomer' a word?"

"Noooo. I would say 'more handsome', as in 'you're more handsome than Adam.'"

"I'm not!" Jeremy was defending Adam, not debating his looks.

"I'm joking. Jeremy, if your mom is expecting you this weekend you should go see her. Don't feel like you have to come to the nature sanctuary."

"It's okay, I'll see her on Sunday. That'll be plenty. She's been kind of weird lately. A little, oh, hostile toward us? It's not like her."

Jeremy couldn't account for it but Pia had an idea what might be behind it.

"Are you her only kids?" she asked.

Jeremy nodded, but then said, "We had an older sister, Sarah, but she died when she was six from leukemia. Adam and I can't really remember her."

"Oh, that's so awful. I'm sorry to hear it." She paused over that information. "Well, if you and Adam both graduated from college recently and are living here, your mother might be unhappy now."

"What do you mean?"

"There were years when you two used to go with your mom wherever she went. You needed her to take care of you and caring for you was a large part of her identity."

Jeremy nodded, "Sure."

Clearly Pia had to continue, as he didn't seem to grasp her meaning yet.

"Now that you're grown, her family has changed and it might be a loss for her. It's just the way it is, but she'll take some time to adjust, that's all.

"Huh. I never thought about it like that. You really think so?"

"It's a definite possibility."

"That's an oxymoron. Talk about a funny word," Jeremy grinned.

Pia had to smile at him. "Anyway, just be patient with her and give her hugs."

Then she rose to leave. Jeremy brought Pia her coat and put his own on. He drove her to her car. Before she unlocked her car Jeremy gave her one of those hugs.

Chapter 8

The next day was cold, but not bitter and with little wind. It was mostly clear with some cirrus clouds in the higher elevation of the sky. The sanctuary had a good turnout for the open house. Pia was set up in a room that had a large doorway leading directly out to some snow-covered hayfields. This was a good area for families to try the snowshoes, as they could break new trails all over it themselves waiting for the program to begin. Also, they couldn't get lost. Pia wore heavy jeans, work boots, and a turtleneck under a favorite old wool sweater. She had a wool hat on that her friend Annie had made for her a few years before.

Pia would wait until there was a group of eight or ten people before she gave instructions on how to get the snowshoes on. During the afternoon she repeated these instructions three times. When she was beginning with a second group she saw Jeremy come in by the front door. He was in a good, warm coat and held a pair of gloves in his hand but had no hat. One of his cameras was around his neck. People were milling around looking at all the stuff in the program room and talking.

Pia took a deep breath to calm her nerves before speaking to the crowd.

"Okay, welcome! Can you all hear me?" she loudly began.

Everyone was quiet then. Behind Pia were many sets of wooden snowshoes hung on pegs.

"Thanks for coming, we hope you have fun today! My name is Pia. On the wall here are several different types of snowshoes. Mostly we have Modified Bear Paws, Hurons, and Ojibwa styles." Pia held up examples of each. "They're different depending on what region of North America they're from and the different types of snow in those areas. These Huron snowshoes are good for carrying heavy loads because they offer great flotation. The Modified Bear Paws are good in any type of snow. Mine are Ojibwa, named for the native tribe in the Great Lakes region that developed this type. They're good in deep snow, so long as you keep the pointed tip up. I like them because they're narrow to slip between trees easily."

"Question: how did you make those? Or did you buy them ready-made?" a woman with her family asked.

"All of these came as kits, with the wood frames ready. Then some of the staff wove the nylon lacing and varnished them. Historically, snowshoes were made with moose-hide lacing. The thinly cut strips of hide would be soaked in water and then woven on. That way when they dried they were very tight. They should have at least three coats of varnish. Oh, avoid dry asphalt because the varnish will wear off quickly."

"Do you have metal ones?" a tall man asked then.

"We don't. These are more traditional, and have the benefit of being essentially silent, whereas the metal ones are noisier. Also, I watched someone with the metal ones, and maybe it was just how that person walked, but the snow was being kicked onto the backs of their legs while they walked. That would not be advantageous in real traveling situations. They aren't as artful as these, either. I guess I'm a snowshoe snob," Pia laughed.

She meant to make fun of herself so as not to offend the man. She was aware of Jeremy taking photographs, which made her more self-conscious.

"But the metal ones have teeth on the bottom. Isn't that a plus?"

Pia tried to keep it positive. "They can be. You can buy the teeth and attach them to these. In normal use, with deep snow, those shouldn't be necessary though." Then, addressing everyone, "Before I hand these out, I'll show you how to put them on. This is the hardest part! They're easy to use and easy to get out of, but if you don't put them on correctly you're apt to lose one and then be up to your knees in snow. There isn't enough snow to hide a garden gnome today, but when it's deep it can happen." People chuckled. "I'm speaking from personal experience!"

She showed everyone how to set their feet in the straps and instructed them that the straps should be as tight as possible.

"Okay, now I'll hand them out based on your general weight since we have different sizes. I recommend you let me check them before we head out."

Pia was interrupted by two children fighting over a toy they had found in one of the bins used for home school programs.

A small boy said loudly, "I want it!"

Another child about two years older told him, "I had it first, Connor. Play with something else."

Connor had a planned retort he must've learned in a daycare setting.

"Sharing is caring," he said boldly.

Connor assumed that would fix the situation. It did, but only because the older one scoffed at him, "'Sharing is caring.' Duh, that's so stupid," as he handed over the toy.

Pia was glad it was over and she didn't have to intervene. She didn't know who was supposed to be watching them. It didn't seem to be anyone waiting for the snowshoes. Connor seemed unsure of how to respond. He had what he wanted, but his face showed that the other boy made Connor feel like he had somehow lost, not won. Pia had a scowl ready for the older one but he didn't look at her or anyone else. He must have known he'd been a jerk.

She continued, "If you want to just stay in the field you're welcome to do so. I'll lead a short hike in the woods beyond there for anyone who wants to come along."

While Pia did her best to keep it orderly, the families were eager to put the snowshoes on and often did it incorrectly. She spent about fifteen minutes just outside the doors with her gloves set under one knee, strapping people in their snowshoes with her bare hands for better dexterity. Jeremy took photos of everything. Pia straightened up, shook the snow off her gloves and watched the happy chaos.

She called out to the group, "You can walk as you normally would! You can pivot your ankles because the shoe is strapped to you and there's a space in them for the toe of your boot to go through."

She demonstrated for people from her spot near the building. Her friend Annie, who was a long-time staff member, came by to see how it was going. Pia had just selected a set for Jeremy. She avoided physical contact with him but he gave her a friendly quick kiss on her cheek. Pia introduced Jeremy to Annie as a former student she knew from the university but was pretty certain she was blushing when she said it.

Annie said, "Nice to meet you, Jeremy. We're so fortunate to have Pia helping out here for so many years. Have you been here before?"

"No, never." Through the wide doorway, Jeremy glanced back at the room, which housed many types of feathers, small animal skulls in containers, shed snake skins, with sets of antlers from deer and moose hung on the walls. "This room is sort of reminiscent of a hunting lodge."

"We did not kill all these animals," Annie said jokingly. "Seriously, they died of natural causes."

Pia laughed out loud. Then Annie went into the field to help some people struggling with the snowshoes.

"The antlers were donated for educational purposes," Pia explained. "Annie's an outstanding naturalist. She also has more integrity than anyone I have ever met. Now there's a good soul," she said as she strapped him in his Hurons, her face at his knees.

"I thought she was a he," Jeremy said.

There was no judgement in his voice; it was just an observation.

Pia shrugged. "Mm, she's androgynous I guess. I think many people are a sexual blend to varying degrees, even though we only have two choices on the outside. Inside doesn't always match outside very well, or in some cases at all. Honestly, I'm a real blend myself."

She looked him directly in the eyes to gauge his response to that.

Jeremy confided, with something like relief in his features, "I'm a blend, too."

They exchanged a look of mutual understanding. Pia just didn't have an issue with it at all.

Finally, she strapped her own snowshoes on and they joined everyone outside. She explained to the group loudly, mostly to keep them from wandering, that hers went on quickly because two of the three straps didn't need to be buckled or unbuckled, as she had them already set up for her specific boots.

"Hi, Pia. How's it going?" Jane called, carrying a load of wood past Pia's group towards the bonfire.

She volunteered at the sanctuary, too.

"Hi, there! You're at the bonfire today?"

"Yeah, I'm in charge of s'mores!"

Pia smiled and had to turn her attention back to the visitors. Then Jane saw Jeremy.

"Hi, um…don't tell me, don't tell me. Okay, tell me?"

Jeremy grinned. "Jeremy. How are you, Jane?"

"Forgetful, but otherwise great. See you!"

Jane's arms were nagging her to keep moving. Also, Annie teased her.

"Get back to your post, Sergeant S'mores!"

Annie took half the wood out of Jane's arms and went with her.

Jeremy said, "Have fun!"

"Okay, everybody ready?" Pia hollered enthusiastically and waved her mismatched gloves.

There were general positive shouts.

"Alright! Who wants to lead for a while?"

An adolescent boy shot his hand up. He asked Pia where to go and she pointed. Then he led the group up the gently sloping hill. Jeremy continued taking photographs periodically.

"How are you doing? It's a good workout, isn't it?" Pia asked the boy after a few minutes, loudly, to include the whole group in the conversation.

It turned out that in the field there was about a foot and a half of snow.

"Yeah, it is." The boy was a little heavy and huffing a bit.

"What you're doing is packing the snow down for the rest of us, breaking trail. The indigenous people who used snowshoes when traveling would take turns being the lead, so no one person got worn out. We can switch if you want, then you'll see how easy it is being second in line," Pia offered, and he nodded.

Some people moved into fresh snow then, to try breaking trail. When they reached the forest, there was much less snow because they were on a popular trail. After a while, the boy spoke to Pia.

"Leader lady?"

"My name is Pia. What's yours?"

"Dante. Leader Pia? It seems like you are trying to avoid stepping on the tree roots."

"Wow, you're very perceptive. I am trying to avoid them, actually."

Then Pia grumbled, "A nearly impossible task in snowshoes." She continued in her trail leader volume. "The trees will be okay, but I personally don't like to step on them. I really like trees," Pia explained pleasantly.

Dante seemed to be mildly autistic, so Pia tried to be clear when she spoke to him.

"Does it hurt the trees?" Dante sounded a little concerned.

"It doesn't damage them, but I don't know if it hurts them. I think the rocks don't mind a bit if you step on them."

"The rocks don't *mind?*" His mother said in a tone that suggested Pia might be pushing what is reasonable.

"I've been told they have energy, so who knows?"

Dante's mother said directly, "They aren't sentient."

Jeremy was near the end of the group and saw someone make the crazy sign for their kids behind Pia's back.

He said, "Everything on earth is made of the same basic elements arranged differently, from people to rocks. But then, not everything on earth is part of the planet. Some so-called rocks are asteroids."

"What do you mean?" Dante stopped to let a few people pass him while he waited for Jeremy to catch up to him.

Jeremy talked with his hands as he spoke to Dante.

"Sometimes meteorites, big rocks from space, become pulled into earth's gravitational field and they come flying right through the atmosphere and land here! Usually they burn up on the trip before they land, and if you see it in the night sky, that's what falling stars really are."

"Why do they burn up?" Dante asked.

The whole group listened as they continued on the woodland trail in single file.

"Because they're traveling so fast they can't keep it together. They travel at about forty-five thousand miles per hour! When an object travels in space, it takes no effort because it's in what's called a vacuum. When it reaches our atmosphere, the air here is a gas. Did you know that?"

Dante did. "Our air is made of oxygen that we breathe. It's a gas, not a solid or a liquid."

"Exactly right! The air in front of the meteorite is being compressed, squashed, because of the speed. When gas is compressed like that its temperature rises, and it gets very hot. In this case it's so hot things catch on fire! If meteorites survive the trip to earth without completely burning, they're called asteroids by astronomers. Geologists prefer to call them bolides, but they're the same thing. Once in a while someone lucky finds one on the ground, usually in an impact crater."

Jeremy clearly enjoyed teaching Dante. Like Pia, he spoke loudly enough so everyone was included, although everyone else probably already knew all this. Pia was just hearing it for the first time.

"Do you work here?" a red-headed man in a down vest and wool sweater asked Jeremy.

Jeremy looked surprised and shook his head. "No."

"You certainly should!"

Jeremy smiled.

Pia said, "I think an asteroid hit me on the head once."

Several people in the group thought that was funny but Dante looked serious.

He said, "I like red ones," the incongruity of which puzzled Pia to silence.

"That's why Dante has a red coat," his mother explained.

"Like red cardinals and red berries?" Jeremy offered some living examples.

"Red pajamas, red toothbrush, red plate!" Dante added those quickly in a row.

For him the focus was now on color and Pia suspected those were his personal things he listed. She was reminded of "red rum, red rum" from an old horror film but she kept her mouth shut.

Then a little girl of about six interpreted the conversation as a game.

"Red crayons, red roses, red…I don't know any others!"

She laughed heartily then and moved around the trees, getting off trail.

"There really isn't much snow on the trail. If we turn here we'll be back in the field and then it will be deeper," Pia directed the group.

In a few minutes they were at the top of the field, on the far side. They spread out a bit. The little girl wanted to know if some animal tracks nearby were made by a bunny. Everyone looked at them.

"No, they're from a squirrel. You can tell a lot about tracks by other hints. In this case the tracks end at the base of a tree, so the animal went up the tree. Bunnies can't climb trees. We might see their tracks soon though. I know they live here. Good job, keep looking!" Pia told her.

"What are these tracks?" Jeremy asked, pointing down at the snow near the forest edge.

There was a long, bumpy, raised line in the snow.

"Those are referred to as 'artifacts' in tracking terminology. What you're looking at aren't actually animal tracks, but chunks of snow that dropped from the branches overhead." Pia liked talking about this with him.

"Do I flunk?" He smiled and his head bobbled faintly.

"Not at all, it was a good question. They made a trail pattern the way they fell in a row." She really wanted to gobble him up then.

The man in the down coat remarked at how lucky Pia was to work at the sanctuary, to have such a rewarding occupation.

"You can work here, too, but most of us don't get paid. We're almost all volunteers," she explained.

"Ah. I'm less envious now!" he joked.

"I get more out of volunteering here than I give. I'm always learning and it's a good way to decompress from my work week. We always welcome new volunteers. You should think about it!" Pia said jovially.

"Leader Pia, fleas," Dante said then. Now everyone followed his gaze.

There were dozens of little black flecks hopping about in some deep impressions in the snow at his feet.

"Thank you, Dante! You could be an excellent naturalist. Those are called snow fleas, because they look just like fleas and they're found in the snow. They aren't really fleas though so they won't hop onto you. We're lucky to see them today!"

They continued down the field towards the program room at the main building. Pia tried to keep them along the edge of the field because that was where they were most likely to see rabbit tracks. When they were almost back she spied some.

"Here are your rabbit tracks! These are probably from an eastern cottontail. They're more common than the native New England cottontail. There are also snowshoe hares, but their tracks are larger and the distance of the stride is longer. You see, there are two big back feet here and two small front ones here. The rabbit went in that direction."

"Are you sure? It looks like they're going this way," the tall man said, nicely, but he was sure she was mistaken.

Pia was used to this and understood why he said it.

"It does look like that. The rabbit starts by pushing off its little front paws, which are set one in front of the other, and then when it hops the big back feet swing forward and the little feet come up. So the small feet then big feet, then a space, then small feet then big feet...." Pia was able to show them because the tracks were clear for quite a way.

Then they came to a spot with rabbit pellets.

The little girl pointed at them and declared, "Poop! That's bunny poop! Hahaha!"

She thought that was the funniest thing ever. Pia glanced at Jeremy to watch his reaction to her. He found her entertaining and smiled broadly watching the girl. He crouched to capture some images of her. His ears were very red from the cold.

"You are a very silly girl!" Pia said playfully to the child. This made her squeal some more.

When they returned to the program room, Pia let everyone know where there was hot cocoa waiting for them. She did her best to accommodate everyone at the same time in the frenzy that ensued. People wanted to leave the snowshoes and go in the main building. Quickly the crowd thinned out.

Dante and his mom approached Pia and Dante's mom spoke to her son. "What do you say, Dante?"

He forced out, "Thank you Leader Pia. I had fun." It wasn't very enthusiastic.

Pia answered, "You're welcome; I'm glad you joined us."

Jeremy was by her side then.

Dante looked at Jeremy. "I like you."

That wasn't said with enthusiasm either but it was spontaneous, so Pia figured that's just how Dante spoke to people.

Jeremy told Dante he liked him too. Dante and his mother were the last of the group to leave the room. Pia then explained to Jeremy that she had to repeat the program once more, so he could see what else was going on if he wanted. There were some new people waiting for the snowshoes already. Pia explained to them that she had to correct the buckles on them, though actually she said it so they wouldn't start before others had a chance to join them. As she fixed the snowshoes, she placed them on the pegs.

"You're good at this; that was very educational," Jeremy told her as he took his snowshoes off.

Pia kept her voice down and continued with her work. "Thanks. I don't really like leading groups. I'm too shy."

Jeremy handed her his pair to hang with the others. "It didn't show."

"I'm glad to hear that. Oh, thanks for the lesson on asteroids! That was neat." She looked in his eyes and wanted to kiss him but wouldn't do that there. "This should take about an hour or so."

When the afternoon activities wrapped up, Jeremy returned to the program room and found Pia on her knees, putting ragged towels under the snowshoe pegs to absorb the dripping melt.

"So, this is my happy place," Pia said as she rose from the floor. With her hands on her hips she surveyed the space. "Did you get to meet the sheep?"

"No. I talked to the guy cutting the ice on the pond and helped him with moving it. He's pretty cool. I took lots of photographs, too."

"That's great! Let's go over to the barn. I don't see them very often anymore."

As they left the program room Jane was carrying a load of supplies she had loaned the sanctuary out to her car. Jeremy caught a door for her so everything didn't tumble as she tried to get through it.

"Thanks, Jeremy. I should've made two trips. What did you think of our winter open house?"

He enthused, "It was great! This place is beautiful and everyone's really nice."

He took some things from Jane as they all walked towards her car.

"Yes, it's pretty special."

At the car Pia took more of Jane's items so she could open her hatch. "Thanks, guys. Are you heading out?"

Pia said, "We're going to visit the sheep first. I miss them."

She handed Jane what she had in her arms and once those items were stowed in the trunk Jeremy did the same. As Jane closed the back of the car she thanked them and said goodbye.

Pia and Jeremy walked a little way down the road to an iconic red barn. Most people were gone and the staff had already moved the sheep inside for the night. Just inside the huge doorway Pia yanked on a weathered string to turn on a bare lightbulb overhead and did the same about three yards further inside. She showed Jeremy the pen where the sheep were kept and raised its latch to let him go in. Eight wooly animals collected in a corner away from him. As they were prey animals, food for predators, their eyes did not blink and their ribs heaved as they breathed.

"This isn't going well," Jeremy said.

Pia was already around a corner lifting the heavy lid from a large wooden bin.

"Hold on, I have a plan."

A moment later she brought him an old coffee can filled with grain to feed the sheep so they'd approach him. Soon Jeremy was surrounded by the animals while Pia leaned on the railing to watch.

"There, you're friends already. If you pet them you'll get lanolin on your hands from the wool. It's an authentic barnyard experience." Then she pointed. "That one there I helped hand-raise nine years ago. Careful, he might butt you."

Jeremy looked at her with some alarm. Pia just smiled at him and mused how much she enjoyed him.

While he was petting some of the sheep and watching them eat he said to her, "This is such a great place. I learned a lot from you today and, I think, quite a bit about you. You're almost a part of this landscape, you know? I think you're really cool." Then he changed the subject, glancing up. "Can we go up into the loft?"

"I don't remember ever going in the loft."

"I think we should investigate it," he suggested.

"I'm learning a lot from you, too. Less tangible things though." Pia added, "I have much more to learn *about* you."

Jeremy's feed can was empty, so the sheep began to move away from him as they each figured that out, but they were comfortable with him being there now.

"Tsk, they're such fickle beasts," Pia noted.

After Jeremy exited the pen, she dropped the latch over the wooden gate and put the can back where it belonged. He took some photos of the sheep before they made their way up a ladder and looked around. The sun was fading and through the windows they could see the pink and blue streaks of clouds stretching far across the sky over a lower field, with bare trees lining the field edge in the distance. As they viewed the scene it changed incrementally into another lovely rendering of itself.

Jeremy whispered to Pia, "I'm glad I have my camera to capture the sky scene from up here, through these windows. It's so beautiful, and so fleeting."

Pia nodded while he snapped away. When he lowered the camera she whispered to him right by his ear, "What we have in mind is going to be cold."

"We don't have to expose much. We'll have another authentic barnyard experience," Jeremy whispered back, grinning.

Pia took his head in her hands and kissed him intensely then.

She spoke quietly, "This place is sacred ground to me. It's great to have you here."

She took off her gloves, pulled Jeremy's coat apart and found her way to his bare belly. She undid his jeans, loosened her shirt and dropped her own pants, all without any hesitation and kissing him often.

He said, pleasantly surprised, "You're awfully lusty this afternoon."

"Mm-hm."

They were hidden among hay bales and they were quiet up in the loft. Pia thought there might be small critters there with them but she didn't mention that. They could hear the sheep making soft, comforting sounds below them and the scent of hay and the animals surrounded them. In the increasing darkness they kept eye contact with their pupils large. Pia was aware that their cars were almost the only ones left in the parking lot, so as soon they finished they hastily hauled their pants up and snuck down the ladder.

"We were looking at the sheep, that's all," Pia said, as much to herself as him.

Jeremy stopped her at the huge barn doorway to pull some hay off her so she quickly checked him for it as well.

"Unfortunately, tonight I'm the one who has to leave too soon," he told her rather apologetically as they walked back to the parking lot. "I told my mom I'd come home tonight, in time for dinner. Sleep over."

"Oh, I'm *so* glad to hear that. That makes me happy."

At his car they hugged and Jeremy gave her a quick kiss on the lips. She made sure he knew which direction to head in to get to a main road.

"I'll talk to you soon, Pia."

"I can't wait. Be safe." Pia smiled at him.

She was so happy, so completely happy. Just as Jeremy drove away Annie walked towards her with Pia's snowshoes in hand.

"Glad you're still here. These are yours, right?" she said.

"Yes. I just wanted to show Jeremy the sheep before he had to leave. Thanks."

She took them from Annie and stood in the lot watching his car get smaller and smaller.

"Okay, thanks so much for helping out today. I really appreciate it." Annie always said that.

So Pia responded with, "As always, my pleasure. Have a good night, Annie."

Chapter 9

Pia didn't see Jeremy for nine days after that. He did text her so she knew he was still there. In the office, she and the other staff were under more scrutiny than usual. Occasionally Sandra would do this, immediately following an incident when she decided people needed watching. Nell and Pia were very lenient with the deadline policies for the graduate students. Some were attending courses but never registered for them and others were registered for courses they didn't actually attend. Pia hated both scenarios. If a student didn't register for a specific course, it could be a full year before it was offered again. She would often advise them to see if the instructor would allow them to register it as an independent study the following semester. They would not be overloaded with work then, because they had already taken the course. They couldn't register for it after the deadline for the current semester, but this was a way around that.

It was more difficult with the students who registered for a course and then forgot all about it. Sometimes these were students who weren't in a program with the university; they were just individuals taking one course for their own benefit. A student might register for a course a month before it began and just never notify anyone that they had decided not to take it after all. Then, halfway through the semester they were presented with a $4,100 bill for, from their perspective, nothing. If Pia dropped the course, the bursar could run a report and see that she had done that and when it happened. So it was a constant battle within her whether to help the student and risk her position. She sent out emails explaining the deadlines to the students which helped a lot but it didn't catch all of them. The ones who never used their university email were the hardest to reach.

Sandra and Ralph were in watchdog mode that week.

The Chinese students in particular communicated with one another often, fortunately. If one person identified a policy they'd let the others know about it. Pia could only imagine how much they had to learn about the culture, laws and regulations here. Pia had helped a few with their late registration changes so more came by the office daily.

On Thursday, a Chinese graduate student came in and Ralph was right beside Pia looking for some forms. The student wanted desperately to drop a course because he should never have registered for it. It was an undergraduate course that wasn't going to count toward his degree requirements. Pia explained to him that she couldn't help him out.

"You may withdraw from the course now but you can't drop it. That means that you will receive a 'W' on your transcript instead of whatever grade the instructor would give you. If you never went to the classes, she would assign an 'F'. You can't receive a refund now, though. I'm afraid it's too late. The deadline was six weeks ago." Pia said it in as supportive a tone as she could, but she knew the information was useless to him.

"Please can you drop course for me? I can pay a small fee," he implored her.

"I can't, I'm sorry. The deadline with the late fee was six weeks ago. Without the fee was seven weeks ago."

"What if I have the professor to tell for you I did not attend any class?"

"No, that won't help." Pia said, worried Ralph's patience was taxed. The student looked truly anguished and he was determined.

"But, but…I cannot pay the course. It is too much money. I cannot pay."

Ralph sighed heavily, made a face and walked away. The student leaned an elbow on the counter to rest his head in his hand while he desperately searched for a way to fix this.

Normally, Pia would tell him to fill out a petition and coach him on exactly how to word it, but Sandra had told all her staff not to do that. She was tired of the petitions and it really wouldn't help him if Sandra made her own decision instead of bringing it to the committee.

Pia took his student I.D. card to look in the database for any chance there might be. Sometimes the student would leave out pertinent information, such as that the course had only begun a week before due to some extenuating circumstance the instructor had, or if it was through the corporate education department, which had their own schedule independent of the campus. She hoped he had registered for it only recently. That would have been against the policies too, so she would try to rationalize that someone shouldn't have allowed it and remove it for that reason. Anything she could use as leverage. His name was Yi Tao. There was nothing in his registration history that would help in this situation.

Pia returned to the counter with his I.D. card. Unfortunately, her taking it and checking the database had given Tao more hope and therefore he continued to appeal to Pia for another five minutes.

"Please, please can you help me? My wife just had baby, it doesn't sleep. I don't sleep. I cannot pay the course. Please can you help?"

"I'm really very sorry, but there isn't anything I can do."

Pia felt tremendous sympathy for Tao but she had no authority on the matter. Ralph had gone over to Mary's cubicle to talk to her for a few minutes but returned to the counter.

"We can't help you. You're responsible for that bill," he said too loudly and with no concern for Tao.

"But, but…what can I do? I cannot pay —"

"That's it. No more." Ralph waved his hand and walked away.

Tao was very distraught. He looked around and then his thoughts took him somewhere else and his eyes gazed at the counter surface without seeing it. After a minute he looked to Pia again.

"I'm very sorry," she said softly.

He seemed to understand that she honestly was but that didn't help him at all. Then Tao left the office, disconsolate.

"What kind of person refers to their baby as 'it'?" Ralph snickered as he wandered back towards Mary's cubicle, where she had been standing with her arms crossed to witness the interaction with Tao.

Mary added, "I was just going to say that, Ralph."

"Most Chinese," Pia told them. "It's not a measure of their affection for their babies at all. They just don't use masculine and feminine terms for people."

Ralph frowned at Pia and Mary rolled her eyes for Ralph with a sneer. Pia felt, as she had many times before, that she wasn't part of the culture there and she wasn't welcome. She went back to her cubicle to look at an email she had printed and pinned to her wall. It was from an alumnus who had referred to her as 'spectacular' a few years ago. Pia would hang onto that until it fell apart. She discovered that Shelly had put the photo of Ben Stiller over it, so she felt a bit lighter.

"Thanks for loaning Ben, Shelly," she said from her cubicle.

Shelly said, "Anytime!" without letting up on her speedy typing.

Jeremy called Pia just after five that afternoon. What he told her lifted her spirits further some while she walked to her car.

"I wanted to tell you that you were totally right about my mom! We talked about how Adam and I have grown and left her. Adam and my father were there for the conversation and now they think I'm so intuitive, heh. She cried though, and that was hard. Hopefully things will go better now."

Pia felt her warmth towards him grow. She hesitated to initiate seeing him because she wanted this relationship to be on his terms. She hadn't convinced herself that he was staying with this and wanted him to lead. However, she was very much hoping to see him soon.

"That's good, I'm glad to hear it. This reminds me of one summer when my nephew told me that his mom was angry with him because she wanted him to mow the lawn around a lone tulip in the middle of the yard. He just mowed over it because he had other things to do and it was in the way. I told him next year, cut the flower and put it in a glass in the kitchen, then mow. I guess he did and my sister-in-law thought he was the most thoughtful son ever. Then she told his girlfriend, so he scored points with her, too."

"Ha, that's cool. Um, I'm trying to think of a time we could get together soon. I'm going away this weekend with some friends to New York. How about next week? Would Monday be good?" Jeremy said.

Pia unlocked her car. She hated waiting until Monday but was pleased he was asking at all.

"Yes, Monday night will work. I can hardly wait."

She felt a pang of jealousy that he prioritized other people in his life, but she understood that, of course, he had friends.

"Okay, great. Call or text me Monday and we'll work out when and where, okay? Or I'll call you if you don't." Jeremy was cheerful.

"Alright. Have a nice time this weekend."

She put her phone in her handbag and turned the engine over. The traffic was backed up so she had to wait awhile before she could even get out of her spot.

Christmas was coming in a week and the whole world seemed busy.

Pia intended to give Jeremy a gift. She had decided to get him a hat that Annie had knitted from the sanctuary sheep's wool. In the sanctuary gift shop, Pia chose one with natural colors and hoped it would be a good fit for him. She boxed and wrapped it and she found an ideal card. It was one of William Wegman's Weimaraners photographed wearing a crown of glass ornaments. She read once that the dogs loved to dress up and pose, but she couldn't see how the photographer got this shot. She hovered her pen over the card for a long time, anxious about what to write and how to write it.

Finally, she wrote what her heart felt. She knew that Jeremy would not mock her even if he didn't feel the same way about her as she did about him. She kept those items in a drawer at work to give to Jeremy on Monday.

Pia was also giving a lot of thought to Yi Tao. She wanted to email him a petition form but she knew she would be in trouble if he told anyone she had sent it. She went back and forth with this in her head all day Friday. In the end she sent it to him. She didn't instruct him not to mention that she sent it, because writing that in an email could end up doing her more harm than good.

On Monday morning Pia was glad to see Tao come in with the petition. She smiled at him, but Mary was at the counter. Normally Mary would have checked with Ralph to be sure it was completed correctly, but Ralph wasn't in the office. Mary accepted it from Tao and told him a committee would review it.

"Mary, may I have that form just for a minute please? I'm supposed to enter the information on the spreadsheet before you take it," Pia reminded her.

"No, this one's for a graduate student, so it just goes directly to Ralph."

Pia knew Mary was incorrect but she didn't wish to say so in front of the other staff.

"Then it can't be properly tracked with the others. No one will know what its status is."

"Don't worry about it, Pia. Ralph will know what to do."

Mary routinely defaulted to Ralph as she wasn't confident in her own abilities. This flattered Ralph.

Pia steamed in her head, "I know what I'm doing and I only wish you did."

She put what little information she had on the spreadsheet. Frequently students would ask how their petition was progressing and no one had any idea, so she had set up the spreadsheet to track them. But it was only accurate if everyone who received such paperwork remembered the new protocol.

The rest of the day proceeded similarly, with progress in most areas and a few steps back in others. Eventually five o'clock came. Pia had made it through another workday.

She was the last person to leave, as it was already after five, so she locked the door behind her. As she turned to make her way to the main doors one of the Venezuelan students approached her. She said hello to him, as they were familiar to one another, and she figured he was probably on his way to her office. All the Venezuelan students were in the registrar's office routinely because their government was very thorough in tracking the students' educational progress. Mario was a lean, handsome young man who was graduating the coming spring. He was wearing black jeans and a tan leather jacket with a wool scarf folded into it and the collar turned up. Pia liked him. She liked all of the Venezuelan students. Actually, she liked most of the students, Venezuelan or otherwise.

Mario stopped walking, rather like a horse with the reins pulled, with his feet settling back a step.

"Hi, Pia. Your office is closed now," he noted with resignation.

"Yes, but I can open up again. What were you coming here for?"

Pia hoped it was just to pick up a form or a letter he was waiting for. Jeremy was heading down the hall behind Mario then. He smiled at Pia and she acknowledged him with her eyes, while speaking with Mario. In a moment he was standing near the registrar's office door with them. Pia had just unlocked the door with her I.D. card.

Mario looked to Jeremy briefly and then answered Pia.

"I am here to take a transcript for my friend if I can. He is Paulo Moreno, you know him, yes?"

"Yes, I do."

Pia adored Paulo; he was a gentle soul. She swung open the door and switched the light on, holding the door open for both of them. Mario looked uncertain as to whether Jeremy should come in.

He said to Jeremy, but with his eyes checking with Pia, "I think this office is closed now."

Pia said, "It's okay. Jeremy, this is Mario. Mario, this is Jeremy. Jeremy just graduated with his master's degree in aerospace engineering."

Jeremy said hello to Mario cheerfully.

To Mario, Pia asked, "You're in civil engineering, aren't you?"

She dropped her things onto a chair and went to the drawer that held the requested transcripts, thumbing through them in search of Paulo's envelope.

Mario ran a hand through his hair. "No, I am in international studies. Paulo is civil, so you are almost correct."

He gave her a weary grin. Pia found Paulo's transcript.

"Oh, Mario, there's no note telling us to give it to you…."

"He only phoned me one hour ago for me to pick it up for him. He said he sent an email to Shelly. Paulo is in Venezuela now, so he cannot get it. He forgot to take it last week."

Mario leaned on the counter and rubbed his eyes. He was clearly tired. Next to him, Jeremy was the Energizer Bunny. He was moving from spot to spot near the counter just because he had that extra energy.

Pia rested one hand on her hip and said to Jeremy, "Can you give us some of that?"

Jeremy stopped abruptly and looked at her quizzically.

Then she tipped her head and said, "Your energy. If you don't need it all?"

Jeremy glanced over to Mario quickly and then said to Pia, "Sure, here?"

His head bobbled and he grinned.

Pia blushed and she glared at him. That was quite out of character for him. Mario was a cute boy, though. Jeremy resumed moving about and he looked at his phone.

Then to Mario she continued, "We have to know you have his permission. It's an important document. I can't open Shelly's email."

Pia's fingers tapped on the counter while she rummaged through her messy brain looking for a solution. Jeremy asked if Mario called Paulo, could Pia talk to Paulo for his permission. Mario looked hopeful. They all knew they didn't want Pia to boot her computer up and wait for an email.

She sighed, "Technically, no. But I know Paulo so I'll recognize his voice. Sure."

Mario used one hand to press down his scarf to view his phone in the other. While Mario's fingers moved swiftly over his phone Pia smiled at Jeremy, grateful he didn't mind waiting while this was sorted out. Mario couldn't reach Paulo. Everyone looked at each other. Pia knew both students but she could not recall if they were friends or if she'd ever seen them together.

Mario looked rather exhausted. "It is okay, I will come back tomorrow. Thank you anyway. I have spent three hours at the automobile, no, motor vehicle, registrar, what it is called. So that is why I am so late." Mario gathered his things that he had set on the floor by his feet.

As usual, Pia regretted the policies. She knew that if Mario wasn't permitted to pick up Paulo's transcript and did something with it that she'd be fired and the university would be in trouble. However, Pia figured the odds of this being the case were astronomical. In the morning she could check with Shelly about the email from Paulo. Pia extended her hand forward with the envelope for Mario to take.

Mario looked at Pia. "Are you sure this is okay?"

Pia shrugged and nodded simultaneously. He took it from her and opened his computer bag.

"*Muchas gracias.*" Mario gave her a tired smile and placed it in the bag securely.

"*De nada, amigo.* Let's get out of here."

Pia yawned as she picked up her handbag, a little paper bag with handles and her bento box. Jeremy held the door as they all stepped out into the hall. They walked together until the first set of doors, where Mario separated from them. He said goodnight and thanked Pia again, but hesitated briefly, as it occurred to him that Jeremy didn't get whatever he came to the office for.

"*Buenas noches,*" Pia said to Mario, as she and Jeremy were headed further down the hallway.

"Goodnight! Enjoy your classes," Jeremy said to him as well. Mario shrugged at whatever dynamic was going on here and left.

On the way down the hall Pia scolded Jeremy. "I can't believe you said that," regarding sharing his energy with them.

"No worries, it was pretty obtuse. I think maybe you have a dirty mind, young lady."

He was his happy self and it made her smile despite herself.

They had dinner at an Ethiopian restaurant. This was a first for them, eating in a restaurant together. Sitting down on pillows on the floor, Pia told Jeremy how long it had been since she'd had this food.

"I remember the first time I ate Ethiopian food. It was when Ethiopia was in the news for having a terrible famine and many people there were starving to death. My friend's dad joked that the restaurant would only have dirt to serve. I believed him and had to be coaxed in the door," Pia recalled soberly.

"I don't remember hearing about that."

"You probably wouldn't have. I was a little kid then," Pia explained.

"Oh."

"I have these conversations with Gordon sometimes, but then I'm the young one in them." Pia couldn't help the comparison, but Jeremy jumped on it and steered the conversation to Gordon.

Jeremy's first question was, "How much older than you is he?"

"Eighteen years." This was always awkward.

His next question was, "And he's disabled?"

"Well, he has a back injury, so it really limits what he can do. It's a shame."

Third question: "May I ask…can you two…you know?"

"Yes we can, thankfully." Pia took a sip of her wine. They hadn't ordered any food yet.

"Why doesn't he have surgery?" Like many people Jeremy asked that as if it were a no-brainer; of course you would do whatever might help you live an active lifestyle.

Pia had told so many people this. "We know someone who had back surgery that made her pain substantially worse and there was nothing they could do to correct it, and it ruined her. Generally, back surgery doesn't work. Gordon's world has gotten small because he's so physically limited now. I couldn't live that way but he seems alright with it."

"Wow, I couldn't live like that either."

"May you never have to."

The subject dropped then. Jeremy redirected his thoughts to the meal and they finally looked at the menus.

"I love Ethiopian food. Lots of choices for a vegetarian," he told her. "What would you like to order? Do you eat meat?"

Pia answered, "I don't have to. I was a vegetarian in college and then I saw a film, *The Life of Plants*, I think it was called, narrated by Stevie Wonder. It made me feel as badly about eating plants as animals. Then I tried to just eat Hostess products and Cheetos but that didn't last."

Jeremy chuckled at that and then he asked her, "Is that why you're so sensitive about trees?" Pia looked at him curiously, so he continued, "You don't want to hurt their roots, you try to not step on them."

"Oh!" Pia said, realizing he was referring to the snowshoe hike. "No, I just love trees. Huh…actually, maybe you're right."

Jeremy said, "So, I really like *atkilt*; it's curried vegetable stew with carrots, potatoes, peppers and onions…maybe some other vegetables. What do you think?"

"That sounds good. Do you like *misir key wot*, the lentils in *berbere* sauce?" Pia suggested.

"Delicious!"

They settled on those and *gomen*, cooked greens. When the food arrived with the spongy bread it was very colorful and aromatic. It was served on a big platter, like a deep pizza pan, and the waiter put it on the low table woven of natural fibers. There were no utensils and Jeremy declined plates. They just picked up the vegetables and sauces with pieces of the spongy bread they broke as they went along.

Pia said, "It's nice that it's communal food."

"Yeah, it is. This is so good! Mmm."

Pia wanted to know more about Jeremy's life. She didn't know much.

"How was your trip to New York?"

He smiled. "It was great, we had a lot of fun! It's such a huge city. We did a lot of walking, that's for sure."

"Did you do any photography?" Pia asked between bites.

Jeremy swallowed his food. "Yes, lots. I discovered so many linear images in the landscape of that city."

"You mean compositionally linear?" Pia asked, although she couldn't think what else he might mean.

"Exactly! I'm so glad you have an artistic sensibility. Lines were everywhere: cables, streets, buildings, really all the structures, and the subway, like here. Perspective and vanishing points, you know."

"On your website, I noticed speed and aperture settings for the images for your exhibit. I'm impressed that you use a real camera."

Jeremy sipped his wine and then asked her, "What do you mean by a 'real' camera?"

"Not a digital camera."

Jeremy frowned briefly. "My cameras are digital. They include speed and aperture, lenses and filters, and a lot of capabilities old cameras lack. It's a different skill set but not less complicated."

He was being informative; he wasn't annoyed with Pia as far as she could tell.

"Oh, I'm sorry. I obviously don't know anything about photography. I tried it when I was about ten because my elementary schoolteacher was really into it and he started a photography club. Our cameras cost ten dollars. I liked using the developer, stop bath and fix-it chemicals, and watching the images develop like magic, but I hated trying to get the film out of the camera in total darkness."

Jeremy was upbeat again and said, "A photography club for little kids? That is so dope."

Pia was grateful he was so good-natured.

"Tsk. You're so sweet. Very much the diplomat."

"What makes you say that?"

He was clearing the platter of the last of the sauce with his bread.

"You just are. I made a total ass of myself and you let it go."

He just smiled.

While they waited for the bill Jeremy asked what else Pia wanted to do with the evening. She had a paper bag with his gift and card in it and was waiting to give them to him. He hadn't asked about it. Besides that there was only one other thing she wanted to do.

"Is your apartment available?" she asked him.

"I don't know if people will be there. It's a little difficult trying to have privacy when my roommates are around." He was thinking. "How would you feel about going to a hotel?"

"Sounds good to me."

During the short drive to the hotel, Pia thought about what Jeremy had said about his digital camera, and then she reflected that she had only seen a small selection of his photos, the ones that had been in the two campus exhibits. As they parked near the entrance to the hotel, she asked, "Would you bring your computer in? I'd like a tour of your website if you don't mind."

"Sure. If you're interested I have hundreds of images. Oh, you haven't seen the ones from your nature sanctuary yet! I'm glad you mentioned the computer or I would have forgotten and left it in the car. I brought it with me today but I don't usually anymore."

They crossed the lobby to the front desk. The concierge didn't ask any questions, but Pia thought they looked odd without any luggage. Just a bottle of wine and a laptop.

Once they were in their room Jeremy took out the computer and set it up on the desk. He pulled down the covers on the huge king bed and knocked the throw pillows to the carpet in the process. He flopped onto the bed.

"How is it?" Pia asked as she went by him.

She took the water glasses out of the bathroom and came back to fill them with wine.

"It's fabulous. I guess I'll spend the night here. Are you going to stay with me?"

Pia hadn't thought that far ahead. She could not imagine how to explain that absence to Gordon.

"I don't think so. I don't see how I could."

She absent-mindedly picked up the small pillows and put them on the dresser. She noticed Jeremy press his lips tight and look down briefly but he didn't seem particularly troubled by her answer.

"Why do people have those little pillows? What are they for?" he asked.

Pia poured and handed him a glass.

"There is no logical reason for the existence of throw pillows."

"My mom has a bunch of them."

Pia thought, "Not mom again!"

Jeremy was stretching his muscles out. His glass was on a table by a clock. His head was hanging off the side of the bed, so Pia was upside down to his view.

"I think tonight maybe you should undress me for a change."

"I thought we were going to look at your website," Pia teased.

She took off their clothes until there were none left. Each item she tossed in a different direction. She had missed Jeremy the week before. This was a little celebration to have him back as far as she was concerned. As he had done with her, she took time to be tender with each section of his body as it was revealed. The king-sized bed was like a playground for lovers and they had a great romp together.

Chapter 10

Afterwards, while Jeremy stepped into the bathroom Pia took out the Christmas present and card and put them on the bed. She perused a book on the desk that explained about the hotel services available while she waited.

Jeremy came back in and asked about the present. "Hey, what's this?"

"It's a Christmas present for you," Pia said distractedly. "Jeremy, there's a piano bar downstairs."

"Cool," was Jeremy's response to the piano bar, then, "Pia, I don't have anything for you. I was hoping to make you something but I haven't done it yet. I'm sorry," he said ruefully as he settled onto the bed.

"Will you play the piano for me? That would be a wonderful gift."

"Um, if you'd like, sure! We can go down and see if they'll let me. Should I open this now?"

"Yes, go ahead."

Pia sat on the bed with him. He opened the gift and seemed to genuinely like the hat.

"If you don't wear hats don't feel obligated to wear this one. I just thought you could use it. Annie made it with the sheep's wool. I have a few from her myself."

Next came the card. Pia watched Jeremy's face as he opened the envelope. He laughed when he saw the photograph.

"This is great, Beethoven's barking dog!" He was being his adorable self. Then he read it out loud, "Jeremy, you have added so much light to my life. I love you very much! Merry Christmas, Pia."

He looked at Pia and his head bobbled, and then he gave her a kiss and embraced her.

"Thank you so, so much!" he told her happily.

When they separated he was smiling.

"Phew," she thought.

Jeremy glanced around the bed and then he asked sternly, "Where are my clothes?"

He scowled at her.

Pia made a guilty face.

"Um, all over the place. Sorry."

Jeremy collected his clothes from around the room and, as he found hers, threw them at her. It was a bit of a treasure hunt and he made it fun. Then he abruptly stopped.

"Hey, we should wear each other's stuff. I dare you."

"Okay, but I hope you realize I can't fit in your pants," Pia replied.

They settled on switching underwear, sweaters, and each wearing one of the other's socks. Jeremy couldn't get Pia's bra around his frame, so she could keep that. She was right about the pants. Pia had no problem wearing Jeremy's sweater. It was the charcoal one, and it just looked big on her. Jeremy stretched out Pia's smoky blue cotton sweater a little. He pushed the sleeves up to his elbows so it was less obvious that the arms didn't make it to his wrists. Finally, he wore Pia's scarf that she had as an accessory. The scarf had shades of blue, green and purple, a sort of hazy blend, in a fine, delicate rayon weave.

She helped him arrange it then stood back to assess him.

"You look pretty good in that; very European. So handsome."

"Do I? Good." Jeremy looked in the mirror. "Huh, not bad."

Lastly, Jeremy ceremoniously pulled his new hat onto her head. They took the elevator to the first floor to see if the piano was available in the lounge. It was rather crowded and lively for a Monday. They approached the bartender.

"It's busier than I expected in here," Pia told her.

The bartender was a middle-aged, middle-weight woman with black hair pulled back in a neat ponytail. She was very well-groomed and pleasant, but she had circles under her eyes. Pia thought that maybe this was not her only job.

"There's a convention here so we're pretty full. Were you hoping for a quiet spot?" she asked Pia.

"No. We wanted to ask you a question."

Pia turned to Jeremy then and he made the request.

"I play piano and I was wondering if, by chance, you wouldn't mind if I played yours for a while? If it's not an imposition."

Jeremy was his usual charming self. It wasn't something he put on, it was just how he was. Most people picked up on that and it made them more inclined to indulge him. It seemed only Ralph was impervious to it.

"It's certainly not an imposition. I wish we could've had someone for tonight but we don't book anyone for Mondays. Feel free! If it seems like it's bringing the crowd down or if someone complains, I'll let you know."

"Really? Are you sure you don't mind?"

"Absolutely, kid. Go for it," she told him as she dried and put away some glasses.

Jeremy took Pia's hand and they went over to the baby grand. He sat and lifted the keyboard cover carefully. He looked at Pia and she looked back at him expectantly. Jeremy divulged that he was a little uncomfortable physically.

"Your underwear is itching me."

Quietly Pia answered him. "Sorry, they have a little lace. I wore them especially for you. If I had known we'd be switching I would've been more practical."

"Alright, I'll accept that and give you a pass this time, young lady." He gave her a quick kiss and then

began playing Pachelbel's Canon. Pia enjoyed watching him play. She hadn't even the most rudimentary understanding of how to play an instrument beyond what she'd learned in elementary school with a recorder. She had easily learned to read notes but that was it.

Some people came over and stood around the piano. Jeremy wasn't shy at all about this; it seemed to energize him. When he finished that piece some people applauded. There was a drunk crowd in a far corner who would rather talk over the music, but that was to be expected in this environment; it wasn't a concert hall.

Jeremy continued with something contemporary. The bartender came by with a large cognac-type glass that she put a dollar in as enticement for others to give Jeremy tips. Shortly after that she brought water for Jeremy and Pia. When Jeremy finished that piece he asked Pia what she would like him to play.

"Can you play 'Ode to Joy'?"

"I can if it's in one of these books."

He perused the most appropriate music book on the piano.

"Hey, here it is. Okay, I'll give it a try."

Jeremy began it cautiously but shifted to more confident playing soon. It wasn't the Boston Symphony Orchestra but it was still moving. Pia loved it.

He continued for another half hour until the bartender loudly asked people to listen to a stout, bald man who had an announcement. He wanted to remind anyone there for the convention that breakfast was at seven-thirty tomorrow morning and registration for the first set of workshops began at eight-thirty. This thinned the crowd down to almost no one within fifteen minutes.

"That was awesome," Pia said to Jeremy.

"Here, let me show you how to play. Sit next to me." He moved over to make room for Pia on the seat so she joined him.

"Hold out your hands like this. Good. Your fingers are numbered one through five, with the thumb being one and the pinky being five. See these numbers on the sheet music? Those tell you which finger to use. These here are measures and these time signatures tell you how many beats are in each measure and that each beat is a quarter note, half note, or dotted half notes, and such."

Then Jeremy looked at Pia to see how she was doing with this information. Pia wasn't lost yet but knew she would be shortly and made a fearful face for him. He was not deterred.

"Let's find a song you know. That will make it much easier for you to follow the music."

He flipped through another music book, then another. Jeremy saw something that made him double back a few pages in the last one.

"Aha! Perfect!" Jeremy tipped the pages towards Pia so she could see. It was 'Three Blind Mice.'

He looked at her like that was fabulous news.

"Jeremy…."

"Here, see the single white keys between the black ones? That's 'D'; there are seven of them." He showed Pia where they were. "This is middle 'C'. Put your thumb on it – good. Here are the other notes, see what I'm doing on this side?"

Pia nodded. He rose and stood over her to hold her hands at the keyboard.

She thought, "Why are there seven 'D's?" but didn't ask.

"Okay, this is a really easy, short song. I'll hold your hands while you try it, one measure at a time. This is a measure, right? Ready, here we go."

The sleeves of the sweater Pia wore slipped to her hands then.

"Oops, hold on."

Jeremy chuckled and rolled them way back for her. She wondered if he'd taught children to play.

"There, that's better. Alright, now begin." Jeremy was really doing it but using Pia's hands. "Now try it without me."

He returned to the seat. Pia did try and it didn't go too badly. She was a visual learner so this wasn't difficult to follow. Jeremy gave her some more information about the music sheet, the ties, the repeat sign, and again about the various notes. Pia knew she wouldn't remember all that.

"Good. It's better to hold your hands with your wrist like this." Jeremy made a little adjustment to Pia's hands. "Perfect! Okay, try some more."

She did as Jeremy instructed. Pia got through it twice more on her own.

"Great! Now we're going to play it together, you there, and I'll be adding something to it here. Ready?"

They gave it a go. With Jeremy's guidance they played it a few times, improving slightly with each effort. Pia was surprised how much the piece changed when Jeremy added his part. Then the lesson was finished. She felt that she hadn't quite begun.

"I can't learn to play the piano tonight," Pia said as gently as she could.

Jeremy looked at her as if she was talking nonsense.

"Pia, you just did."

She didn't think that really counted. "I guess."

"Well? What do you think, did you enjoy it?" His enthusiasm was apparently unstoppable.

"You know, I did actually. Maybe I'll take lessons."

"Good. Do you want to go back upstairs?"

She nodded. Jeremy closed the lid on the keys and brought the big glass of dollar bills over to the bartender. Pia followed him with the small water glasses.

"Here you are, thank you," Jeremy said as they slid the three glasses over to her.

She had her back to them, mopping up something from a counter with a rag, but turned around when she heard him.

"Don't forget your money, kid," the bartender told Jeremy, pulling the tips out so the glass could be washed.

Jeremy shook his head. "It's for you. Thank you for allowing me to play. I really appreciate it."

"But, no, it's your tips," the bartender replied.

"Keep it please, for enduring Three Blind Mice so many times. You're wonderful. Goodnight!"

As Jeremy and Pia walked towards the door, she reflected that he referred to the bartender as 'wonderful', which answered a question she had had months before. He probably did tell everyone they're wonderful. She felt a little stupid for having thought she might be special in that regard.

In the elevator Pia pulled the hat off her head. Jeremy draped his arm around her shoulders in a natural, unconscious way and looked down at her affectionately. He kissed her head and she tipped her face up to smile at him and receive one on the lips. Pia wrapped an arm around his waist, leaned into him and checked the time on her phone.

"I should probably head out soon," she sighed.

Jeremy said incredulously, "What? You told me you were going to look at my website with me."

He pulled away and stared at Pia. She hadn't expected such a strong response and didn't know what to say, since she hadn't gathered her thoughts. The space in the elevator suddenly seemed too small.

"I did, but then we went to the lounge instead."

Jeremy registered that without taking his eyes off hers, saying, "I didn't know I was forfeiting one thing for the other."

He seemed like he was going to say more but then stopped. When the doors opened Jeremy stepped out first and remained ahead of Pia. She felt badly as she trailed behind him down the long, wallpapered hallway to their room, light sconces ticking by. When they were in the room Pia took off her shoes and Jeremy sat down in an upholstered chair, switched on a floor lamp and used his phone. As she passed him on her way to the bathroom, Pia wasn't sure if he was checking messages or texting and she didn't want to pry.

While Pia was in the bathroom she had a change of heart. She felt like a jerk for always giving Jeremy about three hours and expecting that to suffice as quality time. When she returned to the bedroom she went over to the chair Jeremy was in and squatted next to it, so her head was lower than his by a little bit, and she looked up at him. Jeremy put his phone down and turned his head to look down at her. He looked disappointed, possibly even cross with her, and seeing that made Pia feel terrible. She hoped she could turn this around.

"Jeremy, I'm sorry. I'll stay. I do want to look at your website with you. I want to know you better and I can't do that if I keep running off."

"The piano time was a Christmas gift for you," he told her, resting his head on a wing of the chair, disheartened.

"I know, thank you for that. I appreciate it. If you still want me to I'll sleep here tonight, with you."

"You will? Really?" He seemed genuinely affected.

Pia said softly, "Sure. It's what I want too, you know."

She reached her hand up to stroke the side of Jeremy's face gently, and then played with the end of a lock of his hair. It reminded Pia of a paint brush.

Jeremy sat forward with his elbows leaning on his knees and his mood improved.

"What will you tell Gordon?" His head was close to Pia's now.

She thought a moment and then said quietly, "I'd have to tell him the truth."

"How would that go over?"

"I have no idea. Not great."

Pia considered the possibility of being hospitalized and homeless by this time tomorrow. She knew that eventually this relationship had to be identified, clarified, but she had managed to avoid thinking about it so far and didn't know where to begin.

"I haven't been giving any thought to what this is and where it might go. I'm really grateful for this time with you but I think it should be on your terms, however you want it to be." Pia felt that, as she was older, she had some responsibility for him. Conversely, she wanted Gordon to be more independent of her. She hadn't acknowledged how often she left him alone while she pursued her interests. Interests such as Jeremy.

He was brighter now. "I didn't plan any of this, it just happened naturally. It feels good and I think we should just enjoy one another. It's not complicated."

It occurred to her that the situation might be making Jeremy feel degraded. That would be inexcusable. Pia adjusted her legs so she was sitting on one foot next to Jeremy's chair.

"I know what I'm doing is wrong but I hope—"

Jeremy interrupted and was quite clear. "It's not wrong. I'm sharing myself with you and you're doing the same for me."

Fortunately, Jeremy wasn't angered by what she'd said; he was just adamant that she was mistaken. Pia thought he must just be seeing it from his viewpoint, which was fine with her.

Then he wryly added, "Sharing is caring, Pia."

That made Pia laugh and he laughed with her. Pia totally didn't see that coming and needed the comic relief. She was glad they got through that together.

"Can you stay a few more hours, then? I don't want you to stay the whole night if it's going to cause problems for you."

She did stay with him and they spent a long time on the website. Beyond the beautiful photography, it was a window to his world and he shared a lot with Pia. Afterwards they switched clothes back and then reclined on the sofa together for a while.

Jeremy said, "So now you know some of my favorite things: visiting different places, meeting people, and having new experiences. What are some of yours?"

"Mostly little things. Feeling a breeze on my bare skin, sunshine. I love water and swimming."

Jeremy interjected, "Me, too."

Pia kept thinking. "I like spring, summer and fall. My friendships."

Pia sorely missed those seasons though, and it was only December.

Jeremy asked, "What about spending time with me? Is that one of your favorite things?"

"Yes, most definitely, silly. At the top of the list."

"You seem like a very natural person, like you grew up on a farm or in a Mongolian yurt," he said.

"Me in a yurt?"

"Sure."

"No. I was raised by city people in an urban area." Pia wondered about that herself then. "When I was a kid I was always roaming around free in the summer with my sister or my best friend. We were wild children, riding as far as our bikes would take us. I don't know how we always found our way home. My feet were always filthy."

That recollection made her content. Pia could remember how her cheap flip flops would be worn down to nothing by the end of August, and even now, she could almost feel the sting of stubbed toes that inevitably followed. Chicory and Queen Anne's lace were the only flowers able to take root and thrive in the cracks of the concrete sidewalks, below the irrepressible sumac trees growing alongside chain-link fences.

"Adam and I weren't allowed anywhere near that much freedom. We could ride our bikes only about a block or two. No point to that. I know it was for our safety but it was too restrictive. Maybe that's why I can't get enough of traveling now. But we always spent part of the summer on the Cape, in Truro. That was great. We could roam along the edge of the sea looking for stuff and chasing the waves. I suppose the waves chased us! My parents relaxed the rules some there. I remember finding horseshoe crabs, big pieces of seaweed, and skate egg cases…. *The Edge of The Sea* by Rachel Carson is a great book. Have you ever read it?"

Pia had been swept up in his description of the natural world and was happy to realize he loved it as much as she did.

"I'm ashamed to tell you I haven't."

"I'll loan you my copy," he suggested.

Pia nodded, yawning.

"It's time for you to go," Jeremy said quietly, petting her head.

Pia extracted herself from the sofa, gathered her things and pulled her arms through her coat sleeves.

As she gave Jeremy a long, strong hug she said, "I would so much like to sleep with you and wake up next to you."

She felt a little sad as she said this. It would probably never happen.

"That would be nice," he said as he kissed her goodnight.

As Pia was crossing the hotel lobby she noticed an attractive young woman standing off to the side next to a large potted plant. The woman scowled at Pia and then looked down at her phone to text with zeal. Pia went outside and began the long, cold walk to her car. She didn't mind the distance but she would lose time getting home so she walked quickly. There was a crescent moon in the sky which always made Pia feel safe, as if it were watching over her. Since she had finished the Harry Potter books, it had become her "patronus," although one that was shared with all people. It was a ridiculously romantic notion but a comfort anyway.

As soon as Pia was in her car and the engine turned over, she called Gordon. She had given a good deal of thought on her walk about she would tell him, but she knew that if he ever grilled her she would confess. Pia hated lying because she felt it was disrespecting whoever was on the receiving end, but she feared the fall-out if or when she told Gordon about Jeremy. Still, whatever the fall-out was would be exactly what she deserved. But she would put that off for as long as she could. She did realize her falsehoods were to protect herself, not to protect Gordon from emotional pain.

"Alright, where are you? Are you lost?' Gordon was in good spirits as he was joking about her being lost, although it did happen occasionally.

Pia ignored that. "I'm in my car. Sorry it's so late. I'll be home in a little while, honey."

"Okay, see you when you get here. Did you have fun?"

"Yup. Drank too much though."

"Then drive carefully. 'Bye, I love you."

This made her feel lousy.

"Love you, too."

Did she?

Chapter 11

The next morning Pia was late for work but no one seemed to mind or even take notice. There was a lot of energy in the air because the students were leaving today and the offices were closed for over a week beginning Thursday for the Christmas break. The college held a two-hour 'holiday' lunch for the staff and faculty. Pia had piles of work to do before they closed for the break. She would come in one day to get caught up a little, so she wouldn't be totally overwhelmed when they re-opened.

Shelly had the greatest workload because all of the international students wanted copies of their transcripts for their travel visas. Pia did the best she could to help Shelly by covering the phones, email and the main counter. In the late morning Jeremy's friend Paco came in with a registration form that had a special signature from the instructor. He was lined up behind a few other students.

Pia was at the counter going as fast as she could. This pace energized her and she rose to the task. When it was Paco's turn Pia extended her hand to take the form from him.

"Hi, Paco, how're you?" she said, smiling broadly at him.

"Good, thanks."

"Are you traveling somewhere far for the break?"

"Yeah, home to Ecuador. I am leaving this afternoon, in a few hours."

He frowned briefly then and something about his face caused Pia to pause. She looked at him for a few beats and then knew what it was.

"Paco, do you have a sister? I saw someone who looked just like you last night."

Pia remembered the woman in the hotel lobby. There was a definite resemblance.

"Did you? Huh. I do not have a sister here; she is back home. Is that form all set?"

Pia quickly typed some data into the computer before telling him, "Yes, Paco, you're in that course now. Have a great break."

She date stamped and initialed the form while her mind lingered on the woman from last night and how much she looked like Paco.

"Thanks," he said as he left the office.

Pia went back to her desk, still thinking about the resemblance. Very soon she was consumed with work and forgot about it. It irritated her that Sandra had them close the office with a note on the door so everyone could go to the holiday lunch together. She was fairly sure that the reason it was for two hours was so that the offices would stagger their staff's attendance at the event. But Pia wasn't in charge. There was much mingling between departments at this event and there were lines for all the food, so everyone did get to see each other at least briefly. Pia preferred to eat quickly and then tour the huge hall to catch up with people she knew from different offices. Often there were bonds formed with others entirely by email so it was fun to actually see one another.

Shelly and Pia walked back to the office together a bit sooner than the rest of the staff. On their way across the quad Shelly told Pia about a rumor in the office.

"Ralph and Dave were talking last week about you and that kid you like…Jeremy Ronan."

"Oh?"

Pia crossed her arms and held them close. She hadn't worn her coat because it was a short walk, but she was quite cold.

"Yeah. Dave seems to think you're involved romantically with him, for real, not kidding. I just thought you should know." Shelly was cool about it and Pia was grateful for her telling her.

Pia said airily, "Geez, thanks for telling me. That's silly."

Then she couldn't resist asking Shelly's opinion of Jeremy since she was much closer to his age than Pia was.

"Shelly, do you think he's attractive? Jeremy, I mean." Pia meant it to sound like she was curious if Shelly might be interested in Jeremy.

Shelly made a face. "Ugh, no. Not at all."

Pia sufficiently hid her offense at Shelly's swift dismissal of Jeremy. "He's no Ben Stiller, huh?"

"Ha!" Unfortunately, Shelly had more information to share. "Pia, Dave thought he saw you two kissing on the sidewalk a few weeks ago. He told Ralph, who told me and Mary. So probably everyone's heard that by now."

Pia's mind raced to find something to say to steer the gossip in another direction. Unfortunately, she had no skill at this.

"Good grief. That's ridiculous!"

Oh well, that would have to do.

In the afternoon Yi Tao stopped in again. Mary was the person who helped him at the counter. Tao wanted to know if there was any news about his petition. He began very courteously and so did Mary. However, as Mary persisted in giving him responses that were not actual answers, Tao became frustrated with her. He continued to be polite but he was distraught and Mary seemed to take offense at this. Pia understood Tao couldn't help being agitated because he was relying so heavily on the committee's determination and Mary would give him no hint as to what it might be.

As their interaction became more tense, Sandra came in to get something off the printer and she stopped to get involved with this scene.

"Hi, I'm the registrar. May I help you?" To Sandra's credit, she was professional.

Tao explained what he was there for, albeit with interruptions from Mary.

"I can tell you we've received your petition and it went to the committee this morning. Give me your name again and I'll go check in my office; we had five petitions. You can have a seat while you wait." Sandra motioned to the chairs but Tao elected to remain standing.

Sandra was back shortly with his petition in her hands. "The petition has been denied by the committee so you are responsible for the bill. The bursar's office was sympathetic to the situation you're in and is willing to allow you to make monthly payments. That was very nice of them; they don't normally do that. I'll be sending you an email later today with information on contacting them to work out a payment plan."

Tao was obviously devastated and continued pleading with Sandra. Eventually Sandra told him that the determination was final and he had to leave the office. Pia knew that he could go over the committee but she was forbidden by Sandra to tell Tao that, so he'd have to figure that route out for himself. It was embedded somewhere in the comprehensive student handbook but she didn't like his chances of finding it.

The rest of the day was busy and time went by quickly. Pia didn't think about Tao, Paco, or even Jeremy until she was walking to her car after the office closed. They were all a jumble in her overworked mind. She had very strange dreams that night.

The one that stuck with Pia when she woke on Wednesday morning involved being on a subway train and, from her window, seeing Jeremy with some friends on the platform for the other direction. He wore a blue sequined dress and was chatting with two nondescript young men in drag. Because he was so slender it fell remarkably well on him and that made Pia envious, which in turn bothered her. In the dream he had no facial hair, whereas normally he had a perpetual hint of a beard, and his face was made up.

When Pia woke, she knew she should not have dreamt in color; that was supposed to mean you were crazy. In the dream about Jeremy everything was black and white except for the vibrant blue dress. It was distressing, until she remembered describing him as a blue morpho butterfly. She thought with relief that that explained it.

Once she arrived at work, she did her normal routine of revving up her computer, refreshing her memory on the progress of several forms on her desk in front of her monitor, and then making a cup of coffee. She was pleasant to everyone in the office and tried her best to keep a poker face for her gossiping co-workers. By mid-morning she had adjusted to just not caring what they thought about her. She had a huge amount of work to get through. Early on Pia heard other people commenting on one particular email that must've been sent to the whole campus but she hadn't read it yet.

About the time Pia finished her coffee Shelly went to the drawer that contained transcripts waiting to be picked up and went through them a few times, her fingers moving deftly through them as if strumming a guitar.

"Huh, that's strange," she frowned.

Dave heard her and looked up from his computer screen.

"What's strange?"

"I have an email giving permission for someone to pick up a transcript, but it's gone already. It's not in the drawer."

Pia responded, "Just as I was closing on Monday, Mario Alvarez came in for Paulo Moreno's transcript. Is that the one you're looking for?"

"Yeah, that's the one. Paulo left for Venezuela without picking it up.

Thanks."

Shelly dropped her printed email from Paulo into her recycle bin on her way back to her seat.

Shelly was moving on to something else but Dave asked Pia, "Did you get an email from Mario, too?"

Pia panicked and did what was becoming easier.

She lied, "I did."

Her phone was ringing so she looked away from Dave and picked it up to speak with a professor who had a policy question. While Pia was on the phone she received a text from Jeremy. When she had a break Pia stepped out into the hall to call him.

"Hi, Jeremy! I just got your message. Merry Christmas to you, too. Are you going home for the holiday?"

"Yeah, I'll go there tomorrow night. My father's side of the family will be there for Christmas Eve then Christmas Day we go to my grandparents' house. It's about an hour away. How about you?"

"Going to my stepson's house. Lots of people, lots of food. It will be fun. Almost everything's ready."

"Do you have a lot to do for Christmas?"

"Yes. I'm bringing a lot of the drinks and two appetizers and twenty presents. It's crazy but wonderful. I so enjoy the little kids."

She realized she was illustrating the great difference in their roles in their respective families and hoped her stress was concealed.

"Yeah, I have some younger cousins I like to see. Hey, have a great time. I'll talk to you soon. Hopefully this weekend, or Monday for sure. Merry Christmas, Pia!"

"I'll be thinking of you." She softly added, "Bye."

She went back to her office. On her way by Nell's desk, Nell mentioned the email the others had talked about. Pia only knew that there had been something bad involving a student and people thought it was terrible so close to Christmas

"Pia, isn't it awful about that poor student? Imagine his parents. It's such a tragedy. Tsk." Nell shook her head.

"I haven't opened that email yet. What happened?"

"One of the Chinese students killed himself last night. One of the graduate students. Let me see…."

She pulled up the email and reviewed it through her bifocals, tipping her head back.

"It says a graduate student in mechanical engineering took his own life last night…Yi Tao, twenty-five, married with one child. Oh, his son is just a baby."

Nell may have continued with more information, but Pia heard nothing after 'Yi Tao.' She was struck dumb and she couldn't move. Her legs became shaky and apparently her face expressed her shock, because Nell was asking if she was alright.

"What?"

"Pia, are you alright? Did you know him?"

Pia answered, "Yes, he was here a lot recently. He petitioned to have the cost of a course waived and the petition was denied. Jesus."

"It's really terrible." Very quietly, to avoid being heard by the others, Nell added, "Is he the one Sandra and Mary spoke to yesterday?"

Pia nodded. "Mm-hm."

Nell whispered, "Oh, dear. I wonder if that had something to do with it."

Pia gazed at Nell with a pained expression. Nell was so nurturing Pia sometimes wished Nell was her mother. Pia went back to her desk quickly. She opened the rambling email from the president. She was having trouble getting through the tedium of the thing in her distress and just wanted the facts. The president finished with a line about providing more information after a complete investigation. Great. She did her best to continue with her own work but made slow progress.

After a while, Pia decided to go over to the mechanical engineering department. It was close by and she was friends with one of the administrative assistants there. The department head, Khalil Abdullah, was a reasonable fellow, too. Maybe they could tell Pia what the story was. If this was because of the petition, as Pia suspected, she would not be able to forgive this.

When her friend, Janeen, saw her come towards her desk she understood why Pia was there. The mechanical engineering office was buzzing with the news and there were many people discussing the tragedy. Janeen's eyes were red, as if she had been crying.

"Hi, Pia. Did you hear about Yi Tao?" Janeen asked her.

"Hi, Janeen. Yeah, that's why I'm here. Do you— sorry, how are *you* doing?"

Pia caught herself. Sometimes she didn't have good manners.

"Oh, I'm hanging in there, you know. Ooh, bad choice of words, sorry. Khalil is really upset because he worked with Tao and was completely surprised by this. Tao was an upbeat, energetic student. He had a lot on his plate, though. But he was so close to finishing his degree. That's what makes this so tragic. Why couldn't he just hold on 'til then?"

"Was Tao one of Khalil's research assistants on his National Science Foundation grant?"

Pia knew a lot about Khalil's grant. When she had down time in the summer she sometimes trolled the university website reading about the professors' research and interests. She found it much more rewarding than reading People.com or shopping online.

"Yes, he was. The worst part, well not *the* worst part, is that Karen from the grounds crew found him this morning. She was hysterical, let me tell you."

"What do you mean? Where did he die?"

"Pia, Tao hung himself in the lab on the second floor. He left a note and it said he didn't want to do it at home, where his wife would discover him. He did it because of how cold and unreasonable our university was towards him. He made a point to exclude Khalil specifically, but he found the bureaucracy here intolerable. I think that was exactly how he put it."

Pia looked down at the ceramic knick-knacks on Janeen's desk and picked one up absent-mindedly.

"Tao petitioned to have the cost of a course waived. He should've dropped it but didn't, and he learned that the petition was denied yesterday," she said.

Janeen was surprised to hear about that.

"Oh, for Christ's sake! Our department could have worked something out for him if he needed help with his bill. I didn't know anything about that. *Shit.*"

Learning that Tao could've gotten help if more avenues were investigated made Pia feel even worse.

She lamented, "If I didn't know that after being here ten years, how on earth would a student? Poor Tao. His poor family."

Pia sighed and placed the little item she'd been turning in her fingers back on Janeen's desk.

"Yeah, this is terrible," Janeen agreed. "Hey, I have to get back to work, but thanks for stopping by. Try to enjoy Christmas."

"Thanks Janeen, you, too. Say 'hi' to Eddie for me."

Pia made her way back to her office with a very heavy heart. Enjoying the Christmas break seemed out of the question. As soon as she was through the doorway to her office Ralph asked her where she'd been. That was rather out of character, but Pia had been gone awhile and hadn't told anyone she was leaving.

"I was over at mechanical engineering. Did you need me for something?"

Pia tried to sound like everything was normal, suppressing an overwhelming desire to gnash her teeth at him. She continued over to her desk.

Curious, he asked her, "What were you doing over there?"

Pia breathed deeply. Then she replied evenly, "I wanted to find out more about Yi Tao's death."

"Me and Sandra just got out of a meeting about it with the higher-ups. This office will have a meeting about it first thing tomorrow morning. It didn't have anything to do with that petition if that's what's on your mind."

The last sentence was a bit of a warning.

"Sure," Pia said curtly.

Ralph looked at her for a minute before deciding not to engage and walking away. He had sore hips and a big beer belly so he always moved slowly, swaying like an upside-down pendulum. He couldn't help it, but sometimes Pia thought he wasn't invested in anything enough to pick up his pace. Sandra learned to leave for meetings without him to avoid being late herself. Ralph never caught on to the concept of leaving earlier so he'd get to them on time.

On Thursday there was a skeleton crew because everyone was off the following day. It was unusual for the university to make staff work on Christmas Eve day, but that's how it had worked out that year. Only Pia, Sandra, Ralph, and Dave were available to attend the meeting. Nell, Mary and Shelly had taken the day off. Etienne, Larissa and the other work-study students had left for the break as soon as their final exams were over.

Once they were all seated at the conference table Sandra began.

"Okay, I'm going to keep this brief because we all have lots to do and hopefully we can close the office at three today. So, as I'm sure you all know, Tuesday night one of the graduate students, Yi Tao, allegedly committed suicide."

She was about to continue, but Pia broke in then. Her disgust with the whole situation was welling up in her, so she didn't edit herself as she should have.

"He didn't 'allegedly' anything. He left a fucking note."

Pia didn't look directly at anyone; she kept her eyes on the table. It angered her that Sandra cared more about getting out of work early than the death of a student. Dave whistled under his breath and twirled his pencil. Ralph seemed to enjoy Pia getting herself in trouble; he gave Dave a knowing glance and cocked an eyebrow. Sandra stared at her for a beat.

"Pia, watch it. You're being very inappropriate." Sandra waited to see if she was going to dig her own grave any further. Pia was silent. "Okay, so, there's an investigation into what happened that's ongoing and the administration isn't going to make another statement until that's complete. His family has been notified and the counseling office is available for all students, staff and faculty who would benefit from their services. Any questions?" No one spoke. "Good, then we're finished."

Sandra ended the meeting with a cold delivery to Pia. "I strongly suggest you talk with the counseling staff if you have any problem with this."

Then she seemed to think of something else. Sandra might not have said this if everyone else was present but given that Pia was basically outnumbered three to one, Sandra smugly added, "And stop making out with the students or you won't keep your job much longer."

Pia blushed in shock and embarrassment. She had decided long ago that someone else really shouldn't be able to embarrass you, because in their effort to do so they just make themselves look bad. This was a great example of that but it was still a lousy feeling. Ralph kept his face impassive and Dave refused to meet her eye. She thought Dave was basically a good guy but he was not stupid enough to align himself with her in this group. Pia waited for them all to get up before she followed them out and went back to her desk.

She heard Sandra ask Ralph on their walk across the office, "I wonder how she knew about the note?"

Ralph responded, "Does that confirm for you that she's a problem?"

Sandra said, "Oh, she's been a problem for a while, Ralph."

Pia went through the motions of the rest of the day: finishing up some paperwork, making a sign for the door, changing the phone message for the holidays. Ralph and Sandra left before Pia and Dave, Ralph talking Sandra's ear off.

Pia wished Dave would just leave but he wanted to stay with her until the door was locked. She supposed he was being chivalrous, but she wanted to be alone. She also wished she had her book of poetry with her. She hadn't felt this uncomfortable in a while. Finally they turned off the lights and locked the door. Then they stepped out into the cold together. The campus was like a ghost town without the students and faculty.

"Brrr, it's frigid!" Dave said.

"Yes," Pia answered.

"Pia, it's none of my business, but did I see you kissing that student, Jeremy? Or possibly it was someone who looked like you?" Dave cautiously asked.

"Dave, it's none of your business. There was a specific situation and out of context it wouldn't make sense." There, Pia had given a non-answer, much like Mary would have. Pia didn't feel good about it, though. "Sorry, but it is what it is."

"And what is 'it'?"

"It's still none of your business." Pia smiled at Dave in a friendly way, but she wasn't going to give him anything to work with. "Hey, have a great Christmas. Enjoy your son."

Dave shared custody of his young son with his ex, and this year

Dave would have him for Christmas Day.

The moment Pia parted from him, stepping off the curb by her car, her face fell and her lips pursed as if as if she might cry.

She drove home on autopilot, feeling anything but festive. As she approached her driveway, Pia saw that Gordon had put the holiday lights on for her.

"Aww," she thought, "that's nice."

When she came through the kitchen door she felt glad to be home, where it was warm and bright inside. She had a week off from that miserable job. Gordon was in a good mood because she was going to be around. He came out of his office when he heard her in the kitchen moving his debris to its proper locations and throwing out wrappers. It had begun snowing outside in the dusk and Pia was eager to get into pajamas and her soft, warm bathrobe.

"Happy vacation! May I pour you a glass of red wine, my dear?" Gordon hugged and kissed her.

She dropped her handbag in its usual spot and took off her coat.

"Thank you; that would be great. We're having veal piccata tonight if that's alright."

Pia was hanging her coat and Gordon's in the closet. Gordon's never quite made it there without her help. He left his belongings in the kitchen, where they remained until she moved them. Pia had long since given up on expecting this to change.

"What's that again? Is it the one with lemon?"

Every time Pia said 'piccata' Gordon asked her that. For almost seventeen years.

"Grrr, *yes*. Damn."

"Hey, don't growl at me. What's the matter with you?"

It was so easy for one of them to affect the other's mood, it was ridiculous.

Pia stood in the doorway between the kitchen and the dining room, with her back to Jeremy's photograph and her arms crossed. Last night Gordon had wanted to tell Pia about his day. This was a nice change for them and an emotional break for her, so they sat at the kitchen table while she listened to him. She hadn't told Gordon about Tao's death then. She did now.

"Gordon, that student, the graduate student I told you about with the petition to drop a course?"

He said, "I don't remember that."

Her brain translated it to, "I never listen to you."

"Grrr. Well, he killed himself."

Pia turned to go upstairs but Gordon reached out and held her arm. "Wait, what?"

He was genuinely engaged now, so she stayed.

"Yi Tao hanged himself and left a note saying it was because of his terrible treatment at our university. It's our fault," she said forlornly.

Gordon said, "Christ, it's certainly not your fault. You do everything you can for the students, honey."

"Sandra couldn't care less. I don't know how she can sleep at night," Pia said, but then swerved to another perspective. "Ugh, there I go again. I'm so self-righteous. I have to learn not to do that. She's not a demon." After a heavy sigh she added, "I'm gonna change out of these clothes. This bra has got to go."

"Do you want me to come with you?"

Gordon made a special face that included a funny grin and batted eyelashes. This always made Pia smile, and even now she managed one because he looked so ridiculous trying to be coquettish. It didn't match his masculine, hairy self at all.

"Sure but bring the wine, baby."

They were good company for one another the remainder of Christmas Eve. He was glad she would be around for a week and she was glad it pleased him. Gordon was on his best behavior because he knew from experience they would be getting on each other's nerves in about five days.

Pia drank too much during the preparation of dinner. It was a simple, delicious recipe but it required some attention. She allowed the sauce to reduce too much while she thought about Tao. She served it with green beans, which Gordon disliked but still ate. This was the subtle politics of their marriage. Pia knew Gordon would relax after he'd just had sex and Gordon knew that he should appreciate Pia's effort with dinner if he wanted her to stay in a good mood.

On a sunny Christmas morning they savored coffee while they opened their gifts to one another. There wasn't anything creative or surprising under their tree this year. The stockings were rather mundane as well. Pia's mood didn't help things. She felt badly that she couldn't manage to pull this plane's nose up over the clouds for Gordon. She hoped things would be better at his son's house later on.

About eleven they set out with a car full of gifts and food for the hour-long drive. The roads were clear although there were piles of snow banked alongside the asphalt, so one had to be wary at intersections. The holiday usually included between fifteen and twenty people who would vary to some extent each year, depending on how much energy the hostess could muster and who was in town. Once Christmas was hosted by Pia and Gordon, but the living room proved too small with a tree in it so they were assigned Thanksgiving and some birthdays and cookouts.

In sharp contrast to their quiet house with just the cat, Gordon's son's house was a cacophony of adults and children laughing, yelling and joking. It was an occasion to celebrate one another. They gave gifts only to the children. Watching them open their presents was the best part of the day for Pia. Gordon liked the enormous meal best, although he also enjoyed the family.

Beyond the magic and sense of blessings, Pia liked the pagan aspects of the holiday: the tree, the wreaths and garlands. Of course, she had much of the outdoors inside her house all year round. Not much came from a department store. She had giant pinecones, seashells, and dried plants including Chinese lanterns, bittersweet and pussy willow stalks. Occasionally she'd bring in living things like snakes and chipmunks to rehabilitate. Once a neighbor dropped off a gray squirrel that had been hit by a car and Pia kept him for about a month while he regained his strength and audacity. And, of course, there were those two occasions when Pia brought turtle eggs home to incubate and later rear through fall and winter.

Gordon and Pia left for home about nine that night. They were so full of food they were almost sick. At home it was so quiet. Gordon settled into his office while Pia unpacked all their food containers. She fed the cat and stroked her soft fur for a bit. In the living room she picked up the gift wrap strewn on the floor and packed it down in the kitchen trash bin. "Another Christmas is over," Pia thought to herself nostalgically, as she moved like a spirit through the rooms unplugging the window candles and the tree lights.

During the day Pia had hardly thought of Jeremy while she was with all those people. Now she thought of him intensely and wondered what he was doing. She wished she could share him with her friends and family. She had talked about his photograph in the dining room at Thanksgiving the year before. Pia remembered that she had been mentioning him to people when she was involved with setting up his exhibit. That would be coming down in a few weeks. So much had changed since she had hung it.

Pia thought of these things as she undressed. She crossed the room from her closet to the bedside, took hold of the down comforter and top sheet together and turned them only enough to dash under them, switching off the bedside lamp and covering herself up to her chin. A few seconds of bare skin in a fifty-degree room had chilled her. She closed her eyes and curled up like the fetus she had once been as she shivered. She was aware that the cat had jumped onto the bed and was looking for a choice nook to settle in for the night. Pia ventured one arm out to caress the soft animal for a minute. Shortly after that she pulled her arm back under the covers and fell asleep to the sound of purring. Gordon would join them in a little while.

Chapter 12

The next time Pia had contact from Jeremy was two days later, on Sunday afternoon. She and Gordon were reading the paper in the living room.

His text read: "Hi, Pia! Can we get together soon?"

Gordon heard the tone that indicated Pia had a message.

"What's that?"

He frequently asked her what the different tones meant as her phone made them. He almost never had his old flip phone on; Pia was the only person who called him on it anyway.

"Um, that was Jane about a program at the sanctuary. Looking for volunteers," she lied without looking at him. The fibbing was taxing, which is why she normally avoided it, but she didn't know what else to do.

She texted Jeremy back immediately.

"Of course! Let me know when is good for you. J"

"Tomorrow afternoon? At the university, ok?" was his response.

"Sure."

"Meet me in the lobby of the library @ 2 pm. Miss you!"

Pia marveled at how those two little words made her so happy. She deleted the thread and then put the phone down.

"I think I'll go into work tomorrow to use the rec center," she said. "It will be almost empty so I can use it as long as I want."

"You're going into the city just for that?" Gordon asked.

"Well, I'll borrow some movies and a book from the library, too."

She got up from the sofa to sort laundry. Shortly after that their land line rang. Pia heard Gordon pick it up and speak jovially to whoever it was. She hoped he wasn't teasing a telemarketer, a favorite pastime for him.

After a minute he hollered, "Pia, phone!"

Pia came back to the living room and took the phone from him as he held it out to her.

"Hello?"

"Hi, Pia, it's Annie. How was your Christmas?"

Pia had nearly told Gordon it was Annie texting her a few minutes before and realized again how risky lies were. "Hi, Annie. It was fine. How was yours? Did you fly out to Indiana this year?"

"Yeah, but my parents are in assisted living this year, so that was kind of difficult. Since I don't see them very often it's always a shock to see how they've aged."

"I'll bet."

"I'm calling because I was wondering if you're available this week at all. We're having a small meeting at the sanctuary, and we'd like your thoughts on something."

"Sure. I have tomorrow morning or anytime on Thursday."

"Can we make it Thursday, say ten o'clock?"

"Okay, I'll see you then. Take care, Annie."

"Thanks so much."

Pia hung up and returned to her chores, excited about her plans for the following day.

At the university on Monday Pia had no trouble finding a parking spot because most students and all faculty and staff were gone. The international students were hanging around the open common areas in the campus center and the library as if they were life rafts, so those buildings had some human energy but it felt desperate and diffused. Pia walked toward the library from her car. She was ten minutes early for a change. Jeremy was coming up the hill on the opposite side but she didn't see him.

Something was going on in front of the building. There was a campus police cruiser parked there with its blue lights flashing. One of the police officers, a short fellow named Ryan, was on the sidewalk with his hands on his hips. Pia couldn't remember if Ryan was his first or last name. He was speaking with a large man who was quite agitated. Pia knew the big man from her previous job a few blocks away. He would walk in there without an appointment when he had ear pain. He had a cognitive disability, so reasoning with him to come back in a week when his ear hurt then would not work. The clinicians always saw him immediately, but more to be rid of him than from any sense of empathy.

Ryan was becoming annoyed with the big guy but was cautious because of his size. Pia redirected herself to them and quickened her steps almost into a jog.

She called out, "David! David Miller!"

That made the big man look up. She smiled and waved as she approached them. The man was confused because he didn't remember Pia, although she had seen him periodically around the neighborhood.

"Mr. Miller, you don't remember me, do you?" she said.

"No. How do you know my name?"

He was getting tired of holding his many bags of groceries and his shoulders dropped a bit.

"I used to work for your ear doctor on Oak Ave. How are you doing?"

"It's hard. I don't drive a car, they won't let me drive a car, and I have a lot of groceries. They're heavy and I have to walk. And this guy's telling me to go away," Mr. Miller complained.

It was difficult to discern if Ryan welcomed Pia's intrusion or not.

"This is Officer Ryan. It's his job to protect the students who live at this school," Pia made the introductions as if they were willingly spending time together. To Ryan she said, "This is Mr. Miller."

Ryan responded dryly, "So I gathered. I was just telling Mr. Miller to leave the premises, as this is private property."

Mr. Miller became very agitated and raised his voice.

"I don't understand! I'm just walking on the sidewalk! I'm not going in any of the buildings!"

Pia couldn't really blame him. Ryan became tense and tightened the grip on his club and raised it slightly from his side.

Pia told Mr. Miller gently, "Everything within the stone walls is part of the school. You passed through an invisible fence when you came up this street. You couldn't tell, you wouldn't know it from looking. Here, can I help you carry your groceries? We have to go back down the hill and around to that street." Pia pointed in the right direction.

Mr. Miller seemed willing to listen to her but still protested, "I don't see why I have to go back the way I came."

"We have to do what Officer Ryan tells us to because he has a badge and that's his job."

Normally Pia would just let him cross the campus, but she understood that Ryan would forbid it on principle. And it wouldn't help Mr. Miller learn the process. Generally, Pia didn't regard the police very highly but she knew instructing Mr. Miller to show them respect would be in his best interests.

"Come on, you don't live far from here, do you?"

Pia was being her friendliest to him. She was on the verge of being flirty, but not quite.

"I live two more blocks away."

Mr. Miller had the personality of Eeyore. Pia smiled brightly, like they were off to a fun place.

"Alright then, let's go!"

Mr. Miller allowed her to take some of his bags and he began to follow her.

Over her shoulder Pia said, "Thank you, Officer Ryan."

Ryan gave her the hairy eyeball but Pia could tell he was relieved to have the situation resolved. Ryan got back in his patrol car and turned off his lights. Pia was glad to have her thick gloves on to carry the plastic bags. She used canvas bags for her own groceries, and it had been many years since the days she had to walk them home from the supermarket.

"Can I carry anything?"

Pia and Mr. Miller stopped and turned. Jeremy! Pia made a repentant face.

"Oh, I'm sorry, Jeremy. Do you mind if I do this? It shouldn't take long."

"No worries, I'll come with you," Jeremy answered, wearing his new hat. To Mr. Miller he said, "Hi!"

Mr. Miller was having quite an afternoon.

He just asked Jeremy in an annoyed tone, "Who are you?"

Jeremy took some bags.

"My name is Jeremy. Nice to meet you!"

"It isn't nice to meet you," Mr. Miller groused in reply. "I wish I had a car, but they won't let me have a license. I just want to get these groceries home."

And so the three of them set off for Mr. Miller's apartment building. Pia showed him where he made a wrong turn at the bottom of the hill and which route he had to take from now on. Soon they were at Mr. Miller's address and left him after they were sure he had his key in the lock. Then Jeremy and Pia walked away together.

"Pia, I was wondering if we could visit the art gallery at Wilson College? There's an exhibit that I'd like to show you. We're on our way now if we keep going up this street."

"Sure. I'm sorry about the detour. I've known David Miller for a long time. He doesn't remember me, though."

Jeremy stopped walking to face her. "No problem at all. See how nice you are!"

His head bobbled before he gave Pia a lovely kiss and hug. He put his arm over her shoulders and they headed to the gallery.

"You're such a good soul, Pia."

She said, "The truth is I just can't mind my own business."

He replied, "Mr. Miller's good fortune."

"How much of that situation back there did you see?"

"I saw that if you didn't intervene the campus policeman would probably have had to arrest Mr. Miller. Or he'd have to carry all those groceries himself, heh."

After a minute Pia asked, "Have you read *Of Mice and Men?*"

"No, I don't think so," Jeremy answered.

"Oh, it's such a great novel. It's short, by John Steinbeck. He's one of my favorites. Anyway, it's about this huge, mentally challenged man named Lenny and Mr. Miller reminds me of him. People are afraid of him, well, both of them. I suppose if Mr. Miller got angry enough he could do some real damage, like Lenny did. Oh, sorry, I shouldn't have told you that part. Tsk." Pia talked as they walked along.

"But you're not afraid of Mr. Miller," Jeremy observed.

"Nope." Pia didn't know why she wasn't.

It was not too cold out; definitely above freezing, and cloudy. The barometric pressure was trying its best to give Pia a headache but she had evaded it with ibuprofen. Everything was the same monochromatic gray everywhere she looked.

Inside the gallery building was very colorful and bright and Pia was glad for that. Since it was on a college campus there was no admission fee, but they both showed their university ID cards to the security guard when they went into the building. No one would check on Jeremy's to learn it was obsolete. They left their coats on a bench. Pia began viewing on the left to proceed in a counterclockwise direction, but Jeremy directed her to the far wall.

"Check this out! A friend of mine took these photos."

It was a series of images running the whole length of the long wall, about twenty or so. Jeremy and Pia took the whole scene in from where they stood. She could immediately see that they were connected as a whole piece by some colorful tape in each photograph. Then Pia moved to the sign next to the image farthest to the left and Jeremy followed her. It didn't say anything about the photographer's vision. Just her name, the dates it was created, and the medium. The artist set up some bright duct tape and took a series of images with it in them, along the ground. The result was that the viewer connected them all together. In most of them, where one picture's tape ended is where it was picked up again in the next picture even though they were different locations. Each image was a good composition individually, but it was fun to see how they lined up next to one another. Pia noticed that as her eyes followed along, there were some photos where the tape exited the frame in one place and in the next frame it came in at a different place. However, her eyes made them connect.

Pia tried to articulate it to Jeremy.

"See these photographs? My eye is connecting these two here, like this."

Pia showed Jeremy how, from the location of the tape on the edge of one piece, her mind made this big circle and then the tape connected to the next piece, because her eye made the connection where there was none.

Jeremy agreed. "Yeah, that happened to me, too. I think it's intentional. It's so cool."

They took their time looking at each individual image and then stood back to view the complete set again.

"This is a great concept. Really great," Pia nodded her approval.

They moved on to the next artist's work.

In a corner of the large gallery space was a video installation, and the curators had made a partition so the light from the gallery didn't reflect onto the screen. There was a bench to sit on while watching the video. They went in but didn't sit down. The title was "Tree Sequins Sequence." The artist had filmed the top halves of a row of trees. The sky was vibrant blue and the deciduous trees varied from very bright green to more deep green, depending on the species. The camera panned around the area, always focused on the canopy and the sky. There was no audio, but they saw intermittent breezes blowing. When that occurred, it was obvious that the maples, lindens and oaks were disturbed, but the birches much more so. Their leaves flickered much like sequins and Pia assumed they were the sequins referenced in the title, as the others only bent their branches gently.

After about three minutes the video looped again. Pia thought the concept was rather weak but she couldn't take her eyes off the green trees and blue sky. She longed for that time of year when it was warm and she would be outdoors as much as possible.

Jeremy had seen enough of it so politely said, "I think that's it. It's just running in a loop."

"Yeah. It's so…summery."

She was unable to move her eyes from it.

"It's pretty, but I don't know what the artist is trying to convey. I wonder why those leaves flit about when the others don't," Jeremy offered.

"It's because of the leaf stem, how it's designed. The birches are also called 'quaking aspens' for that reason," Pia said, pointing to the birch leaves on the screen. "They have a keeled leaf stem, whereas other leaves' stems are round." When Pia looked at Jeremy she could tell he still couldn't quite see what she meant. "The artist should've left some leaves so people could see for themselves. Here is a normal leaf stem."

Pia put her hands together with the fingertips touching and the thumbs touching, so it looked like she was illustrating the size of a grapefruit; she formed a circle with her hands.

"But this is how a birch leave stem is designed." She left her fingers touching but not her thumbs; she moved the bases of her hands together, like in prayer but with the knuckles apart.

"See, so they're keeled on opposite ends. That results in their constantly flipping around." Pia looked at Jeremy to see if he understood her.

Jeremy smiled and said, "Thanks for that explanation, Pia! I wonder why, though."

"Do you mean the big why, like everything's purpose in life, or do you just mean 'why'?"

Jeremy chuckled at that. "I just wonder why, as in 'how come,' they're shaped differently. If there's an advantage in it, or something in the species' evolution to explain it."

"Oh. Well, scientists speculate that it discourages insects from laying eggs on them, or parasites from establishing on them. Their leaves come out before most others," Pia told him matter-of-factly.

Jeremy was looking at Pia strangely, so she felt self-conscious.

"Sorry, am I boring? I talk too much," she said as she looked down.

"No, you're not boring at all. You fascinate me." After some hesitation Jeremy added something more. "Actually, we need to have a talk though, right now. Have a seat."

A correction snuck out of Pia's mouth. "Have to."

"What?"

"Nothing."

Pia hated the current trend of replacing 'have to' or 'must' with 'need to' and it was her hope that it was temporary.

They sat on the bench and Jeremy swung a leg over so he was straddling the bench and facing Pia. She felt that when someone you've fallen in love with says you have to talk it's never good. She swallowed hard and looked back at Jeremy.

He told her in a kind, playful way, "I've noticed that you put yourself down a lot. It bothers me when I hear it so, if possible, try to never do it again. For me, okay?"

Pia nodded. Was that it?

Apparently not, because Jeremy had a question. "Do you know why you do that?"

"Well, sure, to beat other people to it."

"Pia! That's ridiculous. What if they weren't going to put you down?"

"But sometimes they do. I think that other people can see you better than you can yourself, so I try to see myself as others do, to the extent that's possible."

Jeremy persisted. "Maybe I should ask the 'big why,' as you call it. Why are you down on yourself at all?"

"Oh. I guess my mother, as cliché as that sounds. She was often negative because she was pretty unhappy. She didn't say she loved us and she didn't give hugs. She always told us what was wrong with us."

"Really? Your mother never tells you she loves you?"

Pia had no use for this topic; she had worked through it a long time ago.

"We're using the past tense because she's dead. It's alright; she did the very best she could. I understand that."

Jeremy couldn't grasp this notion.

"My mom always tells me she loves me, and Adam, too. Always gives us bear hugs. She loves us so much."

Initially, Pia didn't know what to say in response but she had feelings about this.

Eventually she said, "Remember that she lost one of you."

Jeremy nodded.

She let out a sigh and then said, "I don't harbor any resentment or anger like my sister does. I just feel so sorry for that little girl." Her mind was in her very distant past, with the memory of hiding and crying and wanting to run away and live somewhere else. "That poor, unloved little girl."

Pia's heart hurt for her as she looked away, to a corner of the space they were in. The little girl was so sad.

"What little girl?" Jeremy asked gently.

Pia returned to the gallery, to Jeremy's eyes, and realized she wasn't making sense to him.

"Me. I guess that was me." She cheered up at the progress she'd made and she smiled for him. "Well, she's doing much, much better now!"

He got back on track. "Pia, how do you see me?"

She cooed, "I think you're fabulous in every way."

"That's really great to know. So I'm fabulous, right? I know everyone doesn't think so, definitely, but many people do. I feel the same way about you."

"Thanks, Jeremy." Pia blushed. Her instinct was to dispute this, but since Jeremy was coaching her on not doing that she refrained.

"I'm telling you so you know you're fabulous. I want *you* to believe it."

"Sometimes I do, but not for very long."

Pia enjoyed the moments when she was proud of herself, however fleeting they were.

He suggested, "Try to keep positive thoughts about yourself."

She replied, "You are such a sweet guy."

"Pia, positive thoughts about *yourself*."

Jeremy feigned exasperation as they rose to leave.

She teased him, saying, *"I'm* spending time with such a sweet guy."

Jeremy shook his head and said, "I guess that's a start. So, what would you like to do next?"

Pia lowered her voice because there were several other people in the gallery then.

"I want to do whatever you want to do."

She wasn't sure why that was her answer. She knew what she wanted to do but had not a clue where to do it.

Jeremy took hold of her hands and leaned in close to her. He swung their arms by his sides, and answered, also in a low voice.

"I want to take you to an old manor on a steep, craggy hill overlooking an angry ocean and soak in a deep tub with you, drink wine out of big goblets and then make love on a thick rug in front of a roaring fire barely contained in a huge stone hearth as night overtakes the sky."

Pia blinked. Did he just come up with that on his own? Was it a quote? She looked at him in surprise.

Jeremy's head bobbled and he smiled at her, saying, "Would that be okay with you?"

"That could work."

Three young women came into the gallery then, rowdy and loud, their voices echoing in the large space. It was an unfortunate distraction.

Jeremy looked at them and said, "Hey, here she is!"

"Here who is?" Pia's heart asked silently.

He went up to one of the women. They greeted one another and hugged lightly. Pia was a bit disconcerted. The woman was young, slender and pretty, light Black, with large almond-shaped eyes. She had several silver beads in her braids, long boots, a short skirt and a jacket that wasn't really warm enough for this weather. She had a heavy friend who had several nose piercings, blue hair and black lipstick, and another friend whose appearance was considerably more traditional.

The woman Jeremy had hugged said, "Hey, you! Thanks for stopping by. Sorry I didn't get to talk to you much at the opening."

"No worries, you had a great turnout! This is my friend Pia."

Jeremy held out his arm to encourage Pia to move into the circle from where she was standing away from them.

Pia extended her hand and the young woman shook it briefly.

"Nice to meet you," Pia said.

"This is Jamila. She took that photo series we just looked at," Jeremy enthused.

"I really like your art. It's a great concept," Pia offered.

She was a little flustered but did her best not to show it. She suddenly felt too old.

"Thanks," Jamila responded. She and her friends all looked around at each other.

There was an awkward moment then, which Jeremy picked up on.

He hastily said, "We have to head out. It's a great show!"

"Sure, be talking to you, Jeremy," Jamila said.

The three women continued further into the gallery together. Jeremy and Pia headed toward the doors.

Outside it had begun drizzling icy cold wetness and a wind was sending it into their faces.

Jeremy said to Pia, "I met her through a friend at our school. She's also an improvisational dancer."

Pia wished he didn't sound so enthusiastic about Jamila.

"She's incredibly beautiful. You both have so much talent." She stopped walking to ask Jeremy, "Do we know where we're heading?"

Jeremy stopped to answer her.

"One of the music professors never locks her office. I was thinking we might be able to borrow her space if we'd like to be alone. I know it's not ideal," he said apologetically.

As they resumed a quick pace in that direction Pia replied, "That's totally fine. I should be coming up with ideas, too. How was your Christmas?"

"It was really great! How was yours?"

Jeremy never offered her much information about his life. Pia figured that was because they were always short on time due of her situation. When they were together, Jeremy was completely present. Pia used to go to lunch with a young co-worker who was always texting on her phone or inviting people Pia didn't know to come along. Multi-tasking friendships didn't work very well, and she appreciated the laser-like focus Jeremy turned on her when they were together.

She remembered Tao. "It was okay." She walked with her head down because of the precipitation.

"You don't sound very enthusiastic. Did you get coal in your stocking this year?" Jeremy gently teased her.

"I certainly should have. No, it's just…oh, a student died last week."

"Another one? Wow, that's terrible. How?"

Pia sighed heavily, saying with downcast eyes, "He hanged himself. I…I should've done more."

Jeremy stopped to look at her.

"What do you have to do with his killing himself?"

"He had to drop a course after the deadline and we didn't let him so he had to pay for it and he couldn't. I gave him a petition form to fill out and he submitted it but it was denied." It all spilled out in one breath. "Now the man is dead. He's *dead.*" Pia's grief was obvious.

"Aww. I'm sorry to hear that, but there had to be more going on."

Jeremy gave her a quick but robust hug and reasoned, "It doesn't sound like you had anything to do with it. You're an administrative assistant so you don't have any authority on these things. That's what you told me before."

The rain hadn't let up, and Pia resumed walking.

"A lot of times I just break the rules, and I could've for Tao. I would've been caught, though, because we were being monitored that week by the bursar's office." She pushed some hair from her face brusquely with a thick glove. "If only I had."

"You'd risk your job again."

"Mm-hm, and I'd lose it this time. That's what stopped me. I cannot tell you how strange it is to have the options of either doing the wrong thing the right way or the right thing the wrong way. It's always like that in my office."

"It really isn't your fault in any way, Pia."

"I realize that intellectually. My heart hurts, though. You know that phrase people use when they hear a bell toll: 'ask not for whom the bell tolls, it tolls for thee'?"

"Sure."

Pia asked, "What do you think people mean when they quote it?"

"I know that's a small part of a longer poem, but I assume most people mean 'you could be next,' or 'we'll all die sometime.'"

They were approaching the building they were hoping to go in.

"Yeah, I think you're right, that's usually what they mean. It's a misunderstanding on their part, though. It's a poem by John Donne, and it goes something like 'If a clod be washed away by the sea/ Europe is the less./ Each man's death diminishes me,/ for I am in involved in mankind./ Therefore, send not to know for whom the bell tolls,/ it tolls for thee.' So, that's how I feel. A piece of mankind is gone."

Before trying the doors Jeremy looked back and replied, "I agree with you on principle but that's a lot of grief. It's fine to feel it, but then you have to let it go."

The front doors were locked, which didn't surprise Pia.

They went around to the side as Jeremy added, "You can't continue to carry grief around because it'll become too heavy a burden. It will just crush you and then you won't be any good to anyone."

Pia was thinking about what he said as they tried a side door and found it unlocked.

"You've got a point there," she commented as they went inside. "That's what cemeteries and shrines are for. I'll make a time to think about Tao, maybe at the reflection pool on campus, and then I'll let him go."

Pia felt herself move away from these thoughts.

"That sounds like a good plan," he said.

They began climbing up an old circular marble staircase.

Pia wanted to assure him that she wasn't completely needy.

"I'm much more vibrant and stronger in warm weather. I get energy from the sunshine. I'm a total warrior then."

"Really, a warrior?" Jeremy laughed over his shoulder to her. "I'd better watch out!"

"No, I'll protect you from dragons and killer robots and such," she joked while she followed Jeremy's feet.

They went up to the top floor and then proceeded down a short, narrow hallway with a red carpet down its center which ended at a heavy, oak door. Jeremy knocked on it loudly enough for anyone inside to hear, but not so much as to attract attention from anyone elsewhere in the building. Nothing. He cautiously turned the knob and found it was unlocked. They went in and Jeremy switched on a lamp and shut the door behind them.

"Hello? Professor Wang?" They paused.

The space had another door in it. Jeremy opened it; it was a small closet.

"Are we in the turret?" Pia looked around the rounded space and decided they must be.

"Yeah, isn't this cool?"

Pia felt like she had been tedious this afternoon and she wanted to change the mood. She began to kiss Jeremy but he fell away from it soon.

"What is it?" she asked him.

She was comparing herself to Jamila still and was afraid he might be as well.

"I don't know, I can't identify it. I think I'm too melancholy now."

Pia couldn't dispute that; she felt it, too. It had been a dreary day and she had exacerbated it with her thoughts about Tao. Pia wanted to apologize but stopped herself.

She said, "I feel it, too. How would you feel about going for a walk in the rec center?"

Jeremy considered it for a minute. "Sure, let's."

So they went back outside where it had stopped raining but it was still dreary. The buildings were not far from each other. They went in through the large glass doors and Pia swiped her ID card. Jeremy held out his obsolete card which the sleepy student worker accepted without issue. They took the stairs up to the track level. It overhung the huge swimming pool. Fencing was installed to prevent anyone from diving from the track. Three Chinese students chatted happily as they walked together but no one else was there. Their voices were high-pitched and light and reminded Pia of birdsong. They sounded very upbeat to her, although she knew not what they were saying.

Jeremy and Pia left their belongings on a bench in a corner. Pia was already in sneakers and yoga pants. She pulled her sweater over her head, leaving her in just her moss green t-shirt. Jeremy was in jeans. Pia got to see his smooth stomach as he pulled off his sweatshirt before he tugged his t-shirt down. Jeremy decided to walk with bare feet. He started stretching his hands to the floor as they prepared to walk.

Pia hesitated before requesting, "Um…I'd like to start with a handstand if that's all right. It won't take more than a minute."

Jeremy's head bobbled a little when he stood up and said, "A handstand? Let's see this."

He rested his hands on his narrow hips.

"I heard that in India people do them daily to try to keep all their organs from drooping or something like that," she told him.

"Stop procrastinating."

Pia went over to the wall in a corner, where the track curved away from it and there was free space. She looked to make sure the students were not nearby so she wouldn't inadvertently kick them. Then, with one swift move, she was upside down against the wall, her heels against it for balance. She looked at the floor between her hands and concentrated on her breathing.

In a beat Jeremy joined her and said, "We're 'upside-down.' One of my favorite Jack Johnson tunes."

Pia remained up as long as she could, which turned out to be only fifty seconds, then curled down. Jeremy was still upside down, so she just looked at him from her seat on the floor. She admired his arms.

"Must…not…tickle you," Pia said mischievously.

"Don't you dare." He narrowed his eyes jokingly at her.

He stayed that way for over a minute and a half before bringing his feet down and rolling smoothly upright immediately. His body could do it but the blood needed a few seconds to re-orient so he swayed slightly.

Pia smiled her approval. "Nicely done! Let me see if there's a radio or CD player over by the exercise mats. Sometimes there is."

They went over to that area together and found the radio tucked in a corner. Jeremy reached for it and brought it over to the track. He waited for the students to come by to ask them if they'd mind. They didn't so he turned it on to something with a steady beat.

"This will definitely keep us moving."

Finally, they were off at a fast pace. After a half dozen laps Jeremy had an idea.

He stopped to say, "Let's finish up with a race! Let me know when you're ready. Once around, okay?"

It was Pia's turn to give someone the hairy eyeball.

She said, "I thought you weren't competitive."

Jeremy smiled widely and replied, "I'm not, it's just for fun!"

Pia was glad to see him smile. She took off without warning him, hollering over her shoulder, "*Go!*"

She ran as fast as she possibly could but in a few seconds he sped past her.

"You're such a brat!" he said on his way by.

That made Pia laugh and she slowed considerably.

When Jeremy finished he went to the side where mats were strewn all over the floor. He drank deeply from a water fountain and then collapsed face up onto one of the mats, panting. Pia joined him after stopping by the fountain herself. She knelt down by Jeremy's head with a knee by each of his ears. She looked down at him and began to massage his face.

Jeremy smiled up at her and then closed his eyes and relaxed his muscles.

"Mmm, this is nice."

Pia had learned basic massage techniques a long time ago and used to give Gordon full massages periodically. It had been a while.

She began with Jeremy's face and neck. It was an opportunity to study his face while he wasn't looking at her and she was grateful for it. She could look at him forever. It wasn't quite as extreme as new parents watching their baby all the time, but it had a similar flavor.

Softly Pia murmured, "You are so beautiful."

Some men might misunderstand that, but Pia knew Jeremy would be fine with it.

"Heh."

When Pia finished, she brushed a hand through his hair gently a few times.

"That's it, unless you turn over and I'll do your back and arms."

"That would be great." Jeremy sat up and pulled his shirt over his head, adding, "Are you sure you don't mind?"

"Oh, I definitely don't mind."

They exchanged another smile, and then Jeremy leaned down to spread his shirt between the pad and his torso. Pia swung over him and began at his neck. Since he was so narrow Pia could straddle him easily. She proceeded slowly and methodically.

"Do you give a lot of people massages?"

"No, you're the first in a long time. Once after work a bunch of us went out for a drink and I gave three people little shoulder massages. It was funny: one was very soft, one was quite skinny, bony really, and one was very muscular."

"Where am I on the flesh spectrum?"

Pia didn't want to tell him he was on the skinny side. "Perfect."

Sometimes, like now, it became a meditation for Pia where she touched every inch of skin with care and attention but with almost no conscious effort. Some more people had come onto that level of the rec center and Pia heard children playing on the track. After a while she could see that Jeremy had goosebumps in the areas her hands weren't directly heating.

"You're getting cold," Pia acknowledged.

Just then some people walked along and stopped at them, so Pia looked up at them. It was Diane and her husband. They all paused while a general discomfort hovered in the air. If it had been two minutes later, Pia and Jeremy would've been standing and Jeremy would have his shirt on.

Pia acted as naturally as she could under the circumstances, saying only, "Hi, Diane!"

She and Jeremy stood up. Diane responded with a drawn out "Hi…." She then addressed Jeremy with a smile. "Jeremy, right? I met you at the reception for your photography exhibit. I'm Diane, and this is my husband Ted."

While Diane spoke, Jeremy put on his shirt. Pia watched Diane watch Jeremy pull his arms through the sleeves and slip it over his head in one motion. He tossed his hair out of his face as he tugged the shirt down over his torso.

"That's right, I remember you!" Jeremy said to Diane, and "Nice to meet you," to Ted.

The kids were noisy but happy in the background.

As always, Pia couldn't think on her feet and said, "I was giving Jeremy a massage," as a meager explanation.

"I see that!"

Diane was saying much more with her eye contact to Pia. Then Diane looked at her husband, saying, "Ted, we should bring the kids over to see Jeremy's show in the campus center."

Jeremy enthused, "That would be so great if you did! I'd really like to know what you think of it."

"It's family day at the rec center," Diane explained, "so we all went swimming. While our hair's drying I thought I'd give them a tour of the facility."

"Are those your girls I hear?" Pia asked.

"Yes. You haven't seen them in a long time; they're all bigger now." Then Diane hollered to her three kids. "Girls! Come over and say hello to Pia!"

And so they did. Pia liked Diane's family. Ted was quiet, but he always was when Pia saw him. They caught up briefly. Then Diane bid them goodbye and directed her family to the elevators. Pia began chewing on a nail once they were gone.

Jeremy raised his eyebrows, saying, "Was that cause for concern?"

Pia turned her gaze on him and stopped gnawing on her nail.

"I think probably, yes." After a beat she added, "Oh well. This isn't the first time we've been spotted together."

"Is your husband going to kill me?" Jeremy asked.

Pia wasn't sure how serious he was about that.

She answered him lightheartedly, "No! I just meant things could get uncomfortable for me on the campus, that's all. Gossipy. Gordon would have an issue with me, not you. Don't worry."

Jeremy nodded and glanced at the windows.

"Pia, look, it's snowing outside!"

He was as happy as a child about it and went over to the glass. Pia joined him. They could see their reflection in it, so it looked like it was snowing on and through them. Jeremy watched the flakes falling for a minute, and then looked at Pia.

"Isn't it beautiful?"

"It really is." Yet her heart sank when she considered what her commute might be like in a few hours, and she hoped it might stop soon.

"Maybe we'll get a lot of snow! We can make angels on the quad, heh."

Pia couldn't resist smiling at his enthusiasm before they returned to the bench where the rest of their clothes were, put them on and headed out.

Chapter 13

"Oh, I have to go to the library to pick up a few films and a book or two before they close." Pia said as they walked into the falling snowflakes. "Is that alright?"

"Sure."

They redirected themselves from the music building to the library. They were quiet for a few minutes, and then Jeremy spoke.

"I'm remembering how you said the snowshoes offer 'flotation.' At the time it sounded odd, but technically that's correct if you're walking on top of snow, since snow is just water."

Pia said, "Yes. You can walk on water."

Jeremy continued his mental wandering.

"A few months ago, I was standing on a bridge over a brook and it looked like the same water over and over because it all follows the same path, like a fountain kind of, making a loop. But every drop was new water going under the bridge. Continuously new water all the time, even though there's only so much on the planet. It got me thinking that maybe some of the water had been there before. If water molecules had memory, maybe they'd recognize the brook if they'd been there after another rain."

"That's an interesting idea. Maybe you drank some of that water before," Pia suggested.

"Yes, and maybe after I drank it, it sweated out of me. Maybe the water molecules could remember they'd met me, my molecules, before if they passed over me again sometime, in the ocean or as a snowflake landing on my hair now. Where else have they traveled? Have they been someone else's tears? Am I stepping on snow that was once humidity in Louisiana?"

Pia mused, "I think you have a poem growing there, Jeremy."

Jeremy turned his face up into the snowflakes, allowing the sharp little bites to melt on his skin.

"I've never written a poem."

She remembered his captions that accompanied his photographs for his exhibit.

"Well, you write very poetically."

"Do you write any poetry?" Jeremy asked as they reached the doors to the library.

He held a door open for her.

"No, I have no skill at that. I've been thinking for years of trying to make a poem about the snow that partly melts when the sun is on it then refreezes each night on my road. As the winter goes on, it seems to graft to the asphalt and becomes hard, smooth, opaque. The winter's bones. But I can't manage to do it right. It makes me appreciate Jane's talent."

Inside they stomped the snow off their shoes on a mat. It was unnecessarily hot but the old buildings were like that. Pia went over to the featured books displayed on a table and grabbed one after only a cursory glance. Then she went to the films where Jeremy was already searching the shelves for something interesting.

Jeremy said from the other side of the stacks, "Hey, here are some old Pink Panther movies."

"That will do if they're DVDs. Grab a couple, would you, please?"

Jeremy selected two and came around to Pia with them in his hand.

She said cheerily, "Thanks, my friend. That was easy!"

On their way to the check-out desk, Jeremy began quoting one of the films.

"Does your dog bite?" he said in a terrible accent.

After so many years, Pia still remembered this. She picked up Inspector Clouseau's part.

"No." Then she followed that immediately with a fierce growling, snapping sound.

"I thought you said your dog does not bite?!" Jeremy said while rubbing his hand from the imaginary dog bite.

Pia deadpanned, "That is not my dog."

Jeremy laughed, "Bravo, Pia!"

Once outdoors, she followed his lead while she stuffed the items she had borrowed in her coat. Jeremy began heading back to the turret but stopped when he remembered something.

"I have something for you in my car. It's right there."

He pointed as he retrieved his keys from his pocket. Jeremy unlocked the passenger side door and took out a cardboard box. Then he locked the door and resumed walking to the turret with it tucked under his arm.

"What is it?" Pia asked curiously as she followed him.

She tried to put her steps into his but his prints were too far apart for her.

"You'll see soon enough! You can put the book and movies in the bottom of the box after you open it. There's plenty of room. But it can't get wet out here."

The snow was coming down a little heavier but the actual flakes were getting smaller as it was colder now. It was dark outside too. Pia thought it was neat how you could almost hide amidst the flakes.

Once they were locked inside the turret office they took their coats off and Jeremy gave Pia the box. It wasn't taped shut, it just had the top folded closed and there was no wrap, so her hopes weren't high.

But as she looked in she let out a small gasp. She looked at Jeremy with delight as she lifted out a complex origami paper sculpture. It was another mathematical, abstract piece. Pia knew immediately that Jeremy had made it specifically for her because it had four colors: blue, gray, yellow and green. She looked at it for a long time, turning it around in her hands.

"Oh, Jeremy, this is so special. I can't believe you made it for me!"

Eventually she looked away from it to Jeremy. His head bobbled slightly while he smiled back.

"I put my copy of *The Edge of the Sea* in the box, too. Do you really like it?" They were both considerably more cheerful than they were earlier.

"Oh, I love it! Thank you. How long did it take you?"

"I've made that one four times before, so it wasn't too hard. A few hours."

Pia stood up from her seat and put the library book and movies in the bottom under Rachel Carson's book, and delicately returned the paper sculpture to it, setting it gently on top. She wasn't ready to fold the lid closed yet, though. Pia set the box near their coats by the door. So far in their brief relationship Pia had been working up her courage to tell Jeremy out loud that she loved him. Now, somehow, she was unable to stop herself. She said it with tender acquiescence.

"Jeremy, I love you. I *really* love you."

His head did the subtle bobble again.

"Hey, I love you too."

As he said it, Jeremy went over to Pia and they embraced. They kissed while running their hands over one another. The intensity level seemed to notch up. Jeremy was not even remotely playful this time. He was somehow able to balance his physical desire with great tenderness. Pia tended to go one way or the other, and she enjoyed learning another approach.

They shed their clothes gradually and left them in a pile on the worn carpeting. Jeremy unceremoniously shoved some papers and office supplies away from the surface of a small but sturdy conference table. Then he embraced Pia again, kissing her steadily and, lifting her, took a few steps to set her delicately onto the table. Pia was aware of a discernable contrast between how Jeremy treated inanimate objects and how he handled her body. He was so gentle with her as he guided her back and head down on the wooden surface. They made intense, pure love.

Afterwards, Jeremy nuzzled Pia's neck as she ran her hands over his shoulders and folded around him. Jeremy kissed the base of her neck at the clavicle, then kissed under her ear. He left his face there, his lips at her hairline behind her ear, breathing her in. They kept each other warm. While Pia stroked Jeremy's hair, she remembered the night on the dance floor.

"Hey, I kissed you like that once, just the same as that," she said quietly.

"Mm, I'll never forget it. You started all this trouble, young lady."

Jeremy gave her a quick kiss there, lifted his head to smile at her, and then moved off of her, reaching for his t-shirt. Pia slid off the hard surface and they held each other affectionately.

Jeremy murmured, "What are you feeling?"

Pia couldn't remember ever being asked this before. Unprepared for this question, she answered in the physical sense, where her hands were.

"Your tiny bum."

Jeremy gave her a brief, patient grin and looked in her eyes.

"No, seriously."

"I'm feeling love for you, and gratitude, too. Actually, both have grown some since you asked me that question. And you?"

"Me?"

"What are *you* feeling?"

"I'm feeling certain that life doesn't get any better than this."

And so it happened again; Pia's feelings for Jeremy grew stronger. She kissed him while they were both bringing up goosebumps.

"We're getting cold again," she thought aloud.

They put on their clothes. She sat in an upholstered chair and he squatted on her lap, facing her, with his feet on seat of the chair so he didn't put all his weight on her.

"Pia?"

"Hmm?"

They were still caressing one another lightly. Pia couldn't resist doing it.

"I didn't mean to be callous earlier, when we first came to the turret."

Pia was confused, saying, "I don't know what you mean…when?"

"Oh, when I said you should feel less grief about the student who hanged himself. I'm sorry about that. It wasn't my place and it wasn't good advice," Jeremy explained somberly.

It was a refreshing change to be on the other side of an apology for Pia. She was often apologizing for something she said or did, and meanwhile people hadn't given any thought about whatever it was. Pia shook her head slowly at him with a small smile.

"You had a good point," she said.

"I just don't function well when I absorb pain. Like at the art museum with you," he said, referring to the photography exhibit about the child soldiers. "I really hate it, I'm sorry."

"It's okay. I know I can personally take a lot of emotional pain. I mean, I obviously don't like it, but I'll survive it. Just the same, I think there's a real strength in accepting your sensitivity level."

Jeremy seemed grateful to hear that, so Pia reiterated it with, "Being sensitive is a good thing."

"But you're sensitive and you can face pain head on. I can't do that."

Pia mulled that over briefly, deciding, "It's the maternal instinct in me, I suppose. Not courageous, just protective."

She wasn't sure that cleared anything up They sat there together in silence for a minute.

Jeremy broke it by stating, "I'm starving."

Pia didn't want to leave the cozy warm space of the turret although she was hungry, too. She also very much enjoyed the time she and Jeremy had together alone.

"I don't suppose we could order food to be delivered?" she wondered out loud.

"Not to this specific location, I don't think. Are you worried about being seen with me again?"

Jeremy said it teasingly but Pia thought he might be serious about it as well.

"No, quite the opposite. I just like being locked in here with you! Look, we've already been seen kissing by someone in my office. It's a risk I'm willing to take. You're worth it."

"Thanks, Pia," Jeremy said and offered her another kiss.

Pia wasn't sure he understood how much was at risk for her. It was best that he didn't.

"What do you feel like eating?" she asked.

Jeremy thought about it for a minute.

"I don't know, anything. Something that pairs well with beer, heh."

Then Jeremy put his hands on the arms of the chair and lifted himself off her lap like a gymnast might, swinging his feet to the floor. They gathered their things and closed up the room, leaving it as best as they could as it was before. Pia let him lead them back out and she folded the top of the box down so the origami gift would be safe and dry. It had finished snowing, to her relief. They passed Pia's car on the way to the pub Jeremy chose so she set the box lovingly on the passenger seat.

"I hope nobody breaks into my car tonight," she said as she swung the door closed.

They only had a few blocks to walk. When they were coming up to the pub there were two young men on the sidewalk. They were asking a couple who had just left if they could have their leftovers they were carrying. The couple promptly crossed the street without responding to them. Pia and Jeremy both watched the incident. When they were right by the young men Jeremy acknowledged them.

"Hey," Jeremy said as he and Pia began to pass them.

One was shorter but stocky, with big brown eyes and thick, long brown hair he kept pushing out of his face. He was exceptionally handsome, albeit in a scruffy way. The other was also attractive. He was taller, blond, with blue eyes and looked remarkably like the late River Phoenix. He was rather reserved.

The one with the brown hair asked, "Hey man, are you going to eat here?"

"Yes," Jeremy answered.

"If you can't finish it all, will you bring us out your leftovers?"

Pia, always practical, asked him, "Should we bring utensils too?"

The young pair was willing to wait quite a while out in the cold.

"Nah, we have those. Just need some food to go with them," the shorter fellow said.

The blond told Pia, "I like your gloves."

He held up his two mismatched gloves: one black leather, one rawhide, so Pia extended hers out in front of her. A family left the restaurant then, and the blond turned to them quickly.

"Got any leftovers?" he asked them.

"Get outta here before I call the cops!" The obese man was startlingly aggressive. His family was arguing, though, as they walked. They continued across the street, but his teenage daughter was looking back at the one with the big brown eyes.

"Someone got up on the wrong side of the bed today," the blond said as he turned back to his companion with a grin. He was unfazed by the verbal assault. Apparently this was frequently the response they got.

Jeremy looked at Pia. She knew looking at his face what he had in mind and nodded once.

"Hey, do you want to join us?" Jeremy asked them.

"Join you?" said the blond with a frown.

Pia answered, "Yes, come in and eat with us. Our treat, of course."

Now it was the young men's turn to look at each other to ascertain a decision. They shrugged simultaneously.

"So it's settled!" Jeremy said, and they all went in and were seated in a big booth.

Jeremy and the other guys ordered a lot of food. Pia ordered potato skins. It was a weakness of hers. Once they ordered, Pia asked them about themselves. She certainly felt maternal then.

She began, "So, what's your story? Are you from this area or traveling around?"

They had full, well-worn backpacks, but considerably less than someone doing a major trail journey. No rolled mattresses, water bottles or spare boots.

"We're traveling around. We're nomads, man," the shorter one said with a lazy grin.

His speech was leisurely, like a pothead's. He was truly as cute as a puppy and he seemed to deliberately use it to his advantage. The waitress flirted with all three young men each time she came by.

"Gypsies," added the blond as if it were a noble title.

"Someone must be missing you?" Pia suggested.

They were silent on that point. Jeremy exhibited better manners than Pia.

"My name's Jeremy, nice to meet you."

He extended his hand over the table and the brown-haired fellow shook it.

"Max. This is Jamie."

Jamie shook Jeremy's hand since Jeremy held it out for him, though he did so somewhat reluctantly.

The beer had arrived so Pia lifted her glass to them. "To meeting Max and Jamie then!"

As soon as she said it, Pia felt that that was the kind of ominous thing always stated at the beginning of ax murder movies; something you might regret.

"Here, here," said Max. "What's your name?" he added.

Pia was pleased she wasn't a backdrop as she felt she had been when she met Jamila.

After swallowing a sip she answered, "Pia."

Max continued with, "Are you Jeremy's mom or something?"

Pia blanched while Jeremy answered, "No, we're friends."

"That's cool." Max said it as in 'no problem' and drank deeply from his beer mug.

Pia had to ask Jamie a question.

"Has anyone ever told you, you look like River Phoenix?"

She had expected Jamie to say, "all the time" but he answered, "Who?"

"He was an actor," she said, bringing that topic to a close.

Pia was getting antsy to leave but didn't know how to do it without disappointing Jeremy. He noticed that the food was distributed inequitably amongst the four plates. He met Pia's glance and looked to her plate and then back to her. She only had one lone potato skin. Jeremy cut the one on his plate in quarters, jabbed a piece with his fork and held it out for Pia to eat. She hesitated.

"C'mon, open up!" Jeremy enticed her, grinning broadly.

Pia ate it.

Then, as he picked up another for her, "Would you like some sour cream on this one?"

"Oh, sure."

Pia ate that piece, too. Jamie shot Max a look.

Then the men waxed philosophical on various topics as they ate the main courses voraciously. Jeremy was delighted by their company and the camaraderie shared between Max and Jamie.

"I'm hoping to get to Provincetown tonight," Max told them.

Pia thought he had his work cut out for him. That was three hours away on clear roads. And that's in a car, which they didn't seem to have.

She asked Jamie, "Are you going too?"

Jamie scowled briefly.

"Of course. I'm his extra set of eyes." He made a motion with two fingers that his eyes watch Max. "I watch out for him."

"I do the same for you, too, man," Max said nonchalantly as he ate. "We just have to acquire some more money."

Jeremy wanted to help them out so offered, "I can give you a ride for a portion of it if you want. There's a highway that curves around the area, so I could bring you south of here, about a third the way, then I'll just circle back up."

"You sure, man?" Max interrupted his eating; he understood that this was very generous of Jeremy.

They all did. The question of why hung in the air. Jeremy was a generous, friendly person with the energy and the time, which Pia knew, but it seemed foreign to Max and Jamie.

"Works for me, dude," Jamie said to Max, as if to finalize the deal.

This seemed to be a practiced routine for them. Max reeled people in for their mutual benefit. At this point Pia really had to get home and it seemed that Jeremy was interested in their new friends.

She said as nicely as possible, "Jeremy, I should get going. Do you mind if I head out soon?"

He checked the time on his phone.

"Yeah, sure. I didn't realize how late it is. You have all your things, right?"

He looked around the seat quickly.

"Mm-hm."

"Let me walk you out," Jeremy said to her while she stood to leave and, "I'll be right back, don't let the waitress take my plate!" to Jamie and Max as he stood up.

"Be safe, guys," Pia said to them.

Max gave her a thumbs-up sign as he bit into a meatball.

Jamie said, "Peace out."

Pia was glad Jeremy walked her to the sidewalk. She didn't approve of his giving them a ride, possibly because of Jamie's looks. This was reminding her of a film River Phoenix was in, *My Own Private Idaho*, where he and Keanu Reeves portrayed male prostitutes. Pia found her wallet at the bottom of her handbag and opened it as she checked again that Jeremy was comfortable with her leaving.

"Do you mind if I get going? I'll stay if you want. You seem to be enjoying their company."

"Yeah, that's totally fine. I understand," Jeremy assured her.

Pia handed him all the cash she had, which would cover most of the bill, saying, "Jeremy, be careful. I don't want something to happen to you."

"I think they're stoners. Peaceful people." Before he put the bills in his wallet he motioned with them and said, "thanks."

"Yes, I vaguely remember that from high school. Still, there's only two ways they can get money from people. One involves seriously compromising themselves and the other would be stealing. Please, please be careful."

Jeremy raised his eyebrows. "Or they could just ask."

"Ask?"

"They could ask people for money."

"Oh, right." Pia nodded but looked down.

Jeremy saw that this didn't resolve her apprehension.

"Do you want me to text you later?"

"Yes, that would be terrific! Thank you."

She appreciated Jeremy saying that, and not making her feel like a mother hen. She knew she'd continue to worry about this.

"Hey."

Jeremy wrapped his arms around her then, so she held onto him, too. He pulled back and held Pia's head in his hands like the first night they were on a cold sidewalk together. Then he gave her a few of those quick, gentle kisses on her lips and looked into her eyes reassuringly.

Pia reluctantly bid Jeremy goodnight. "You're precious, remember that."

That made Jeremy grin, "Bye, Pia."

"Bye. Oh, thanks again for the origami!"

Pia drove home and made dinner. She had marinated some chicken and other ingredients in advance, so they just had to go in the oven. She made rice and green beans while the main course cooked. She told Gordon that she ran into Jeremy and he made the origami creation for her to thank her for working on his exhibit. Gordon liked it possibly more than Pia did. He essentially made it his own, carrying it into his office and setting it on a corner of his desk. Pia suspected she'd have to visit it there from now on.

They watched one of the Pink Panther movies. They'd eaten late, but Gordon didn't mind. Pia always fit a lot into a day, so this wasn't unusual. After three hours had passed she received a text from Jeremy. She had been checking her phone covertly with it silenced.

"All ok. Dropped them off at rest stop on 93. Will call you tomorrow."

Pia sent a message back: "Thanks for letting me know. Godnight."

Oops, a little mistake there. Pia groaned but didn't bother herself further over such a little thing. Jeremy wouldn't like that.

Chapter 14

The following day Pia slept in late. That was a treat but later she reproached herself for missing several hours of daylight when so few were available this time of year. After a few chores around the house and a French toast brunch ("not really French," she thought), Pia went out for a walk in the forest. She could directly reach trails from her road without having to get in the car.

Pia kept her phone with her. Sometimes she listened to music on it, but not in the woods during hunting season. It was very cold and breezy but clear and blindingly bright. Pia's eyes were relieved from squinting only when she was beneath the hemlocks. It took her a few years to become totally comfortable walking alone in the woods and getting the cell phone helped. Gradually these solo walks became almost a need, like water and warmth.

She waited to hear from Jeremy. Pia realized she was overly attached to him but she couldn't help herself. Again she thought of the relationship between her former coworker Wanda and that woman's young lover. Pia had left that company during the summer so she didn't know how it resolved. On some level Pia suspected this time with Jeremy would be temporary. He was going out into the world and whether he knew it or not, he would be leaving the past behind him eventually for all the opportunities unfolding ahead. But Pia wanted to be with him for as long as possible, for however long he wanted her.

Then, finally, a text. "May I call you now?"

Pia pulled off her chunky gloves and tucked them under her arm from where they promptly dropped to the ground by her feet. She smiled at the inanimate phone lovingly as if it were a kitten and typed, "Yes."

In a minute Jeremy's voice was in her ear.

"Hi, Pia! How are you today?"

"Fine, thanks. How did it go last night? Did you guys have fun?"

Pia was curious how much of the time which had elapsed last night was spent with Max and Jamie.

"Not so much, actually. Apparently they saw us kiss goodnight from the restaurant window, so once we were in the car Jamie referred to you as Mrs. Robinson and then they started singing songs from the film *Harold and Maude*. It got old fast, no pun intended. I tried to keep it positive, but I let them out sooner than I would have if they had behaved better."

"Well, as long as they didn't do anything worse than that I'm glad. I'm surprised you're familiar with *Harold and Maude*, " Pia said, blushing at the thought.

A shadow of a large bird passed between Pia and the sun, but when she looked for it, it was already gone.

"Oh sure, I saw it a few years ago. It's kind of a cult thing in college. You actually do remind me of Maude —"

Pia groaned audibly.

"—because you care about trees! I can totally see you trying to save the ones in the city."

"Some of them are wretched. The ones along the sidewalks choke on the salt used to melt the ice. I wonder about the ones on top of buildings, like penthouse gardens… if they have big egos, or fear of heights…." Pia trailed off.

She had put her gloves in a pocket and hopped from one stone to the next in a seep area, where the ground was always wet. Pia avoided stones covered in moss because they were slippery and, of course, she didn't want to hurt the moss.

"You are so weird! So when can we get together again? Are you free tomorrow night?" Jeremy asked.

Pia thought. Tomorrow was Wednesday and Thursday night was New Year's Eve. Pia figured Jeremy would be doing something age-appropriate for that such as partying until all hours.

"Pia? Are you there?"

"Yeah, I'm thinking what my schedule is. I have to look at the calendar when I get home."

Pia stopped and looked all around her. She had the forest to herself.

"Where are you now?"

"I'm in the middle of the woods," she said with a grin because they'd been discussing trees.

"Oh, you have the whole week off don't you? I'm at work."

Pia pictured him sitting in front of a computer at a desk in a cubicle, in an office suite in a building that was part of a larger office park off a highway. He was about as far away from nature as you could get.

"I'm sorry you have to work. Oh, I promised someone I'd babysit tomorrow night."

"Hmm…how about Saturday?"

"A group I'm involved with is holding a town hall and vigil to honor Sharelle Jackson and protest her murder. I can just help set up though and then leave. I'm making a bunch of posters and bringing pens and candles. So, yes, whatever time is good for you. I'll work around it."

"Could I go with you to that?"

Pia was pleasantly surprised he was interested.

"Sure, that would be great! It starts at two, so we should be there for one-thirty. We can meet up earlier if you want to."

"Okay, I'll text you Saturday morning."

On Thursday, Pia drove over to the sanctuary for the meeting with Annie. She didn't have any details about it and assumed some other volunteers would attend. Jane had just gotten there but no one else had arrived yet. The secretary was a new part-time employee. She welcomed them in and offered them some tea, which they both declined. Pia complained to Jane about the bitterly cold wind that was blowing outside. Presently Annie came down the nearby stairs.

"Hi, thanks for coming. Since it's a small group we'll fit in my office. Please, come on up."

Jane and Pia followed Annie up the steep, creaky staircase and down a short hall to Annie's office. They sat down beside each other in old wooden chairs and Annie shut the door before taking a seat across her desk from them. They were silent for a moment while Pia took off her gloves and unzipped her coat.

She thought, "This is a little unusual. I sure hope Annie's not leaving."

Once she was settled she looked at Annie expectantly.

Jane and Annie glanced at each other, and Annie unconsciously played with a string on her sweatshirt. Jane began the conversation.

"Pia, we wanted to talk with you about something."

Pia's face was receptive with a pleasant expression. She was always eager to help them out.

Then Jane added, "I want you to understand that we're doing this because we love you and we care about you."

Pia frowned slightly, not following where this was going.

Annie chimed in, "Absolutely. There's no judgement here whatsoever. We very much respect you and this is only out of our concern for you." She added good-naturedly, "You can definitely tell us to go to hell, but please hear us out first."

Pia swallowed hard as she prepared herself for an inquisition.

Jane continued, "This is regarding Jeremy."

Pia felt her cheeks suddenly burn. "What about him?" she said weakly.

"Again, we're only bringing this up because we care about you," Annie said gently. "I don't know how you feel about him, but he's clearly enamored with you. I saw him kiss you a few times when he was here."

Pia noticed that Annie made the action Jeremy's.

Jane added, "Pia, what's going on? What are you doing?" She rubbed Pia's back supportively.

Pia always loved Jane's soothing voice but her first reaction was to be defensive. "So you two colluded on this? Jeremy and I are friends. Is that a problem?"

Jane continued, "You can do whatever you want. 'Follow your heart' as the saying goes. We just want you to think about what you're setting yourself up for, that's all. Are things okay between you and Gordon?"

"Yeah, fine. I mean the same as always," Pia replied gruffly. "Our marriage has nothing to do with my friendship with Jeremy."

Annie persisted, "I noticed you blushed when you introduced us, too. Like you are now."

Jane added, "You did tell Sam and I that you're infatuated with him. Are you two already involved?"

Annie looked surprised by that information.

Pia grumbled, "Why do you ask?"

Jane sighed, "Because you might be sorry in the end, that's all. Think about what's at stake."

"That's really our whole message to you," Annie added. "We became aware of this situation and we felt we should intervene. What you do is your choice and we're here if you want to talk to us. We don't approve of what's happening but we support you regardless."

They became quiet. They looked to one another and then back to Pia. Pia just looked down at her hands in her lap for a few minutes in humiliation. She heard the phone ring downstairs several times before the secretary picked it up. The clock ticked on the wall. Annie's cell phone vibrated on her desk. She lifted it to glance at it and then set it back down.

Keeping her head down Pia said sincerely, "I'm sorry to be a disappointment to you."

A bit of her hair fell in her face so she tucked it behind an ear but her eyes remained down.

Jane responded with, "Don't be silly, you're not a disappointment. You're a concern. Just think about what you're doing."

Both women looked compassionately at Pia when she lifted her eyes, causing her to pause.

She said to them with wonder in her voice at the realization, "You really aren't judging me."

Jane said, "Of course not."

Pia relaxed and confessed to them, "I am seeing him. I realize I'm messing up, but I love him so much it hurts." She looked to each of them as she added, "The real ache comes from wanting him all the time. Just thinking about it makes me…."

She exhaled audibly and ran her palms along her thighs.

Annie threw her hands up and turned quite pink herself.

"Okay, I know we asked, but that's really more information than we were looking for." Then she smiled, shifted in her seat and shook her head. "*God*, Pia."

Pia felt contrite then, lifting her brow and biting her lip.

Annie continued to shake her head while Jane rubbed Pia's back again and asked, "Are you going to be alright, my friend?"

With that, Pia felt the support and love they were trying to convey. Tears of gratitude moistened her eyes.

"I'm sorry, Pia. I didn't mean to upset you,' said Annie, distressed.

Pia shook her head. "I'm not sad, I'm grateful. I'm so lucky to have friends like you. You're both such remarkable people. You're the best."

Annie scowled, pointed a finger at Pia and said sternly, "And don't you forget it!"

Pia smiled at that and got up from her seat. She gave them each a strong hug.

"Thanks, guys. I'll try to stop but I can't make you any promises," she said as she opened the door to leave. "Oh, and please don't feel like you have to lie for me or cover this up. I wouldn't want that."

She figured they would want to do some sort of post-mortem together so she shut the door behind her. While Pia was feeling tremendously loved, she also felt like a failure. Downstairs she quickly waved good-bye to the secretary and bustled out the door.

Right about the time Pia meant to leave on Saturday, Jeremy called to say he was behind schedule and wouldn't be ready until one o'clock. Pia drove to his address to picked him up since he was entirely unfamiliar with the neighborhood they were going to and her car was full of supplies for the event.

After she found a parking spot within three blocks of his address she ascended the outside steps and went into the old building's foyer. She scrutinized the apartment numbers by the mailboxes and pressed the button for Jeremy's apartment, kicking some restaurant flyers into a corner. After a minute she heard the obnoxiously loud buzzer indicating the interior door was unlocking for her.

"Move it before I lock again," it seemed to threaten. She hadn't heard that since she had lived in the city herself many years ago.

Jeremy was at his door when she reached the landing of the interior stairs, with his hands on the door frame and swinging his torso forward.

"Happy New Year!" Jeremy said before they exchanged a long kiss. "I'm almost ready, come on in!"

Pia followed his bare feet inside. Jeremy closed the door behind her, moved a pair of boots out of the way and then bounded down the hall. She hovered in the living room. Jeremy moved with energy, bouncing from place to place. Pia wondered to herself how much coffee he drank. The shades were pulled to almost the bottom of the windows. Pia heard a television or computer in one of the bedrooms behind a closed door. The apartment smelled of recently baked food. It was more cluttered than the last time she visited, but still not too bad. There was a big potted poinsettia on a side table looking all dried out. Pia couldn't resist the temptation to water it so she went to the kitchen and returned with a full glass.

Jeremy came back with shoes on, wearing his hat and pulling on his coat, saying, "I thought you were following me to my —" He stopped, watched her as she watered the plant and grinned. "Thank you, from the poinsettia!"

He took the glass from Pia and was about to set it on the coffee table when she said, "It smells good in here, like someone baked."

Jeremy explained, "I made a coffee cake. Would you like to try a piece?"

"Sure!" she said with surprise.

Jeremy brought the glass and Pia back to the kitchen. The bowls, spatulas and other baking accessories had been washed and were drying upside down on a dish towel. The counters were clean. The coffee cake was in a pan covered with foil on the kitchen table. Jeremy brought it to the counter and cut a slice for each of them, and they ate it standing by the sink.

"What do you think?" He filled the glass again with water from the tap.

"This is delicious! Do you bake often?"

Jeremy drank some of the water and slid the glass towards Pia.

"I usually make something on the weekend if I have time. I think I'll make zucchini bread next weekend. Adam says this is the third coffee cake in a row, heh."

When Pia's piece was finished she brushed crumbs off her fingers over the sink and helped herself to a long drink of water. Jeremy finished the water and put the glass in the sink, then took a final bite of his food. He covered the coffee cake back up with its foil.

"That was nice. Thanks." Pia loved baked goods.

"It will be devoured before I get back. Okay, we'd better get going."

Once they were on the staircase Pia said, "Thanks for coming along for this. I hope you like it." Their feet caused a slight echo tapping down the stairs together.

"Hey, we'll see! I don't know what to expect. What exactly is a 'town hall' held by a non-governing group?"

Pia smiled and explained, "A community gathering. It's really an opportunity for people to speak their minds about what's been happening and how it affects them. Hopefully we'll recruit new members. We sure could use more help." She opened the passenger door on her car for Jeremy.

"Well, thank you, Pia!" he said with some surprise.

She laughed. "You're welcome; the handle doesn't work."

She went around to her side and got in. Jeremy seemed crammed into the little car. The mileage was fantastic, but the leg room not so much. He didn't complain.

"Your car is so clean. Did you do anything for New Year's Eve?" he asked.

"No. It's not a big deal to me and I can't really stay awake that late. How about you?"

"Yeah, I went to a party with some friends. There were about eighty people crowded into the house. It was a great time!"

"Good."

"I want to go to Times Square next year."

"I did that one year, with my roommate and a friend of ours," Pia recalled. "I'd love to go to First Night somewhere warm, like Florida."

Jeremy said enthusiastically, "First Night originated in Boston, you know."

Pia had to grin. "Yes, that's right."

She could remember the first First Night.

"What's your group called?" Jeremy asked as they drove across town.

"Right now it's 'the New Justice League' but there's a rumor DC Comics is going to challenge the copyright to that."

"They'd probably win."

"Mm-hm. We're thinking about changing it to just 'New Justice.'"

It was about twenty minutes from Jeremy's building to the community college where the group had rented a huge conference space. Jeremy helped Pia get everything out of her car and they lugged it all into the building. It was so unlike their university, very bare bones.

"Oh, I forgot the pens. I was supposed to bring a bunch. I swear I have oatmeal for brains," Pia said.

Putting herself down was a difficult habit to break.

She added, "Oops, there goes my New Year's resolution already."

"To stop saying 'oatmeal'?" Jeremy teased.

That made Pia laugh. "Exactly; it's 'hot cereal.'" She giggled again thinking about it. "You're funny."

Jeremy smiled at her. They brought everything up a flight of stairs and looked around for the room. One of the founders of the group was in the hallway.

"Hi, Pia, how you doing?" Damien greeted Pia. "We're setting up in that room on the left. We're waiting for a few people, though. Zara is picking up Anton and Maria at the train station. If you can help set up the chairs that would be great."

He looked at Jeremy.

"This is Jeremy, a friend of mine. He wanted to help out today."

They shook hands.

"Good to meet you. Sure, we can use all the help we can get. We're hoping to have at least two hundred people attending, but you never know. Four hundred would be a great problem to have."

Damien took some of the supplies and walked them into the room to explain the set up. Then he went off to a corner and made some phone calls.

Pia and Jeremy arranged the tables for a speaker panel at the front, covered them with tablecloths, re-arranged the chairs so that they were all facing the panel, and set up food tables in the back. Some other people were setting up the sound system then joined them on chair duty. The group was primarily Black, but included a kind old Indian woman, a few Latino people and some white people. Some were veterans of the civil rights movement in the 1960s. Pia introduced Jeremy around to everyone as they interacted.

Finally, some appetizers and beverages were laid out and the panelists were ready. Pia, Jeremy and some others posted signs along the route from the parking lot to the room so people would know they were at the right place. Jeremy was catching the enthusiasm of the group as their mutual work energized them all. Everyone was excited about the event. Slowly, people from the community began to fill the room. The group had a table outside the room for greeting people, asking them to join their e-mail list and requesting that they sign a petition about a pending case.

Pia explained a little about the process to Jeremy.

"Because this event is an opportunity for people to voice their concerns and tell their stories, we don't want any police listening. It would erode the trust we've been slowly building here. The people manning this table will turn away anyone who looks, well, like a cop."

"Why don't the neighborhood people trust your group?"

Pia paused before she replied. This was a nuanced issue.

"Some other community groups have a problem with this group because it includes white people. Damien loses some credibility because of it. We're perceived as joining the fight for philosophical reasons, on principle."

"Sure. What's wrong with that?"

"Black people are in this fight because it directly involves them. I could be a Jewish lesbian who works at an abortion clinic but people wouldn't know any of that from looking at me, necessarily. If you're Black, racist people can see that. Then too, I'll get back in my car later and resume my privileged life. I can go wherever I want. For them, there's prejudice."

Jeremy replied, "Huh. I know there's some racism but is it really as prevalent as you're making it sound?"

Pia lowered her voice to say, "Last year I attended a round table discussion on this at our school. The Black students all said they're called 'n*****' every day."

Jeremy flinched at the ugly word.

She continued, "I want to help, but I'll never know what it's like to be in their shoes. You'll begin to understand it when people get up to the mic and talk. It's been quite an education for me."

Loudly Damien called out with the mic in one hand and the agenda in the other, "Hey hey, what up? Mic check! Alright, welcome!"

His posture indicated he was totally comfortable with a microphone and an audience, and he smiled broadly.

Everyone quieted down. Damien thanked everybody for coming, although there was a steady stream of people still coming in and looking for seats. He explained who he was and what the group's goals were. Then he introduced the five Black panelists. There was a lawyer from the American Civil Liberties Union, a professor of sociology from Harvard, a local activist and community leader with a 'history' who turned her life around, someone representing ex-prisoners, and the director of the neighborhood outreach organization run by the city.

Damien detailed how a police officer in Louisiana had recently killed Sharelle Jackson in her home, while she was brandishing only her sick three-year-old son, no weapon. Rumor had it that the boy had projectile-vomited on the cop, which set the cop off. Of course, no one knew what really happened. There were over a hundred and fifty people gathered in the room, and every one of them was familiar with this news. Damien then reminded them that after the town hall there would be a walking vigil from here down to the police headquarters. Pia kept looking to Jeremy to see how he was handling all of this. He was keenly attentive to everything. Damien ended by reminding everyone that they could speak at the microphone after the panelists wrapped up, but to please try to keep it to two minutes per person.

Each of the panelists had something valuable and different to say. They all garnered respect because of the work they did. Some of them had useful information about handling various situations for a better outcome. Others beautifully articulated so many of the things people felt and the issues they faced, as the audience responded with encouragement and agreement, until the room began to feel like one giant heart beating. Pia was profoundly touched by this.

Jeremy and Pia helped set up lunch for the break, and after the speakers and audience were fed, the organizers ate. Jeremy and Pia sat at a table in the back with three old Black men. It was good to sit down. The men told them about the union they were in. When they were going out for a cigarette break, they slowly lifted out of their seats and one told Jeremy and Pia to "be safe, be safe".

Jeremy directed his attention to Pia.

"You work so hard. Do you ever just relax and hang out?"

"Oh, sure. I read, go for walks and hikes. Gordon and I go on short trips to the ocean or New Hampshire, Vermont. But for me, working towards goals with people is a great way to spend my time. A reason to get up in the morning, I suppose. Do you consider baking work or something you enjoy?"

"Hmm…it's work I enjoy because it's creative. So I guess I would consider it relaxing."

He looked around at all the people. Some of the volunteers were picking up plates and cups off the tables. A thought occurred to him.

"Oh, I should've brought my camera! I could've documented the event for your group."

"Thanks, Jeremy, that's very kind of you to offer," Pia said, pleased. "Maybe for the MLK day march coming up? We had press from three papers here earlier. Now no cameras are permitted and hopefully no one records anything with their phones."

"Why?"

"Because people are going to talk openly about how police treat them. That takes some courage and the aforementioned trust."

They locked eyes for a bit.

Jeremy's head bobbled slightly as he asked, "How do you know all this?"

"I've been learning it for the past seven months. I had absolutely no clue before." Then Pia said more softly, "Just wait 'til you hear what they have to say."

It was a pain to bear, just listening. Pia couldn't imagine being subjected to this inequity.

Damien returned to the microphone at the front of the room. He took it out of the stand and walked with it as people settled in for the second portion of the program. The panelists remained in case anyone directed questions to them. Jeremy and Pia sat down in the audience.

Damien announced, "Thank you all again for coming today. We're going to begin giving folks a chance to speak momentarily. I want to stress that we want everyone to feel comfortable talking. So in that spirit, I request that no one videotape, record, or photograph anything that transpires in this room." He let that sink in as he glanced around the audience before continuing, "Additionally, if you are a current or past member of any police force, or if you are now, or have ever been, a corrections officer, we ask that you respectfully leave this space immediately."

Again Damien paused with the microphone by his side. Three people stood up and walked out: a Black man, a Black woman, and a Latino man. Jeremy looked at Pia with great surprise. She had seen this before. Some people had already lined up at the mic stand and Zara was keeping order there. Damien brought the microphone over and set it in its stand and then sat near the panelists.

The first person to speak was an old man propped up with a cane.

"We got to see some change. I been in this fight since the bussing, and ain't been no real change yet. It touch my heart seeing so many young brothers here. We gonna need everybody. I'm getting too old for it really, but what else you gonna do? This killing business got to stop! It give me hope to see some white people here, too. I jes' about give up on y'all. But you here now. God bless."

Behind him was a woman of about fifty, well-dressed, with great hair. She was fiery.

"Let me tell you a story. One day two years ago, there was an officer on the street outside a CVS. I'm not sure what was going on but he was out of his patrol car and addressing four children. They weren't older than maybe ten or eleven. I went up to him and I asked him a question he couldn't answer. All I did was *ask* him a *question*."

A young man seated near her side interrupted with, "Was it 'Do you know who your daddy is?'" People laughed.

The woman appreciated the humor but continued. "He said 'shut up, bitch, I'm gonna arrest you.' That's exactly what he said and how he spoke to me. I said, 'What are you going to arrest me on? What's the charge? I only asked you a question.' He said he was going to arrest me for assaulting an officer. I was like, 'What? I didn't touch you.' His partner came over and said he was going to be the witness. I told him, 'That's ridiculous because I didn't touch him.'"

She paused, and when she continued she was considerably subdued.

"The first one hit me and I fell to the ground. His partner kicked me and they pulled my arms back and handcuffed me. They really did arrest me. I'm still trying to undo the charges and in the meantime that's on my record. It's cost me hundreds of dollars and I've missed a lot of work for court appearances. I'm telling you, as God is my witness, I did not do *anything* wrong and I certainly didn't break any laws."

Jeremy looked incredulous; Pia was solemn and looked to the floor. Around the room were murmurs of support. The woman sat down and a lanky man possibly in his thirties stood up to the mic.

"I got a history, you know. So I used to get beat on by the cops routinely. They got to know me by name; they'd holler, 'Hey Jerry' then come over and kick my ass, pardon the language. When I was a teenager I used to do some bad shit, sorry for the language, and I deserved what I got but—"

He was interrupted by Zara, who moved in front of the microphone. Her temper flared a bit.

"*Excuse* me. Regardless of what you did, you did *not* deserve to be *beat up* by the police!"

Then she gave the floor back to him. Lots of folks were snapping their fingers in support of Zara's point. It was like clapping but less disruptive.

Jerry gave her a crooked grin. "Well maybe not, but it happened all the time. I got no love for them, that's for sure. I just want to say I support what you all are doing and keep up the struggle. Much love!" He raised his fist in the air before he finished.

Another man was next. He was tall and slender and a bit effeminate. At this point half the room was in line for the mic, so the audience was thinning out. But everyone was listening.

"I moved to Boston from Detroit a year ago because I thought it would be safer for me here. It turns out I'm probably wrong about that. Where I'm from I was almost killed by the cops. I was at a nursing home visiting my grandmother, and when she's not taking her meds she gets kind of crazy. We were out front of the building so she could sneak a cigarette and a nurse, or an aide rather, told her to put it out. So Gram gets all crazy on her and I was trying to calm her down. Next thing I know, there's two cops beating me with their clubs. They maced my face and then they started tazing me. They only had to taze me once, y'know what I'm saying? But, no, they tazed me like thirty times. I was just trying to help someone; I wasn't doing anything bad. I wasn't breaking a law and I wasn't hurting anyone. They almost killed me, man. I was in the hospital for three weeks. You know, they wonder why some Black men run when they see cops coming. They nearly killed me, so I'm afraid of them. Thank you."

He respectfully stepped back from the mic for the next person. A wiry young Black man began speaking next.

"Yeah, so, what you're doing is righteous, but how do I know that some of these white people aren't in the KKK? Or maybe they're cool, but they have relatives who want us dead, you know? Just saying we don't know who to trust, right?" He paused before concluding, "That's all I got."

A middle-aged Latino man took his turn speaking. As his story began to unfold, he was transported back to the event and his eyes looked far away, back in time. Gradually his hands began folding over each other repeatedly. Pia thought he might be mentally challenged.

"Once when I was about twelve or thirteen, I was hanging out in the playground across the street from my house. The cops come around because there's a lot of gangster activity and drugs going on there. So they come around one afternoon and there was some kids in the park, but I wasn't near them, and this cop says to me, 'Ritchie, we gonna arrest you for selling drugs' and I says, 'I ain't selling no drugs' and he says, 'you know there's drug deals in this park all day long,' and I says, 'I know but I don't do them or sell them. I'm just a kid.' He says he's gonna arrest me anyway, so I says, 'I live right across the street, you know I do. That's my house right there' and I point to it. Just then Ma come out and asked them why they're bothering me. She yelled across the street to them that I ain't doing nothing. Then they left me alone. If Ma was working at the store that day, I don't know what woulda happened to me."

Then he slowly returned his mind to the town hall.

"Thank you for listening."

He sat down, still wringing his hands.

Pia thought the police might have been cruelly teasing Ritchie and it obviously left an emotional scar on him. Jeremy looked like this was beginning to take a toll. Pia rested her hand on his knee and he looked at her appreciatively.

She moved her hand to Jeremy's back as she whispered in his ear, "Let me know whenever you want to go."

She looked in his eyes questioningly while she put her hand back on his knee. Jeremy nodded once and took her hand. Then he turned his attention back to the person at the mic.

Next was a heavy woman with two boys fidgeting beside her.

To them she said, "Go sit *down!*"

She didn't notice that the boys had no idea where they should sit. They reluctantly sat together where they found empty seats near her.

She began with an observation. "If y'all had put on your flyers that there was day care you would have way more people here."

The group didn't think about that until it was too late to arrange it. They understood she was right on that point.

"Anyway, I'll tell you something that happened to me a few months ago. My neighbor in the projects called the cops on me 'cause she heard yelling and screaming. That's me, I turn up the volume sometimes, I'm sorry to say. Then two cops knocked on my door. I looked through the hole in the door, and I saw they were city police. I knew something wasn't right, so I called the station. I told the dispatcher that there were two city cops at my door and shouldn't there be housing police instead, 'cause it's their jurisdiction. She asked me if I could see their badges, so I looked in the peephole again and I told her who they were. Meanwhile they're still knocking and telling me to open up. She said their shift ended ten minutes ago, that right then there were other cops on duty. She told me 'do *not* open your door; I'll have them called back.' I don't know what those two had in mind, but I didn't want no part of it."

She wanted to say more but Zara told her she had used her time up.

Jeremy indicated to Pia that he wanted to leave his seat. The two of them went into the hallway and around a corner. Jeremy was looking overwhelmed.

Pia didn't want to keep him there any longer than he wished. "We can leave now if you want to."

"No. I'm okay. I just had to take a break, though. It's a lot to take in at once, you know?"

"Sure, I understand. We can go sit downstairs."

The town hall went on for another hour or so. Everyone had an experience of ill treatment. None of it was justified legally or morally. The overarching message was that the police in their neighborhoods are terrorists in the eyes of the community. When it wrapped up, quite a few people stood around waiting for Pia, Jeremy, Anton and Maria to get all the candles ready for the vigil. Pia had made holes in paper cups the day before so the candles would have the cups blocking the breeze. They handed them out as quickly as they could just inside the main entrance. Soon other volunteers took over for them. Pia didn't think of bringing more than one lighter, but several others were procured from the crowd to help move things along.

Pia waved to the man who'd been tazed.

"Hey, Aaron!"

Jeremy was confused. "You know him? Was this all contrived?"

"Not at all. Everyone else at the mic was spontaneous and we don't know them. Aaron joined our group a few months ago." Pia leaned in close to Jeremy and continued more quietly in his ear, "He always tells his story now, at every action we hold. I think it helps him heal."

Aaron came directly over to them.

"Hi, Pia!" He gave her a solid hug.

"Aaron, this is my friend Jeremy."

Jeremy said genuinely, "I'm really sorry for what you went through. That sounded so terrible."

Aaron replied, "Thanks. I took them to court but in the end we settled. It was a learning experience. The whole system is corrupt, believe me. The defense lawyer and the judge use hand signals in the courtroom."

Jeremy couldn't conceal his surprise at that.

Aaron continued, "For real. That's why the prosecutor's table is behind the defense's. They aren't side by side, like on television. Pia, do you have the posters?"

Pia pulled out the stack from behind her where they were leaning against a wall.

"Yep, right here."

Aaron hoisted them from her.

"Thanks."

Aaron quickly flipped through them to see what she had done.

"These look great! Did you make one that says 'Yo, don't taze me, bro'?"

They all laughed. Jeremy seemed relieved that Aaron could joke about it.

Pia responded somberly, "Then they might decide to shoot you."

"But you've got my back." Aaron smiled and gave her another hug.

"Thank you for helping out, man," he said to Jeremy and shook his hand, locking fingers and leaning in with a quick shoulder pat.

Then Aaron disappeared into the crowd to hand out the posters after leaving one with Jeremy.

"He's working on his master's degree in education now. How are you doing? Do you want to walk in the vigil, or just head out now?" Pia asked, but then their conversation was interrupted.

"Heyyy, Pia! Good to see you! I couldn't get out of work sooner. Do you need help with anything?"

Another founder of the group was hugging Pia and smiling and talking simultaneously. She was a ray of sunshine, and a great speaker who worked so hard for this cause.

"Hi, Janet! I think we're almost ready. You might want to check with Damien. He's in that corner." Janet

moved in that direction, and Pia focused her attention back on Jeremy. He was smiling.

"This is really cool! Everyone's so friendly. I definitely want to stay for the vigil."

The two of them went back into the room upstairs to clean up although most of that had already been done. They packed up what they'd carried in except for the candles and posters which Pia could collect after the vigil. Jeremy found and ate several slices of cold pizza. While he ate leaning against a wall, he watched Pia make a few trips from the room down the hall to the stairway.

"I really like the way you walk," he told her after he swallowed the last of a slice.

"The way I *walk*?"

"Yeah. You walk very purposefully. With a slight swing in the hips. It's very sexy," Jeremy said, smiling. His head bobbled a bit. "I so love your hips."

Pia knew what Jeremy liked most about her hips and it wasn't her walk. She shook her head and waved her hand at him, saying, "You crack me up."

They loaded everything in Pia's car and then joined the group on the sidewalk. Almost immediately people began the march down the street, with the lighted candles bobbing and flickering in the darkness throughout the crowd. Unfortunately, Pia didn't have enough for everyone. There were about ninety people and Pia had only brought seventy candles.

"That college is so different from ours." Jeremy said. "I don't know if I believe what Aaron said about the courtroom."

"I've been to some hearings for a local victim and the physical layout wasn't like he described in his courtroom, but I believe him. Can't speak on the corruption, but I don't doubt it," Pia said as she walked. "The case we're working on right now is for this woman who's in jail pending a hearing because she hit a cop with a ruler. The very same weapon wielded by Catholic nuns with impunity for decades."

Jeremy looked at her rather strangely. Over the chanting around them she asked, "What? Are you alright?"

She didn't know what else to do but continuously take his emotional pulse.

"This seems like a different you than the one at the nature sanctuary and at school, that's all. People who hit cops with anything, even rulers, are going to get in trouble for it."

"I suppose you're right. But she's mentally challenged and she's been in a cell for four months, waiting to find out if the charges will be sustained or dismissed. What's the point in having the charges dismissed after spending all that time in jail? She's lost her Burger King job and her apartment."

Now Jeremy could see the connection to the Pia he knew. She sympathized with the person suffering the unfortunate consequences.

She continued, "Anyway, I promise I'm not militant or extremist or anything. I got involved with this cause because of people like Eric Garner, Rakia Boyd and Tamir Rice. To me there's clearly a huge problem that I cannot in good conscience ignore. This is otherwise not how I would want to spend my time. I have a low tolerance for injustice."

"Okay," Jeremy said. Then he smiled, picking up on something she'd said and connecting it to one of their earlier conversations. "Hey, you promised me just now."

Damien used a bullhorn to let spectators know who the vigil was for and who the organizers were. In no time at all, the group was flanked by police cruisers. Damien had obtained a permit, so the police attention was under the auspices of escorting the group to clear the road of cars for them. The marchers were getting louder and bolder, energized by one other.

"It's kind of nerve-wracking to be surrounded by police when you're holding a sign calling for an end to racist policing," Jeremy said somewhat tensely.

He kept his sign up in the air, though. Pia didn't consider them 'surrounded' by any stretch, but she was accustomed to this and Jeremy was not.

"This is my tenth action with this group and nothing's happened yet. We have a permit so the police are only an escort. I think the new mayor directed the police to be very passive. No one wants the bad press. Let's switch. Here, you take the candle."

Jeremy handed Pia his poster and cradled the candle's flame as he took it from her since the paper cup had burned away.

"Is there a plan if things get violent?"

Pia realized she had to increase her assurances, but she was growing a little weary of it. She retracted her idea of Jeremy having courage. She wanted to tell him, "*My* plan is to stand between the cops and the Black people."

Instead she said soothingly, "Our group is peaceful. It's a vigil, not a rally, so the mood is more solemn than angry. Believe me Jeremy, if I thought there was a reasonable chance of violence tonight I would not have let you come along."

She remembered his trip to the university rooftop and what might have happened.

"Would you still participate if you thought there was a good chance it could get dangerous?" Jeremy asked.

"Absolutely. This isn't about my welfare. We have some volunteer legal witnesses from the ACLU, one in front and one in the rear. See the man in the blue pea coat near Damien? He was on the panel. They wear tags identifying themselves as such, so the police are probably aware of them. There are two street medics as well; they have red armbands and red crosses on their backpacks. There's one over there. Oh, and I'm a first responder and so is Zara."

Jeremy was considerably calmed by that news, saying, "You really know what you're doing. I'm impressed."

Pia responded, "Damien and the other leaders have been at this for a while. They're inspirational."

They continued the remaining blocks with everyone around them chanting. Lots of people came out of their homes and hung out windows to see what the commotion was. As always happened, members of the community spontaneously supported, and in some cases joined the group. One older, heavy man standing on his stoop asked for a candle in Sharelle's memory, so Jeremy ran up the steps with his own to give. Pia was distracted and didn't see this. She kept moving with the crowd.

A few minutes later, Janet approached her with Jeremy in tow.

"I found your young friend and I might just keep him," Janet teased.

"No, sorry. You're a goddess and I love you but he's mine," Pia joked back.

"Please don't fight over me, ladies."

Jeremy stayed between them as best he could. The sidewalks weren't cleared in this neighborhood so it was narrow and sloppy going. Some of the participants spread into the street because of that. Before long the sidewalk was completely clear of snow because they had reached their destination, the police station. Damien ended the vigil by leading everyone in a simple yet powerful way.

Into the bullhorn he said, "This is for Sharelle Jackson. We must not forget her. Say her name."

Members of the New Justice League were sprinkled throughout the crowd and responded, "Sharelle Jackson."

Damien repeated with his head down solemnly, "Say her name."

Approximately ninety people called back, "Sharelle Jackson."

The people with candles raised them higher.

"Say her name."

"*Sharelle Jackson.*"

Damien concluded the vigil by thanking the participants. People dispersed immediately. There was a subway station across the street and a bus line nearby so the crowd disappeared like water down a drain. Pia held out a bag to collect the candles from people who didn't want them anymore. It was six-thirty.

"So, that's that," Pia said to Jeremy as they began their walk back to the community college.

Others from the organization walked with them since they were heading back to their cars. Jeremy offered to carry a rolled-up banner. He kept it over his shoulder like a bayonet, with the extended end up high. Everyone was evaluating the strengths and weaknesses of the day's events and their spirits were high.

As the uneven pockets of snow under their feet slowed their progress considerably, Jeremy noted, "The snow isn't shoveled here but it was outside of the police station, on that block…."

He thought he was speaking only to Pia.

Damien overheard Jeremy and looked back at him briefly as they continued walking, adding, "Right? Funny thing about that! This is the main road too, not a side street."

Zara said, "The buttons at the crosswalks don't work either, so don't even bother."

She had an edge to her voice whereas Damien had sounded glad that Jeremy noticed the inequity. Pia recognized that Zara wasn't angry with Jeremy; she was disgusted with the status quo.

"Oh, I took photos of a bunch of intersections that don't have them at all," Pia said, remembering the little project she had spontaneously taken on a few weeks prior. "I sent them to the mayor three weeks ago. I'll try to follow up soon."

"Really?" Zara and Jeremy said at the same time.

"Yeah. I don't think I'll get anywhere but I'll keep emailing him about it," Pia said as she watched her footing.

"All right! Pia's *on* it!" Zara was pumped again.

"Well, they put all the money into the commercial areas of the city and don't do much for these residential neighborhoods," Pia said.

Damien concurred. "Exactly right."

Downtown and the wealthy neighborhoods were maintained. To Pia it certainly seemed that the Black neighborhoods were being deliberately neglected. Many Black people had told her that they had the distinct impression that white society considered them worthless. The community activists and parents constantly struggled to keep that sense from affecting the children and perpetually instilled their own pride in who they were.

Once they were back at the school everyone said goodnight and parted ways. Jeremy and Pia collapsed into her car's seats and rested for a bit. It had been an eventful and emotional afternoon, and it was good to sit down and just be with one another.

Chapter 15

Jeremy had a plan.

"My friend gave me the key to her studio apartment while she's away. Would you have any interest in going there with me?"

Pia rolled her head to the right and looked at him.

"Why, certainly. That would be lovely."

She started the car and pulled away from the curb.

"Great! If you can get us back on Mass Ave. I can show you the rest of the way. Oh, that reminds me: she's Indian, so I asked her about the handstands. She said in India they do headstands. They have tons of health benefits!"

"Ah. I'll try that."

In about fifteen minutes they were on the outskirts of the city, in a residential neighborhood behind a major street. Jeremy's friend lived in a tiny attic studio apartment over a one-family house. The homes were packed in tightly, but they were old and well-built, with little details that newer houses lacked. Jeremy led Pia to the rear of the property through the light and shadows cast from a streetlamp in the front. There was a staircase built onto the back of the house. He had no problem finding his way and unlocked the door easily.

Once inside, he reached for the light switch to the right of the door and took off his coat and hat. He hung them off the back of a kitchen chair. Pia noted on a subconscious level that Jeremy was quite familiar with the place. She pulled her work boots off and left them by the entry on the tile floor since they had crud all over them. When Jeremy noticed her do that, he did the same.

"Good thinking," he said.

The apartment included a little entryway with pegs along the wall, a small kitchen with a table and two chairs, a larger, main room containing a bed, loveseat and two night tables and, out of Pia's line of vision, a bathroom. She had lived in a studio for one year when she was a student. It had been claustrophobic and lonely.

"Can I get you anything? Something to drink? I think she just has juice." Jeremy looked in the refrigerator. "Yeah, orange juice and Mountain Dew."

As Pia slung her coat over the other chair she saw a snapshot on the refrigerator of Jeremy and a young Indian woman smiling together. Probably a selfie she took. There were other photos of her with more friends.

"No, I'm fine, thanks."

Pia walked into the main room and looked around. She pointed to a photograph on a wall. She had seen it before. It had hung in the café at the university almost two years ago and it was on Jeremy's website.

"That's one of yours, isn't it?"

"Yes, it is. I'm going to use the bathroom. Back shortly!"

Jeremy kissed her and went into the room on the other side of the kitchen wall. Pia continued to look around while she listened to Jeremy empty his bladder. She felt odd about using a friend of Jeremy's bed. She asked herself if it made a difference to her that the friend was a woman. It seemed to, but rationally it shouldn't.

Apparently Jeremy had an idea while he was in the bathroom. When he opened the door, he was grinning mischievously.

"Want to take a shower together?"

He went over to Pia and rested his hands on her rear so their pelvises neatly collided.

Pia looked at him dreamily as she looped her arms around his neck. She tucked his hair behind his ears.

"Before or after…?"

Jeremy wrapped his arms around her, considered the options, and then suggested, "During?"

His hands settled on her rear again.

Well, that solved the conundrum about the other woman's bed. They took off their clothes in the main room. Pia followed him into the bathroom. It didn't have a tub, but it had a good-sized shower stall and an enormous mirror over the sink. Jeremy's friend had some fancy soaps and lotions on the sink, a hand towel and a Waterpik machine for her teeth.

Jeremy let the water run until it was hot enough. Pia liked hers extremely hot, more than Jeremy could stand, so they decided to keep the door closed so she would be warm with the lower temperature. Jeremy stepped under the showerhead first and Pia drew the curtain. They took turns under the force of the water. They caressed each other and kissed. Then they soaped one another's hair and bodies.

"We're having good, clean fun, huh?" Jeremy said at one point.

Bubbles were all over their faces and they were happy to be relaxing after the day's activities. They turned in place a few times to rinse, still kissing as much as they could.

Pia thought that the space was wonderfully intimate, but she couldn't really conceptualize how they could make love in the stall, despite their otherwise constant contact. She kissed all over Jeremy's torso, and moved down his line of hair leading from the navel to the pubic area. Pia loved that area on Jeremy; his smooth, taut belly with the hair down the center. Pia crouched and slid his aroused penis into her mouth.

He rested his hands on her head, checking with her, "Is that alright?"

She nodded and vocalized, "Mm-hm."

Jeremy's hands pressed her head to him more firmly. He checked once more.

"You sure about this?"

Pia nodded again and was more deliberate with her actions. She couldn't get over how polite he was. Jeremy let himself enjoy it fully then. After they had finished, Pia stood up and Jeremy stepped aside so she could cup her hands to collect water to slosh in her mouth. Jeremy soaped himself there again and rinsed. After that, he held her face in his hands to meet his eyes. Pia smiled at him and they kissed. He turned off the water.

Pia wrung her hair as she stepped out first into the fog. She reached for the only towel, plush and extra-large burgundy. Jeremy followed and helped wrap Pia in it while hugging her, so they were both benefitting from it. Jeremy was facing the wall with the towel rack and a small, framed painting of an exotic city, and Pia was facing the mirror, while Jeremy was playfully trying to dry her hair with a corner of the towel.

Pia glanced up at the mirror and she caught her breath. She stopped moving and her smile eroded. For a few seconds Jeremy didn't know what the problem was so he tipped his head to Pia's face, which was still staring at the mirror.

Still holding the towel wrapped around Pia, Jeremy bit his lip while he turned to look at the mirror with her. The two of them were barely visible, like ghosts in the mist covering the glass. Jeremy opened the door part way and then he brought that hand to Pia's head, petting it gently. The only part that was clear was something that had been put there after a previous shower. On the mirror someone had drawn with their finger a big heart with an arrow, and in the heart was written 'Jeremy loves Ishra.' And within it was the reflection of Jeremy and Pia, wet and nude, becoming clearer as the vapor rolled around and out the door. Increasingly the moisture began to drip from the writing, making it look as if the heart was crying.

"Imagine that," she thought to herself.

Eventually Pia lowered her gaze, tugged the towel out of Jeremy's hands and went into the main space where she began drying herself in earnest. She didn't do a very thorough job before she started getting dressed, so her panties and bra gave her trouble when she tried to get them on. She was frustrated by that and struggled with them a little while she shivered.

"This is not my finest moment," she thought.

"Pia."

Jeremy picked the towel up off the floor and dried his hair a bit, wiped himself down, and then wrapped it around his waist.

Pia continued dressing silently. She was nearly hyperventilating but hoped that wasn't obvious. She kept her back to him.

"Pia, let me explain."

"Wow, that was classic," she thought. Pia said quietly, "Sure, explain," while she kept dressing without looking at him.

She felt like an idiot; all this time he'd been referring to her as his 'friend' rather than his 'lover' she'd assumed was due to her wedding ring. She was grateful her wet hair shrouded her face. She wondered what Ishra would think of this.

Jeremy sighed and came around to face her.

Very tenderly he said, "Hey, come here. Come here."

His gentle manner made her want to collapse into his arms, but he was the one who hurt her. She made no move towards him.

"So, I'm in a relationship with Ishra," Jeremy explained. "I probably should've told you that at the start. There just hasn't been an opportunity where it made sense. I was going to tell you when we were in my bed, when you talked about the word 'exclusive', but then Adam came home."

"Uh-huh."

As far as Pia could tell they weren't making any progress.

Jeremy took a seat on the edge of Ishra's bed and continued.

"Pia, you and I…we aren't exclusive. I'm seeing Paco as well. I'm not sure how much of this is a surprise to you or how much you already understood."

Pia was still numb and silent. She sat in the upholstered loveseat near the bed to put on her socks.

"This is not that uncommon with my generation. Paco knows about you both and he's fine with it. Well, he thinks you're not my type. Ishra knows about Paco and you, I think. I'm not sure." That seemed to be an aside. "For a while I was with Ning, too, but that ended before you came along. Partly I didn't tell you because when I'm with you that's what I'm focused on, not other people. We…well, things just started to happen with us." He motioned to Pia and back to himself. "I thought you wanted to be with me and so here we are."

"Stop. Please just stop."

Pia looked right at Jeremy wearily. Was he suggesting that this was Pia's doing? Perhaps it was. She felt completely exhausted. Finally she took a deep breath and released it slowly.

"Ning, Paco, Ishra. You've slept with half the United Nations."

"Heh, I guess."

Jeremy looked at Pia with hope in his face, as if her humor meant she was going to be fine with this news. In fact, she was completely distraught about it. She was just in shock.

She ran a hand through her hair. Soon it would dry on its own.

"Paco?"

"Yeah, we've been together a few years. Again, not exclusively though. Pia, we've talked about our orientation; you know I'm bisexual. If I understood correctly, you are too."

Pia had understood that intellectually but the reality of it felt bizarre. She also envied his level of self-knowledge. She nodded her affirmation about their both being bisexual and recalled the last time she saw Paco. It was in her office, the day after she and Jeremy went to the hotel.

She thought aloud, "That's why Paco doesn't like me."

Jeremy said, "I wouldn't say he dislikes you, it's just…."

Pia couldn't care less what Paco thought of her, she was only stitching pieces together.

"At the hotel in the lobby…I saw someone, a woman. Paco?"

She wasn't looking at Jeremy, her eyes were on the area rug's elaborate pattern.

"Yeah, that was him. Sometimes he cross-dresses," Jeremy said straightforwardly.

Still in a tired tone Pia slowly asked, "You're telling me that he was waiting for me to leave so he could go up to our room?"

"Um, yeah. My room. See, I texted him when I thought you were leaving me around eight-thirty. I didn't want to spend the night alone in a hotel room. He had already asked me earlier in the day if I was going to be around. So I let him know I was…all by myself."

Pia raised her voice a little.

"What if I had decided to stay overnight with you?"

Jeremy was confident in his response.

"You can't really do that. Your situation doesn't allow for it."

He was considerably more astute than Pia had realized.

"You slept with Paco after me?"

Jeremy nodded.

That was disturbing news to her.

"I can't believe this. Why didn't you tell me?" Pia got up and began pacing. "Why are you even seeing me?"

"I told you already: I thought you wanted to be with me and I wanted that, too. I still do."

He was right on that point. Pia didn't realize how obvious she had been. She understood then that she hadn't been giving Jeremy enough credit.

"How can you see several people at the same time?" Pia was still pacing. "Doesn't that get confusing for you?"

Without answering her directly, Jeremy said gently, "Pia, take it easy. It's alright. There's nothing wrong."

"There *is* something wrong. Hello, you're seeing someone else!" Pia's tone was becoming mean.

"You're seeing someone else, too."

"What are you talking about?"

"Gordon, your husband. Remember him? You're having an affair, Pia. You can't judge me for seeing several people at the same time. You are married to Gordon and involved with me."

They had never discussed the potential effect of their relationship on Gordon and Pia had assumed that Jeremy hadn't been considering him in the equation at all. She realized then that of course he had. Of course.

Her defense of her position was weakening and her volume came down.

"You said you loved me."

Very sincerely Jeremy said softly, "I do love you."

"Well I'm not the only one, apparently."

Pia regained a little anger because what he told her was incongruous with how he behaved, as far as she was concerned.

Jeremy stayed his course.

"No, you're not the only one. You're one of my lovers. I'm so glad you are. Seeing two or more people doesn't detract from the relationships. It's like having several friends or loving your whole family."

He made it sound like this could work out fine.

Pia was totally lost now.

"Well what is this? What are we doing?" she asked with her hands turned out in a plea for something to make sense.

In his same gentle tone Jeremy told her succinctly, "We're sharing a very special relationship together."

"Are you patronizing me? Are you mocking me or what?" Pia asked miserably.

"Not at all, I'm completely serious. You should know me better than that, Pia. I never lied to you, and I don't believe I misled you in any way. I love you and I care about you. You aren't the only person I love, though. I really don't understand why you're so upset."

"Really? It's not complicated. I thought I was special to you. I thought…."

Everything Jeremy said was logical. She was having a hard time arguing with him, mostly because he wasn't fighting the facts but confirming them rationally. She gave him her diagnosis.

"Jeremy, I'm in love with you. You let me fall in love with you."

Pia was being a bit of a drama queen by putting the responsibility for this on him with that last sentence. On one level, she was aware that her behavior might send him away. She knew Jeremy well enough to know that he wasn't trying to hurt her. He was kind and thoughtful. She was being a beast but she just couldn't stop herself. Many years ago, she and Gordon would fight with all their weapons but they had learned to stop it since it was pointless and hurtful. So it had been a long time since Pia vented like this. It was oddly familiar to her but she knew it was bad.

To his credit, Jeremy got up and tentatively approached Pia to embrace her.

"Can I hold you? I want you to be okay."

He put a hand on her shoulder and caressed it tentatively.

"Do you want to not feel guilty? Is that it?" Pia asked cruelly.

She was feeling like a demon but she couldn't seem to stop herself from saying these things.

Jeremy removed his hand from where it was touching her then, as if it had become burning hot.

Now his voice revealed real annoyance with her.

"I don't feel guilty; I'm not guilty of anything! I haven't done anything wrong! I'm really, really sorry this is hurting you but, honestly, I didn't do anything to you, Pia. You have made this place where you feel wronged."

He went into the kitchen where he could have some space and waited to see if Pia might relent. She was settling down, but slowly. There was no denying everything Jeremy had said. Pia knew she was being ugly and it was making her more insecure. She thought that if he did love her he wouldn't much longer.

After a minute or so she joined him the kitchen to say, "I'm sorry. I shouldn't have lashed out at you. I'm too reactive."

Jeremy was standing, leaning his backside against the counter by the sink.

"I'm not your property. I don't know what else to say, Pia. I'm in over my head here." The last sentence was the only thing Jeremy said about how he was faring. After a heavy sigh he said, "Look, I think it's best if you leave. Can you find your way out of the neighborhood okay?"

Pia was quite surprised her apology had no impact. She had expected it to help smooth things out, but it appeared to have meant nothing to him.

While she put on her coat she said, "You should call Paco."

"I'm picking Ishra up at the airport in a little while."

Pia levelled her eyes at him and snarled, "Good. Maybe you can get another blow job."

Her aim was excellent. Pia had managed to insult all of them by insinuating it was about getting enough sex. Jeremy looked at her with a level of sadness and hurt Pia couldn't recall causing before. She immediately wished she could retract her words but she couldn't; they were out there already, working like venom.

Jeremy took a step towards her and roared, "I *care about* the people I sleep with! There are a lot of assholes in the world, Pia, but *I'm not one of them!* I'm *not* one of them!"

His face was red with anger and a few tears were pooling on the rims of his eyes, held by his long lashes.

Pia was very ashamed of what she'd done and her face reflected her deep remorse. The tenant below knocked on the ceiling with a broom handle: thud, thud, thud.

"*Please* leave," Jeremy pleaded. He rubbed his arms; whether it was from being chilled standing there without a shirt or to comfort himself Pia didn't know…maybe both.

She went out the door quickly with her face down, stirring a concoction of self-pity, heartbreak and anger in her mind. She stomped to her car, kicking at soot-covered snow piles along the way. There was a ticket on her windshield for parking without a residential permit, which she ripped as she grabbed it. "Of course," she thought. She pulled her driver's door open with unnecessary force, and when she went to slam the door shut she didn't lift her foot inside quickly enough so she shut it on her ankle.

"God frickin' damn *shit!*" she cursed in pain.

Pia's spontaneous curses were comical and she loathed them. At least no one had heard her. She made the engine suffer for her misery when she turned it over and pulled out of her spot.

Once she was on the road Pia cried freely in privacy. Snot and tears flooded her face. At a red light she reached for some paper napkins from out of her glove compartment and flushed her nose. Still she cried, but it slowed down to a trickle as she breathed heavily. Pia continued allowing herself to feel that Jeremy had done something bad to her but her subconscious knew better. Partly she was upset with herself as she always seemed to be for her own terrible behavior.

Further, Jeremy's words about Gordon ricocheted around in her mind. She had to own that she was as dishonest as the next person. She was ashamed. She turned on the radio, and when she heard Florence + the Machine singing "did I build this ship to wreck?" she left it on. It was going to be her mantra in the coming weeks.

Pia texted Jeremy the next morning, "I'm sorry."

About four hours later he responded to her.

"Thanks."

That was it. Pia moved through her day in a daze. She kept herself from texting or calling him again, although the impulse was strong. She went into work to get through some of the several hundred emails waiting for her. She tried to focus on them, as they were a good distraction and had to be answered. She made substantial progress since she had no interruptions. There were some grateful responses from professors who were also working.

She meant to stop by the reflective pool for Tao but she ran out of time. She had promised Gordon chicken fajitas. She also had more pressing concerns which, to her regret, diminished the importance of Tao's death.

She was swinging wildly from one feeling to the next. She was sorry for how she handled the news about the other lovers and wanted to be with Jeremy. She longed for him. But then she would remember that they didn't have the relationship she thought they had. The idea that he was sleeping with others he loved made Pia extremely jealous. She simply could not bear this knowledge. She was an emotional wreck.

At home she may or may not have concealed all her feelings. Gordon paid so little attention to her that she could have caught on fire and gone unnoticed. Sometimes she entertained herself by wondering if she should die sitting on the sofa, how long it would be before he realized she was a cadaver beset with rigor mortis.

Flies. Gordon would definitely notice if flies were around the body.

The following day was Monday and it was time to resume normal work hours. Pia took down the 'closed for the break' sign from the door and put the normal response on the main phone line. Everyone had the same conversation they have every year, about the kids and presents and food, and how disappointed they were to have to be back at work. Pia wasn't very talkative. By about four in the afternoon she gave in to her impulse to text Jeremy again.

"Please forgive me. I'm sorry about Saturday."

About nine o'clock that night Jeremy responded, "No worries."

This was similar to the communications Pia would have about once a year with her sister Nancy. To Pia's thinking they were pointless.

She gave the situation a great deal of thought and reviewed all of the events until she was able to reduce it to the key elements. She and Jeremy had been romantically involved only for a few weeks and that had been sporadically. Jeremy wasn't deliberately keeping secrets from her. What he did with the rest of his time was his own business. Pia felt she had been particularly immature when blaming Jeremy for her falling in love with him. Your heart does whatever it wants. Pia could only shake her head at how she had behaved and how much she expected from Jeremy.

All she could do was try a few more times. She couldn't really see them continuing with their relationship if Jeremy viewed her in a new light, but she hoped to at least patch it up. Pia also reprimanded herself for believing that she meant as much to Jeremy as he meant to her. Now it seemed utterly ridiculous that he might fall deeply in love with her, of all the people he'd met in the world. Silly, silly girl.

Chapter 16

The following Tuesday, Pia continued to catch up on her work at the office. The students were still on break so the staff had few interruptions. There were professors making grade changes throughout the week, though.

As Sandra's admin, Pia could see on the phone system that Sandra received several calls from Mike in human resources. Sandra must've coordinated the times with him because she always picked up before Pia did so. Pia was a little concerned over this. She could see from a shared electronic calendar that Mike and Sandra were scheduled to have a meeting later in the week.

At lunchtime Pia called Jeremy's cell phone number, gnawing on a nail while walking on the indoor track. He didn't pick up so she left a message for him.

"Hi, Pia again. I'd really like to see you to apologize in person. I'm sorry if I hurt you. Well, I did hurt you, I mean. You didn't do anything wrong. My expectations were unfair. Jeremy, I'm really sorry," she said as her voice cracked.

She hung up. There was nothing more to do.

When Pia returned to her desk she realized she had, once again, forgotten to go to the reflective pool.

"Tomorrow," she vowed to herself.

She had an email from Diane wanting to get together for lunch sometime soon. Normally Diane exercised at lunch but she wanted to sit down with her. Pia had an idea about why, thinking back to their awkward meeting in the rec center over break, so she ignored the email.

In the afternoon one of her favorite professors came in the office. Austin Carr was a gentle soul who wore wire-rimmed spectacles and dressed in classic professor garb: corduroy, tweed, wool vests. He seemed like he couldn't get out of his own way sometimes. Austin always benefitted from extra assistance from the staff when it came to paperwork and procedures. Shelly had no patience for this and would never coddle him. She had been trained by Ralph, after all. Ralph was friendly to Austin when they were face to face because they'd worked together for twenty-five years, but he would usually complain about the professor after he left the office.

Austin was hoping for some of Sandra's time to discuss a student of his.

"Hello, Pia."

"Hi, Austin. Nice to see you!" Pia greeted him warmly.

"How've you been? Is Sandra available?"

It was good to see a friendly face. Pia couldn't respond about how she'd been. "Let me check her schedule." Pia looked at Sandra's calendar and she was free. Pia could tell from her own phone that Sandra was on a call, so she messaged her that Austin was there to speak with her. In a minute Sandra sent a message back that she would not meet with him, she knew what it was about, and Pia should tell Austin that she was booked the rest of the afternoon. Pia hated it when the boss told her to lie and she tried to rationalize it by figuring that Sandra was the one initiating the falsehood. Pia was only the messenger, but she was still lying.

"I'm sorry, she has meetings all afternoon."

Pia definitely was sorry, but because Sandra was blowing off Austin.

"I heard her voice when I walked by her door. Can't I wait? This will only take a minute. It's about one of my students," Austin said with some annoyance in his tone.

Pia asked, "Can you tell me what the situation is? Maybe I can help."

Ralph had someone in his office, and Pia could hear them talking, and Shelly had stepped out. Mary and Dave were also absent. This made it possible for Pia to have a frank conversation with Austin. Nell was on the phone but Pia wouldn't be uncomfortable with her listening.

"One of my students, Brian Corcoran, is locked out of registration," Austin explained. "Something about his financial aid being held up. He told me he can't get the financial aid until he's registered, and the bursar's office blocked him because he hasn't paid."

Pia had heard Sandra and Ralph discussing Brian's situation in the office. Pia told Austin that he was correct; Brian had been unable to register for spring classes because, since his financial aid was pending, he hadn't paid his tuition bill. The financial aid was contingent on Brian being registered as full-time, but Brian had waited until he was certain he wanted to return in the spring, so he'd missed early registration.

Austin said emphatically, "That's completely unacceptable; it doesn't even make any sense. I'm supposed to be somewhere else right now but I want to resolve this first. Can you please let Sandra know I'll wait until she's free?"

This was exactly the type of situation students fell into that Pia could not tolerate. Austin found it preposterous as well. The student had petitioned to register, but Sandra was against it.

Pia came around to Austin's side of the counter and pulled some forms out of a wall pocket. Austin sat down in a chair roughly, so Pia sat next to him and quietly confided to him, keeping one ear listening for Ralph.

"Austin, Sandra isn't going to meet with you. She hates confrontation so she's avoiding you."

What a terrible administrative assistant she was.

Austin said with exasperation, "What confrontation? I just want to discuss Brian with her!"

Pia had to stop herself from shushing him.

Right after that Shelly walked back into the office saying, "Hey, Austin," as she passed him.

Pia lowered her voice. "That's just how she is. Brian hasn't missed the registration deadline yet. I recommend he take one of these forms for each class he hopes to get into and see if the instructors will sign them. That way he has a definite seat in them when the financial stuff gets resolved."

Austin took the forms and looked at Pia.

He didn't lower his voice as he replied, "I realize it's not your fault but this is totally asinine."

Fortunately, some students came in and went to the counter so Shelly was distracted by their questions and wasn't listening to the conversation. Pia nodded.

"I know. If you could let someone on the committee know to expect Brian's petition that might help. One is the dean of undergrads. Your friend Professor Romanov is, too. In case Sandra decides not to bring it to them. Sometimes she denies them herself. The good news is the committee meets tomorrow. Oh, and I'll email Brian to see if he needs anything clarified."

"All helpful information. Thanks, Pia."

About fifteen minutes after Austin left, Sandra came into the office to rinse her coffee mug in the breakroom sink.

"Oh good, you got rid of Austin. He's such a bonehead."

Pia kept it neutral. "He wants to resolve Brian Corcoran's situation."

"I don't know how he's going to do that," Sandra said as she continued to the break room.

There had been occasions when Pia would register a student for a course outside of the dedicated dates, specifically because of this predicament. Catch-22: you have to pay in order to register, but you can't pay until you have registered if you're using loans to pay. Ideally, students completed their course registration before the tuition was due but often they didn't. Most recently she had done it for a woman who was in her last semester and needed everything to fall into place in order to graduate. As long as Pia had the instructor's permission she would do it. Every action she took in the database was date-stamped with her initials. If Sandra and the bursar were looking for something to use against Pia, it wouldn't be difficult to find.

The next day, while Pia was walking on the track in the rec center during her lunch hour, Jeremy called her cell phone. She had just about given up on him.

"Hello?"

"Hi, Pia. This is Jeremy."

"Oh, thanks for calling me back. I'm sorry."

"I know you are. Um, we should get together. Sorry I didn't get back to you sooner. I was sorting through a lot of stuff in my head. Can we meet tonight after you're out of work?"

Pia was supposed to run home, cook, and head out to a committee meeting.

"Sure."

"Okay, how about meeting at Mickey's Brew Pub, where we ate with Max and Jamie? I can get there for five."

"Okay. See you then. Thank you."

Pia called Gordon and said she would be home late and then would make dinner. She would skip the meeting. She was painfully aware that the exclamation points were missing from Jeremy's speech. She suspected their relationship couldn't be salvaged but she still wanted to see him to do the best she could at righting it.

Later in the afternoon, shortly after two o'clock, Sandra came in from the committee meeting where Brian's petition was on the agenda. She walked briskly over to Ralph's office doorway and vented loudly about how the meeting went.

"Ralph, you're not going to believe this."

Ralph looked up expectantly. Everyone in the office held their breath to hear what she would say.

"Austin Carr paid Brian Corcoran's spring tuition bill!"

"Really?"

"He put it on a credit card so the bursar would open up Brian's course registration again. I was so mad! So I have to allow him in closed courses now if he can get the instructors' signatures. I hope all the courses he wants are full."

Then Sandra continued to the break room to get herself some yogurt.

Pia didn't know if Sandra was aware that all the staff, and Etienne as well, had heard her.

Etienne came over to Pia's desk and whispered, "That was very weird and unprofessional."

Pia nodded. She rubbed her face with her hands. Within an hour Brian came in and handed his approval forms to Etienne and waited while he put Brian in his courses for the spring semester. Pia gave Brian a smile and thumbs-up from her desk, where a partition blocked everyone else from seeing her. Brian smiled back.

Pia sent Austin an email shortly afterwards.

"Brian is all registered now. His financial aid should kick in and you'll be reimbursed soon. You're the best! I'll bring a jar of homemade strawberry jam to you later in the week! Warm regards."

Pia realized that she fashioned her emails like Jeremy's these days, since his were so nice.

Soon Austin replied, "I think you should keep the jam for yourself. You are always a big help to the students and faculty. Glad you're there. Best wishes."

Sandra's meeting with Mike from human resources was underway. At four-thirty Sandra called Pia into her office. When she arrived, Mike was seated at a small table. Pia knew then that she was being fired. She took a deep breath and sat with them.

"Pia, you have consistently overridden the university's policies to suit your own whims. I have a stack of instances of that here in this folder. You were given a warning a year ago, which you apparently didn't take very seriously. So we're letting you go." Sandra looked up at Pia then over to Mike.

Pia wanted Mike to know where each of them stood, so she replied, "In each of those situations in your folder I was helping our students."

Sandra clarified, "You were ignoring our policies."

"For the students."

Sandra went off, "You still don't get it, do you? It's not about helping the students; it's about maintaining the policies!"

As soon as she said it, Sandra seemed to realize she hadn't worded that very well. Mike cleared his throat and shifted in his seat but remained silent.

Pia calmly responded, "Those shouldn't be mutually exclusive."

Sandra looked at her like she was an idealistic idiot.

As condescendingly as possible she said, "Good luck, Pia."

Sandra rose and left Pia and Mike alone so he could give Pia information on her health coverage and last paycheck. Then Pia went back to her desk and collected her things. Everyone else in the office was brought into the break room for a brief meeting, so no one watched Pia put her things in a box and walk out with Mike. She was glad for that. Mike must've told Sandra to arrange it. While Pia was leaving everyone else was being told she was doing so.

Now there was a new storm of thought in Pia's head. Janeen had told her months ago that a warning is the first step to being let go. Pia had thought the warning was isolated and resolved, but Janeen had seen it happen to others over the years and advised her to start interviewing elsewhere. So Pia had updated her resume and sent it out to a few schools, although she didn't want to leave. Even though she had been forewarned it was still a shock. Like putting your hand in a shark's mouth and then feeling its teeth clamp down. Ouch.

Walking away from the building she was surprised to feel an overwhelming sense of relief. That was something she had not anticipated at all. But it made sense; it had been taxing, working for people who seemed to do everything in their power to avoid helping the people they were meant to be of service to.

Pia started to get in her car before she remembered Jeremy. She tossed her belongings in it and walked over to Mickey's Brew Pub to meet him there. He was waiting by the door on the sidewalk. Pia didn't want to hug him because her emotions were as delicate as thin glass; a hug might send shards everywhere. She could hardly meet his eyes.

Jeremy said only, "Hi."

He paused briefly and then initiated an embrace.

Pia made a conscious effort to be strong. It occurred to her that this might be the last touch she was going to get from him. They went inside and the host led them to a small, two-person booth. Jeremy ordered a beer and she chose lemonade. She thought Jeremy must expect this to be brief since he didn't order any food. She could see that he was anxious by his fidgeting.

"So, I've been thinking a lot about what happened and some of the things you said," he began.

"I wish you could ignore all the things I said," she offered.

Jeremy looked at her as though she'd misunderstood and then

continued.

"I wanted to make sure Ishra understood exactly what was going on. I sat her down at the airport before we even got to the car."

"How did it go?" Pia asked.

"She only knew about Ning, so I told her everything. It made her sad but she accepted it. I stayed with her that night and we slept in each other's arms. I think that helped both of us. So she's okay with it. We feel love between us."

Pia thought that would have helped her through it, too. She felt great angst about them being together. Still, Ishra was so young and so accepting of the terms of her relationship with him that Pia couldn't think ill of her. Pia's having been fired also had a numbing effect on her response, but all the same, she had to swallow hard before speaking. "That's really good."

"Pia, I do understand that the news was hard on you. I wish I'd told you initially what the situation was. I will in future relationships, for sure."

He drank deeply from his pint and then set it down on his coaster. Pia suspected that Ishra wasn't particularly comfortable with this situation. Jeremy's lovers just didn't want to lose or disappoint him. She was fairly sure Paco resented her involvement with Jeremy. In any event, she was there to make amends.

She laid her palms on the table and said, "I know there is no malice in your heart. You would never intentionally hurt anyone, much less someone you care about. You are the kindest, sweetest, most thoughtful person I know."

Jeremy's posture relaxed as he leaned back in his seat. Pia tipped her head down to her straw and drank some lemonade. She moved the straw in a circle absentmindedly and returned that hand to the table. Jeremy leaned forward again and took her hands in his, something she didn't expect.

His thumbs ran lightly over them as he said, "I could tell before you left that you regretted that totally crappy thing you said. I'm sorry I hollered at you."

"I drove you to it," Pia said, adding in almost a whisper, like a tiny prayer, "Please don't hate me."

"I don't hate you, not at all. Um, I just don't know how I feel about…." He let the sentence drop off.

Pia knew where this was going.

"I know. If I were made of earth, I'd be a minefield. If I were made of air, I'd be a storm. If I were fire, well, you'd have to be a phoenix."

Jeremy looked at her with one eyebrow raised.

"I guess. I'm not sure it's all that bad, heh. I just think…I'd be watching for another land mine, you know?"

"I haven't behaved that way in a long, long time. I thought I had learned not to do that at all, but obviously I haven't. I understand what it must look like from your eyes. It was caustic. Hopefully it won't happen ever again."

Earnestly Jeremy said, "I want to keep this relationship with you. Could you promise it won't happen again?"

Pia looked in his hopeful eyes. She wanted so much to make this right and have him back again. All she had to do was say 'yes'. Continuing to be involved with him meant she would have too much invested to tolerate being one of several lovers, though. She wouldn't be content with that and she would probably sabotage it again soon. Her face became pained briefly. She squeezed Jeremy's hands before withdrawing hers to her lap and she shook her head. She could not promise Jeremy that.

He looked down at his glass.

"That wasn't the answer I wanted, but it was what I expected."

Pia suggested, "Maybe you can keep me in mind for seeing art exhibits or going on hikes if you'd like some company."

"That sounds good," he said without much conviction.

"I'm leaving it up to you because I don't want to push you, but please know that I'd like to spend time with you."

"Okay."

He drank more of his beer. Pia took a ten out of her wallet, left it on the table and stood to leave. She put on her coat and leaned down to give Jeremy a kiss on his cheek, but he turned his head at the last second, so a lingering kiss on the lips transpired. They hesitated. She licked her lips and straightened.

Jeremy maintained eye contact and said in a low tone, "Pia, I don't want to end this. If you could, I don't know…."

Jeremy would not change anything on his end and she couldn't either. She allowed silence to communicate an impasse.

After a moment she said softly, "Alright then."

Pia dragged her eyes from his gaze. She wrapped her scarf around her collar, slipped her hair out from under it and left, appearing to have found grace.

The second Pia went through the door, she abandoned that appearance. Her face and heart crumpled and she began to cry, a fist pressed to her lips. Pia had kept it together rather admirably while she was with him. Now she felt the loss of too much at the same time. She thought then of the reflective pool but wasn't sure she was allowed on the school grounds now. Her heart physically hurt. She thought about how she had lost Jeremy and her job at the school she was so devoted to despite her best efforts. She wondered how much worse things could have turned out if she had made no effort at all to nurture these relationships.

When she arrived home she set about making dinner. She had lots of things to think about and she didn't talk much. Pia rarely missed a committee meeting, so Gordon thought that was unusual behavior for her. He figured she wasn't in the mood to spar with Thatcher. Pia had left the box with her belongings from work in her car because she didn't know if she was ready to tell Gordon about that yet.

While they ate Gordon told her about a bobcat he had watched in the yard and a problem with a prescription that wasn't ready at the pharmacy when it should've been. While Pia was cleaning up after dinner, he asked her if she would like him to run any errands for her the next day. She was normally short on time and Gordon liked having little assignments from her to add an increment of variety to his routine. Pia realized that she had to let him know she would be home tomorrow. She put some things in the dishwasher. She washed and dried her hands and then turned to him.

"Let's sit down. I have some news," she said reflexively, forgetting he was already seated.

"Uh-oh!" Gordon said jokingly.

Pia kept her eyes down as she joined him at the kitchen table.

Pia said wearily, "Gordon, I've been fired."

"What?"

"I was let go today."

"You're joking."

"No. I'm really sorry. I'll get something else as soon as possible. I had a lot of vacation time, so I got a big check today."

Gordon was stunned for a moment, then asked her, "Aww, how are you doing? Are you okay?"

That was a relief to Pia, as she'd expected him to hassle her for screwing up. Gordon knew she didn't play by the rules when she thought they were wrong but he wasn't like her and couldn't understand why she didn't just go to work and do her job. Pia was grateful for his good nature.

"It was a shock but I was warned it would happen sooner or later, right? Thank you for being so good about this."

"I know it must be tough for you. You love that school."

After a minute he glanced at the day's mail on a chair near him, where he spied his favorite magazine. Pia sensed his attention waning. It was remarkable that he had focused on her as long as he had, but of course this was big news and affected them both.

She decided to share all her news with him. She might as well lose everything together. Maybe she would begin a whole new life tomorrow. He was standing and reaching for the magazine.

"Honey, there's more."

"What do you mean?"

Pia took a deep breath and began.

"I have a confession to make to you. This is really bad. Are you ready?" she said sheepishly.

"I don't know. Depends on what it is."

He was assuming she was overdramatizing this and it was some little thing. He sat back down, employing a hand on the arm of his chair to ease his back pain.

"Gordon, I…. You know Jeremy Ronan?" Pia asked, knitting her brow anxiously.

"Sure, the little shit who ratted you out to the president," Gordon snickered.

She hesitated. Under different circumstances she would admonish him for calling Jeremy that.

"I, um…I became attracted to him. Romantically. Kind of like a crush. I'm sorry."

Pia tried to gauge how Gordon was doing. She was making circles with a forefinger on the smooth wooden surface of the table and glanced up at him furtively.

"I know that," he proclaimed.

Pia was perplexed.

"You *do*?"

"Honey, you talk about him all the time. I knew you liked him. I didn't know if he caught on but then you had his cologne on that one time. That's why it bothered me; because you like him so much. You didn't have sex with the little bastard, did you?" Gordon joked.

This was something Pia would never have foreseen. It made her feel worse, and like a fool. She looked away from his gaze.

"You didn't, did you?"

Pushing a tiny boat from the safety of the shoreline into a tremendous current, Pia found herself nodding.

"A little. Yes."

Off it went, tossing wildly as it was carried downstream, perhaps to splinter into pieces.

"Are you serious? What exactly is 'a little'? You just kissed, is that what you mean?" Gordon said.

His smile disappeared, and he seemed to be drinking in the reality of what she had just told him. His expression changed to great disappointment. Pia had betrayed their commitment for a crush on a college boy.

Pia shook her head. Little tears began rolling down her cheeks, maybe for him but possibly just the stress of the conversation. It seemed as if she'd cried more in the past few weeks than she had in her whole life.

"I'm sorry. No, I slept with him. A few times over the past month or so. I'm really sorry, honey."

"*You let him fuck you?!*" he bellowed, on the edge of his seat.

Ducking her head into her shoulders, cowed, she murmured, "Don't say it like that."

She'd reacted instinctively to the crude term and realized too late that that was a mistake.

Gordon held a palm out and replied in tone filled with disgust, "Oh, *pardon* me. You 'made love'? Have I got that right?"

There was a silence while he stared at Pia. He looked at her lap as if he were visualizing the deceit, and Pia reacted subconsciously by crossing her legs. She avoided his eyes when they returned to her face and wiped some tears away with her sleeve. She thought to herself that life was too exhausting. She clearly wasn't qualified for it. She lifted an elbow onto the table and cradled her forehead in that hand.

Looking down she mumbled, "I'm sorry. I'm so sorry."

Then Gordon's face fell. Actually, his whole posture slumped. He looked much older than he had at dinner.

"I trusted you. Where does this leave me? Do you want a divorce?"

"What? No! I mean, I don't want to. That's up to you."

"You're not sleeping with him now?"

Pia shook her head while tears continued to down her cheeks. "No."

Gordon stood up and went over to the counter, with his back to Pia. She didn't know if he was going to switch to anger as she had with Jeremy, but she knew if he did she would deserve it. Mustering all of her courage, she got up from the table and went over to him to see his face. He looked so miserable. Then he reached for Pia; she braced and shut her eyes tightly. He wrapped his arms around her, hugging her firmly. She felt a blend of tremendous relief and guilt and hugged him back. They held each other a long time.

He told her, "I don't want to lose you."

"I thought you'd kill me."

"I should, you little whore," Gordon said teasingly.

So many little things came up throughout their marriage where he'd been an insensitive ass. Now when there was a serious issue he was a shining star. Pia was seeing him from a new viewpoint that would not have been possible had she not presented him with this situation.

She wiped her face with her sleeve, saying with relief, "This is not what I expected your reaction would be at all. You're being so tolerant."

"Pia, I'm an old man in case you haven't noticed, and in bad health.

You're so much younger than me and you're so cute. I've known for a long time to watch out for something like this, that your desire might wander. I'm not stupid."

She rested her head on his big broad chest and he rubbed her back.

He said, "I just don't want you to abandon me."

"I'm not going anywhere."

Because she was so grateful for this unexpected outcome, Pia continued, "I really don't deserve you. Thanks for putting up with me, honey."

Over the years, Gordon's behavior had chipped away at Pia's love for him and she'd assumed those pieces were gone for good. But apparently they could grow back, like a lizard's tail, or a sea star's foot.

During the next few weeks Pia and Gordon connected more than they had in years. Since she had plenty of free time and didn't know how long that would be for, they took small trips to all of their favorite places on the North Shore, in Vermont and New Hampshire. One favorite place on the Rhode Island seacoast was Beaver Tail, a park that jutted out into the ocean with great views on three sides and a lighthouse at the farthest point. They sat on a bench wrapped closely together watching the lively sea and the indomitable gulls interacting. It was much nicer in summer when there were sailboats tacking, people flying kites and the wind providing relief from the heat instead of this frigid coldness. Now the wildness of it was more pronounced, which seemed to suit them, somehow.

After sitting silently for a long while, Gordon asked, "What are we having for dinner tonight?"

Pia replied, "Lemon chicken."

Gordon said pleasantly, "Good! I like that dish."

"That makes two of us."

Pia intended to do her best to make up to Gordon for cheating on him and for the time she had been emotionally absent from him. She filled her days spending time with him to assure him she was no longer spending time with Jeremy. Gordon was understandably insecure about it.

None of this helped her to miss Jeremy any less, though. Her thoughts wandered to him frequently and she wondered what he was doing. What made her most sad was thinking that Jeremy might not miss her or didn't think about her. She would retire to bed early but sleep didn't come easily. This loss was debilitating and she spent hours looking at the ceiling wondering what a positive outcome would've been like. Pia felt she was only pretending to be alive. She didn't disclose to Gordon that the relationship with Jeremy ended only because he didn't want her anymore.

Chapter 17

In late January she sent Linda an email when it was time to take down Jeremy's exhibit. Linda had emailed and phoned Pia at work and the email had come back as undeliverable. Pia explained to Linda that she had been fired and she would go to the campus center after hours to take down the photographs. She decided to leave the images and the book of comments in Linda's office for Jeremy to pick up at his convenience. Linda agreed to email him for her. Pia didn't want him to know she had left the university.

When the exhibit closed and still Pia heard nothing from Jeremy, there was a sense of finality to things. Pia wanted to update Annie and Jane so they wouldn't feel burdened with this any longer.

She decided to start with Jane, at a poetry reading in their town. It was one of a series by a poetry association and Jane was a friend of the featured reader, Dan Lewis. During a break Jane sidled over to Pia to catch up.

"Hey stranger, how's it going?" Jane asked with a meaningful stare.

"Good. Jeremy's gone."

"Really? And that's good?"

"It's awful but…. Anyway, Gordon knows all about it. I don't want you to feel like you have a secret from him."

Jane asked apprehensively, "Did you tell him or did he find out another way?"

"I told him the same time I told him I was fired."

"You've been fired?" Jane kept her voice down but her face showed surprise.

"I'm afraid so. Gordon was just so good about everything. I'm still amazed with him," Pia said, thinking that her glass was half full.

"So I don't have to ask if you want to stay with us?"

"No, we're doing pretty good. That's very generous of you, though. Thank you."

People were beginning to regroup as the poet was ready to continue with the second half of the program.

Jane said, "I'm so sorry about your job! Let's go for a walk later this week, okay?"

Pia said, "I'd really like that, thanks."

At the end of the event, as Pia was leaving, Jane said, "I'll call you tomorrow."

Pia nodded before Jane turned her attention to another friend. After saying goodnight to some acquaintances, Pia went out into the cold parking lot. There was neither a moon nor clouds, so the rural night sky was filled to overflowing with stars. It was stunning and she admired it for several minutes before getting in her car.

The last lines of Dan's poem *That Damn Apple Again*, spoken in an intense, cautionary tone, stuck with her on her drive home: "In the dark/ all the lights/ look like/ home." He was a master at reducing complex ideas down to a handful of words so his work often went over her head, but this she connected with. It brought to her mind how sea turtle hatchlings and young puffins lose their way if any light from land competes with the moon. After a few minutes Pia had another thought: perhaps that's why she went the wrong way.

The following day she made a trip to the sanctuary to seek out Annie. Looking across the lower field she saw Annie jogging with all the sheep trailing behind her through the sodden snow and the brittle remains of milkweed stalks. Pia headed towards the red barn to meet her. Annie waved when she saw her. Pia knew to wait far off to the side lest she frighten the sheep and send them running in the wrong direction. Annie led them in a wide loop and eventually back to their daytime winter pen which was adjacent to the barn. Pia shivered and shifted her feet while she waited. When they were close she could hear all their hooves crunching heavily into the wet tangles of the field. Once the gate was shut behind the sheep Pia went briskly over to Annie.

Annie's face was red from the raw wind and she was nearly out of breath. Nothing seemed to stop her from being outside. In fact, she relished it.

"Hey, Pia. How's tricks?" she said, huffing.

"How's what?"

"Never mind, figure of speech," Annie said to Pia, then to a sheep that hovered just inside the fence by her side, "Go on girl, go on now."

The sheep reluctantly meandered towards the others.

"Can I ask you what you were doing with them?" Pia enquired.

There was nothing to eat in the fields. Their winter diet consisted of pale green hay stored in the loft subsidized with grain pellets. It was a tedious season for the sheep as well as for Pia, but at least they were well insulated.

"Uh, well...."

"I'll tell you mine if you tell me yours," Pia persisted, as she crossed her arms, stomping her feet lightly to try to keep her toes from becoming numb. In her mind she asked herself, "Was that obnoxious? It was, wasn't it?"

Annie consented with a grin. "Well, in that case, I was walking them."

Pia looked at her blankly.

"I feel badly that they're cooped up so much, so if I have time I take them out for the fun of it," Annie confessed bashfully while she played with the latch.

"Aww, that's so sweet."

Pia acted like she was teasing Annie, but she really was touched.

Annie smiled, saying, "Yeah, yeah. So what've you got?"

Pia looked at her and took a breath. She wasn't eager to resume this topic.

"I want to tell you that Jeremy is out of the picture and Gordon is aware of what happened."

Annie just blinked at her with eyebrows raised.

"That's it, that's all. I feel like a shit about everything and I didn't want you to feel like you were keeping a secret. So it's not a secret anymore."

"Wow. So what's the status of you and Gordon?"

"Same. Actually, better than before. I lost my way for a while, I guess."

They started to walk towards the office together. Annie didn't say anything for a minute but then she sought clarification.

"He knows about your relationship with Jeremy and you're still together?"

Apparently that was incomprehensible.

"Yup. I was as surprised as you. I married a better person than I realized. Life's funny."

"Is that why Jeremy's not around anymore, because Gordon found out?"

"No, it ended and then I told him about it." Pia didn't know how to explain it. "I'm not being evasive, it's just…Jeremy spreads his love around."

They stopped at the parking lot, where Pia's car was close by and she could hardly wait to get out of the wind.

"Oh. But all's well?"

"Yes, it is."

"Glad to hear it."

There was a large noisy group coming out of the office. Pia decided to save the news about her firing for another time, to let Annie get back to work.

"Thanks for being my friend, Annie."

"No problem."

They held each other's gaze for a moment.

"Hey, I gotta run and check if those people need anything. I'll see you soon."

Annie walked quickly towards the sanctuary office and greeted the visitors.

As Pia expected, she didn't hear from Jeremy, with one exception. About five weeks after their last talk he phoned her.

"Hi, Pia. I'm so glad you answered!"

It was after nine o'clock at night. Pia was reading in her living room in her toasty bathrobe, with the cat on her lap and her feet tucked under her. She'd been texting Jane, so the cell phone was beside her on the sofa. Pia's heart picked up its pace at this surprise.

"Jeremy? How are you?"

The cat reluctantly left as Pia shifted her feet to the floor.

"I have a baby owl and I want to know how to take care of it!" Jeremy exclaimed happily.

Pia knew a little about owls and she could bet it wasn't a juvenile.

She asked, "How'd you get a baby owl? Only great horned owls are nesting now, in heron nests over water. Where was it?"

"We were driving on this winding rural road and we slowed way down because of a thick patch of fog, and it flew against the car. I think we're in Lincoln. There aren't any signs around. I have it now!

It's beautiful… but it isn't moving. Its eyes are open; it's alive. What should I do?"

Pia felt jealous of whoever was with him but moved on from it.

"It's probably just stunned if it isn't obviously injured. Can you send me a picture of it?"

"Yeah, sure. I'll send it and you call me back once you look at it."

He hung up. Very soon Pia received a photo of it. She thought it was a screech owl and confirmed it with her field guide before calling him back.

"It's an adult screech owl. How's it doing?"

Jeremy had an update. "It recovered and flew into the woods. I hope it's okay and won't die out there. It didn't weigh anything at all, Pia! Are you sure it wasn't a young one? It was so small."

Pia had to smile to herself at Jeremy's enthusiasm about his chance meeting with the creature.

"I think it'll be fine. They're so light because their bones are hollow. Birds grow very rapidly, so young birds are downy and clumsy even when they're the size of their parents. Your little friend had adult plumage. Screech owls aren't our smallest owl species, either; the saw-whet owl is even smaller than your owl."

Jeremy didn't say anything, so to bring her point home Pia added more information very directly.

"If you were holding a baby bird of prey you would feel parental talons ripping across your skull in a matter of seconds."

"Yikes, Pia, you don't have to be so graphic!"

Pia heard him relaying to his companion what she'd just said. Someone laughed.

"Were you able to get many photos of it?"

Jeremy had. "Sure, probably a dozen."

"I'm trying to think of who at the state division of fisheries and wildlife you could contact to let them know you saw it. Screech owls are an elusive species so I'm sure they'd want to know where it was. Oh, I have an idea! They have a little magazine they publish, *Mass Wildlife*. The editor will definitely print one or two of your photographs if you send them in. He can also forward your information to whomever it should go to for their records."

"That would be great! Who is it again?"

"I'll send you his contact information by email. Gordon has a subscription so I'll let you know when I see it in the magazine. You were lucky to meet it."

"Yeah, that's what we think too, heh. Hey, thanks, Pia."

"You're welcome."

Just before they disconnected she said, "Wait, Jeremy?"

Pia was conflicted; she didn't want to spook him but she was so glad to hear from him. He was still there.

"Yes?"

She sounded desperate, clingy. "I miss you." Pia was trying to tell him she loved him but there was silence from him so she repeated, "I just miss you."

She watched her fingers looping around the end of her bathrobe belt.

"Uhh...I...."

This was quickly becoming unbearable so Pia said with an artificial smile, "It's okay. You take care."

She moved her thumb over the little "hang up" icon and pressed it. She exhaled and replayed the conversation in her mind.

After a while she got up from the sofa and went into Gordon's office. In an effort at being forthright, she told him about the call. Gordon wasn't happy about it. She suspected that, for better or worse, it was an isolated event and expressed that to him.

She emailed Jeremy the information about the magazine. She kept it light and encouraged him to submit his photos. She wrote that the editor was an acquaintance and someone Jeremy would like and included a few anecdotes about him. Now Jeremy had her personal email address, which was good, because if he ever emailed her at the university he'd figure out that she was no longer there. Then again, he might never send anything to either address.

Unfortunately, that conversation with him set Pia back in her effort to move on without him. He was at the forefront of her thoughts again. She waited eagerly to hear from him for several weeks even as she knew she probably wouldn't. Eventually, she returned *The Edge of the Sea* to him by mail. The last time she saw the book of Billy Collins' poetry it was in the back seat of his car, untouched.

Pia took her walks around the city park and at the wildlife sanctuary more often and hardly ever on the wooded trails near her house. She kept alive the possibility that they might run into each other and he would be happy to see her. Occasionally she would permit her imagination to construct a scenario where Jeremy wanted to contact her but was hesitant, afraid. Perhaps he missed her but didn't know how to approach her. She understood that unless Jeremy was deliberately looking for her she wouldn't find him, but still she hoped.

As time went on though, she increasingly let go of those notions and returned to reality. Again, finally, little things gave her pleasure. One afternoon her friend's ten-year-old daughter joined her spontaneously on the sofa to snuggle; Pia didn't know what prompted it, but it was joyful. When the neighbor's adult son came home for a visit from the west coast there was a party for him. Towards the end of the evening he came over to Pia and told her he still had the gift she'd given him years ago when he left for college. She was pleased by the fact that it had travelled with him to six apartments but also that he wanted to share that information with her. There was an old lady who rode a bicycle past her around the city park in bright clothes and funny hats on dry days. Each time she passed Pia she would wave and smile. It would get them both laughing as the woman would pass several times.

In each instance Pia was struck by the clarity with which she was aware that these were reprieves from her normal emotional state. They were little gifts for her, crocuses pushing up through the snow, and she savored them.

When *Mass Wildlife* printed Jeremy's photos and a paragraph about them Pia was thrilled. He had taken her suggestion seriously. She was sure he would be excited when they sent him his complimentary copy. Pia reprimanded herself on being such a fool for allowing the distraction with Jeremy to lead her away from her life. Soon she forgave herself, though. Life would go on.

During meetings and public events held by the New Justice League the conversation was always about racist brutality and it often spun into an exploration of the root cause, which boiled down to fear and/or hate. This would eventually bring them around to the solution, love, which was a positive way to end. Pia wondered why so many people attached themselves so securely to the disliking and distrusting of strangers when they could initially approach them with love instead.

At one rally she stood next to a slovenly, drunk old man who wasn't interested in the event but stayed since it was in his neighborhood park. Pia humored him in an effort to keep his noise level down while she managed a table with a donation box and petitions for people to sign. Aaron gallantly stopped by to see if Pia was uncomfortable with the man there and she assured him it was alright. The drunk veered close to her face each time he spoke, and his stinking breath and red, watery eyes reminded her of Neil, her first husband. She had to fend off a creeping gloom until the end of the afternoon when things changed. He was difficult to understand because he had an accent and was slurring his words but Pia caught some of it.

"Did you say you have a turtle?" Pia asked.

"Oh, yes, she's beautiful. I live a block away."

He motioned in the general direction of an intersection before his arm flopped to his side.

"Her name is Missy. She lives in a box in my apartment."

"How big is she?" Pia asked.

The man set his feet apart to steady himself and showed Pia with his hands.

"When I got her she was only this big, but now she's *this* big," he told her proudly.

Apparently she had tripled in size.

"I've had her a year now. She's so beautiful. I have something for her. Look."

His pants almost fell down as he took a stone he had found out of his right front pocket. He showed it to Pia but wouldn't let her touch it when she reached for it.

"See, it's shaped like a heart. It's for Missy to show her how much I love her. Do you think she'll like it?"

Pia replied seriously, "I'm sure she will. That's nice of you."

He teetered a bit as he proclaimed, "Oh, I love her. I would do anything for her. Would you like to come visit her?"

Pia smiled, thinking that while that sounded like a pick-up line it wasn't one.

"Yes, I would. I really like turtles."

"Okay, you can come visit soon. You will love her. I should go home and bring her this rock."

With that he stumbled away.

Pia's attitude changed from tolerance to affection for him and she was sorry she had initially been dismissive of him. He probably wasn't properly caring for Missy but she brought him so much happiness Pia could forgive it. And Missy had managed to live with him for a year already. The idea that somewhere in the noisy, urban neighborhood there was a little apartment with a turtle in a box providing joy for a lonely drunkard lifted Pia's spirit tremendously and her gloom dissipated.

One day it occurred to her to try this positive approach with someone she knew she didn't like, as a way towards peace with him. At the next meeting about the snow-and-skate park, Thatcher was still hoping to obtain the land parcel he had set his sights on even though the committee had recently received a final, emphatic 'no' from the landowners. He could sense it slipping away when the other committee members had all tentatively agreed on an alternate site.

After the new proposal had been discussed in detail, Thatcher shook his head.

"I just don't understand what the issue is with snowboarding on that other parcel. What a waste."

Across the table from him Pia leaned forward and suggested with a sincerely open heart, "Thatcher, I wonder if you would do something with me."

Pia couldn't blame him for looking skeptical.

She continued, "I would like to go for a walk on that property with you. Whenever you want. This weekend?"

"What do you mean by a walk?" he asked warily.

Pia was a bit puzzled, as she couldn't imagine being more direct, but she tried again.

"A walk together through the woods and fields."

Pam added, "Hey, we could all go. That would be nice."

Pia agreed with a nod, although some of the others didn't look as enthusiastic.

"Why?" Thatcher asked, still eyeing Pia with suspicion, waiting for a punchline.

"I want to see how you like it. We can talk."

Thatcher scoffed and then met her eyes and realized she was serious.

"Okay. Sure."

They set up a Saturday morning to meet. Pam would go with them. They met at the small gravel turn-off that served as a parking lot for the preserved land. It was late March and the heat from the sun was finally beginning to reach the earth in New England. It was too early for black flies and mosquitos but warm for the season. They took turns being the lead and Pia or Pam would loan Thatcher their binoculars when they sighted birds. When Thatcher led he went quickly, as if to get the walk over with as soon as possible.

"Thatcher, slow down a little, please," Pia said at one point.

She sat on a rock in the sun at the forest edge. Pam joined her. Thatcher turned and came a few paces back to them.

"Sorry, I usually hike much faster than this."

"Well, I'm old," Pia quipped.

"In your thirties isn't old," he answered.

"I'm not in my thirties. But thanks!"

Pam lamented how muddy it was in places although she was in appropriate footwear. Thatcher was in expensive running sneakers and Pia had hiking boots.

"It's all part of the experience," Pia said absentmindedly.

She picked up a scent.

"I think we have company; I feel like we're being watched. Do either of you smell anything?"

"Actually, I do. It smells like a skunk here," Thatcher said.

There came a strange sound from the woods, a bit like someone slurping from the bottom of a glass through a straw but more high-pitched.

Thatcher took no notice of it but Pam heard it and said, "What was that? I've never heard that sound before." She looked through the trees in the direction of the noise.

Pia said, "I only heard it for the first time last fall, on a walk with Annie at the nature sanctuary."

Thatcher said, "So what is it?"

They heard it again. Pia stood up and looked around.

"Not sure just yet. Hey, may I lead for a bit?"

They continued on the trail alongside an old stone wall. In a minute Pia stopped and pointed to the ground.

"There. That's scat. And more here."

"No kidding, Pia. I would never have known that without your help." Thatcher said sarcastically, but he was grinning.

Pia berated herself in her head then: "Why did you say such a stupid thing? Who doesn't already know that?" Then, remembering Jeremy's request to be kinder to herself, she tried to let it go.

She noted more scat a few paces ahead along the trail and saw it was fresh.

"Hmm…just mice to eat now," she thought aloud to herself.

There wasn't any evidence of fruit in it, only bones and hair. The smell was stronger here.

"So a red fox lives here. That's the sound and the scent, similar to a skunk."

She looked all around the woods beyond the wall.

Pam questioned Pia, "That's the scat we smell?"

"No, it's a musk scent the fox secretes from glands to delineate his territory. They also use urine to do that, but that's not what we smell. So this is his home area."

The women scanned the area with their binoculars, back and forth slowly. Thatcher started to walk away.

When he was a few yards from them Pam said to Pia, "Aaannnd… there! There he is!"

She pointed enthusiastically and Pia located him in her own binoculars.

"Hi, little fella," Pia said to the fox.

"Oh, neat. He's so gorgeous! Just watching us," Pam said.

Thatcher came back and Pia showed him where to look. Just as Thatcher located the fox it turned and loped further away from them along the forest floor in the dappled light that reached through the pine trees, but he got to see it.

He said, "The tail's as big as the rest of him."

"So we found him with our ears, noses and eyes!" Pam added cheerily.

Pia stopped to take off her socks and shoes and then Thatcher led some more. He pointed out a red squirrel running along the stone wall carrying a pinecone almost its own size. A few minutes later he pointed to a white-breasted nuthatch upside-down on the side of a tree.

"I'm very impressed, Thatcher," Pia told him.

She had tied the laces of her boots together and stuffed the socks in them and periodically switched which hand carried them.

"I was a Boy Scout, you know. I don't spend all my time in an office."

"What did you like most about being a Scout?" Pia asked.

While Thatcher gave it some thought Pia passed him on the trail.

"I would have to say camping out. Cooking over a fire…telling ghost stories…and peeing in the woods. Peeing in the woods is the best thing ever."

Pia stopped to turn to him. She realized he was ribbing her about the peeing because he had a twinkle in his eyes and was grinning.

Pia smiled back. "Uh-huh."

Pam said, "I'd rather not until the leaves are out, myself. There's no privacy yet."

Pia responded, "True that."

Thatcher's phone rang, so Pia reminded him that they had agreed to ignore them on the walk. He reluctantly left it in his pocket. Pam was able to identify some early spring migratory birds calling in the area.

They continued to walk and talk until they reached a ridge, and then they looked all around for a few minutes. Together they watched the clouds float overhead and felt the breeze on their faces. They squinted when the sun came out from behind a cottony cloud.

Pia quoted Rachel Carson. "'Underlying the beauty of the spectacle there is meaning and significance.'"

Thatcher asked, "And what is the meaning and significance?"

It sounded like a test.

She continued the quote. "'It is the elusiveness of that meaning that haunts us, that sends us again and again into the natural world.' That's from Rachel Carson."

She closed her eyes to the sun, then looked down at her feet and wiggled her toes.

"That's so true," Pam said, then asked her, "Aren't your feet cold?"

"Yeah, but the sun is heating them up now."

Thatcher asked, "Why are you barefoot?"

"I like to feel my feet touching the earth. It makes me think about gravity and the depth beneath here to the center of the planet."

Pam said, "I like it too, especially on soft grass, but I'll wait until June. Geez, I sound like such a sissy today!"

They all laughed.

Thatcher reflected, "Maybe I'll take the family hiking in the White Mountains this summer. It's been ages."

The three of them then continued downhill and followed a loop that eventually brought them back to the parking area. On the way Thatcher told them about his sons' activities and what the rest of the weekend had in store for him. Pam and Pia listened with interest.

At the cars they said their good-byes. They each seemed hesitant to be the first to leave; it had gone well. Pia knew part of the reason was that Thatcher had made an effort at diplomacy. He had met her halfway and she appreciated it.

She said, "Thank you, Thatcher. I really enjoyed this."

Pam added, "Me too. It was a great idea."

"Yeah, it was nice. Well, see you."

Thatcher got in his car and drove up the road towards the affluent section of town.

Pia thanked Pam as well and then headed for home feeling good. Maybe it wouldn't make any difference, but she and Thatcher had managed to enjoy each other's company for a morning.

Chapter 18

On a Thursday night in April at about eight-thirty, Pia was writing out bills at the kitchen table and Gordon was in his office watching a show. The phone rang and he picked it up. A moment later Gordon hollered that it was for her.

Pia picked up the extension. "Hello?"

"Hi, Pia. This is Jeremy."

If Gordon was listening, his blood pressure was certainly rising.

"Jeremy? Hi!"

"I tried your cell but couldn't reach you so I Googled you and found your home number. I hope that's okay."

Pia didn't understand why he was telling her that and mentally brushed it aside. "Sure. How are you?"

"Um, I was wondering if I could ask a favor of you. I'm kind of stuck for a ride. I'm at the train station. Is it possible by any chance that you could come get me?"

"Down by the library?" Pia was puzzled.

"Yes. I know it's out of your way. If it's any trouble don't worry about it, really," he said.

He sounded like he was reconsidering his request.

"Sure, of course. You'll have to give me about a half hour to get there."

"That's great, thank you." He said and then hung up.

While Pia put on her coat and scarf she told Gordon that she was going to give Jeremy a ride, she didn't know to where and she'd call him when she had some idea what the situation was.

He grumbled, "That's absurd. You are not doing that."

"Yeah, I am."

"No, you're not. I forbid it."

Pia put her hands on her hips and looked at him hard. "Ex*cuse* me?"

"Don't go get him," Gordon pleaded.

"I'm going to do this for him. Look, I spend every holiday with your ex-wife."

Gordon flicked that argument away expediently, saying, "I hate her and you know it."

This was the truth. Pia tried again.

"Every time Bill has a party we hang out with a woman you've slept with."

"I don't care; this is different."

"It's no different! You're making a double standard. I'm going to help him out. Gordon, you have to trust me."

He was cornered. "I do trust you. It's just hard to."

Pia looped her arms around his neck and looked into his eyes, saying, "You can trust me, honey."

This seemed to help him. She gave him a kiss and left the house.

She drove into the city wondering what this might be about. Pia understood that he wasn't contacting her to re-ignite their romance. That was over. Nonetheless, she was glad that Jeremy felt he could count on her if he needed her.

She found a parking spot relatively close to the station. It was very cold outside with a raw wind, so Pia went inside the concourse to look for him. Jeremy was standing off to one side and watching the entrance. As soon as he saw her he came over to the doors. He was wearing just a thin, ragged hoodie over a t-shirt, with the hood over his head. Jeremy had a huge black eye and a busted lip. Pia tried to not look horrified, but his face was a mess.

"Thanks for coming to get me," he said.

His delivery was uncharacteristically flat. He didn't embrace her, but just stood with his hands in the pockets of the sweatshirt.

"No problem at all."

She hesitated, waiting for some explanation of his condition. He didn't offer any and she didn't want to pry.

"Okay, well, I'm parked just outside," she said after an awkward moment.

Pia led the way to the car and noticed that Jeremy stayed quite close beside her, bumping into her lightly the whole way. It was a bit annoying but she figured that his vision was impaired. Once there, she unlocked and opened his door and started around to her side. Jeremy paused as if considering something, began to get in, and then seemed to think better of it. He looked over his shoulder and back to Pia.

"Um, I think I would rather lie down in the back, if that's alright," he said.

Pia just looked at him with a question on her face.

"Really tired," Jeremy weakly offered as a reason while he shivered.

He seemed so peculiar; he wasn't himself at all. Pia hesitated briefly before stretching into the back to move her canvas grocery bags out of the way. She wished it weren't a two-door car.

"You must be freezing in just that sweatshirt. Here, now there's room for you."

Jeremy, it seemed, was still considering the best approach to the back seat and not actually getting in it. He looked around again. Pia was so confounded that she finally tried to get the facts.

Over the roof of the car she said, "Jeremy, I'll help you in any situation because I adore you. Am I hiding you from the police?"

She tried to make it sound like she was joking, but she wanted to know what was up with him avoiding the front seat.

"No, I promise. Nothing like that."

He looked so not right, jittery with his arms folded tight to himself and he looked over his shoulder yet again. He didn't look Pia in the eyes. He was procrastinating on sitting down….

All of a sudden a terrible, horrific thought occurred to Pia. It transformed the situation. She went back around the car to stand in front of Jeremy. She tried to stare into his eyes, although one was almost bruised shut.

"Jeremy?" Pia began to ask. He saw the stricken look on her face and quickly looked away. A couple walked by them laughing loudly about something.

"Jeremy."

He looked at her then. She gathered her courage.

"Have you been…."

She was afraid she was being intrusive but she had to know.

"Have you been sexually assaulted?"

Pia had expected Jeremy to say no, but he didn't answer. With her heart beating fast she re-phrased the heinous question as he looked down at the sidewalk.

"Did someone rape you?"

Jeremy's body seemed to calm then; he met her gaze and his face reflected what was going on in his head.

"Two people, actually. But I'm fine. It's okay, really."

Once he said that, he collapsed under the weight of his misery. He bit his lip trying not to cry. Pia embraced him and he began sobbing.

"Oh, Jeremy, I'm so sorry…. I'm so sorry this happened to you. You poor thing."

Then she began to cry with him.

"Poor thing…. God, I'm sorry."

She brought one hand up to cradle the back of his head, saying, "How could anybody hurt you?"

"I fought." She could barely make out his words in her shoulder. "I fought."

"Oh, honey. I meant you're so kind. I'm so, so sorry." She thought to herself, "So this is what agony feels like."

They stood there like that for a few minutes, until Jeremy was drained of all his tears.

Pia helped him lay down on his side in the back seat and she pulled a bunch of paper napkins from the glove compartment for them both to dry their eyes. Then she took her scarf from around her neck, rolled it and set it under his head. She took off her down coat and put it over him, tucking it gently between his back and the seat. Jeremy winced. When she was in the driver's seat she put the heat on and twisted around to talk to him.

"Can I bring you to an emergency room?"

"No."

"Jeremy, there's—"

"*No.*"

That settled that. The last thing she would do was go against his wishes.

"Well, shall I drive you home to your mom?"

Jeremy considered this, then, "No. I don't want her to see me like this. And my father...."

He let the thought drop off.

Pia asked, "Should I take you to your apartment then?"

She was running out of ideas. Jeremy groaned a bit and stared at the back of the passenger seat, looking forlorn. Besides his brother there were the two other roommates. Pia let out a long sigh.

"You can come back to my house. We have a spare bedroom. Besides me it's just Gordon and he spends most of his time in his office," Pia said in as upbeat a voice as she could under the circumstances.

Jeremy looked at her and asked, "Would that be okay?"

"Of course, my friend. Of course it would."

Then she started for home. She hoped she could be a strong caregiver for him and not a wreck. Besides caring for her mother, Pia had worked in a nursing home and was capable of caring for another adult's body. She could change the sheets on a bed with someone in it, but that wasn't a skill Jeremy would benefit from. She didn't know trauma like this at all.

Pia called Gordon and told him that Jeremy was coming to stay for a while. He started giving her some grief since it was now approaching nine-thirty and, of course, because she had slept with him.

Since she didn't want Jeremy to know that Gordon was not enthusiastic about having him in their home, she just said, "Great, thanks honey! We'll see you soon."

She sorely wished she could coach him ahead of time on not bringing up the past.

At her house, after the arduous job of getting Jeremy out of the back seat with as little discomfort as possible, Pia threw her coat and scarf on and they followed a flagstone path to the side door. Gordon sauntered into the kitchen when he heard them come through the door and Pia anxiously introduced them to one another.

"Gordon, this is Jeremy, the student whose photography exhibit I worked on. Jeremy, this is my husband."

Jeremy looked mostly at the floor, avoiding Gordon's eyes, with his hands again in the pockets of the hoodie. Gordon folded his arms across his chest. Neither showed interest in a handshake. There wasn't much of Jeremy's face to see, what with the hood, his long hair and the bruises, but as Gordon saw Jeremy's condition he smiled broadly.

"Wow, that's an impressive black eye! How many times did you get hit?"

Gordon's face told Pia his hidden thought: "The little bastard must've slept with somebody else's wife."

A flash of interest went through Pia as she learned Gordon knew something about fights. He made it sound like it was a macho source of pride to participate in them.

Jeremy mumbled, "I'm not sure…a few."

"You're not sure?"

Gordon sounded like he was goading Jeremy and Pia went on alert, ready to intervene. Jeremy didn't need any grief from him. Maybe he couldn't stay here after all.

Jeremy explained in a low voice directed at Gordon, "I was momentarily distracted when I got kicked in my balls."

Gordon was clearly pleased that someone had beaten Jeremy and smiled again, but said, "Whoa, I'll bet! I'm sure the other guy looks worse though, right? Your nose isn't broken; you're lucky."

Jeremy didn't say anything to that.

Pia dropped her handbag onto a chair wearily while she explained absentmindedly to Jeremy what Gordon meant.

"If your nose was fractured it would have to be re-hit to set it right."

"It's no fun. We have some ice packs from my knee surgery. There might still be one in the back of the freezer," Gordon said to them both.

He just could not help grinning and Pia hoped that Jeremy thought he was being friendly.

As she hung her coat and Gordon's in the closet Pia responded, "Good idea, thanks. I'll put the others in there in a little while."

After pulling several frozen foods out, Gordon found the pack in the freezer and handed it to Jeremy, who immediately set it against his face before Pia could unfold a dish rag from a nearby drawer.

"Thanks," he said to Gordon.

"Hold on a sec," Pia said as she moved Jeremy's hand away from his face.

She placed the towel around the pack and then nodded that he could press it to the eye.

She showed Jeremy upstairs. She set out some towels and gathered some clothes that might suit him best. Definitely not Gordon's underwear: they would just fall to the floor from Jeremy's small frame. She explained this to him and left some of hers instead. He didn't say anything one way or another. At least these were comfortable cotton without any frills. She had some loose flannel pajamas he could use, and she left with him her big, soft bathrobe. Jeremy remained standing in the guest room, which was feminine in blue, yellow and white florals on the quilt and the curtains, and Battenburg lace throw pillows. There were two upholstered chairs and an old, refurbished dresser painted yellow with a mirror over it. Sanguine landscape paintings made by local artists hung on the walls.

Without thinking Pia suggested, "You can have a seat, you know."

"Or not."

"Oh…right."

She felt stupid and looked down but then thought of a solution.

"Hey, I have an idea."

Pia went to her bedroom and Jeremy followed. In contrast to the guest room, this one was in taupe and mauve with antique cherry furniture that had belonged to Gordon's parents. Pia brought a small, wooden chair to the front of her closet with one hand, opened it and switched on the light with the other. She stood on the chair and rummaged through some travel bags on the shelf over her clothes. One bag nearly tumbled out but Jeremy caught it with his hand so Pia could shove it towards the back of the shelf. In a minute she found what she was looking for and held it out for Jeremy to take.

"You think it'll work?" she asked him.

Jeremy looked unenthusiastic but he took the U-shaped travel pillow designed for supporting a head. When Jeremy returned to his room he paused at his grim reflection in the mirror for a minute. He pulled his gaze away and then dropped the pillow onto the bed. Pia was in his doorway in a moment.

"Are you going to try it?"

Jeremy spat out, "I'm disgusting and filthy. I shouldn't touch anything until I've had a shower."

He looked away from her.

Pia said as evenly as she could, "What happened to you is disgusting and filthy, but *you* aren't, understand?"

"I'm not exactly clean."

Softly she told him, "You will be soon."

Before she left Jeremy to his shower Pia got clinical enough to give him instruction on looking at places with a hand mirror that he couldn't otherwise see. She told him she would collect various medicinal items from the downstairs bathroom, such as bandages and antibiotic ointments, and leave them in his room. Then she cautiously asked Jeremy about an idea she had been considering on the ride home.

"I have a friend who's a physician. I would like to call her. Someone really should look at you," she gently requested. Jeremy didn't give her an answer. "She could prescribe something for pain, too."

He was getting physically restless, so Pia could see he was uncomfortable about it.

As kindly as she could she added, "She won't judge you. You're— okay here."

Pia nearly said he was safe there, but it was too late for that.

Finally, he nodded.

"Thank you," Pia said with relief.

She turned and went back downstairs. Jeremy took a long shower. The first thing Pia did was go into Gordon's office to discuss Jeremy.

She told Gordon he had been in a fight and robbed outside a bar. She also told him that Jeremy didn't know she'd been fired or that Gordon knew about their affair. She didn't want Gordon to spill either of those last two pieces of information to Jeremy. Pia made him promise, and he reluctantly did so.

Carla assured Pia it wasn't too late to call. When Pia explained the situation Carla said she'd done the right thing to contact her and she would be there right away. When Pia heard Jeremy move from the bathroom to his bedroom, she went up to let him know Carla was coming. He was enveloped in that soft, peach bathrobe. His hair was wet so he was toweling it, but only half-heartedly. The eye was getting much worse. He began pacing from nerves when Pia told him her friend was on the way. She did her best to calm him.

"Jeremy, she's really nice and she has three sons of her own. If at any point you want her to stop or leave just say so and I'll make her go, I swear."

"Okay."

Just then the doorbell rang. Jeremy resumed pacing in the small room. Pia put her hand on his arm briefly and went downstairs.

Carla exchanged pleasantries with Gordon as Pia took her coat, then he went back in his office and the women went upstairs. Pia carried glasses of water for Jeremy and Carla. On the way Carla told Pia it would've been best if Jeremy hadn't had a shower before she saw him. Pia said she knew that but she thought, given the circumstances, it was more important to allow Jeremy his choices. Carla understood.

Pia introduced Carla to Jeremy as 'Dr. Young' and referred to him as 'the patient' for confidentiality. Carla had a wonderful smile and positive disposition but Pia had never seen her in her role as a physician before.

Carla asked her to assist, perhaps to ease Jeremy's nerves. It was clear they were taut. Because she was a midwife as well as a primary care physician, Carla was accustomed to, and prepared for, house calls. She took a seat in a chair opposite from Jeremy. He sat on the end of the bed on the travel pillow.

Carla leaned forward and began to speak soothingly. Her words were measured.

"I'm so sorry for what you've been through. I'm here to help you heal as best I can. I'll give you some pain medication and we'll attend to your injuries. I'll also give you something to help you sleep. I'll leave enough for five nights. Your body will heal much better with lots of rest, and it will give you some emotional relief, too."

Jeremy appeared to be listening closely. Pia wanted to stroke his hair back from his forehead but stayed focused on what Carla was saying.

"I want Pia to fill out the paperwork so you'll have it if you decide later you need it. The name on the forms will be John Doe, but the date and time and nature of the injuries is important documentation. It's really good that you're allowing me to see you. Thank you for letting me help."

Jeremy nodded with almost a smile for Carla and Pia was relieved to see him relax a bit. Carla was doing great. Then she threw a curve ball at them.

"Are you gay?" Carla asked very matter-of-factly.

"No!"

Jeremy jumped up and basically unraveled, repeating, "No!"

He moved in a tight circle nervously.

"Because…" Carla tried to continue.

Pia stood next to Jeremy, mortified.

She spoke very quickly and her tone was warning, "That's a boundary 'no', not an answer to the question, Carla."

She was about to tell her to leave.

"My point is that that doesn't matter, but if you were gay, you might be thinking that had something to do with causing this event," Carla said.

"It's not his fault!" Pia stressed, meaning the assault.

Jeremy was staring at Carla like he wanted to run but was confused by her.

"Exactly what I'm getting at," Carla said to Pia.

Then back to Jeremy, "It's *not* your fault. Your choices or lifestyle, whatever they may be, are not responsible for what happened to you tonight," Carla said earnestly, holding Jeremy's fearful stare.

Pia was catching on, and she repeated in a hushed tone to Jeremy, "It's not your fault."

"I'm sorry; I didn't mean to upset you," Carla said more gently. She paused, brushed imaginary lint from her pants, and then continued. "When I was seventeen, I was sexually assaulted by a 'friend of the family.' I spent years trying to figure out what I had done to make him decide to do that to me. I don't want you to waste one more minute thinking about what you did wrong or what you should've done differently."

Jeremy was showing signs of relief which Pia was glad for. Now she understood why Carla was so willing to come over. Jeremy sat back down gingerly on his pillow on the bed.

"Nothing you did is responsible for this. Nothing. Two horrid people preyed on you. Actually, you might not be their only victim. As Pia just said, it's not your fault, hon. You know that, don't you?"

Jeremy seemed like he might cry again. He looked down, shuffling his bare feet on the carpet briefly.

Carla added in a warm, friendly tone, "I'm sorry, I couldn't hear you."

Jeremy's throat only managed to produce a squawk, so he nodded, still looking down. Then some tears quietly slipped over his cheeks. Pia held out the box of tissues for Jeremy and lightly caressed his shoulders as he pulled out a few. Carla allowed time for the message to settle around him.

"Alright now. With your permission I'd like to start with that eye. If you've done an assessment in the shower you can show me what else needs to be looked at. It's at your discretion. Oh, let's give you that pain medication now. I also brought a tube of cream I can leave with you for localized relief."

"I helped myself to three Tylenols a while ago," Jeremy informed them, "but it hasn't touched the pain."

"That's fifteen hundred milligrams," Pia said, mostly for Carla.

She replied, "Okay, good to know. You may start writing now, beginning with that."

Carla tended to the eye, then the lip, verbalizing anything she wanted in the notes.

She asked Jeremy, "Where next?"

"My back is killing me."

Jeremy slipped off the sleeves of the robe, with it still tied at his waist, while Pia and Carla moved around to situate themselves behind him. He didn't have the pajama shirt on. Jeremy had substantial bruises on the front of his torso where he'd been punched, and his back had a huge area that was terribly bruised, swollen, and lacerated. He must've been slammed into something with a sharp edge. Pia recoiled when she saw it, not because it was gory so much as because it was on Jeremy.

"How're you doing, you alright?" Carla asked softly when she saw Pia's reaction.

Jeremy responded, "Yeah."

Carla laughed softly and touched his arm saying, "Sorry, hon, I was talking to our nurse. She might need a minute."

This made Jeremy turn his head to look at Pia, and Pia wished he hadn't. She composed herself quickly. He gave her an understanding look.

They proceeded to do the best they could for him, including fifteen stitches. When Carla was finished with Jeremy's back she draped the robe up over his shoulders and he adjusted it around himself.

"How about your legs and arms?" she asked.

Pia was seated in one of the chairs catching up on her notes and only half listening.

Jeremy pushed back his sleeves to reveal a few bruises and said, "My legs are alright."

Carla gave his forearms a look over and then indicated that they were not of great concern by gently brushing the sleeves back down over them.

Aware that Pia was still writing she said to Jeremy discreetly, "There's more?"

She held his gaze. He blinked a few times and gave a tight nod. Carla straightened and stretched her back, waiting for Pia to finish.

"The antibiotic cream is twice a day?" Pia asked without looking up.

"Right. If that wound gets any worse let me know right away and we'll try something more aggressive."

Jeremy quietly said, "Aggressive?"

Carla found a gentler phrase, saying, "I mean something more effective in fighting infection."

Pia finished writing and sat there cluelessly.

Carla pressed her lips together and then said, "That'll be all, Pia."

Pia looked at her blankly.

Carla added, "Thank you."

Then Pia realized she was being excused so Jeremy could have some privacy with just Carla.

"Ah."

She put down the pen and papers and left the room. She waited at the bottom of the stairs, sitting with her legs crossed, one foot wagging. Gordon came to check on things and she stood up to embrace him but he would have none of that and pushed her hands down. He was not happy about this arrangement.

"Thanks for letting him come here. He's been hurt pretty badly." Gordon didn't have a say in it but Pia wanted to acknowledge that he should.

"I don't want him here."

"I know, I'm sorry."

Gordon walked away and Pia sat again.

After a while Jeremy came out of the room and went back to the bathroom. Carla gathered her things and was about to head downstairs when Jeremy came back out to the hallway.

"Thank you, Dr. Young. I really appreciate your help."

He looked at her as though they had something that bound them together.

Then, after a pause, "My name is Jeremy Ronan."

He leaned forward to hug Carla and she returned it, being as careful as possible with his back. Both Carla and Pia understood that he was showing trust and gratitude by telling her who he was. Pia was touched by that.

"You're most welcome, Jeremy. Pia knows where to find me if you need anything else. Take care with yourself."

That was an interesting thing to say, Pia thought, 'take care with yourself.' Before Jeremy was back in the bathroom Pia asked up the stairs if she could check on him in a little while. He nodded.

Once Carla turned to descend the stairs she looked overwrought. Pia directed her around the corner to sit on the living room sofa together. Carla set about writing two prescriptions on the coffee table before her.

Pia didn't know quite what to say to the physician but saw that she was affected by tending to Jeremy.

"Are you alright, Carla?"

Carla paused but returned to her writing before she spoke.

Once she finished she snapped her pen down and said, "That boy, Jeremy, is seriously suffering."

Pia was about to press her hands to her ears as she could not bear any details, but the two women stood toe-to-toe at the invisible barrier that was patient confidentiality. Pia would not ask more and Carla would not say more.

"I'm sorry, I had no idea this would be so hard on you," Pia told her genuinely.

Carla said through clenched teeth, "It makes me so angry."

"You've been such a great help to him," Pia said to console her. Carla looked doubtful about that, so Pia added, "Really, he's much calmer than he was earlier."

Carla smirked and rubbed her brow.

Wagging one of two pill packages in front of Pia she explained, "He's not calm, he's heavily sedated. He could fall asleep brushing his teeth."

"Oh."

Carla provided Pia a schedule for ice packs and medications. Then she wrote out a doctor's note. This would excuse Jeremy from work for up to a week. Carla could follow up with another if necessary. Pia brought Carla her coat and then walked her to her car. She hugged Carla and thanked her, so sorry for what Carla had experienced. Then she described for Carla what Jeremy was like before this.

"He was so positive; a person light shone from. I can't understand how anyone could hurt such a sweet person."

Pia rubbed her hands over her face for a minute.

"This experience doesn't have to define him," Carla said gently. "He will find his light again." Pia clung to this hope.

She offered to pay Carla but she refused it.

After Carla left, Pia went back upstairs and knocked on Jeremy's door, which wasn't completely shut.

"Come in."

He was in bed under the covers. Pia sat in the chair next to him. As an ice pack was balanced on his face over the eye, she couldn't really see his face.

"Thanks for letting Dr. Young see you. I think she was helpful," Pia told him.

What she actually thought was that the woman was totally amazing and they couldn't have asked for a better doctor. This would be written in a notecard to Carla, sent along with some flowers later in the week.

"She was great. I'm glad you talked me into it."

He was much calmer. Pia didn't care if it was the sedative causing it, she was just grateful for it. He yawned.

"She did scare the shit out of us for a minute, though," Pia recalled.

"Yeah. Um, I think I ruined some of your towels…there was blood. Maybe these pajamas."

"Don't worry about that. If the bleeding becomes a concern, we can call Dr. Young; she's ten minutes away. I told Gordon you were in a fight outside a bar. I can stuff a pillow behind you to keep you from rolling if you want."

Jeremy said sleepily, "Uh, sure, that might help."

Pia got him set up so that the back injury and the eye were not pressed against anything. Then she gently set the ice pack on a face cloth over his eye.

"Oh, there's one thing I should warn you about," she said as she sat again. "A long time ago I went through a rough time, although nothing like this. Anyway, I found that when I woke up was tough. I can't remember for how long this went on but, tomorrow at least, you'll have one or two seconds when you first wake when everything's fine, like it was before. But they're bittersweet because just then you'll remember your current reality. That third second really sucks."

"I didn't know you swear so much," he answered in a groggy voice.

Pia thought to herself, "I didn't know I loved you so much."

She stroked his hair gently. The thin old cat jumped up on the bed.

"I'm sorry; I can keep her out of the room if you want."

"She's fine."

As he petted the cat she licked the top of his forehead with her tiny, serrated tongue and purred before moving down the quilt to find a comfortable nook. He yawned again.

"Can I get you anything?"

"No, I'm good."

They both understood he was merely using a figure of speech, and that this was in fact the worst night of his life.

"Alright. I hope you have peaceful sleep."

Pia rose, turned on the closet light and left its door open a little bit. She went to leave, switching off a lamp, but then hesitated halfway out the door. She thought for a minute about what to do.

"Jeremy?"

"Yeah."

Pia revealed, "I don't want to leave you."

"It's okay."

"No, I mean I would really like to stay with you, if you don't mind. Just until you're asleep?"

"Sure. When I'm alone…it all comes back."

Pia returned to curl up in the chair with her head resting on her arm. She observed the cat, so content and oblivious. After a bit, Pia removed the ice pack for the night and thought Jeremy might have been looking at her with his one good eye. She couldn't be sure in the darkness.

He mumbled, "Do you have a lullaby?"

"Hmm…. I have a song I used to sing to the turtle hatchlings."

"You sang to them."

"Yes. They liked it," Pia said sheepishly.

Then she began singing Joni Mitchell's 'River'. Jeremy closed his eyes when she began and it wasn't long before he was sleeping.

Chapter 19

Pia gathered Jeremy's clothes and towels and rinsed them in the large sink in her basement. There was a tear along the back of his t-shirt but she didn't think it was her place to throw it away. She held each item under a strong stream of ice-cold water until Jeremy's blood snaked out of the fabric and down the drain to her septic system in the front yard, far beneath the new grass coming up. She roughly rubbed the fabric even after the dark red was gone. Afterwards, she put them in the washer and finally the dryer.

Gordon would not acknowledge Pia when she came to bed. She rubbed his neck but received no response. They slept with their backs to one another.

Jeremy slept deeply and, as far as Pia could tell, soundly. In the morning she carried his clothes upstairs and quietly placed them in his room and then returned to the first floor. She phoned Jeremy's employer to let them know he would not be in. She conjured her medical secretary persona from her past to explain that he had been injured and would call them later on.

She showered and put on jeans and a cotton shirt under a thick gray sweatshirt. She walked around in fluffy lavender socks. Gordon and Pia had coffee without conversing. She put on some soft instrumental music in the living room. She tried her best to read a magazine but her mind continually wandered back to the previous night. Without knowing how to best deal with this crisis, Pia felt an undercurrent of anxiety all morning. She spiraled down to a dark contemplation of all the horrors some people routinely inflicted on others.

Jeremy came downstairs at about noon. He was still in the pajamas and the robe. At the bottom of the stairs he stopped to look around and he found Pia in the living room sitting in a big stuffed armchair with her feet tucked under her. It was partly cloudy outside, but the room was bright and welcoming when the clouds gave way.

"Hi," he said.

Pia saw him taking in their surroundings through the four windows, the wooded land, the isolation, the distance from where he'd been assaulted.

She returned from her gloomy musings to say, "Hey there. Let me make another pot of coffee; this is old," as she rose from her seat. "It's time for another ice pack, my friend."

She stopped in front of him, the eye injury being the central feature of his face now, although his lip was bad too. He was not doing any better at all.

Feeling unable to comfort she said only, "I wish there was something I could do for you."

"You are helping, thanks," he said rather mechanically.

Jeremy was still thoughtful, even though the light was extinguished from his eyes and spirit.

He sighed, adding, "I have to call my company."

"I called them around eight. I told them you had an injury and you'd call them yourself later. I hope that's okay," Pia said as she walked to the kitchen with Jeremy following her.

"Who did you say you were in relation to me? If there's coffee in the pot, I'll have that."

So Pia poured that for him and then started a fresh pot. She moved along the kitchen counter, reaching for the coffee and filter out of the cabinet.

She slid the sugar and milk over to him, continuing, "I told them I was calling for Dr. Carla Young on your behalf, because you couldn't. You can tell them you're under her care. How are you doing?"

They both stood leaning against the kitchen counter then, each holding a coffee mug.

Jeremy spoke quietly.

"Oh, the same. Nothing hurts less today. I feel like there is some tiny amount of space now between me and what happened. I wish I didn't think about it constantly."

Jeremy looked at his coffee and then drank some. His face was pained as he stared at the floor.

Pia said quietly, "Come back here."

Jeremy looked at her and she gazed at him compassionately. After a minute she went over to a small roll-top desk in a corner of the kitchen and retrieved his prescriptions for dosage details.

"You can have more pain medication now."

Jeremy looked over her shoulder and said, "How can you understand any of this? It looks like hieroglyphics."

Pia handed them to him so he could look at them with his one good eye.

"I worked for surgeons so I know the shorthand. This triangle means 'change', the s/p is short for 'status post,' which just means 'after,' and that P.O. means to take the medication orally, ingest it. 'TID' means three times a day."

Jeremy looked surprised by her knowledge. Pia took his medication out for him because Carla had suggested she monitor the doses if possible. She also thought the more clinically she behaved and spoke, the easier it would be for him to be responsive to her assistance.

He swallowed the pills with the coffee and then asked, "Would it be okay if I had another shower?"

She said, "Of course. Would you like something to eat? Maybe not."

When Pia was going through her divorce she could not eat for three months.

"Sure." He seemed as surprised to realize this as she was to hear it. "I'm not interested in food, but I'm very hungry."

"Good. Brunch will be ready when you come back downstairs."

Gordon was pleased that Pia would be making a huge brunch with scrambled eggs, English muffins and some sausages just for him, since Jeremy didn't eat meat. She peeled and separated eight clementines as well. She didn't have much energy but was still glad to have a task.

Jeremy came back downstairs in a while and they all ate together. His hair was wet again, and he had the robe on.

After some silence Gordon said, "Pia made this strawberry jam. She says it's like summer in a jar."

Something in his tone made Pia feel that he was meaning to convey that he knew her much better than Jeremy ever would.

"I'll try it, thanks," Jeremy said as he reached for the jar in the center of the table.

"Yep, she's been making it every summer for years. My son's family loves it so she always gives them some. You could say it's a family tradition."

Jeremy gave him a weak and brief smile.

"The grandchildren love it. Did you know we have grandchildren?"

Jeremy paused from eating to respond.

"Uhh…I don't think I knew that, no." He changed the subject. "Do you follow the Patriots?"

"I didn't watch them much this season."

They were at a dead end.

Pia watched Gordon size up this young man dressed in his wife's bathrobe, with an eye swollen and purple. Jeremy was having some difficulty eating with his damaged lip, making it slow going. Gordon must've done his best not to think about their history. It seemed so improbable.

Pia said, "Gordon likes baseball. My sister's a classic football widow." Then, quizzically she asked Jeremy, "Do you like football?"

She doubted it but didn't know for sure.

Jeremy shrugged. "No. I just figured most people do. Not my thing." He shifted in his seat frequently. "Pia, after we eat would you mind looking at my back? I think I'm going to need some bandages or something."

Pia began to get up, saying, "Let me look."

"No, that's alright, later's fine."

Pia sat back down. She was resisting a desire to tend to him. When her plate was empty, she brought it to the counter and picked up Jeremy's paperwork. She wanted to refresh her memory about the back. She rejoined them at the table with it.

Gordon asked, "What's that paperwork?"

"It's Jeremy's documentation. I just want to go over how to treat his back."

Then she glanced up at Gordon with a look that said 'drop it.' Unfortunately, Gordon never picked up on subtleties. He looked over towards the papers so Pia abruptly placed them face down between herself and Jeremy. Gordon would select a parking spot next to another car in an otherwise empty lot. He just had no sense of personal space.

She noted, "It's almost twenty degrees warmer today than yesterday."

"I shut the window you opened. It's still only fifty-five degrees," Gordon said. "So how do you know Carla, Pia?"

This wasn't a strange question because Pia knew about a hundred people in town through various groups and Gordon didn't participate in them. Jeremy seemed surprised by it though. Shouldn't Gordon know this?

"Isn't she a friend of yours?" He asked, looking at each of them.

Pia explained, "She's an acquaintance of mine. We're on the open space and recreation committee together. We like each other, I think."

Trying to be funny, Gordon said, "You *think* you like her?"

"I know I like her. I have trouble understanding if people like me. You know that," Pia said before finishing the last of her juice, thinking Gordon was being an ass.

"Well, I like you," Gordon proclaimed.

"Thanks," Pia said. "Good save," she thought.

"Me, too," Jeremy added.

He looked directly at her eyes, although only briefly. When Gordon looked over at him, Jeremy was again involved with getting his eggs into the uninjured side of his mouth. Gordon glanced at her as well. To Pia's relief and surprise she hadn't blushed.

Gordon said, "There, it's unanimous."

When they were finished eating Gordon went back to his office. Pia and Jeremy went upstairs so she could tend to his back injury. With Jeremy's approval, Pia pushed the cotton curtains aside and opened a window slightly before she looked at his back. The pajama shirt was stuck to the dried blood of the injury, so it was a process to remove it by re-wetting it. Jeremy's back needed several things: ice for the swelling and bruising and bandaging for the substantial cut. Pia delicately and methodically cleaned away some pus and blood, applied the antibiotic cream, then the bandages. They didn't talk, so the room was silent except for the sounds of spring coming in through the open window. Pia was much gentler with Jeremy than she would've been with her own body.

After she smoothed the final piece of tape securing the last piece of gauze, she moved Jeremy's hair aside and kissed the back of his shoulder very lightly. The gesture was something she had to do for herself and she hoped he didn't mind it. He looked at her then, like he had the night before when Carla asked how she was doing.

"Pia," he said softly.

If she gave any thought to Jeremy's assault she would lose control of herself. Unfortunately, that's what happened next. Pia took several deep breaths trying to contain her grief before her face distorted and she began to cry.

"Don't cry."

Pia wiped her eyes with her sleeve, but they weren't finished yet.

"I'm not; my eyes are leaking."

"They're leaking tears."

She didn't want to make this about her; she didn't want to do this. She continued to suck air in gasps, and she pulled her sleeves into her fists, which she pushed against her eyes. Pia cried much like a five-year-old.

She explained to him while sniveling, "Pain and love are two sides of the same coin and I love you so much. I can't stand thinking about what you've been put through. It's breaking my heart."

Jeremy stood up but was in no shape to console someone else.

She continued, "I myself caused you to suffer once. How could I? I'm so sorry."

Without having to give it a thought he replied spontaneously, "You're still my friend. I knew you would help me if I asked."

Almost magically, Jeremy's words soothed her. She hadn't thought at all about why he called her. She had been concentrating only on what to do for him. Pia was comforted by the idea that they were friends and she pulled herself together. She used more of the facial tissues that were supposedly for him. She collected the items she had spread across the quilt while tending his back and put everything on the dresser. Pia tossed the used packaging in the trash while Jeremy pulled on a white cotton t-shirt and she helped him put on a loose sweatshirt over it.

"If you can lay on your stomach I'll keep some ice on that for a while. You can stretch out on the sofa and watch T.V. in the living room, or there's another sofa on the porch. Or stay here?"

"The porch."

Feeling like a failure, Pia said meekly, "I apologize for losing it."

Jeremy had a revelation for her.

"I would have been a little disappointed in you if you didn't, actually. You've been so stoic."

They went downstairs again and Jeremy settled on the sofa on the three-season porch. It was sunnier now so that room was comfortable even with the windows open slightly on either side for a cross breeze.

Pia carefully placed some ice packs on his back, between the shirt and the sweatshirt, and on a facecloth over his eye. She sat on the floor keeping that one balanced. A variety of male songbirds had arrived from the south and were vocalizing throughout the surrounding woods. There weren't any deciduous leaves out yet but there were buds ready. Occasionally the breeze would ride along the tops of the pine trees and they announced the wind's presence, one after the other all the way down the hill. You could hear it coming well before it reached Pia's address and well after.

Jeremy noticed something else about it, saying, "The wind sounds a lot like the ocean on a beach."

"I never thought of it like that. The wind collides with the pine trees, just like the waves hit the sand. Without something to break its stride, it wouldn't make noise, I guess. Once, in Florida, I saw a cyclone because it picked up sand and dirt. If it hadn't, I wouldn't have seen it in time to move."

Jeremy told her, "Once on the Cape I saw a waterspout."

"Really?"

Gordon came to the doorway between the porch and kitchen and asked Pia, "Are you going to bring the paper up?"

"Sure. Jeremy's seen a waterspout, Gordon. Have you ever seen one?" Pia asked, knowing this would interest him.

"No. That would be something. Where was that?" he asked Jeremy.

"It was on the Cape a long time ago. I think I was about twelve or thirteen. It was like magic."

Pia rose to walk down the driveway for the newspaper. Before she reached the bottom step she looked back to the porch to see Gordon retreat to the kitchen. She didn't want those two alone together. The cat was there in his place and she scented Jeremy's outstretched hand when he offered it. She purred for him.

Pia returned moments later with the paper and the mail and was pleased to see the cat still with Jeremy.

She remarked, "The poet Pablo Neruda would call her a 'diminutive parlor tiger.'"

Jeremy coaxed the animal, "Diminutive parlor tiger…diminutive parlor tiger."

The cat moved to the center of the floor and began licking her tail.

"She doesn't care much for that title," he decided.

Pia brought everything into Gordon and they talked about what to have for dinner.

Soon she returned to the doorway to ask Jeremy, "Do you need anything?"

He had his phone on the floor and his left arm swung down to it tapping the screen.

"I don't know what to tell my supervisor. What would you recommend?"

Pia could barely see Jeremy's good eye looking at her from the cushion.

"Well, I'd say I was in an auto accident, in the passenger seat."

"That would be lying, though."

Pia sighed heavily. "Carla wrote that you 'sustained injuries', so stick with that. Your employer knows not to ask any details. I agree with her that you should take a few more days."

She thought of Jeremy going to work with a busted-up face. Apparently he had the same thought.

"I don't want to show up with a black eye. I feel like the rest will be transparent."

"My suspicion was based on how you behaved, how different you seemed," she said, meaning to be helpful.

"Great. I guess I'll work on that."

Pia turned to go inside so he could make whatever phone calls he wanted without her there. Something occurred to her then though, so she turned back to him, closing the door.

"Jeremy?" she asked hesitantly.

He replied cautiously, "Yeah?"

She went over to him and dropped to the floor, sitting on one foot. She tipped her head near his so she could look at his good eye.

Quietly she asked, "Do you know them?"

Jeremy looked at her for a long moment before lamenting, "I thought I did. I'd met them before. I'm not pressing charges, if that's what you're thinking in that head of yours."

Pia's face showed she had another concern. She frowned and bit her lip.

"What is it?" Jeremy prompted her.

"Do they know where you live? Or where you work?"

Pia was becoming worried that he had not seen the last of the brutes. She began to gnaw on a thumbnail with vigor.

"They don't," he assured her. Jeremy's relief about that was reflected in his tone.

Pia was comforted and she strongly exhaled, "Good."

She was about to get up when Jeremy had a new thought.

"Jesus, now you have me thinking. I should warn people. But I can't do that without telling and I just… can't."

He was becoming panicky and sat up. Sitting caused him to wince but he managed it. Pia was sorry she had started this conversation so soon. The ice packs fell away from him.

He shook his head slowly as he told her, "Pia, I can't tell. But I don't want them to do this to someone else. Dr. Young said something about this, didn't she?"

"That there may be other victims, yes." She collected the ice packs from around him, saying, "I'm making things worse for you."

Jeremy didn't seem to hear that. His mind began racing while he struggled with this miserable impasse. He looked at her, searching for some resolution.

"Jeremy, you're a trauma victim. Give yourself some time to heal. Later you might have the strength to help others but you don't have to think about that now."

"I can't just turn off these thoughts. I don't know what to do," he said, jittery and tense.

Gordon noticed this activity through the window of the kitchen door and opened it, asking, "What's the matter?"

Jeremy looked down quickly.

Pia said cautiously, "We're considering how to warn other people that they might get jumped too."

"Oh. It's called a police report. You're right to be thinking that it isn't an isolated incident. No one steals one wallet, right? Once somebody speaks up, others will come forward."

With that Jeremy looked at Gordon, who reached for a bag of potato chips from a cabinet and walked away.

"Thanks for the wisdom," Pia said sarcastically. He was already out of hearing range.

Jeremy said, "Hey, he's right. Maybe someone else has already reported them."

Pia suggested, "We can look into it."

"That means I don't have to," he concluded.

This thought calmed him considerably so Pia left it at that.

Gordon hollered toward the porch from inside the house, "Pia, did you open any windows upstairs?"

"Yes!" she called back.

"Would you close them already?"

To Jeremy Pia said, "Excuse me."

She rose from the floor and went inside, swinging the kitchen door behind her but it didn't shut all the way.

Gordon said gruffly, "Don't be an idiot. You're letting bugs in."

"Simmer down, I'm shutting them," she said as she passed Gordon and headed up the staircase.

She let Jeremy be. He did a lot of texting and later watched an old movie on television with her. Pia hoped it was a distraction for him but he might have been indulging her. Gordon ran some errands. For dinner Pia made a tuna casserole and a salad with lots of good things in it: chickpeas, cucumbers, spinach, carrots, radishes, sunflower seeds and tomatoes. Pia didn't plate the food, she put it all out on the dining room table. She poured Gordon some red wine. Jeremy asked for water.

After a while Gordon commented, "I guess you could've made Swedish meatballs after all."

Pia looked at him questioningly. Gordon motioned to Jeremy's plate, which included the salad and two rolls. Jeremy had been scoffing down his large helping of the salad, albeit with difficulty due to his injury, but stopped eating when he realized they were discussing him. He looked at each of them.

"I don't eat meat."

Pia began, "I'm sorry. I thought tuna —"

Jeremy snapped at her, "Fish are animals, Pia. I don't eat animals."

Gordon intervened, "Hey, watch your tone."

Pia moved a hand towards him, murmuring, "Gordon, don't."

Jeremy said, "Sorry."

He didn't sound sorry, he sounded hostile. Jeremy put his napkin on the table as he got up and left the room. Pia became glum. She didn't understand why he ate dried fish in Africa but not her tuna. When she cleaned up the table she left Jeremy's plate in case he wanted to finish eating. She microwaved some leftover Indian rice from a few days ago and set it on the table in a covered earthenware crock. Gordon went back to his office to watch television. Shortly after that Jeremy came in the kitchen where Pia was transferring the leftover food to plastic containers.

"I'm sorry. I was feeling really angry but I don't know why. I should apologize to Gordon, too," said, looking in the direction of the office.

There was still some remaining tension in his voice and the apology seemed forced.

Pia said pacifyingly, "No, Gordon and I were rude. Being in pain is also taking a toll on you."

Then she thought that while that was true enough, the whole situation was misery for him.

"I stopped eating fish three years ago but you wouldn't know that," he explained.

Pia said kindly, "There's biryani rice on the table for you. If you've had enough of today you can have your sedative as well."

He had only been up for about eight hours.

"Just the sedative, please. Can I have Dr. Young's number? I have to ask her about something I just thought of."

"Sure, let me get it," Pia replied, putting down a pot.

She brought the paperwork to Jeremy. "You should hold onto these papers, unless you'd rather I do. Here's her number," Pia said as she pointed to where she wrote it in her notes.

He lowered his voice, "I'd prefer it if you could keep all this if you have a good hiding place for it. Just don't read the last page in Dr. Young's handwriting. Would you mind?"

"No, that's no problem."

Eventually she would put them in a manila envelope in the back of her closet behind a shoebox. Jeremy took the pills for sleep as prescribed and went up to his room with his phone and papers. In a short time, he came back downstairs and into the kitchen.

"Pia?"

She was at the sink washing dishes. "Hmm?"

"Would you mind picking up a prescription for me? Dr. Young called it in to a pharmacy in the next town over. It's kind of urgent so I don't know why she couldn't use one here."

Pia shut off the faucet and turned to him while she dried her hands on a towel, explaining, "Because there isn't one in this town."

Jeremy looked incredulous.

"I'll leave right now. Do you want to come for the ride?"

"I'd better stay here."

"Okay. It takes fifteen minutes each way so I'll be a half hour if it's ready when I get there. Will that be alright?"

Jeremy looked a bit concerned but nodded. Pia went to Gordon to tell him that she was going and he offered to finish the dishes so she gave him a kiss and hug, both of which were met with resistance.

Just before she left the house Jeremy said, "Wait."

Pia paused at the open door, keys in hand, expecting a request for something additional from the pharmacy. Jeremy came across the room and silently gave her a quick peck on her cheek, jumping back a step immediately and looking contrite. She looked at him with sympathy before she closed the door behind her.

Pia drove as fast as she could. After she left the pharmacy and was waiting at a red light, she glanced at the product. It was a hydrocortisone enema, Pia presumed to help process his meals without pain. When she arrived home she thanked Gordon for doing the dishes.

"Oh, I forgot."

"But they're all washed."

"Then Jeremy must've done them," he replied, turning his attention back to his show.

As soon as he heard Pia's voice, Jeremy came downstairs to greet her, rather bleary from the sedative.

"Thanks, Pia. I really appreciate you going out for this."

He took the paper bag from her and turned to go upstairs.

Pia wanted to explain how the medicine worked and why it might not be as effective for Jeremy as he expected.

"It works by being absorbed through the thin lining of —"

"No-no-no," he said firmly, surprised and embarrassed that she knew what it was.

Pia blinked, saying, "Alright, but just take this pencil."

She pulled a stubby one from a cup full of pens near the phone and held it out to him. He looked puzzled so she clarified its purpose.

"To bite down on."

Jeremy was losing patience, saying, "You're incorrigible, you know."

He snatched the pencil, turned and went upstairs.

Pia called after him, "You'll thank me later." Then she quietly added, "Godspeed."

While Jeremy was upstairs, Pia pulled out her laptop to read her email at the kitchen table. That always took longer than expected. Jeremy never came back down. After about two hours Pia went up to check on him. He had left his closet door ajar and its light on and was fast asleep in his bed, delicately snoring. It was rather like the cat purring. She sat down on the carpet with her back leaning against the wall and watched Jeremy sleeping. Another time Pia would be pleased to have this gift. As it was, she appreciated it, but the cost had been too great. Pia's eyes adjusted as she sat there and gradually she saw more of his features. The eye itself was less swollen now, but the swelling was moving down his face, which made him breathe through his mouth.

She thought about their relationship in all its different expressions. It occurred to her suddenly that her fever had broken. Pia still liked to gaze at his face but it was different now. She loved this person very much and was glad she had told him so today. Jeremy was precious to her and she had missed him terribly since she last saw him. However, her romantic interest in him was gone. Pia might possibly be able to invoke some of the passion she previously had for him if she thought about it long enough, but she would not meditate on it again. Possibly she had finally outgrown it.

She heard the stairs creaking and saw the light come on in the hall. Then Gordon was standing in the doorway.

"There you are," he said.

Pia motioned for him to be quiet, bringing a finger to her lips.

He ignored that, saying, "Come to bed."

There was no reason not to, so she got up, closed the door to Jeremy's room behind her and followed Gordon down the hall. After brushing her teeth Pia switched on a nightlight in the bathroom in case Jeremy got up during the night.

Once she was in bed Gordon began caressing her. She was glad he was interested but weary and pushed his hands away.

"I'm too tired, honey."

The hands returned immediately and deliberately.

"Gordon…."

He was being uncharacteristically aggressive.

She thought, "Well, this is not how we normally play." It then dawned on her that this was because she had brought Jeremy to their home.

"Oh, I get it. Gordon's being the alpha male. There's no need for him to feel threatened by Jeremy. Can't he see that? So perhaps this is, not punishment exactly, but penance." She was a realist, figuring, "I suppose I am putting him through some difficult days." She wasn't excusing his behavior, just explaining it to herself. By the time she finished her thoughts he rolled over, satisfied. Shortly after that he began snoring.

The next morning, Saturday, went similarly to the first, but Pia slept later, assuming Jeremy would as well. She made coffee and brought Gordon a hot mug once the coffee maker gurgled that its task was complete. Normally they toasted to the morning and Pia was willing to but Gordon still had something bothering him.

"Pia, is he leaving today?"

"I don't know, Gordon. We haven't talked about it. He can stay as long as he wants."

"Why is he here anyway?"

Once Gordon said that, it surprised Pia that he hadn't asked it sooner. It was certainly a valid question.

"Well, initially he wanted a ride but then when I saw his condition, I invited him to stay with us. He can't take care of his back by himself," Pia explained.

He kept at her, "Why are you taking care of him?"

Why, indeed. There was the difficult question again.

"You know that I've always wanted to be a mother."

"You want to have a kid with him?" he said meanly.

"No, Gordon. He is the child," she replied in a tone that suggested the man was a slow study. She continued, "If I had a son, I'd want him to be just like Jeremy. Let me take care of him while he needs my help. Please. It won't be much longer."

Gordon picked up the newspaper that had slid to the floor from his lap, grunting from the pain the action caused his lower back.

"You can't do with a son what you've done with him."

Pia was mortified that he was bringing that up. Really though, while Pia and Jeremy knew that that aspect of their relationship was permanently in the past, she couldn't expect Gordon to believe it. She realized then that it was extremely magnanimous of him to allow Jeremy in the house at all and it demonstrated enormous faith on his part.

Pia leaned over and kissed Gordon's cheek.

"You're the best, honey. Thanks for your patience."

Pia's affection disarmed Gordon and made it difficult for him to remain angry.

He conceded, "He's not what I expected…but I still hate him."

"All of the responsibility for what happened between us is on me. Be angry with me. He's just a kid."

Gordon lifted the paper to read so it blocked their view of one another, saying, "Whatever. If you get any more maternal you're going to start lactating."

"Eww. That's gross."

Gordon chuckled to himself.

She went out to the deck to enjoy her coffee. It was about fifty degrees but mostly sunny. She hadn't put out any outdoor furniture yet, although it was almost the season for it, so she carried a chair from the porch and sat with her feet on the seat, with her hands around the mug balanced on her knee. Hot coffee on a cool morning was such a pleasure. She tried to think of something Jeremy might want to do today. If he were feeling up to it physically, maybe they could go for a walk at the sanctuary or in the woods behind the house.

There were big, white, cotton clouds moving slowly overhead. The same kind that Pia envisioned herself floating on during meditation. The birds were singing and there were a few insects flying. After she finished her coffee she went upstairs to take a shower. It was about ten, so, based on yesterday, she figured Jeremy would still be asleep. Of course she didn't know for certain if he'd been sleeping yesterday at that time or was in fact awake. She only knew he remained in his room.

Before showering Pia was in her bedroom choosing clothes, still in pajamas and her thin summer robe, when she was startled by sounds from Jeremy's room, a series of banging noises and then a vocalization similar to the cat when she made a mad dash around the house, a broken loud cry. She went to investigate, as did Gordon. When she hesitated at the landing, outside of the room, Gordon was at the bottom of the stairs. He was about to say something. Pia held her palm out for him to stay there, and she paused at Jeremy's door; it was quiet. Then another banging noise, maybe on the wall.

Gordon demanded, "What the hell is he doing? Tell him to knock it off!"

"Just hold off a minute," she hissed at him.

Without knocking Pia stepped into the room, closing the door behind her. She wanted to keep Gordon separated from Jeremy's real troubles.

Jeremy was turned to the far wall with his fists and head against it, kneeling in the flannel pajama pants. The quilt and covers were thrown to the floor and the pajama shirt was on the bed. He seemed to be wrestling with the wall, his muscles taut and flexing. Pia quickly came to his side and squatted there. She was afraid to touch him without his permission.

"Jeremy, hon. Hey, sshhh."

Jeremy flattened his hands to the wall as he vomited on it, the baseboard, and the carpet. After retching three times he looked at her with a string of bile hanging from his lip and terrified eyes. Pia was alarmed because he was looking at her with that fear on his face as though she had brought it on. Jeremy stayed that way for a few seconds with a fresh injury to his bad eye.

He acknowledged her, "Pia."

However, it was as if he was in two places at once and he ordered, "Go *away*."

Her head told her to do as he said, that that was very important to respect, but she was too shocked to physically act on it. Jeremy was highly agitated and shot up to circle about the room with his arms wrapped into himself, then flung out around him, flexing, flexing.

"Don't look at me. I can't…oh, God."

He circled this way and that. Pia rushed to leave him alone, but as she passed by him she gently ran her hand over his lower back and an arm, hoping he'd understand she was leaving for him, not because of him.

When she was at the top of the stairs she took two steps down and lied to Gordon, who was still waiting at the bottom.

"It's a spider. We got it," she said loudly enough for Jeremy to hear, so he'd know Gordon might intrude.

That worked.

"All that for a spider?!"

She lied again, "It seems he's phobic about them. It's dead now."

Before he walked away Gordon replied, "Tell him we have a lot more of them. Maybe he'll leave then."

Pia frowned at Gordon with disappointment because Jeremy might have heard that.

Then "Pia" came from Jeremy's room.

She took a deep breath and cautiously opened the door to peek inside. Jeremy looked completely defeated but he was back in the present, holding the pajama shirt in one hand. Pia came back in, closing the door again, and stood a foot from him. She'd never seen his shoulders slumped before. Tears rolled down his face slowly, two at a time.

"I don't know if I can do this. God, I don't know," he said as he pulled his arms through the shirtsleeves.

He wiped his good eye with a thumb quickly and reached out for a hug.

Pia returned it, saying softly, "Shhh. You poor thing. You've got a long road ahead."

He held on increasingly tightly. The irony of being hugged to death would suit her, Pia thought. She would just have to wait this out, but it was difficult to breathe now.

"Why did I go with them?" he despaired, seeming angry with himself. If Pia could speak she would've reminded him it wasn't his fault.

When Jeremy did release her, abruptly, he was emotionally exhausted and dropped into a chair holding his head in his hands. Pia brought him the tissues as she had before. It was a ritual at this point. She couldn't think of any response to him. It was Jeremy's journey and one she knew nothing about. She wasn't going to say anything trite, so she sat on the bed in case he had any use for her.

After about two minutes, he lifted his head, looked at the vomit and then said to her, "Sorry. I'll clean that up."

"No, I will. Do not apologize. Do *not.*"

Pia's tone implied she'd be angry if he did so again. He just sighed.

He looked at his hands and noticed a little blood from his eye area that had cut open.

"Shower," he said, getting out of the chair and walking towards the bathroom.

Pia spent some time putting the summer furniture on the deck, dusting it off and arranging it the same way she always had. She made grilled cheese and tomato sandwiches for lunch, with ham added to Gordon's. Jeremy ate three of them and finished their milk. Pia was running low on food. She remembered Carla once referring to her boys as eating machines. Later Jeremy and Pia sat on the deck in the sunshine and Gordon again retreated to his office. A rabbit was under a maple tree nibbling bright yellow dandelion heads.

"Good bunny," Pia encouraged it. Then she lamented, "I suppose I'll have to mow the lawn soon. I hate the first cut. It's like cutting a baby's hair."

She felt the following silence acutely.

She assumed Jeremy must be thinking, "Who cares?"

A breeze came along and blew their hair in their faces then back away again. Jeremy's body jerked suddenly, as if he was momentarily epileptic, causing Pia to start herself.

"You okay?" Pia asked softly.

He looked at her sadly and shook his head. She ran her hand over his forearm, which was resting on a small café table between them. One of his feet bounced, causing his knee to move up and down as fast as a sewing machine's busy needle. He crossed his arms and looked wistfully at the spacious back yard surrounded by forest.

Then he declared with resolve, "I want to cut my hair. Will you cut it for me?"

"Um, sure. Are you certain you want to do that? You could try a bun like Citizen Cope has. I've seen them on a lot of young guys."

He shook his head and repeated, "I want to cut it."

"Okay, we'll do that, then."

Pia went inside for her hair scissors, a mirror, a broom and a towel and came out again soon.

As she put the towel around Jeremy's shoulders to keep the hair off his shirt she said lightly, "It's only fair I warn you that I have no skill at this."

Pia held up the scissors and thought about how to proceed. When she hesitated to use them Jeremy reached for them and she let him take them. Pia was just then thinking about what he'd said in his room about not being able to get through this and that perhaps he shouldn't have scissors. But he had them already. He held them near his neck and proceeded to cut off what hair he could in short order with no regard for how it might look. She thought he meant a trim but it was all going. Pia felt pain in the process, but not her own. She waited until he finished and then she made revisions.

"You'll have to go in the bathroom to see the back," she advised as she held the mirror out for him to take.

Jeremy didn't touch it, so she positioned it in front of him. He looked at his head briefly and then looked away, back to the grassy yard. Pia lowered the mirror and gazed at him for a minute with concern. She thought that perhaps the condition of his face was difficult for him to view. He stood up, shook off any remaining pieces of severed hair from the shirt and went inside without a word. Pia moved his chair aside and swung the broom in slow sweeps, brushing the surface of the deck so the hair fell incrementally through the spaces between the boards to settle on the dirt below. The blond hair disappeared into the perpetual shadow underneath where nothing grew. She paused before she pushed the last bits down.

In the late afternoon Jeremy told her it was time for him to return to his apartment. He had changed into his own clothes after his shower, so Pia expected this but was a little sad about it.

She assured him, "You can stay here as long as you want. Am I getting on your nerves?"

"No, of course not. I just have to go back to my life. I can't hide out here forever."

She located Gordon and told him she would drive Jeremy home soon. He reminded her that she was welcome to baby him whenever she wanted to. Generally, it annoyed Pia when he asked her to take care of him because she felt he was perfectly capable of doing that himself. But sometimes she would concede. After all, it was part of who she was.

Chapter 20

Pia put all of Jeremy's medical supplies in a bag. She packed the leftover salad also. She wondered if he would throw it away like his mom's cooking. Jeremy shook Gordon's hand and thanked Gordon for hosting him. Gordon was decent, mostly because he was getting his routine back. Jeremy and Pia began the drive into the city to the apartment. One neighbor flagged her down to talk about an upcoming town meeting. Further down the road Pia waved to Jane's husband Sam. He was at his roadside mailbox as they drove past. Sam's gaze followed the car after he waved.

Jeremy took note of the surroundings: the pond, the fields, some old farmhouses, and the forest. The area had lots of hills and valleys with old stone walls stitched throughout.

"So this is where you live. It's nice," he said in a subdued tone.

Pia concurred, "I love it here. We're not far from the sanctuary."

He frowned. "Sanctuary?"

Pia's heart sank. Did he not remember?

She said weakly, "The nature sanctuary with the snowshoes and the sheep."

"Oh."

He lowered his window, tipped his head out and softly repeated "sanctuary" a few times to himself. His words lifted into the air and were gone.

After a minute he turned his head back towards Pia and said, "Gordon doesn't treat you so great."

Surprised, Pia replied, "No?"

"No."

"Well, at the end of the day he's pretty good. I'm no angel myself."

Pia almost launched into her ideas about the complexity of relationships but had no energy for it. Jeremy certainly wouldn't want to hear it either.

"He's like my father. You deserve better."

"Thank you."

She was touched by Jeremy's sentiment but he didn't know the whole story. Pia's phone chimed that she had a text message.

When she didn't respond to it Jeremy asked, "Aren't you going to check that?"

"I don't text and drive."

"You're kidding me."

"There's a tree on a curve of my road that's been hit about ten times from people doing that. You can read it to me if you want. It's in the outside pocket of my bag."

Jeremy reached for her phone as it chimed again and tried to figure it out.

"This thing is archaic. Wait, here we go…I got it. It's from Jane: 'Sam wants to know if Gordon punched Jeremy'. Why would Sam think that?"

Quickly Pia said, "Sorry, let's ignore it." She thought, "*Shit.*"

Right after Pia spoke she saw out of the corner of her eye Jeremy typing something.

"What did you just do?" she asked him.

"I answered her."

"Jeremy!"

"What?"

"Well what did you write?"

"I wrote 'No, I did.'"

Then he grinned briefly and replaced the phone. Pia was so glad to see him grin that she just shook her head at his mischief while he looked out the window.

As she drove, Pia recalled pieces of her time with Jeremy. About fifteen minutes into the trip, she remembered something that startled her, while she merged onto a major road.

"My God," Pia groaned quietly to herself.

She was coming to a realization about something.

Jeremy asked, "What's the matter, Pia?"

Pia hesitated but decided to tell him her thoughts.

"Oh…I saw Max and Jamie panhandling last week on my lunchtime walk and they asked after you. Something about Jamie gave me the creeps so I told them you moved away…."

She looked at him with worry on her face. Jeremy nodded to Pia in confirmation and then looked out at the asphalt ahead.

"Yeah. I almost told you yesterday when you asked me if I knew them. My intuition told me to stay clear of them." Morosely he added, "I'll listen to it from now on."

"Jeremy, you couldn't know how rotten they were."

After a minute passed he said, "I know why I went with them."

Pia had a hunch. "Because Max is so attractive."

"Yeah. *Was*. Not anymore."

"Still not your fault."

Jeremy sighed, "If you say so."

Pia reached over for Jeremy's hand and he offered it to hers. They were quiet for a long time, holding hands with fingers entwined and moving forward. She didn't know what he was thinking, but she was contemplating all sorts of ways to kill those bastards.

After a while Jeremy turned on the radio, but it was playing a commercial for a car dealership so he switched it to a CD. Pia couldn't remember what was in there next, as the player had six CDs in it. She hoped it was Jack Johnson, since she knew Jeremy liked him. It was Melissa Etheridge. While 'Keep It Precious' played Pia felt a bit uneasy. It was about allowing her lover to move on and sincerely wishing her the best, like Wanda may have. It was an intense, passionate goodbye song. Fortunately, the next song was much more fun.

When they were almost to Jeremy's neighborhood he said, "Thank you for all of your help." It continued to lack the verve his 'thank you' formerly had.

"I'm always here for you."

Pia was going up Jeremy's street and saw Adam on the front stoop of their building.

She said, "Hey, there's Adam."

"He's expecting me. I told him I've been in some trouble. I don't know if I'll ever tell him what. I'm glad you figured it out but I don't want him to be burdened with it."

"It's good that you and Adam are so close."

She pulled over about four buildings up because there wasn't a spot closer.

"Yeah, he's a great brother. We definitely love each other."

Jeremy sounded okay then.

After a moment she said, "Alright, then. If you need me for anything just let me know. Do you mind if I check on you in a few days?"

She didn't want to smother him. Jeremy looked down and was quiet. He wore a frown.

"Sure."

"Okay, out you go."

Pia wanted to leave. She was certain she was losing something today. She could feel it heavy in the air.

He sat there, so she asked quizzically, "What's wrong?"

Jeremy turned his gaze up and looked straight out the windshield. "Are you leaving me? It sounds like you're really *leaving* me."

Or maybe she wasn't losing something today.

Pia softened, asking, "What do you mean?"

"Maybe because I'm damaged goods now."

"You're not 'damaged goods'. Please don't say such a thing."

"But I am. I'm so damaged. You're not going to check on me for a few *days*? 'If I ever need anything'?"

He was so dejected now. Pia got out of the car, shut her door and walked quickly, very 'purposefully' to use his word, around to his side and opened his door. Adam watched but waited in front of their building. Pia left a hand on the car body and leaned in near Jeremy's face.

"Sweetie, I would like to call you when I get home, and before I go to sleep tonight, and while my coffee is brewing tomorrow morning. I promise you won't leave my thoughts. You are always in my heart. I just thought that you wanted space from me and that you have Adam now."

"I need all the help I can get. I need all the love I can get," Jeremy said. "Just because I have Adam, and Paco will be back next week, doesn't mean I don't want your help, too. And they don't know what happened. I'm going to try to act okay around everyone except you, since you know about it. You're my confidant."

She felt badly that he had to ask her for more help. If she were more intuitive, she'd know he still needed her, wouldn't she?

Cautiously she asked, "You aren't going to tell Paco?"

She was surprised to hear that, but then she thought that Paco's reaction might include blaming Jeremy's choices for this. That would only hurt him further.

"I don't think so. I'm ashamed, somehow." Jeremy saw that she was about to reproach him about that so he added, "I know I shouldn't be, but right now I am."

He ran his hand over his fuzzy scalp.

Pia said sympathetically, "I'll help you any way I can. I'll come back tonight to put fresh ointment and bandages on your back. I'd walk through fire for you."

She felt awful for Jeremy, but relieved that he didn't want to be rid of her. She made a mental note to ask Carla to call him as additional support.

"Come on now," Pia said as she helped him ease out of the seat. He stood by the car and wrinkled his nose as if something smelled bad.

"Did you call me '*Sweetie*' a minute ago?"

"Sorry, it slipped out."

She swung the passenger door shut. They waited for traffic to pass before crossing the street, walking towards Adam.

She asked in a low voice, "Why did you call *me*?"

"While I was in the train station trying to figure out what to do I remembered when we first met them and you were so worried about me," Jeremy explained as he looked over at her appreciatively.

"Ah."

Jeremy was so glad to see Adam that he smiled, albeit feebly, and eagerly hugged him. Pia had to avert her eyes when Adam patted Jeremy's back heartily. Adam looked over his brother's beaten face.

"Crap."

Pia looked sympathetically at Adam; she knew how he felt.

Adam was definitely the older brother. He recovered from the shock and asked genially, "Where'd you get that sorry-ass hoodie and what happened to your coat? Remy, where's your *hair*?"

He rubbed Jeremy's head and smiled.

Jeremy hesitated so Pia came up with, "He lost the coat and hair playing poker."

Adam responded, "He doesn't play poker."

Jeremy was ready then and said, "I realize that now, heh."

Adam asked, "Did you lose a lot of money?"

"Yeah, and I gambled more than I had, thus the ensuing brawl. Some people take poker very seriously."

Pia hoped that Adam would believe Jeremy since he wasn't one to fib. She was troubled that she'd made him lie to his brother though.

Just as she was absorbing this new sadness Adam said, "So, Pia, how've you been?" She didn't answer and he continued to them both, "It's so nice out today, huh? Too bad we don't have a porch or deck."

It was in the low 60's and mostly sunny.

Pia agreed, "It's gorgeous. Spring is finally here! Well, I'm off."

"I'll see you later," Jeremy said.

It sounded like an expectation.

"You bet," she replied.

"That's a poor choice of words under the circumstances," Adam noted without humor.

Pia felt chastised. She watched the brothers go up the steps and into their foyer, with Adam carrying Jeremy's things.

She phoned Jeremy a few hours after she was home, at about six o'clock. Jeremy tried to persuade her to stay home and come back in the morning to change the dressing on his back. She agreed but later reconsidered and returned that night at about eight-thirty.

One of the roommates, a chubby, tall fellow with a beard, let her in without any introduction. The roommates and a third friend were in the living room bowling with Wii while drinking beer and enjoying buffalo wings. Pia shut the door behind her and stood in the entryway.

The other roommate said, "Hi, I'm Mason. The rude one there is Stubby and this is his friend Seth."

He pointed to each with his beer bottle.

Pia replied, "Nice to meet you."

"Want a beer?" Mason asked before taking a swig from his bottle.

"No thanks. I'm not staying long."

"Alright, suit yourself. If you change your mind let us know!"

They turned their attention back to the game.

Pia walked to the end of the hallway and when she reached Jeremy's open door she knocked lightly on the jamb. He looked up from his computer and his head bobbled slightly while he briefly grinned at her.

"Dr. Young called a little while ago to check on me," he told her.

"Did she?"

"Was that your idea?"

"Maybe."

He had just taken some pain medication. That conflicted with Pia's plan for him to take something for sleep soon. They went into the kitchen so he could make a sandwich and they talked for a while about little things. Mason made several trips to the refrigerator for beer, leaving empty bottles in the sink. After an hour Jeremy decided to try sleeping so he stopped by Adam's room to tell him he was calling it a night. A few minutes later they overheard Adam asking the others to try to keep the noise down.

Jeremy took one sleeping pill, half the dosage. Pia set him up with fresh ice packs. She turned off the lights so only the light from the hall shone in Jeremy's room through the slightly open door. She sat on his bed and held an ice pack to his back injury. Occasionally they would hear the roommates laugh or belch.

"This isn't working. I'm wide awake," Jeremy admitted after about twenty minutes. He sighed and added, "I hope I don't freak out in front of any of them. I really hope I can handle being at work."

Pia advised, "Try to settle your thoughts. This is your place. It's a good place to go to sleep."

After another ten minutes Jeremy lifted the ice pack from his face and glanced at Pia. He was sleepy but not asleep. She looked back at him without any ideas. Pia didn't know what she should be doing, but she decided her presence might be the problem.

She was about to suggest she go home when Jeremy said, "Don't leave until I'm asleep, okay?"

She nodded. Five minutes after that she made an executive decision. She set her ice pack aside, tucked the covers all around Jeremy snuggly, and got up. She closed the door and went around to the other side of the bed. Pia eased herself across the covers to him, where she curled around him with an arm over him. As usual, she wasn't sure her intentions would be correctly understood so she lay somewhat stiffly.

In a whisper Jeremy said, "Thanks."

Pia relaxed and nestled in.

For a few minutes she softly hummed a tune. She stayed there for about an hour and then quietly got up. She wasn't sure if Jeremy was sleeping and didn't want to wake him if he was, so she sat on the floor watching him for a little while. Adam came down the brightly lit hall, brushing his teeth and shirtless. He pushed the door so it swung slowly open and he took a peek in. He acknowledged Pia with a nod. Shortly after that she went home.

Pia returned the next day, Sunday, about noon. She changed the bandages on Jeremy's back wound and applied more antibiotic cream. He convinced her he'd be okay so she left to take care of some other responsibilities. She returned again that evening. Mason was out but Adam, Stubby and Jeremy were watching television in the living room. Jeremy had already taken a full dose of sleeping pills so on this night he was unconscious by nine o'clock. Once he was asleep Pia shut his door behind her. As she walked through the living room Adam asked her to sit down next to him on the sofa. She heard Stubby in the kitchen washing a large pile of dishes, singing happily. She sat.

Quietly Adam said, "You know what really happened to him, don't you?"

It wasn't really a question; it was an assumption.

"I don't know what you mean," she said, not convincingly.

Adam was a bit agitated and looked at her intensely, clarifying, "Pia, Remy's my baby brother and I want to know what happened to him. Something's very wrong here."

Pia's face conceded defeat as she asked, "Have you tried asking him about it?"

"He says he's fine. He won't talk to me, which is making me more worried," he replied. "We're buddies."

He looked like a more masculine, conservative version of Jeremy. Pia felt his frustration and she could tell he was much stronger than Jeremy. He would be able to handle the truth, but it was not for her to tell.

"Adam, it's not my place…not without his permission." She rubbed her thighs and tipped her head to one side, revealing, "He's been hurt."

"No kidding," Adam sarcastically replied.

Pia realized people said that to her rather often.

He asked with mean eyes and a set jaw, "Did your husband do this?"

Pia said, "Oh, *that's* what you think? No, he didn't." She grinned briefly, adding, "But that's a good guess."

Adam wasn't amused. "What happened then?"

She shook her head saying, "He doesn't want to burden you."

Adam's eyes bored into Pia's while he leaned forward and said, "I'm his brother; that's in the job description."

Even amidst all this misery, a tiny piece of Pia envied Jeremy his brother's love. She didn't have that in her family.

Finally she sighed, "How's this: I'll leave him a note. If he doesn't want to tell you himself, I'll ask him if I may. Okay?"

Adam reluctantly agreed to consider the discussion over. Pia left Jeremy a note letting him know that Adam wanted to help him and that she believed he would be able to bear the news. She tucked it next to his pillow.

The following day when she called Jeremy, he told her that he and Adam had talked about his assault. Adam was completely supportive and was more than willing to take over Pia's physical role, which was dwindling anyway, so Jeremy didn't need her to keep coming into the city.

Two days later Pia called again and he told her, "Adam's sleeping in my bed now. We used to do that a lot when we were kids."

She heard a smile in his voice when he said that, but it was gone when he added, "He wakes me when I have bad dreams."

Jeremy was working again and finished with sedatives but was suffering from flashbacks and nightmares. He was avoiding Paco. He talked to Pia about it during a phone call when she asked if Paco had returned from his trip.

"Yes, I went to his place the day after he got back. It was so nice to be back in his arms and he's such a great kisser." He caught himself and gently added, "I'm sorry, Pia. Is this difficult for you to hear about?"

That was the closest he came to acknowledging their previous involvement.

"It's okay. My feelings for you have changed, matured," she answered. "So you were saying?"

"Oh, yeah. So it was fine until he wanted sex. It's weird because I love and trust him, but…I might never be able to…. Anyway, I asked if we could just be together and he of course said it was fine, and it was. It was wonderful. But I can't keep doing that. He doesn't know why I wouldn't, but I think it bothered him."

"He might have sensed you were keeping something from him," Pia suggested.

"I'm sure."

"And you don't want to tell him."

"No, I really don't and I've been avoiding him since then. I don't exactly know how to manage it."

This being foreign territory for her, Pia changed the subject, asking, "How about Ishra?"

"She moved to the west coast for a job." He was pensive for a minute before adding, "I started seeing this woman a few weeks before this happened. She wants to see me so I've gone over to her apartment a few times. It's going alright…." It seemed like he was deciding how much to share.

Pia tried to be positive, saying, "Well, that's good."

"No success with the physical intimacy there either, though," he confessed.

"You associate sex with violence now."

"I suppose so. Besides that, I'm afraid she's finding me to be bad company in general. She said I'm boring lately."

"Oh."

"So we'll see how long it lasts."

It was a gradual conversation but eventually Pia was able to persuade Jeremy to see a therapist. With his approval, she did the work of searching for therapists in the area and determining if they were contracted with his health insurance plan.

She accompanied him to the first appointment. It took a little doing to get the therapist to consent to Pia remaining for the session, even with Jeremy's approval. She was a person who seemed neutral in every way, which Pia thought might be a good sign. However, Pia concluded that she was not going to be particularly helpful. Pia didn't know if the woman was new to the profession, not interested in Jeremy's issue or just not very good, but she wasn't giving him any tools or assistance as far as Pia could tell. Jeremy was surprised when Pia didn't let them schedule a second appointment.

As way of explanation she told him on their way down the hall only,

"We can do better than that."

The next therapist they tried had a gleaming, modern suite in a high-rise office building. Jeremy filled out paperwork in the waiting area before being seen. This therapist was an older man who dyed his hair black, with a goatee and sharp features. He resembled a raven and Pia hoped that indicated his high intelligence. He also objected, quite firmly, to Pia's presence, but she would not back down.

Once they were seated together in his office, the therapist quickly looked over the paperwork and, determining the reason for the visit from it, began asking Jeremy for information about his ordeal.

"These are people that you knew?"

"Yes, acquaintances. I didn't really know them well."

"But you went with them somewhere."

Pia didn't like this man's approach already.

Jeremy answered, "Yes."

"Why?"

"Um…they asked me if I wanted to smoke a joint with them, so I said 'sure.'"

"You take drugs then?" He said, scratching a note on the papers on his clipboard.

Jeremy frowned. "No, I mean…occasionally, socially. Just pot. It's not my lifestyle."

"I know it's not his habit to," Pia interjected.

The therapist crossed his legs, seemingly ignoring her.

"Where did this take place?" he asked Jeremy.

Jeremy cleared his throat before answering, "It was very cold out and they said there was a place nearby they knew that was warm, indoors. It was some sort of electrical storage room in a warehouse."

"That's odd."

"They're vagabonds, kind of."

The therapist made another notation before asking, "So how did this happen? How did it unfold?"

Jeremy began to get jittery and stammered, "Uh, well, once we were inside I took off my coat and slung it over a stool because it was hot. I sat down. Then I saw one of them bolt the door and lean against it, which made me nervous."

The story seemed to end there. He certainly didn't want to continue.

The therapist prompted Jeremy, "And then what happened?"

Jeremy hesitated a moment before answering, "Uh, then what happened, happened. It's on that sheet you have."

Clearly he was pushing back against continuing in this vein but the therapist insisted, stating, "You're going to have to share more than that for me to be of any help to you. What happened next?"

Jeremy hesitated again. He became increasingly uncomfortable and his right foot began to bounce.

He swallowed and answered, "The other one said, 'drop your pants.'"

"How did you respond to that?"

"I was a little panicky but tried not to show it. I said, 'why would I do that?'"

The therapist prodded him along. "And then he said?"

Jeremy's foot bounced faster. "He said…he said…'so I can fuck you up your ass, you idiot.'"

The therapist raised an eyebrow, so when Jeremy looked up at him he clarified, "I'm not calling you an idiot, that's what he said, that's what he called me."

The man's eyebrow relaxed. Jeremy maintained his habit of running his hand through his hair even though it was short now, and he did that a few times. He was too naïve to know this grilling was not necessary and far too polite to voice an objection, but Pia did.

"Can you back off now? This is too much for him," she entreated.

Jeremy took a deep breath and exhaled audibly. The therapist was not deterred and just softened his tone with his next question.

"I must know exactly what happened in order to facilitate progress. Please tell me what happened next."

After a minute Jeremy reluctantly continued, "I wanted to sound confident even though I was scared. I told him that wasn't going to happen."

Then silence. The therapist sighed as if he was weary of having to keep prompting Jeremy.

"And then he said…?"

Jeremy continued to fidget and looked at Pia to check if he must answer. She saw a bit of fear in his eyes. She shook her head no. Jeremy swallowed hard and his face twitched.

He looked down and answered, "He said, 'oh, it's gonna happen.' Then he lunged at me."

Pia thought, "He can see how hard this is for Jeremy. He'll stop now, won't he?"

Then, with shock she realized that must've been Jeremy's idea with Jamie and Max. Pia caught a lewd glint in the therapist's sinister eyes that she found repulsive. It wouldn't stop.

"How did he—"

She launched from her seat and flung her thoughts at the man.

"That's enough! He didn't come here to be victimized by you, too!"

"I *beg* your pardon?" the therapist replied, clearly offended.

She grabbed a stack of his business cards from a polished brass container on the richly veneered coffee table. Several of them fell to the table surface and some others to the floor.

"I'm going to have my attorney investigate you. You probably do a lot more harm than good in this room."

Jeremy took that as a cue to rise from the sofa.

Pia wasn't done yet. "He came here for some *help*, you *dick!*"

Jeremy seemed considerably more surprised by her at this appointment but was willing to leave as soon as possible and headed towards the exit.

With his elbows on the arms of his chair the therapist tented his fingers and said coolly, "Ah, it's inevitably about the penis."

He sneered at Pia, but she was already holding the door open for Jeremy.

As they strode quickly past the administrative assistant's desk, Pia told her loudly, "Your boss is a pig."

Two people waiting looked up at Pia and Jeremy and then to each other. Pia dropped all of the business cards into a trash bin by the exit.

"Aren't you going to keep one for your attorney?" Jeremy asked as they continued through a set of doors.

He had to keep up with her for a change. Pia kept walking towards the elevators.

"There isn't really an attorney, Jeremy," she replied in an annoyed tone that wasn't meant for him. He was silent then.

At the elevators she pressed the button repeatedly as if that might hasten the machine's descent. Once inside they joined three business-men so they didn't discuss the appointment. Pia reached for his hand and he clasped hers tightly...a hand hug, as it were. She didn't let go until the doors opened to the lobby.

When they were outdoors and walking at a slower pace on the sidewalk Pia was still distraught and apologized, "I'm so sorry about that."

"It's fine, I felt the same way. I don't know what I would've done if you weren't there. You're a real pit bull, heh."

"I mean I'm sorry I brought you there. Jesus, that was rough. Are you okay?"

"Yeah. But I'm confused. I should talk to the therapist, right? That's why I went?"

"Yes," Pia was going to add more but Jeremy hadn't finished his thought.

"But I didn't want to; I was very uncomfortable. This is so personal. Am I doing something wrong?"

Pia scoffed, "No, that guy was a creep." Then she added more calmly, "The best way to rid this of its power over you is to talk about it when you feel ready. It might come out in increments or a flood, but it has to be when you choose to."

They strolled down the busy downtown street towards the subway station.

After a minute she said, "I know I said I'd do anything for you, but please don't tell me unless you truly must."

He expressed no such intention, quickly replying, "No worries there."

Pia grinned and bumped his arm with hers to direct him to a café. "Let's get some coffee."

While waiting behind someone else to place their order Pia said, "I'll line up another appointment. There's four more names on my list."

"I don't know, Pia. Maybe it's not such a good idea."

With heartache she observed him continue his new habit of frequently looking over his shoulder in public.

"Please try one more. Then I'll stop nagging you about it."

Jeremy didn't reply so she took that as a 'yes' and booked an appointment for him for a few days later.

This office was in a run-down five-story building that was built in the 1960's on the edge of town. There was one receptionist and a central waiting area for a half dozen professionals, each one with a plaque next to their respective doors. Jeremy and Pia checked in with the receptionist and then took seats across from each other. They waited for ten minutes past the expected time, and when the receptionist felt Pia's eyes on her she explained that this was normal.

Finally the therapist opened her door. She was an older Jewish woman in poor physical condition, flabby and with a limp, her form reminding Pia of the cooled wax drippings around a well-used candle. She was short and her hair went in all directions. Her clothes were old and funky, and her eyeglasses hung from a string of colorful beads.

"A hippie," Pia thought to herself. "I hope she doesn't use essential oils and stones with sayings on them."

Then she reproached herself for her cynicism.

In a voice rich and melodic the woman greeted them, "Welcome! You must be Jeremy. I'm Edie. Please, come in."

"Um, I'd like my friend to come in also, please," Jeremy responded as he rose.

Pia stood up and prepared herself to be forceful if necessary.

Edie asked him, "Would you come in alone briefly first?"

He looked to Pia for guidance.

Edie repeated, "Just for a minute, hmm?", extending her hand out for him to go in before her.

He did so and Edie, with some effort at bending down, activated a noise-reducing machine by the door before closing it. Pia waited anxiously, chewing a nail. She decided she'd allow five minutes before she would walk in. In two minutes the door opened and Edie warmly invited Pia to join them.

When they were all seated, surrounded by houseplants in need of bigger pots and more water, Edie asked Jeremy what brought him there. His knee was bouncing.

He kept his eyes down, gathered his courage and murmured succinctly, "I was raped."

Pia hadn't heard him say it before and it hurt like a bee sting.

"I'm so sorry to hear that," Edie said sincerely. She leaned forward, looking at him attentively, her brow deeply knit, with her notepad and pen on her lap. "I'm really so sorry for you. What a terrible, terrible experience that must've been."

"I've…I've been having a hard time since. I have a lot of flashbacks and, well…." He tossed his head about and looked at her.

She responded, "I'm not surprised by that at all. How do you feel today?"

"I feel like I'm a stranger to myself. Like I'm not me anymore."

His knee stopped bouncing. Edie leaned back in her chair.

"Mm-hm. So, how does *that* make you feel?"

"I feel so lost. What am I if I'm not me?"

It unsettled Pia that he said 'what am I' rather than 'who am I.'

"You're the survivor of …" Edie began, thoughtfully considering her next words.

Jeremy gently interrupted, "Excuse me, but I think that's a little inaccurate. I'm *not* surviving. I'm drowning here."

His pain was clear to see.

Their eyes met, a connection was made, and Edie replied softly, "Fair enough." She began again. "You've experienced a severe trauma that was deliberately imposed upon you, as opposed to, say, a fire burning down your house or a parent dying from disease. So there's malintent involved that should be dealt with. But you're still you, underneath that." Then she said with assurance and a slight smile, "We'll find you; you'll see."

The woman offered him hope. Hope, which Pia then realized had been absent.

"There's a very special person there," she told Edie.

Edie turned to Pia and replied generously, "I got that sense."

Jeremy looked down at his hands while Edie asked, "How much time has gone by since the event?"

He said, "It's been about four weeks. Is it normal to still be having so much trouble now?"

Edie offered a different perspective. "I assure you anyone would still be having a difficult time this soon afterwards."

Jeremy looked slightly relieved by that information. His posture relaxed.

She continued, "I just ask because sometimes after the physical manifestations, meaning the bruises and cuts, have gone away, sur— victims— think it's time to be over it." Jeremy nodded and Edie added, "But oftentimes that's when you find yourself having more difficulty; when you no longer have the physical injuries to tend, that distraction, as it were. Your spirit is not healing at the same pace as your body. The damage is much deeper there."

Her voice was as soothing as Carla's and her manner was respectful. She was focused on Jeremy, as if she had nothing else going on in her life. During the ensuing pause Pia reached over to him and touched his arm. Jeremy spun his head to look at her.

In a low voice he urged, "Pia, don't. I like this one."

The therapist looked at them curiously.

Pia smiled wanly. "I was just going to say I'll wait outside the building for you."

"Phew," he gently teased her.

Pia was so glad they had found this woman. She rose to leave, saying to Edie only, "Thank you," with as much gratitude as two words could conjure.

Before closing the door behind her Pia heard Jeremy explaining to Edie that she was their third try.

Pia went outside and sat on the front steps in the warm sun, watching five English sparrows taking a dirt bath underneath a bench nearby. She watched people walking by as well.

Jeremy found her there an hour later and they walked together for a while as he gave her some thoughts on this new experience. Pia listened to "Edie thinks this" and "Edie said that" from him.

She could see he was more upbeat after this first session with his new therapist, and she continued her candle metaphor that started with Edie's figure. Edie provided light for her patients and probably at great expense to her own well-being. Pia became aware of how exhausting this process had been. She thought it must feel so much more so to Jeremy. Perhaps now he could begin to heal and turn his heart, like a sunflower, gradually back towards all the aspects of life which he loved. This was Pia's greatest wish.

On her way home that afternoon Pia stopped to pick up groceries so it was nearly dusk by the time she reached her neighborhood. Coming around a curve in her road she slowed to a stop. Before her were three deer browsing the abundant, fresh greens growing alongside the crumbling asphalt. Her heart rejoiced at the sight and she lowered her window. They looked up at her car as she talked to them.

"Hello, there! You shouldn't be on the road, you know. It's not safe for you."

They remained, flicking flies from their ears and nibbling grass.

"So how does that taste? It's been a long wait for grass, hasn't it?"

Another car approached from the other direction, causing the animals to startle. They flashed their white tails as they disappeared into the woods. The other driver, an old woman, smiled and commented, "Wasn't that nice?" before they passed each other.

At home, as Pia lifted her heavy shopping bags from the trunk of her car she was humming. She remembered the last time she saw deer, after the late night working on Jeremy's exhibit. There had been tracks in the snow, but she had not seen the animals themselves this past winter. She set the canvas bags down on the driveway as she contemplated the full circle of her relationship with Jeremy. It had become what it should: they were friends, good friends, and she was pleased by that. While it had waned somewhat on its own, she consciously chose to put an end to her pattern of deception and lying as well. Her sky was clearing and she felt peaceful.

Gordon came out of the house onto the porch.

"Do you need help with those bags?"

"No, thanks, I've got this," Pia answered pleasantly. She picked them up with strong arms, muscles flexed, and walked confidently towards the stairs.

The End

Afterword

About the Author

Ren Rosso lives in rural Massachusetts with her husband and cat, within a larger community of profoundly talented people. She has worked in higher education, medical offices, and retail. This is her first novel. Rosso enjoys experiencing the varied natural habitats of the world. She encourages everyone to believe in their art in whatever media most helps them flourish.